Pirates, Scoundrels, and Kings

WILLIAM LYNES, MD

iUniverse, Inc.
Bloomington

PIRATES, SCOUNDRELS, AND KINGS

Copyright © William Lynes, MD.

All rights reserved. No part of this book may be used or reproduced by any means, graphic, electronic, or mechanical, including photocopying, recording, taping or by any information storage retrieval system without the written permission of the publisher except in the case of brief quotations embodied in critical articles and reviews.

This is a work of fiction. All of the characters, names, incidents, organizations, and dialogue in this novel are either the products of the author's imagination or are used fictitiously.

Scripture taken from the Holy Bible, New International Version®. Copyright © 1973, 1978, 1984 Biblica. Used by permission of Zondervan. All rights reserved.

iUniverse books may be ordered through booksellers or by contacting:

iUniverse
1663 Liberty Drive
Bloomington, IN 47403
www.iuniverse.com
1-800-Authors (1-800-288-4677)

Because of the dynamic nature of the Internet, any web addresses or links contained in this book may have changed since publication and may no longer be valid. The views expressed in this work are solely those of the author and do not necessarily reflect the views of the publisher, and the publisher hereby disclaims any responsibility for them.

Any people depicted in stock imagery provided by Thinkstock are models, and such images are being used for illustrative purposes only.

Certain stock imagery © Thinkstock.

ISBN: 978-1-4759-6561-2 (sc)
ISBN: 978-1-4759-6562-9 (hc)
ISBN: 978-1-4759-6563-6 (e)

Library of Congress Control Number: 2012922826

Printed in the United States of America
iUniverse rev. date: 01/29/13

Acknowledgments

I began writing this book over 22 years ago. At the beginning, my family and I would read this together, often at bedtime story time. It is a book created with and for the love of my family: wife Patrice, and three sons Christopher, Alexander, and Nicholas.

I would like to acknowledge Connie Parkinson for her wonderful artwork that graces the cover of *Pirates, Scoundrels and Kings*. http://www.connieparkinson.com/

Also by this Author:

Luger Rounds, a Medical Mystery; iUniverse, Inc.; Bloomington, In.; 2012.

"Cody," A Short Story; Narrative Medicine Anthology, 3rd edition, Permanente Press Book, p.92.

"Colic," A Short Story; The Permanente Journal, Fall 2008, 12(4): 84.

"Flustrated," A Short Story; leaflet, Vol. 1, No. 1; The Permanente Press.

"606 University," A Short Story; leaflet, Vol. 2, No. 1; The Permanente Press.

Contents

Chapter 1. Oh, Cruel World 1
Chapter 2. Far Away Now 18
Chapter 3. The Pitlings 21
Chapter 4. Sir Alexander of Alucemet 26
Chapter 5. The Boar's Hoof 41
Chapter 6. Autumn Bienville 57
Chapter 7. A Pirate's Life 82
Chapter 8. The Laughing Lion 102
Chapter 9. Ambushed 130
Chapter 10. Prisoner 145
Chapter 11. A City Alucemet 185
Chapter 12. A Precipitous Quandary 237
Chapter 13. No Gum till I'm Three 256
Chapter 14. A Boy in the Sea 265
Chapter 15. The Straits of Abaddon 282
Chapter 16. A Fine Mess 296
Chapter 17. A Twisted Quirk of Fate 308
Chapter 18. The Cloaked Rider 316
Chapter 19. The Cautious Messenger 324
Chapter 20. Digital Severance 337
Chapter 21. The Spilith Shoot 351
Chapter 22. Once a Fool 367
Chapter 23. Ambush in Devil's Pass 379
Chapter 24. The Beast 413
Chapter 25. Dogs are People Too 419
Chapter 26. We'll Play in Heaven 429
Chapter 27. Good Bye 435

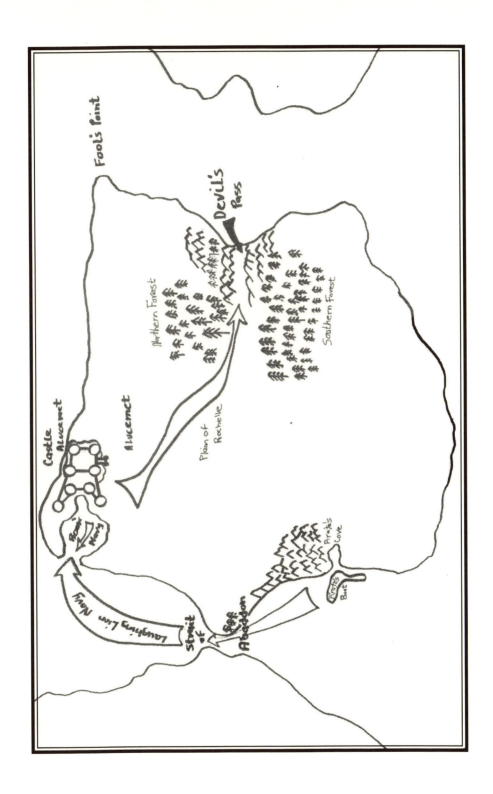

Chapter 1
Oh, Cruel World

> HE WHO GUARDS HIS MOUTH AND HIS TONGUE
> KEEPS HIMSELF FROM CALAMITY.
> **PROVERBS 21:23**

Nothing good can be said about Mondays, Christopher thought. Except for those with a Monday birthday, no one would really complain about its absence. On the other hand, Tuesday would just become Monday and nothing would really be accomplished anyway. If pressed, he would have to admit that at least Monday was only one day and not any longer. Besides he concluded, Monday was the first day of the end of the week.

This Monday had been a particularly foul one for the ten-year-old, blond-haired boy. He had such a wonderful weekend, and now the beginning of the week weighed upon his grumbling heart. Disneyland on Saturday did not help, nor playing in the castle playhouse his father finally finished by Sunday. Being jostled awake with five days until Saturday, fun now gone forever, was more than a youth could take. Unfortunately for our hero, here began a vile day in the life of a boy who had everything, took it for granted, noticed primarily the bad, forgot quickly, and acknowledged little in the way of joyful matters.

Stepping off the bus in the rain and slipping to his posterior in the muck, accompanied by jeering laughs, was the first telltale sign. His next memory permanently ruined his fragile psyche forever. What a grinning blue eyed fool he was with his debonair glance to the smiling girl with the long blond hair, only later to catch a horrifying glimpse in the mirror of her motivation, the perfect vertical brown crust of mud upon his rump. He may as well have had a wad of toilet paper tucked into his waist celebrating his bathroom forays, he decided in elementary school agony.

At that moment he felt the same overwhelming burning feeling as when he realized the meaning of his mom's personalized license plate. His urologist father dealt with a subject too embarrassing to fathom! His sense of humor mirrored that shameful profession. Only he would think the personalized license plate, 8-NUTS-N-I, attached to his mother's Suburban which ferried him to all his activities, humorous. When he realized that it referred to his family of four males and one female, he recalled the soccer practices, school events, and drive-thru restaurants with a burning sensation in his head. Perhaps it was like someone from the Ozarks realizing that a mullet haircut was way not popular in California, or committing some similar unforgivable social miscue. He prayed daily that no one would guess the meaning as the presence of his mother's car announced his humiliation to the world. Urologists. Why would someone be an urologist, he thought for the millionth time! I can't even stand urine, Chris thought. My Dad always does stuff to bug me, he concluded.

And so the terrible day continued. A spot quiz on last week's spelling first thing Monday morning continued his disaster. Mrs. Knapp had this way of doing annoying things like this at just the wrong time. As she walked down the aisle on her clunky heels, she smiled ghoulishly at Chris as if he was carrion, personally delighted with his discomfort. This proved the boy's theorem: like positive poles of two magnets, kids and adults have equal and opposite feelings about everything.

His nose also posed a recurrent problem that day. The big kid hated Chris, and he should have known as much when he smiled so mischievously at him during math drill. Five minutes later he realized his mistake, when the boy said just loud enough to engage the entire room, "there's a big bugger hanging from your nose dip wad!" However, why did Michael tell him at lunch about Rachel's brother eating dog food just as he took that big drink of milk? Any other time would be just fine, but to laugh with milk in your mouth and then have that milk come out of your nose was not in keeping with the superior social air he strove for.

At least the day disappeared quickly, Chris thought. However, as soon as he began to feel comfortable with three o'clock approaching, he remembered something that made him shudder, the tortuous bus ride home.

Delores was a fine, albeit dull bus driver. At the time, he did not know how fine she was. He even felt some remorse, mercilessly laughing at the woman who mistook Michael Jordan for the ambassador to England.

It was odd then the way that Delores disappeared from the bus route. One day she was there smiling and dull; the next day she was just gone. It was as if she met with some foul play. Knowing what he now knew of her replacement, Chris was certain of it. That first day when Hurley appeared he thought it was a bad joke. It was not that he was ugly, fat, and filthy; those things the boy could accept because those characteristics the man had no control over. The term: man, a loose description for the vile creature. Hurley was a rank personality and very frightening. He had a particular dislike for Chris as well. If anyone in the bus made a sound, Chris was sure to catch it. Hurley could sense his thoughts, the boy decided, and what he sensed he loathed with a brutal intensity bent on viscous retaliation. The more Chris saw of the man the more grotesque he became. His face appeared fatter and fatter and his eyes beadier and beadier. His clothes always too small, seemed to shrink daily, stretched over a protruding bouncing belly, producing folds of fat which could conceal a forgotten moldy sandwich with ease. Stained from his last several meals, which were myriad, his clothes were doused with greasy streaks of filthy slime. When he stood up and bent over, that crack with curly hair soared uncovered in the air, a sight the boy would rather forget. Hurley must have cultivated that foul and tainted breath, for nothing of this world smelled so repulsive. As a matter of fact, rotting flesh was a distinct possibility! Yes, that was it! Delores was trapped inside of the man somewhere, kicking at his guts trying to escape. And sweat like a pig, why did he always have to sweat? Even when it was cold and rainy outside, beads of cloudy perspiration punctuated his slippery, pink, pig-like hide.

The bell sounded ending a wicked Monday of school; however, his misery was just beginning. Chris slowly walked to the bus knowing what to expect. The scowl that greeted him did not disappoint the boy. He tried to make himself small, hoping to slip by Hurley. Trudging up the steps slowly, he passed by the driver with his head lowered. Not to be disappointed, he was just past the driver when he heard that familiar nicety. "Get in the back butt lips!" Today he added , "Way in the back you creep!"

Chris plopped down in the seat and stared in utter anguish. This guy was getting worse. He was about to go nuclear. He suspected Hurley as a serial murderer. The being made Chris so mad he could spit! How could this guy exist? How in America could someone so vile be such a tyrant? Hurley was his personal, very own, nagging persecutor! This wasn't right. It wasn't constitutional. Some old crusty document in DC would prove this for sure. His civilian rights, well for that matter his humanly rights, they definitely were not being respected by this person of interest, this plague of pestilence, this, this curse of a clown man.

Students passed by, filling the bus. Hurley seemed to only notice our hero. As they began to move, Chris forced himself to forget. He sat near the back, away from the driver, and he felt much safer. Maybe it was not such a bad day after all. His mind raced back to the past weekend and all the fun. Disneyland, now that was where he wanted to live. Thunder Mountain and Space Mountain had always frightened him but now he was old enough and they were fun. The Pirates of the Caribbean was the entire family's favorite. "That world of pirates, ships and cannons, oh why can't we live in a world like that?" he thought?

With the start of their ride, there was some jostling for seats. Chris returned to the present and began to worry, for down the aisle he caught a glimpse of a little walking, talking nightmare. He was sitting alone on the window side of the bench seat. If not careful, the free seat would fill with the inquisition itself. Then there he was, Robbie, standing in the aisle staring at Chris with that blank look.

"Can I sit here Chris-toe-fer?" Robbie wondered.

The boy was a kindergartener, with white blond hair, blue eyes, and red-rimmed thick glasses, which always sat slightly crooked on the boy's little nose. Today he was dressed in a ridiculous, yellow, hooded raincoat that was much too large for the small boy. With his usual blank stare looking at Chris for an answer, he appeared as if he might cry. Chris knew that the boy looked up to him, but the boy was a non-stop question waiting to ask the next question. He would rattle along about eating chocolate fairies, or snakes invading the playground, diamond door knobs, or some other crazy thing. Besides, sitting with such a youngster ruined the reputation that was so important in the fifth grade social structure that Chris traveled in.

"Uh, I got books Robbie, why don't you sit over there," Chris said, pointing hopefully down the bus as he pulled his backpack across the empty seat.

Robbie looked at Chris's books dejectedly. He puffed out his lower lip, and for once straightened his glasses, which began to fog.

Oh no, he is gonna cry, and his nose looks full of runny snot. Chris grimaced now considering his options. He remembered the time that the same boy had wet his pants when there was some thunder on the bus ride home. He could just see a strong stream bursting out of the boy's rain coat catching him in the face as the boy agonized over his rejection. Against Chris's better judgment, he lifted his backpack and made room for the young boy.

"Fhank you," Robbie said on the edge of tears. He flopped down on the seat. Quickly his tears dried up, and a smile returned to his little oddball face.

Good thing little kids get happy pretty quickly Chris thought, as he watched the boy out of the corner of his eye. He was a little ashamed of not wanting him to sit down for he seemed like a nice, though a bit dorky boy, unstable bladder and all, but at the same time today was not a day that he wanted Robbie to brighten up too much. He could only hope for some silence and a quick bus ride home, Chris thought without much conviction. Then predictably the barrage began.

"When I grow up I'm going to make the world's largest donut."

"That's nice, Robbie," Chris said, trying not to laugh.

"Yes, I am...I definitely am. I'll take lots and lots of flour, put it in a circle on my driveway, and cover it with tons and tons of chocolate. Donuts can float you know, and they are very easy to sell, but I wouldn't sell this one just leave it forever. My mother loves chocolate, me too. I love Dalmatians, do you?" Without waiting for an answer, he went on. "I don't have 101 Dalmatians, but I definitely have more than five," he said referring to his stuffed animals at home.

Chris made the mistake of entering this conversation. "How old are you Robbie?"

"Five years old," he responded.

"Kindergarten, huh," Chris responded, easily calculating his grade.

"How did you know that?" Robbie questioned, staring at Chris in amazement. "How old are your friends?"

"Ten, maybe eleven," Christopher said, without interest.

"How did they get so big? Did they grow like that? What's it like to be old? Can you still have a mom and eat milk and peanut butter? Do they have their own houses? Why are their feet so big, do you have five toes? I am going to stay in my house forever. I will make lemonade and cookies with lots of milk on my driveway."

Chris just blanked out at this point as the boy rattled on, closing his eyes. He suddenly was very tired. The last thing he heard was, "Do dogs know they're naked?"

It happened just as it did every day. Hurley stood and turned to walk down the aisle. It seemed as if lifting his massive, grotesque, overweight body was just all his scrawny little legs could do. Still, he continued down the aisle staring with a sickening smile as he walked toward no one but Chris.

However, the beast was different today. The closer he got to the boy the more disgusting he became. Belching and grunting as he walked, Chris realized that he really did not look like a man, but more like a pig. His face was a rounded doughy mass, and his eyes were almost invisible, sunken into their fat-filled orbits. That nose, always pug-like, was much more so today. Chris knew that at just the right angle, he would be able to look through his nostrils and into that horrible skull, the contents of which were certainly few. His hair, always thin, was curly, coarse, and almost nonexistent. No longer wearing those torn blue jeans with the top two fly buttons open by necessity, he had tight black leather pants on. As he lumbered down the aisle, Chris noticed that his shoes were different as well. He had always worn those black scuffed shoes, the type the Sears repairman had worn. Today he had shiny, black, knee-high military boots, curiously new. As he walked, his stubby arms swung in soldier like rhythm. His chest was exposed, some stubby hair in the middle just above that massive rotund belly, which hung over his leather britches. Black leather suspenders with skull and crossbones were in place, without which the security of his leather pantaloons would have been unstable.

With the entire bus oddly silent now, the menace stopped predictably in front of Chris, clicking his heels as if at military attention. The smell of the obese sweaty body was overpowering, and Chris felt an overwhelming desire to vomit and lose his lunch to this man who might just be happy to consume the emesis. Wheezing and heaving, the man raised his arm in front of the boy slowly, bringing a riding strap just below the tip of his nose. Chris focused on the strap's distal end, making his eyes cross. As if by a secret force within the belching beast, he was forced to draw his gaze up along the black leather strap. He could then not help his eyes from meeting the stare of his tormentor. Hurley had that stupid grin so often seen as he opened his mouth to chastise him. An upper and lower row of decaying yellowed teeth began slowly to form the words, "Wake up mush for brains."

The bus jolted to a stop, awakening Chris. He was soaked with sweat, and his heart was pounding. Hurley was as usual perched hopelessly on the tiny driver's seat that had seemed so satisfactory for Delores but so feeble for the present occupant. He had turned in his seat and seemed to enjoy and understand Chris's recent foul dream. Grinning foolishly, Hurley yelled, "Your stop butt breath," his entire fetid conflagration directed without question only to the boy. Curiously after the plague of his daydream, Chris received the insult with joy. He jumped out of his seat, stopped on his way out of the bus, thanked the man like an idiot, and jumped down the stairs out of the bus past his nemesis. The boy noted that Hurley was again dressed as usual, too tight unbuttoned jeans, but now still dreamlike in his spit-polished military boots. He noticed the boots just in time to avoid the predictable trip over an outstretched leg in his path. He was halfway up the hill towards his home before his heart started beating again.

The birds were chirping and the sky a beautiful blue that spring day in Temecula, but Chris did not notice. Brooding situations had a way of doing that to the boy. He slowed to a walk as his fright passed. It had been a completely horrible Monday, even as Mondays go. Christopher agonized, reviewing his terrible fortunes as he continued a dejected trek home.

CHRIS' BROTHER ALEXANDER WAS FIVE years old. He was home from Kindergarten now for several hours. He loved his bus driver, Miss Rebecca. She thought he was special. Birds would chirp as they would sing and circle her lovely head. She would drop him personally at the door and wave, "Good-bye Alexander." Alexander would make it a point to mention this to Christopher some day, he thought.

Alex loved to invent things and today he was doing so in a prolific fashion. With sticks, string, and baseball cards, the ninja-powered spaceship was nearing perfection. He wondered that day, as he often did, why big people bought so many new things for kids when an old discarded piece of plastic was so much more fun and useful? He decided against informing the Mom and Dad adult world however, what with Christmas and all; yes, safer to say nothing for now. He must make a note of that.

The invention was nearing completion, needing just one more thing, he realized. It was obvious, that yellow, bent, double-sided construct would be perfect. "Let's see, where is that perfect final piece?" He realized it was stored for his use in Chris' room and went to retrieve it. Pushing aside debris from under his older brother's bed, he strained, grabbing the perfect item that he knew would be there. At last the invention, his gift to the world was complete, and he went downstairs proudly to show it to his mom. She was probably waiting just for that purpose, he decided.

Nicholas was in the entry at the foot of the stairs making war. Nothing fazed the boy. He was always smiling, and fun was his middle name. He was three years old, a crusading brawling pirate through and through. Dressed in his favorite black muscle shirt with skull and crossbones he looked the part. He had used his dad's bathrobe tie for a sash and had a broken sword from Disneyland tucked into it. No such sword had ever remained intact for more than two days after their visit, but he still insisted on one each time. He wore the usual shorts, blazing blue with pirate stripes of black. While they fit nicely at the waist, they hung well past his knees. He wore his favorite foot wear: black and red *Heelys Rebel* roller shoes several sizes too big. With twists like a Kung Fu warrior and kicks like a Ninja turtle, Nick was easily outdueling all invisible invaders who would dare enter his domain.

Just as Alex arrived down the stairs he encountered Nick, and just as they encountered each other, the front door flung open. It took four seconds for Chris to spy out of the one hundred or so parts in Alex's spaceship, that yellow construct. He knew immediately it was and always had been his. His mind knew exactly where he had filed it, under his bed. A blood-curdling scream could be heard at that time, "Give me back my junk you dirt bag".

Alex would have nothing of this as he turned and ran towards the kitchen. Chris reached him and grabbed his leg bringing the boy down with a crash. Baseball cards, legos, old balloons, and more flew everywhere.

Nicholas dove quickly into the fracas, not to be left out. He yelled a "Kow-a-bunga dude" as he dove headfirst with vigor onto the two boys. "You want me to punch your lights out?" he said as he wrestled in Alex's defense.

It was Patrice's swift and sure response to the situation which saved this from becoming a bloody battle. She stepped quickly into the entry and measured the situation. With a calm only a mother of three could produce, she efficiently took care of the dilemma. At the top of her lungs, with all the authority she could muster, she screamed, "Knock it off or I'll tear out your vocal cords you monsters!" It helped for a fraction of a second but then the fighting continued. Patrice took immediate responsibility for discipline. "Heads are going to roll; you're all going to get it when your father gets home!" Finally the battle stopped.

Alexander never cried, but how could his brother do this to him? His mother would never appreciate the delicate creation that lay on the floor destroyed. Nicholas certainly did not want to get it, but he could never resist a good battle. For Christopher, this was just one more insult to that day of a day that was Monday. The verdict was in swiftly. Patrice sentenced the criminals to their rooms until dinnertime. They each marched gloomily up the stairs in silence.

To Nicholas, his room was the playroom. For years, the three boys had shared a room. In the new home, however, each boy had the luxury of having his own. Nick tried sleeping alone for a time, but nighttime characters that inhabited the room made this frightening. Therefore, for now, he slept in Alex's room. Nick knew from his mother's tone of voice that *your* room meant *his* room. While he did not sleep in the room, the décor reflected his style. Posters of Mickey and Minnie Mouse decorated the walls. Pictures of bulldogs were everywhere. On the floor the *HEE-HEE*, or now that he was mature the rocking horse, given to him when a friend moved away, looked concerned. Nick loved the bookcase, which was now his after being communal. Built by his father, it was red, white, and blue. His animal friends inhabited it, now looking at the boy with reassuring but mischievous looks. The feeling of discouragement fell over him as he closed the door. He slid down with his back against the door, resting on the back of his shoes in despair.

Alexander climbed the stairs in anger, furious with his hopelessly insensitive and brutal brothers. He was not pleased with his mother as well. He thought of the adage: *step on a crack and break your mother's back*; wishing for a crack at that time. Unfortunately, the home was carpeted, and stepping on a seam would not have the same intended effect.

Alexander's room stood at the top of the stairs, across the stairwell from Nick's, sharing an adjoining bath with the demon Chris's room. Everywhere pieces of puzzles, cars, baseball cards, and more lay ready for use at a moment's notice, a stylish room in the mind of the inventor boy. To his parents his room seemed a hopeless mass of junk. To Alex, however, each piece lay carefully categorized for future projects. On the wall hung an important poster-Teenage Mutant Ninja Turtles, featuring his favorite, Donatello. Now there was a hero, Alexander thought, staring at the image. This serious and business-like turtle would never tolerate the insult the boy experienced today. At night, Nicholas insisted on sleeping in the room as well. The poster made him angry, but he decided to just tolerate it for the time. Alex did not like the baggy shorts worn by his brothers. He was an individual and preferred very tight jeans. As he grew, it was difficult for him to part with them, so much so that the jeans became even tighter, making fastening after a bathroom trip a major project. Today he wore his favorite tight black-colored pants complete with high top sneakers, intentionally big for his growing feet. The shoes were black Lebron James Reeboks, a present from Chris. Curiously, the present allowed his older brother to receive Etnies skateboard shoes just months after the Reeboks seemed the ultimate purchase. Alex did not mind the donation, however. For him they were new and fit his style.

In his bedroom alone, Alex felt misunderstood. The loss of his invention was hard to take. He closed his door slowly, turned, and slid down with his back pressed to the door to sit on the heel of his shoes and think.

Christopher's room by contrast was neat. His bed was always made, a fact so important that he chose not to sleep under the covers. This trick allowed him to neglect making the bed each morning. He had the old desk in his room and each item had its place. To keep it so, he reserved any playtime for the other boy's room. "How would anyone know the difference anyway, their rooms so jammed with junk," he reasoned. A *Ninja Turtle* poster with his favorite, Michelangelo, the party dude, flanked the wall confirming the sad state of his nonparty-like day and understandable despair. From the wall poster, Kobe Bryant yelled his outrage at the boy's situation. In misery, he closed the door and as with his two imprisoned brothers, slid down to rest on his heels. Christopher reflected on the disaster that had been his day. Days such as these were all too common of late. His school was unfair, Monday a true conspiracy, the bus driver his personal demon, and his family a tortuous burden.

It was in that gloom when a sliver of hope entered the boy's mind. Dinner loomed ahead, and it could be his favorite, *pizza* tonight. Oh, to salvage his vanquished day, that meal would mean instant happiness and satisfaction snatched from the throes of unfair circumstances beyond the wronged boy's doing. From the wall, his Turtle friend echoed this desire. He deserved this, the inanimate hero seemed to say, and yes, Chris decided it was so. He stood reluctantly and pressed the intercom button to the kitchen where his mother had retreated. In his nicest voice, he asked slowly, "What is for dinner, mother?" The delay and silence that followed was overwhelming. He knew but did not think of the fact that each brother in his respective cells could hear this question as well.

Pirates, Scoundrels, and Kings

Alexander and Nicholas both knew the importance of the question. Hearing his question and knowing the intent they both thought simultaneously, "Oh pizza please!"

Patrice drew out the suspense, as mothers are so apt to do. With a poignant pause, finally she answered in a disgusted tone, "Meat loaf."

Chris now knew the great tribulation had begun, and meat loaf, what a perfect sequel to an exasperating day. What exactly was in meat loaf? As he thought, he imagined his mother slowly opening the freezer. With thick deep-freeze gloves and long iron tongs, she pulled out a Wonder Bread wrapped item complete with white plastic wrapper and balloons. Removing its contents with glee, a meat-colored congealed mass of something shrouded in a freezing fog and cast in the shape of a bread loaf appeared, topped off with a roughly-hewn, large, stew bone in the center. He imagined his mother laughing in a wicked frightening manner, looking at their dog Gidget who retreated quickly, having nothing to do with this tasteless monster. All he needed now was a headache, he thought.

Alexander's hopes came crashing down with a thud. Dinner, a possible bright light on the hopeless horizon, was now ruined. He knew of this meat loaf, a shapeless, foul-smelling, brown package full of floating substances never itemized for fear of their publicity. Catsup and lots of it was the only tactic that could possibly save him when forced to down this gruel against his will. Child abuse described what awaited the boy that night, Alexander thought.

Nicholas was not sure. "Did she say: beast toast? Would she really pulverize an old beast and force that down his little throat?" he wondered in horror. Imprisoned in the bleak dirty dungeon, Nicholas the pirate would fight to the end, never cry nor ask for a blindfold. He would not gag, but he would resist. He would fight to the end. The anticipation of combat improved his outlook on the day.

Christopher's day was now complete with no hope for salvage. He realized that escape was the only solution. To sit next to the ancient oak tree looking out over the valley would settle the boy somewhat.

He had considered dropping down the laundry shoot ever since moving in to their new house. It stood tempting him each day, its door yelling that he could just fit, sliding down a slide made obviously for his purposes. Besides, his parents would not really mind its use. What good was it for laundry, he reasoned? Until now escape was not tempting, but the day required actions only reserved for adversity. Slipping quietly out his door, he stopped at his brothers' doors, listening for any sounds. If they suspected his intention, they would report him for sure. For once, he seemed in luck. He quickly gathered up his most treasured possessions: skate board, basketball, and Walkman-containing backpack, and quietly exited his room. If he decided during this time away that his escape should be permanent, he was ready with all the essential items. Outside of his door he quickly opened the shoot. Within a heartbeat, he was in the laundry room, out the door, through the backyard, and up the hill toward his place of peace. Gidget knew, but she was cool with it. The Shar-Pei just smiled with her wrinkled face and told him to go for it in dog-to-boy language.

As Christopher climbed the hill behind his home, a feeling of relief fell over him. It was cooler now as the sun began to fall. The air was fresh, and if one was prone to pause and think about the view, the weather, and his new found freedom, he might have to admit to some joy. Chris did not see the beauty of the moment, however, for today had been such a trial.

The old oak tree had fascinated Chris since his family's move to their new house. While nearly everything in Temecula was new, every area leveled for construction led by the hopes of a robust economy, here stood an untouched and ancient tree. It was gnarled and thick, rising to the sky with long twisted branches. The boy thought of it more as a wise old man than a tree, emitting peace, seeming to possess wisdom, and standing as a silent witness to the world for so many years. Where the trunk met the ground a huge rotting branch lay, having fallen from the tree because of its weight sometime in the past. The branch made a perfect chair for him as he reached the top of the hill, slightly out of breath and needing to ponder his tormented existence.

Sitting, he gazed out over the Temecula Valley. Long rolling grass-covered hills stretched out before him. In the distance stood a row of houses. From here, their red tiled roofs and white three-rail fences suggested old farms with hay-filled barns. He was missing Nickelodeon Theater that afternoon, and imagined Andy Griffith and Barney would be at home in them. Distracted by the thought for a moment, he wondered why such a great show, funny, contemporary, and consequential,1 would be broadcast to the enquiring world in black and white? Hollywood corporate decision, he concluded.

He had often imagined a castle sitting alone in the distance, rising solemnly from the grassy meadow. Rose-tinged stonewalls rose to massive, peaked, roofed towers flying brilliantly colored banners. If he squinted, he could see a cloud of dust trailing a noble knight riding from the castle through a closing drawbridge. He wanted to be that knight, riding away to adventures and excitement, and away from this trudge of a life.

Chris believed that God loved him, but if so, why was life so hard? God had the keys to the city, but why was the city such a drag? Important thoughts flooded the young boy's mind. Why couldn't we play all day and sleep through school? Who invented school anyway? Why are all the good foods bad for you? Why did all the healthy foods make him gag? What's up with bedtimes? Do we have to endure little brothers? Why can't we do anything we want all the time? What brilliant person created only two days of weekend but five days during the week? The more he thought the more confused he was, and the more confused he was the more demoralized he became.

It began quietly at first, only a slightly audible noise interrupting his thoughts. When he first realized the sound, he dismissed it as the wind and returned to engrossing self-pity. The noise would not go away, however, and it continued every so often each time louder than the first. When Chris realized it was a voice, he stood up and looked into the tree expecting to see one of his friends laughing at his introspection. He heard it again, looking to the sky when he first made out the words, "Christopher." The voice continued, becoming more frequent. It was audible now and he realized it was a voice repeating his name, now obviously not coming from the tree.

It was about this time that the boy first noticed the overcast sky in what had been a bright and beautiful day just a moment before. A single gray cloud hung above, so visible that he wondered how he had missed it until now. "Clouds can't just appear can they, or can they?" the boy wondered aloud. The boy was not sure and he suddenly did not care because the voice continued and it seemed to come from the direction of the cloud. He turned skeptically and sat again on the branch. Chris was sorry he did because the roar of thunder and the crack of lightning were the immediate result, and he was sure that this cloud was like no cloud he had ever seen before.

"Christopher, it is to you that I speak. The problem is not valuing that which is given so freely," the cloud said in a now booming voice. "Expecting only satisfaction, you do not see character in a day's difficulties."

Only Uncle Bob could have dreamed up a joke like this, but even he could not make a cloud talk, he thought. He began to imagine the beginning of a face on the all too close meteorological mass.

"You must level your values and realize your blessings," came next from the strange cloud.

Chris had been a little frightened until now, but suddenly he burst out laughing. Challenging the voice he bravely yelled in his most authoritative tone. "What do you know? You're nothing but a cloud." Chris now stood looking into the sky with a smirk on his face. The day's events poured out of the boy in defiance. He grabbed an acorn and tossed it at the cloud.

It was humorous, the boy standing and staring at the philosophical cloud. Something about it recalled a scene from one of his favorite movies, Bill and Ted's Excellent Adventure. Here the two heroes stand before various people from the future, each repeating a silly phrase of their personal philosophy. In Chris's future he would lament his next action, repeating their words to the cloud. "Be excellent to everybody," Chris said, reciting Bill's phrase of meaning. He paused, and while he could not be sure, he detected an air of approval in the cloud's face. He should have stopped at that point, content with appeasing his adversary. His favorite line remained to be related, however. In his best Ted impersonation he continued, "Party on- DUDE!"

Before the last word was out of his mouth something told his brain that he was in trouble. He turned to run before he was even aware of the cloud's displeasure. It was one of those times when everything seemed to go so slowly, like a horrible dream where your feet will not move. A roar of thunder like none he had known before was his response. He had taken just a single step when next to his foot the first electrical charge hit the ground. The cloud was not talking in English now, but rather in wrath. The sky became dark, and the wind blew. Lightening was cracking, bolts landing around the boy. He ran as fast as he could but the ground seemed to move with each crack. Chris stumbled several times before he could really get going. Running now downhill he was out of control. There was a sudden drop-off ahead covered with rock, something he avoided before. With little choice, he dove headfirst, landing on his face. He didn't care that his nose was bleeding as he picked himself up and ran for safety leaving the squall behind.

"Dude, one bad cloud," the boy thought as he ran for his life towards his home, now hoping to slip back in undetected.

Chapter 2
Far Away Now

> A GENTLE ANSWER TURNS AWAY WRATH,
> BUT A HARSH WORD STIRS UP ANGER.
> **Proverbs 15:1**

Alexander was asleep and dreaming of greenhouse-powered submarines, video games, and micro-machines. Now that he enrolled himself in school, his profession was school, and somehow that period of sleep that had seemed so wasted now was much nobler to the boy. He insisted, however, when asked, that he never slept and was just pretending to do so.

Nicholas was awake as always with the first ray of light. A big person couldn't possibly understand how important it was for animal friends to all sleep together on a kid's bed even to the point of appearing to leave no room for their person friend. But room he had and a good hearty sleep as well. He jumped out of bed afraid that he might miss one precious moment of the new day. To the boys, sleepwear merged with the garments of day. Long ago the jammy bottoms and tops became mismatched and their shorts often seemed like the perfect wardrobe for bed. This morning Nick was wearing pajama bottoms now becoming too small, reaching to mid-calf. When his bare foot hit the ground, he was off as always to his oldest brother's room. He grabbed his black sweatband and placed it on his head.

While asleep, Christopher was an angel. When awakening he was a grinch, a fact that Nick loved. While Alex would awaken so nicely, Chris was always worth waking up. As was Nick's routine, he entered silently and pulled up the kiddy chair to sit and stare at his brother's face, now just inches from his. To Nick, this was the time of ultimate control over his bigger brother, and he would sit for some time savoring the moment. At just the perfect time he would strike his brother across vulnerable body parts with his best judo chop. Christopher's response was predictable. He would be startled awake and with eyes wide open. Suddenly arising he would yell, "M O M he's bugging me again!"

Much to Nick's disappointment, this morning was different. Chris opened his eyes, blinked several times, and in his quietest voice said, "Good morning, Nicholas. Thanks for waking me up. I need to get ready for school."

The shock was followed by disbelief as Nicholas watched his usually cooperatively disagreeable brother rise and begin getting ready for school. Nicholas rose from his chair, returning with despair to his bedroom. He couldn't believe his sudden change of bad luck. "Something serious was wrong with Chris," he was certain. "Alex would understand," he concluded.

Whistling was not Chris's usual entertainment, but that was exactly what Chris was doing this morning. The sky was blue, birds were chirping, and Chris for once noticed. When faced with escaping death, a new outlook is often the result for the survivor. He walked down the hill towards the bus stop trying to forget yesterday. For a moment he recalled his fearsome journey from the oak tree to his home. How did he explain his condition to his parents? He really couldn't remember! He knew that what had happened to him was not real and suddenly he was happy again. This change was rudely interrupted with the sudden memory of his possessions left yesterday at the tree. His skateboard, basketball-Shaquille signature model, by the way, backpack, and Walkman had been left in his sudden haste to leave the area with his skin unfried. He glanced to the hill behind his house. At this distance his beloved tree seemed small. If he returned to the tree he might miss the bus. While torn, he went on towards the bus thinking that even with that evil goon driver, it was preferable to leave these items than to miss the bus and have to wander himself to school.

The day seemed to last on and on, and Chris was fearful of the loss of his irreplaceable items. So preoccupied was he that the absence of Hurley on the ride home was scarcely noticed. He ran most of the way to the base of the tree after being let off at the bus stop. The final approach was done with caution. What happened yesterday certainly couldn't have been real, but the bruise and scab on his forehead suggested otherwise. He was taking no chances today and thought he was safe. The sky was clear, an observation of importance to him. When he reached the tree, not one item was gone or damaged. He was just bending down to reclaim his goods when the light in the sky grew dim. Thunder followed and Chris wondered why his Dad had ever rented that stupid *Bill and Ted's* video! Why had he watched it over and over to the point of memorizing the dialog? He was sorry that he had even dressed like them in his Ted period. He scooped up his things just managing to get them into his backpack as he turned to run. As before, he was met with a bolt at his feet. This time he wasn't as quick or the cloud was more resolute. He heard his name as before, loud and definitely a little pushed out of shape. A second burst struck him on the back with a crack. A yell could be heard as he fell to the ground twisted and incoherent. He would never be the same.

Chapter 3
The Pitlings

> BETTER A PATIENT MAN THAN A WARRIOR,
> A MAN WHO CONTROLS HIS TEMPER THAN
> ONE WHO TAKES A CITY.
> **PROVERBS 17:5**

To awaken with a mouth full of dirt was not Christopher's idea of comfort, but somehow it happened. The boy lay on the ground, his left arm twisted beneath him, his head rotated and resting on his eye. His mouth was open and a twisted tongue protruded between dirt-caked lips pressed to the dirt ground, as if he was licking a muddy chocolate chip cookie dough ice cream cone in some comedic skit.

When he awoke, his field of vision was narrow, seeing only the few inches before him. As his mind cleared and his vision broadened, the boy saw an oddly-clad foot perched by his face, supporting a muscular limb. Behind this stood its partner foot attached to a young, green-clad boy. Surrounding him, Chris became aware of a group of a half-dozen or so other boys, much the same age and size all looking at him with interest, or was it annoyance?

Chris lifted his head slowly, both eyes widened and fearful. He pushed his bruised, twisted body to sit up on a scorched patch of dirt. The circle of boys tightened around him, some appearing suspicious, while a few with the beginning of curious smiles on their dirty faces.

Overlooking him, the obvious leader examined the boy skeptically. As his mind cleared, Christopher returned the stare, looking the boy over. He was dressed like a character from the pages of an illustrated book. His shoes were green felt-like material, loose-fitting without laces, and pointy like an elf. His legs were covered with tights in the same forest-green color. On his torso, this character was dressed in a rough finished leather coat, tied at the waist, with a silver-buckled leather belt. Over one shoulder was quiver of arrows, and in the opposite arm a menacing crossbow. The boy had a light blond complexion, his hair sandy brown, bushy on the top, cropped closely on the sides, and longer in the back. The eyes were blue, focused, and direct. His expression was inquiring and serious, and while the crossbow in his hand now directed at Chris confused this issue, he still seemed friendly somehow.

Christopher realized as his hearing returned that he had been in dead silence for some time, the quiet now broken by an accusation from one in the circle. "He's a wizard, Manzell, for sure. Them mustn't be trusted!"

The leader boy named Manzell first turned and looked at the accuser. Turning slowly back to the boy he questioned the boy, "Do you be a wizard?"

Chris wasn't sure at that point just what he was, but a wizard, certainly not! Had he been a wizard then some relief for a dratted headache that was slowly boiling his brains out of his ear canals would be on its way. Oh, and by the way, Prince Robin Valiant Hood, Chris thought, would a freaking wizard sit here intimidated by a bunch of elves in green booties? The foreigner he was wanted to yell out. He wanted to explode, maybe retch all over these goons, but a recent lesson told him the peace and love approach was safer. Chris lifted a hand to his aching head, and tried to force a smile, without much success. He was afraid.

The lightning bolt had left every inch of his body on fire and aching. It was the feeling of a gigantic fever with Hulk Hogan sitting on him mixed with Judge Judy yelling and spitting for order in the Court. The boy tried to speak but his mouth was dry and full of dirt. He spit before he could think, hitting Manzell's foot. It shocked him after the fact, imagining an arrow striking him immediately, but Manzell and the others seemed not to notice or care.

"What have you to say," Manzell remarked?

A long pause followed, Chris swallowing a dirty gulp and glancing around the circle. The boys did not seem inclined to help. They were about the same age as their leader and dressed in similar garb. Weapons hung from scabbards at their sides: swords, knifes, and serious looking bows. Their clothes, in general, matched those of Manzell, earth colors, browns, dark reds, and greens. Chris noticed increasingly the contrast to his clothes; a navy blue T-shirt, board shoes, and orange shorts seemed to fluoresce annoyingly in the sunlight.

A response was obviously expected and the next statement by the group demanded a swift one. "Do him in, Manzell," could be heard from the leader's back. It unfortunately was met with nods of agreement by most of the band.

"I'm not a wizard," Chris finally said, nervously.

"Would you dare tell us? Who be you then?" Manzell wondered.

"I'm Chris...ah, ah... Christopher from Temecula," the latter said with some emphasis. Seeing little recognition he continued. "You know... California, zip code 9-2-5-9-1; ah, ah, Schwarzenegger, the Lakers?" he remarked with his best salesman smile.

"Temecula? Where be Temecula?" Manzell asked.

Chris pondered the situation looking down again towards the boy's feet. He frowned, rubbed his temple, stumped for the moment. He knew intuitively that these were people to whom zip codes, the Staples center, or even delivery pizza probably meant nothing. Then it dawned on the boy; he really had no idea where Temecula was or where he actually lived.

Trying to answer the boy he began to freelance. "I live in the pink, no, wait...not pink, salmon colored Mediterranean house up the hill from the bus stop near the school. You know, two lights after that soccer field, past that Squiggy guy's house." Receiving no acknowledgement he went on. "You know, past the skate park with the awesome grind rack, to the left of Carl's. In T town, the city with the Promenade... lemonade... cool in the shade...the best that can be found, T town's really tall mall. Ya, that's where I live, Manzell."

Somehow, Chris was certain these boys wouldn't understand. Looking around he saw trees and dirt, nothing that was even close to the modern day utopia that he was from. He was forming his response when the entire group suddenly disappeared without a word. Manzell returned, and with a strong arm grabbed Chris by the collar, dragging him roughly into the surrounding shrubbery. On his face again, with one boy on his back, he looked up through a small break in the bushes, seeing the source of their concern.

A band of horsemen had arrived and now stood no more than inches away from where Chris lay, exactly over the parched patch of ground the group had encircled minutes before. One huge black horse was dark and fidgety, pawing the ground as if wishing for the hunt. His mane was cropped closely and his dark sunken eyes with yellow jaundiced sclera spoke of evil. If the horse was fearsome, the rider was more so. From Chris's vantage point as it was, with his face again on the ground, the horse's rider seemed to sit ten feet in the air. His black boots were caked with miles of mud and he wore shiny spurs of silver sparked with gold. A saddlebag of weathered worn leather with gold trim was thrown over the horse's rump, and Chris could just make out the initial R.F on the buckle. The apparent leader of the group, the frightening man, was clothed in dusty black. A flowing cape of purple with a black lined collar was secured to broad shoulders with a golden clasp engraved with the shape of a hoof. His hair was brown and flowing, tied in the back in a ponytail. He was a tall man, especially so towering in his saddle, yet still slight of build, wiry, his features somewhat gaunt. His face was intent and serious. His eyes darted to and fro, looking for something or rather someone, Chris soon realized.

The rest of the group was mounted as well, except for one unfortunate merchant who stood out from the rest of the group. He was middle-aged and somewhat portly. His outfit was more colorful, with a vest over a white long sleeved shirt. While the others had purpose in their gaze, his was unsure and frightened. "They're sure to be just up ahead, Master Fordem," he said with an anxious, unsure voice.

"You've led us astray. We shan't forget that," accused another voice.

The leader circled his horse to return. He said nothing but his face was intolerant and full of vengeful hate. With a wave of his head, he signaled silently to his group. The portly man closed his eyes in fright as a rope was thrown over his shoulders and cinched up to secure his arms. A hopeless look came over the captive's face as he was led away in the direction the group had come.

One serious dude, Chris thought.

With the horsemen gone the boys picked themselves up and appeared in the clearing again. One boy helped Chris to his feet as Manzell spoke. "Surely there is evil, more so each day." Looking up the boy continued: "Alucemet...be wary! The stench rises. We must return." With that statement, Chris was aware for the first time of an odd, foul, smell.

One of the boys asked, "How goes the wizard, Manzell?"

The leader turned, aware again of Chris. Manzell's friendly smile and laugh broke the tension. "Sir Alexander will judge him" he was heard to say. "We must be off. We request your presence Christopher of Temecula," he said as the group turned and moved on.

Had this experience been less peculiar or distracting, Chris would have surely seen the similarity, for the site of the prior scene was altogether and curiously familiar. The land was more overgrown for certain. In the distance, there were no paved roads to be seen or homes pushing up on the horizon. Still, the small knoll, the rock-covered ridge, and the rolling hills; if not overwhelmed by his harried arrival, it would have been unmistakable. Absent was the massive and ancient oak, but what stood in its place, if not by its small size, overshadowed and covered by the dense brush, a small sapling from a casually tossed acorn was growing happily.

Chapter 4
Sir Alexander of Alucemet

> He who fears the Lord has a secure fortress,
> And for his children it will be a refuge.
> Proverbs 14:26

Christopher found himself in a bizarre and different land. He had been totally dazed by a relentless, vengeful cloud, and now the black riders had finalized the disturbing day's events for the freighted boy. Chris by now considered himself a prisoner, an unwilling participant of some unfolding violent civil dispute. His memories of the terrorized merchant and those foreboding pursuers made Chris shudder as his gut began to throb with peptic protest.

Chris was surrounded by Manzell and the boys, and the entourage headed towards somewhere, in search of someone, this Sir Alexander. Their pace was quick and direct with little discourse. Given the recent visitors, Chris assumed that they were looking for him or even more likely his present captors.

Manzell wore a sleeveless tunic and for the first time Chris noticed a wide keloid scar over his left shoulder. While in his own world the scar would have indicated boring shoulder surgery, given the setting, the scar suggested to the boy past exciting battles with flashing steel, mighty steeds, evil enemies, and the use of cautery in its treatment. The boy was the tallest of the group and quite muscular for a boy not more than ten years old. The others were as young as six to ten years of age. They were dressed in similar fashion as their leader, rough cut leather-type tunics some with light shirts underneath, while others like Manzell had bare shoulders. Many had loose-fitting trousers which stopped at mid-calf while others wore tights. The colors of the group were earth tones and somewhat drab by Chris's standards. Each boy wore shoes like their leader, loose-fitting pointed toe and elf like.

What distinguished this group in Chris's mind, however, were the weapons: knifes, swords, and bows of different sorts possessed by each. It impressed the boy, the weapons, for they implied a life of fighting, one where the day to day decisions were made with force.

One of the boys walked with a limp, one leg seeming to be shorter than the other. His hand on the same side was shrunken and nearly useless. The boy was named Martin and Chris could see that he suffered none with his disability. No one seemed to single him out or treat him differently. He never seemed to be without a large friendly smile and as Chris watched him, he winked to him as if to say that even though he was a prisoner, everything just might work out all right.

The evil of the horseman was still fresh in Chris's mind, but this odd group seemed to take it all in stride. It seemed inappropriate but a sense of joy and happiness was obvious in this curious band. They seemed to skip rather than walk as they made their way on the journey.

For a while they moved in silence. Martin was the first to speak. "May we have us a song, Manzell?"

Manzell turned as he walked and held his hand in the air. "Start it off my friend," was his response.

And so Martin began:

> A mighty band of soldiers,
> the Pitlings goes our name.
> We shan't be fooled upon,
> and so will go our fame
>
> Our future is upon us,
> all of Alucemet does know.
> From near and far among us,
> we'll take on any foe.

The entire group joined in the chorus:

> We're the Pitlings, the Pitlings
> the good shan't fear us now.
> There's not a cause not for us
> Sir Alexander will show us how.

Another boy broke into verse:

> Them's not too bad acoming,
> we'll take them dare we say.
> When the Pitlings are a finished,
> all the enemy will lay.
>
> It's to we people look,
> we protect them from all who come.
> When the evil comes upon them,
> we'll knock then on their BUM!

The chorus was sung with laughter, loudly by all. Fists and arms were seen raised as the boys joined in singing the chorus:

> We're the Pitlings, the Pitlings
> the good shan't fear us now.
> There's not a cause not for us,
> Alexander will show us how.

The verses and chorus continued each louder and with more energy than before. It soon became Manzell's turn and he sang:

> Alucemet be wary,
> The Boar directs your fate.
> Alex vows to free you,
> our time is growing late.
>
> The Pitlings swear they're honor,
> Sir Alexander will direct our test.

Pirates, Scoundrels, and Kings

Alucemet need not worry,
Until so we shan't rest.

As if choreographed, the last word was met with a violent turn by the songster. Without a word his crossbow was drawn, an arrow loaded, the apparent target the modern day boy. Chris shut his eyes, the arrow launched now straight for his head. He could feel the brush of the feather graze his cheek. In the instant that followed, as he became aware, he was sure that his survival was a mistake. He opened just one eye and saw his presumed aggressor smiling but looking somewhere past him. A cheer went up, and one of the boys returned with a rabbit, its neck pierced by the arrow. The group was delighted and Manzell congratulated. Proud of his accomplishment, and looking for a feast, the group went on. Their excitement was as if the Dominos man had just delivered, Chris thought, and strangely he found himself anticipating a meal as well. Suddenly he realized his hunger and touching his upper abdomen realized that this feeling meant that this unfortunately wasn't a dream. He noticed the sun was setting and shadows were beginning to appear. An incredible sense of exhaustion set over him. "Jet lag," he thought.

During the remainder of the journey, the group captured other items for dinner. Small birds and another rabbit were to be that night's meal, Chris realized. His hunger increased to the point that even these looked delicious. His mind turned to meat loaf, the horrid meal suddenly delectable.

Chris was amazed at the mood of this band of boys. They were an apparent orphan group, but yet they were happy. Chris wondered how? Dressed poorly, having to hunt for food, and no housing tract in site, like the homeless he had seen on occasion in his world. His world. The thought made him sad.

The terrain now climbed through rough overgrowth, dense bushes and trees. The group was on a narrow winding trail, the end of which seemed to be just ahead. Here several of the boys pulled away some large brambles which had been covering an opening into a rock cave.

The group moved upon a path lit by oil-burning torches on the wall. The walls of this apparent hideout were carved from stone. The air was moist and cold as they entered a large room decorated with wall mounted tapestries, a large wooden table with thick legs, surrounded by matching chairs. In the center of the room on the far wall sat a large straight back wooden chair with fixed arms, the seat upholstered with dark material. Above the chair hung a shield, with a complex crest of a strangely smiling lion. Just to the left of this chair a door-sized opening was apparent covered with a drawn curtain. At the head of the table a large open fireplace could be seen burning wood, casting eerie shadows.

Manzell walked the length of the room to the curtain. He drew it back revealing a door. He entered and returned briefly with a boy a few inches taller than Manzell. Chris suspected that here was finally the Sir Alexander he had heard about. From the moment he entered the room, it was apparent that he was their leader. The group was quiet and directed their attention to him. The large chair had not struck Chris as a throne but with Alexander now sitting on it, royalty was apparent.

He had a chestnut complexion. His hair was of a similar color, short on the top and sides, longer in the back just touching his collar. His face was oval in shape and there was a hint of a dimple on his chin. His maturity seemed beyond his young age. His smile was friendly as Manzell whispered something in his ear. In principal at least, he dressed the same as the others, but there was an air of refined dignity surrounding him. A dark leather doublet covered a long sleeved white shirt. The sleeves were loose, the collar open. His trousers were covered to mid-calf by soft leather boots with a flat heel. What was most distinctive about the boy though, were his eyes. Dark brown, they seemed to shine in the candlelight. An air of caring, intelligence, and understanding were apparent in them, and he looked Chris in the eye as if reading some hidden message in his soul.

The group led Christopher around the table for an audience. As he approached, he noticed for the first time a medallion hanging from a thin gold chain around his neck. It glinted periodically, appearing to be made of glass. At this distance, Chris could not make out the details. A large friendly smile came over the leader as he faced the capture.

"Christopher of Temecula, I hear you are a wizard." As Alexander spoke Chris thought he detected an air of humor in his countenance. "I am Alexander of Alucemet. The charge of wizardry is one of significant consequences now in the days of the Boar."

"The Boar!" Chris recalled Manzell's song with reference to this animal character. All eyes were now on him and he realized that though Alexander seemed friendly, he expected a response to these apparent charges.

"I am not a wizard, Alexander of Alucemet. I'm just a kid, and I'm really lost." Christopher then started to recount his arrival but stopped, realizing that he didn't really understand how he arrived or where he was.

Manzell spoke next. "A wizard I am certain, Alexander. He appeared as if from nowhere, lying at our feet! Look to him, where in Alucemet can such garments be taken? And may the Lord strike me down, Alexander; with my own eyes I have seen him eating the dirt that we walk on!"

Alexander quietly examined Christopher, looking at the boy for some time. A suggestion of a small smile could still be seen on his face. He rose and walked to the prisoner. Christopher was very careful in choosing his clothes. Usually he was quite proud of them. Today, however, as Alexander looked him up and down he was suddenly aware of how out of place he must have looked. Alexander spent a great deal of time eyeing his shoes. Skateboard shoes they were called, navy blue low tops with a flat rubber sole, and they now were the object of the leader's curiosity. At home he was the pillar of fashion; here his fashionable shoes began to support Manzell's charges. His shorts were suspected as well. These boys had never seen such a vivid orange color.

Alexander crossed the room, quietly returning and sitting in his chair. He shook his head slowly. "He is no wizard, Manzell".

"My lord, how can you be so certain!" Manzell objected politely. "I saw his entrance to our land with mine own eyes, gone one moment and in our world the next, his orange trousers lighting the way. If he be no wizard what be he then?"

All eyes focused on Alexander as he pondered the situation. He looked Chris over again, slowly judging him. "Master Christopher, a Wizard I am certain you are not. I must listen to my men who disagree, however. You come upon a sorrowful time in Alucemet. The Hoof of the Boar is ready to step on all that oppose him. Only we can right this failing Kingdom, and our destiny is to do so. It is foolish for me to trust my inner judgment in these manners for if incorrect, I jeopardize the cause."

Suddenly Alexander did not look like the supporter Chris had thought he was. "As always in this world, a test is needed to prove the truth. I ask you now Christopher of Temecula, how may you prove your harmlessness?"

Chris dropped his eyes as he realized the trouble brewing here. He remembered one of the group saying, "Do him in Manzell," when first captured. Suddenly, doing him in was looking like a possibility. He had to do something quickly, but what? An idea lit up and he thought to himself. I'm a kid, and I'll show them I'm a Kid. Moving, perhaps too quickly, he picked up his backpack and basketball.

The group hit the floor, rolled away, and drew their weapons. "An imploder, he has an imploder, one of the group yelled!" Another added, "Alexander, make haste!"

Several of the group hid under the table. Others had rolled behind chairs. Most were cowered, with weapons drawn.

Chris turned to Alexander, slowly putting his possessions on the floor. The boy was unfazed, sitting in his chair calmly. A smile came over his face and Chris was sure that unlike his friends, Alexander had seen a basketball.

"An imploder?" Chris said. "What is an imploder?" Slowly picking up the ball he said, "This is no imploder; its a basketball! You know Kareem Abdul Jabbar, Michael Jordan, Magic Johnson!" As he talked he turned to each member of the group offering the object of their fears. There were no takers. The names of Chris's heroes carried no weight in this land he realized.

Chris sensed a tragedy. He was outnumbered by a band of boys who were in fear of him. He realized that swift action was necessary or he, like the rabbit, would be dinner. He found himself for the first time talking as if of this medieval world as he said, "Alexander, a test you demand and so with your permission, a test I will perform. A kid like you I am, but of a different world. From where, I have no idea, but I have no weapons, and ask that your dedicated band disarm theirs. Objects of fun are all that I possess. May I not prove my honesty?"

Alexander nodded his approval to Chris. He turned to Manzell and without a word the Pitlings lowered their weapons and cleared out from under the table.

His idea seemed simple. How could a wizard behave like a kid? he thought. But do kids behave like kids here? The thought brought some questions to his plan, but what options did he have? He took a chance.

Like a globetrotter, he spun the basketball on his finger. Maybe it was fear, maybe just this world, but for whatever reason, he did this many times better than he had ever done before. He grew confident and was even able to switch hands with the ball still spinning. Looking to the crowd he realized they were not convinced. Next he bounced the ball.

As he dribbled, a deep breath in unison was heard from the crowd, anticipating an explosion.

Taking a chance he continued, again with unusual success. Dribbling back and forth between his legs, he sensed a calm excitement come over the room. There was a wooden box some twenty feet away over by the fireplace. It appeared to be a container for firewood, at the time empty. With a perfect skyhook he launched the ball across the room, the ball swishing into the container.

The boys stood, staring in silent awe. His next trick was easy as he gained confidence. He remembered his skateboard strapped to his backpack. He took it out and placed it on the rock floor, a surface perfect for boarding. Around and around the table he went, using kick turns and coming up on the rear wheels. As he moved, he would turn the skateboard from front to back and back again. He at last pulled in front of Alexander, stepped off the board, and with his left foot shot the skateboard into the air catching it about eye height. The applause that followed was relief to his ears.

Alexander stood and raised his hand for quiet. A friendly smile came over his face. "Christopher of Temecula, I know not where your land is, but a wizard you are not." Manzell and the others voiced their approval. High five's from all followed. Chris had just become a Pitling.

After congratulations, preparation for dinner began. Relief now in his marrow, Chris realized an overwhelming hunger. With this hunger, Chris realized again that this was no dream.

Alexander left the room, going through the door behind the curtain. The group busied itself with preparations for the night's meal. Chris felt out of place and thought he should help in some way. He asked Manzell if he might do so; however, he was told that tonight he should just relax. If he decided to stay he would be expected to pull his own load in the days to come.

A fire was going in the hearth, and meat was cooking on a spit. A kettle hung in the fireplace as well and a rich smell could be appreciated. Several boys set the table, placing rough-carved wooden utensils and bowls for their use.

Alexander now returned to the room and took his spot sitting at the head of the table. He motioned for Chris to join him and the boy thankfully sat, taking a chair beside him. Bowls of steaming liquid were placed before each seat and the rest of the group took their places. Alexander said grace asking for guidance and giving thanks for their safety and this meal.

Pirates, Scoundrels, and Kings

Chris was now extremely hungry. He eyed the steaming bowl in front of him with delight. In the candlelight it appeared to be a light-colored broth with a vapor rising. It had a light but pleasant aroma, and he wasted no time using his spoon quickly.

He suddenly realized that all eyes were on him and he heard a few giggles. He looked up to see every one staring at him. They unlike Chris had their hands within the fluid. While they laughed at him, it wasn't with derision but with understanding.

Alexander chuckled. "Christopher of Temecula," he said. "Fate has shown well on us today. A rabbit with a full bladder was captured by Manzell. It has a detergent like property and speaks well of our future. We in Alucemet generally cleanse our hands after boiling it whenever luck brings it to us. I don't think it bane however; feel free to use it as is your custom."

The last swallow was just entering his throat when Chris realized his mistake. Like with the dirt this afternoon, he spat before thinking. Everyone was now laughing uncontrollably.

Even Alexander for once seemed out of control. He looked at Chris and said, "I will have to watch you more closely my friend."

The laughing continued. It really hadn't tasted that bad. Oh how could he think that? he wondered silently to himself He watched himself for the remainder of the dinner. After watching so as not to be the first to taste anything, he finished all that was given to him. A stew of meat and potatoes, and dark hard bread was eaten quickly, the meal quite tasty. He couldn't believe his hunger and he remembered all those meals at home that he had left unfinished. Sweat ale was served to drink and he finished it to the last drop.

Around him were the boys. As he ate he watched them. In many ways they were different from him, their dress, their dialect. In other ways, however, they seemed the same. Like kids anywhere they kidded, but it was obvious as well that they cared about one another. These boys seemed so happy. These kids could have lived down the street, Chris thought, as they laughed and joked.

Chris now turned his attention to Alexander, who sat at the head of the table. As Manzell recounted to him the day's events, Chris tried to politely listen and learn of his New World. There seemed to be an ever-growing presence of evil in Alucemet. Apparently the sign of this evil was represented by the mark of the Boar's hoof. It reminded the boy of the engraving on the horse rider leader's clasp which secured his cape. Apparently, the dark forces were not new, but becoming a more prominent presence. Their objective was not in doubt; they were looking for the Pitlings and their leader.

A boy named Cyrus drew back his chair and rose to address Alexander. He was one of the youngest of the group. He had blond hair, longer than Manzell's and pulled back into a ponytail. As he stood he said, "My Lord, an uncommon day is upon us. One year our group has lived together for our common good. A feast is before us and the presence of our new friend can only speak of good times. What sayesth to a night of song?"

Alexander was up with this request. With his glass in hand he signaled his approval of this. "Cyrus may you do us a favor!"

The boys pulled back their chairs as Cyrus stepped upon the table as if commanding a stage. The boy sang a light melody to the cheers of the others. Several of the boys accompanied him on instruments. A boy named Jason strummed a stringed instrument, while Alexander played a flute. He recanted a story of Knights, chivalry, and castles. All of the boys were clapping as the rhythm of the song picked up.

After the song, Alexander took his place and recited a long poem full of humorous references to the boys. The night continued in this fashion as each boy took his turn, as if each was a skilled entertainer. The fun made Chris forget his world and the confusion of the day.

When the last of the boys had finished, Chris found himself sorry that the entertainment could not continue longer. He had never been on a stage, always quite bashful. Tonight, he almost wished he could entertain. As he thought, he realized much to his surprise that all eyes were upon him.

Pirates, Scoundrels, and Kings

It is easy to wish to entertain a crowd, but frightening when the opportunity presents itself. The group seemed to have no concept of his dilemma as they waited for his performance. What could he possibly do for the crowd? Chris wondered as he reluctantly stood. He was standing on the table before he really had any ideas at all. Searching his memory, the boy recited what he could.

> Skunk in the Barnyard-
> Pee you.
> Somebody ate it-
> that's you.
>
> When did it happen?
> Last night.
> How did it taste?
> Just right.

The boys sat in silence, his poem confusing the group. How could he say that, he thought? The confused stares reminded him, where in the world am I? Out of desperation he babbled on.

> I won, I won;
> I won, the BB gun.
> You lost, you lost;
> you lost the apple sauce.

There was little improvement in the response of the crowd. He recalled his backpack and reached for it. Inside, to his relief, he found his sunglasses and Walkman. Would batteries work here? he wondered in silent desperation as he set the modern apparatus up on the edge of the table. The group was shocked as a rap beat blared from the small device, making a wizardry charge more likely. Standing now on the long table, he slowly slid his wrap around bright magenta sunglasses on. Without effort he rapped like he had never rapped before:

> I guess I dropped in from T Town
> A little sorry dude who'se hopin to get found.
> Chill, no thrill, hey why all da fuss?
> Me, a kid, I took a wrong turn on the bus.
>
> I woke in the dirt, mouth full, I be spittin
> Opened my eyes, surrounded by ya pittlin's
>
> I'm in trouble, missin, I must be far from home
> Found on my face, crashed down on my dome.
>
> A wizard, ya kiddin that never would be me.
> I got no magic, when you know me you'll agree.

As the chorus began, the boy's approval was obvious. Alexander and the others were on their feet clapping. Chris could get to like this, he thought as he yelled, "E X C E L L E N T! " Pointing to one of the boys, he motioned for a half-eaten drumstick. He used this as an imaginary microphone as the chorus began:

> I just dropped in from T Town
> A little sorry dude who'se hopin to get found.
> Chill, no thrill, hey why all da fuss?
> Me, a kid, I took a wrong turn on the bus.
>
> Starved, thirsty, I jumped the food with my scoop
> But gee…phooey, it was rabbit urine soup.
>
> But say, who they, the black guy on da horse.
> Mad, demented? I hope that dude's a hoax.
>
> What's up with all these Pirates, Scoundrels, Kings
> Here, I'm rhappin, cause I can never sing.

On his toes he turned to his right then his left as he made his way down the length of the table. Rock and roll was so far removed from these times and places but yet the boys danced as if American bandstand was on every day. It amused Chris to see these apparently medieval friends grinding to his every word as he sang:

> I just I dropped in from T Town
> A little sorry dude who'se hopin to get found.
> Chill, no thrill, hey why all da fuss?
> Me, a kid, I took a wrong turn on the bus.
>
> I know, this verse is nutt'in short of crime.
> Now, my brain's got nothing left to rhyme.

A loud howl went up from his audience. He jumped from the end of the table and sang the chorus again. He danced and twisted as a guitar solo from the Walkman began. He was surprised as Martin handed him a guitar like stringed instrument to use as a prop. He hit each note with perfection and timed histrionics. His confidence was growing. Maybe entertainment was for him, he thought.

With the last verse, he ran the length of the room and like Bo Diddly slid to a stop on his knees, his hands raised. The crowd was going wild. Several of the boys and Alexander were dancing on top of the table. As the final verse ended, and the chorus began to fade, Chris slowly walked to the table. He slid his sunglasses off, bowing to the crowd.

Alexander met him and with the others surrounded him now as if a hero.

When the applause died down, Alexander said, "A great addition to the Pitlings are you, Christopher of Temecula."

Chris felt a warm feeling of acceptance. The boys congratulated him just as if he one of them. He was beginning to like this world after all.

The night died down and the time to sleep was upon them. After the excitement of the day, Chris thought of how hard it was going to be to fall asleep. There were several chambers adjacent to the main hall, and the boys adjourned to their rooms.

Alexander handed Chris a bedding roll and led him to his room. For the first time Chris could closely see the medallion around his neck. Approximately an inch in length, when viewed from the front it had an hourglass shape, from the side crescent. It appeared to be of glass but was not transparent. A mirror like finish could be seen on the concave surface which faced his chest, and it hung on a thick golden chain. As Chris stared, Alexander placed it slowly within his shirt. An odd expression of seriousness came over the leader. Chris was afraid that he had violated some sense of privacy and glanced away to prepare his bed.

Alexander reached gently to his shoulder and turned him back to face him. "Christopher of Temecula, a burden I carry with me to which your innocence should not be troubled." With a silent expression nothing further was said. While the boy could not know the details at the time, for a land so friendly and happy something in this world was occurring, the nature of which he hoped he would never confront. He shuddered as he reclined in his bedding on the stone floor recalling the black riders. The toll of the day soon took effect as the adopted Pitting dropped off to sleep.

Chapter 5
The Boar's Hoof

>WHEN THE WICKED THRIVE,
>SO DOES SIN,
>BUT THE RIGHTEOUS WILL SEE THEIR DOWNFALL.
>PROVERBS 29:16

On a rocky perch stood the massive castle Alucemet, dominating the land from which its name was derived. Its charm and former nobility was overcome now by an apparent blight, as if infected by a purulent phlegmon. Towers at each corner of the surrounding fortress walls rose to the sky. Ragged purple garlands, adorned with a Boar's Hoof of oppression, vexed a hopeless message of subjugation high above its spires. Protecting the northern periphery were fearsome cliffs, stained white by years of seagull droppings, crashing to an unrelenting sea below. To its west, a perfect natural harbor allowed sea access to this apparent military fortress. Surrounding the castle's southern and eastern flanks sat a moat filled with foul, gray, stagnant water, the last barrier for any brave or ignorant soul calling for an audience within this despotic bastion.

In finer times, Alucemet stood unquestioned as a principled citadel, representing majesty and beauty, a symbol of strength and love. Now, along with its proud people, this was replaced by despotism, the fortress reflecting this sorry change and reluctantly becoming a symbol of hatred and anguish. As the sun set to the west, the disappearing sun was appropriate, for it lit the fortification's neglected rose-colored stone walls in a foreboding manner, the sun's disappearance over the horizon personifying the kingdoms demise.

As if on the wind they rode, a shadow of dust exploding for miles behind the horse mounted column. A menacing cause seemed to guide them, a punishing frustration apparent in the eyes of their commander and his mount, as they made for the castle in the waning hours of the day. The dark rider drove the jaundiced-eyed stallion mercilessly, the horse oddly content with the abuse, while foam, drool, and a shining coat drenched with hard won sweat dripped, as the group galloped along the winding rock-carved road leading to the fortress gate. By hidden signal, the drawbridge slowly lowered to span the moat as the riders approached. With an air of arrogant entitlement, the leader flew over the wooden bridge and skidded into the courtyard, his mount kicking mucky gravel across the guardsmen without regret.

While anger and frustration described the delegate's leader, the peasant's countenance reflected horror and dread. He was bound around his trunk as before, now sitting imprisoned on one of the group's recently arrived delegation of tiring horses. With his lonely eyes cast down, the man sat with resignation unaware of anyone or anything around him. Soon he was pulled roughly from the horse, his face planted on the rock courtyard, as a small crowd gathered to feed like vultures on his misfortune. The habitually jolly man looked up with a bloodied and scrapped face as the muddy boots of one Richard of Fordem, rudely greeted him. Fordem planted a heavy foot on one of the man's hands and twisted with glee. Here was the first emotion other than anger and frustration appearing in the ruthless man, and the peasant howled in pain. Fordem motioned to one of his men, and the peasant was forced to his feet. The leader threw his purple cape over his shoulder and turned to leave, saying loudly for all to hear, "Mark him as ours!" The simple man with bound arms dangling began crying out in fear, anticipating something dreadful about this phrase, as obedient soldiers led him impolitely toward an unpalatable experience across the castle grounds. Crude jostling and curses came from the subordinates, as they scampered, securing the horses and moving to other duties. Fordem marched with hate as he hastily crossed the castle courtyard. An unfortunate villager crossing his path fell to the ground cowering in response to a strong forearm.

The delegation's arrival had disrupted the village activity. These disruptions were becoming the norm of late, and no one spoke of them out of fear of reprisal. The courtyard market was officially closed by this hour, but this center of society and commerce still bubbled with life, albeit a very ill life. Each citizen of Alucemet had adapted in their own manner to the spreading of an evil mist within their society. Some with ruthless efficiency flourished; others sadly did not. Tonight, as darkness fell over the entire kingdom, the sad tried to forget, the ruthless didn't care, but all gathered their belongings. The black smith, the grocer, and the cobbler all closed their shop gates, and with heads lowered, quickly left for their countryside homes speaking naught of the rider's arrival.

The soldiers of the Boar's hoof by selection had evolved towards the ruthless side, and one could still hear the laughs of derision and conceit from them as they stabled their mounts. If one was to characterize their attitude it would be: "I have mine, now. I've got it made. Anyone who dares opposes me will be eliminated!"

Majestic even in a state of disrepair, Fordem's destination, the royal lodgings, towered above the northernmost edge of the courtyard. He entered the palace through two massive oaken doors, opened for him by silent sentries dressed in dirt soiled white tunics. He passed them without a tip, and quickly walked along a once grand marble-floored hallway. Paintings and statues lined the walls, some improved for all time, retouched with crude and graphic graffiti. A crystal vase was overturned and cracked, and several paintings hung obviously ajar, completing a newly inspired crass motif. At the end of the hall were two massive gold-laden doors, markedly contrasted with the image, still polished and shining. Dominating these doors, sprang a curiously smiling lion crest, looking upon the chaotic scene and appearing to know something no one else was privy to. Guards dressed crudely as the horsemen, stood parallel to the door and completed the scene.

Without acknowledgment, Fordem passed the golden doors and guards, turning and climbing a narrow staircase with steps hewn from stone. He stopped in his tracks, with a quiet hiss, wishing he had not heard the call of his name.

"Richard!" The name echoed in the hall.

As only a guilt worn man might, with resignation and fear, the man slowly turned to face a beautiful woman who had heard him pass. She stood now in the doorway holding open the heavy doors, staring and confronting the man. His countenance of fierce insolent determination now melted into one of quiet submission. Fordem could not meet her stare, but rather dropped his gaze to the floor as he slowly acknowledged the presence of the woman, with a reluctant servile nod of his head.

She was slight of frame, and would have stood only to the man's chest in height, but his respect for her was obvious. The woman dressed in a rose-colored, silken gown; her dark hair pulled back in a silver ribbed chignon. She possessed a complexion like milk, and a feminine carriage draped over an extraordinary strength of will. Her green eyes dazzled, but a deep concern was evident in them as well, as she examined the commander, demanding his respect. She stood in golden slippers and carried herself with a regal maturity which connoted the best of royalty.

His eyes lifted, for the first time making eye contact only briefly, and then looking away he responded, "Yes, my lady?"

"Richard, what becomes of the Kingdom? I fear for our King! Any word to speak of him?"

Tense silence followed for what seemed like minutes. The man hung his head betraying obvious shame. Eventually he stammered out, as a child caught by his parent in some transgression. "No. No.... No news, my lady," the cowering man offered. He shook his head slowly trying to appear sympathetic and honest. The man shot a quick glance at the woman betraying his discomfort, and quickly dropped his gaze to the floor again. It was cold that night in the stone castle except on Fordem's brow, which proceeded to produce a flood of sweat sheeting down into his eyes. The man blinked his stinging eyes rapidly, refusing to wipe them in the presence of his Lady.

"Can you speak of my children, Richard? What has become of Alexander, what of Nicholas?"

The names betrayed his discomfort by producing a gasp that he quickly swallowed. "There is no word, ah…ah… sadly as before," he whispered, intensely focusing his attention on the muddy, black, riding boots which for some reason had just gathered his entire attention.

"I scant trust him Richard. This smells of Michaelis!"

He glanced quickly at her, sadness now covering the brave woman's face. She turned with a tear and reentered the chambers, closing the golden doors behind her.

Fordem cringed for sometime after the lady's departure. He was flummoxed; his posture collapsed and he actually lost inches of stature. Perhaps he was on the edge, a good man considering evil, still able to turn back. He stared silently, with a deep sadness at the once so glorious golden doors, and reflected upon some prior dignity that had been his. The fearsome commander, so insensitive to the cares of others, had been profoundly affected by this woman in a curious, childlike manner. While the final choice had been made, he still was deeply conflicted between his natural state of honor and duty, and what he had become: a man of opportunity and shame. But alas, his destiny was cast irreversibly toward evil, and he made a decision to resist the good.

Richard of Fordem collected himself, pulled his arrogant visage together, regained those lost inches of posture, wiped his brow, turned upon his heel, and quickly climbed the stairs. The heavy boots covered by silver spurs tipped with gold, echoed on the stone-hewn steps, as Fordem ascended the many floors.

The man finished his long climb on a dark floor lit by a single oil lamp. Adjoining the landing stood two heavy, black, walnut doors, adorned by a crudely carved image of a Boar's Hoof. He was still very distracted and began to shake mud from his boots before realizing how useless cleanliness was in this new world. Fordem gave up his futile process, threw open the doors, and marched into a dark chamber, filled with a foul and rank stench.

Fordem stood in a hall that had a moist dead feel to it, though an open window was apparent across the room. The ceiling was a high cathedral vault, decorated with freshly spun spider's webs. Across the room, on its northern wall, stood an intricately tooled wooden desk, set on thick legs, in front of a Romanesque arched window which looked out over the sea far below. Behind the desk sat a high-backed, black, leather chair, turned to face the rising moon over the horizon.

The chair rotated and confronted Fordem as he crossed the chamber, revealing an obese, wrinkled, boulder of a man: Michaelis. He was short and squat, with little dangling legs, which touched the ground only because of exaggerated high heels on his curiously shiny and clean black boots. He had a huge square head, topped with a few shards of coarse, wiry, black hair. The man possessed a long snout, beginning at the top of his forehead and diving between two lifeless, black eyes. It was tipped by a wet pug nose, with greasy, black, monstrous nostrils. His mouth was filled with filthy, snaggletoothed canines, much too long to be closed inside of his mouth. His skin was oily and pink, and he had two short ears filled with burls of wiry grey hair. The ears had pointy tips and were separated by his furrowed frontal cranium, so that in the dark room and lit from behind, the man had a silhouette of a craven heavy metal sign, (also known as the sign of the goat), a hand signal used by fans proudly at a Metallica concert.

Fordem stood in obedience, towering over the man, after he had risen to greet the commander. When fully upright, the pig of a man's legs never fully extended at the knees. He dressed entirely in soiled, black, military garb, had a huge belly that shook in continuous harmonic motion, and was stretched over a thick leather belt. Stubby fingers possessed the same coarse hair on each knuckle, and he drummed them to an unheard rhythm on the desk. The beast wore ornate golden rings on each digit, two on both index fingers, a large golden ring engraved with the same Boar's Hoof on his right thumb.

Fordem spoke first. "Your honor Michaelis, I am told of your summons, I regret that all did not go well with our outing. We found no evidence of either boy or their groups at this time."

A high pitched raspy voice responded. "It surprises me not. Where goes that worthless peasant. Recall my warning of him, Fordem? Is he mine as of yet?"

Fordem did not acknowledge the leader's recollection, as if the warning was Michaelis's creative memory again. He quietly responded, "He is being marked presently, Sire."

Michaelis turned and walked out from behind the desk, now standing in front of Fordem. The condition of his high black boots starkly contrasted with the rest of the Kingdom, for they were carefully polished to a mirror like shine. A high heel placed the short man on a perch, and he appeared to exercise considerable caution while walking, as if his foot did not completely fill out the toe of the boot. The beast whined along. "Truly the peasantry deserves no concern. They are merely refuse," he said with a disparaging wave of his ring-laden hand. "Waste product, fecal matter carries the same value in my kingdom. Soon the Boar will have supreme power. No one will oppose me. The puzzle of the Mirrorlass will soon be mine."

"What of Alexander, Sire?" Fordem questioned.

Michaelis barked back spitting. "You dare mention this insolent fool! My superior mind is rapidly discovering the solution. No mind broader than I exist. No one has ever possessed a brain quicker or more definite than the Boar." Each phrase came louder and more rapidly than the former. "I am the future, and destiny is my middle name. Of what use is a small, frail, spoiled, brat boy? As with his weak father, he has no future."

"You speak the truth, of that I am certain, Michaelis. But Queen Patrice, her concern grows with each light and she asks of King William." Fordem stated now with caution.

"She will soon be of no use. Women are so simple to manipulate! They are so predictable and weak. Console her with... I don't know," he said, looking down admiringly of his boots. Present her another pair of shoes. She will worship me for that! Yes, another pair of shoes will gain us more than enough time! You were her trusted manservant. How could you not see this? Once secured, the power of the Mirrorlass will make the Kingdom mine. She will be marked like the others. I will personally destroy all of her possession, I will burn each and every one of her shoes for my satisfaction, and she will beg to swear her allegiance to me."

Michaelis returned and gazed out the window. He spoke quietly, as if to himself. "They will remember me, that royal family. I have broken their spirit and cast out the children." He continued on more rapidly in an angry fury. "Disbelief awaits them all. I Michaelis, their lowly servant of Refuse, will shortly rule their Kingdom, and yes, the entire universe."

He whirled to face Fordem. "Leave me now," he said with a dismissive wave. "At first light, send a scribe to my chamber. The King, under my direction, will issue the first proclamation soon. Have ready the army as well. Your next attempt must not fail. The people will see brother against brother and their last air of rebellion will be broken!"

Michaelis dismissed his commander with another thoughtless wave of his stubby hand. Fordem turned and marched out the doors. They closed loudly and he could be heard descending the stone staircase by the click of his spurs.

As Michaelis returned to his desk, a young steward with empty eyes entered the chamber, pushing a cart overflowing with a bountiful fare. The boy prepared a long dining table, setting serving places for only one. His mutilated ears were visible only when the unfortunate boy was viewed laterally, the posterior auricle flat, as if clipped sharply with pruning shears. This resulted in pointed, pork-like appearance to the top of the external ear. This anomaly was not congenital, for the wound was deeply scarred and irregular, as if cautery had painfully closed a surgically created laceration.

The boy finished his chore and stood at attention, asking silently for disposition. With little acknowledgment, Michaelis lifted his left arm and cast the servant away.

    The Boar walked to the long dining table. He washed his hands superficially and with disgust, a custom only, not acknowledging any purpose. The man then sat at the table, dwarfed in a tall, straight-backed, wooden chair; dried his hands with a cloth towel, and forced it deeply into his collar. Michaelis was surrounded by food in abundance, and using primarily his bare hands, proceeded to feast in a rapid, disgusting fashion. An entire roast turkey and a delicate leg of lamb were consumed in minutes. Fruits, sauces, and soups followed in rapid order. What followed next brought him special pleasure, as he consumed a platter of buttered corn, cobs and all. The boar ate consistent with his appearance, slovenly and sloppy, as sounds and smells emanated from his room like a trash compactor. He ate rapidly, as if he would lose a moment of precious eating time. Swallowing was completed with scarcely a bite, as if chewing a needless delay. A portion of each mouthful could be expected to fall to the table and the floor below, the largest of these quickly recovered and devoured on the rebound. The napkin soon gave way to his tunic, as both became smeared with grease and sauce. Here was a culinary maestro, directing a feast that took on the appearance of brutal war with bones, sinew, hide, and torn meat all falling to the floor becoming a mass grave. He stopped for a breath, but only when forced, and he would gasp at that moment irritated for the delay. Finally, a large jeweled goblet was lifted to his mouth. He downed the contents to the last drop. Bursts of echoing flatus, followed by a large gaseous belch, signaled the finale of his proud composition. He pushed himself away from the table, scattering food, silverware, as well as delicate china, all crashing without a care to the floor.

    The boar collapsed as with narcolepsy into a postprandial sleep on a large cushion next to the table. Lying on his side, he drew his limbs up, and began snoring like a freight train. Sporadically his limbs would jerk in a violent convulsing manner, and he had soon thrown himself off the cushion onto the bare floor. A black crusty tongue lay between barred teeth, as he rhythmically respired, in and out, casting forward and back a most foul-smelling breath. Sweat was beading on his oily brow, a metabolic result of the large meal. The beads would grow until their weight would cause them to roll slowly off his face and onto the pillow. One bead found itself rolling down his long snout, and came to rest precariously on the tip. As it finally rolled off, a perfectly timed inspiration drew the drop deep into his lungs. With an explosive projectile cough, he awoke with a start, jumped to his feet, and drew a short pearl-handled knife in defense. The use of perspiration as an alarm clock was nothing new to the man, for once he became aware and awake, he slipped the knife away in its scabbard, wiped his brow, and smiled, oh so happy with himself.

Now rested after his carnage, the Boar walked across the large darkened room. He inspected himself briefly in a long mirror, totally enraptured by his own glory. Turning to a green velvet curtain, the man cast it aside revealing a small door. Using a golden key, he opened the door which revealed a second door opened with a second golden key. Michaelis removed an object covered with black silk and carefully placed it on a small wooden bench. A sphere, fashioned of cloudy black, semi-translucent material, sparkled in the moonlight, and sat upon a golden stand. The Boar lifted the globe and inspected its underside. Here was a small hourglass opening. The crude man squinted, first with one eye then the other, trying to see within the globe through the opening. A stubby finger tried unsuccessfully to probe it. He lifted an oil lamp inspecting every single area of jewel like surface, as if trying to reveal its secrets. Michaelis stared at the globe for several minutes with an increasingly jealous rage. He sat the globe down roughly on its stand. Grabbing some parchment, he rolled and placed it through the hourglass opening. Using this as a wick, he lit it from the oil lamp, and observed with curiosity. Nothing happened to the device. Impatience was obvious, as he began to spit and curse. He clenched his stubby fist and struck the table. As he did so a portion of the wick fell, burning to the floor.

Pirates, Scoundrels, and Kings

Michaelis shifted nervously from side to side as if in an angry fever. He spun the object on its stand without effect, now more and more livid.

He struck the table a second time, inadvertently burning his hand on the smoldering piece of parchment. With squeals of pain, Michaelis made a mad dash to the site of his prior meal and stuffed his burnt hand into a platter of jam, cooling his burning hide with a sizzle. Free of the smoldering flesh he returned to the table again, only aware of the curious object. Now beginning to become flustrated, he stared and cursed turning the object on its stand. Sweat rolled off the man's brow, and he wiped it with his jam stained hand leaving a heap on his brow.

As he impatiently examined the sphere, an interesting maneuver began. Here he would seemingly fall on his boot shanks, the shiny focal point of his costume now folded over. Without a thought and as if practiced the man would lift his leg and shake the shank outward, righting himself and standing on the elevated black heels.

A comical figure, he examined the sphere with impatience. Complete with a jam smeared face, he became more flustrated by the moment, as his apparent inability to accomplish something with the device became a point of anger for the porcine man. Finally, with violence he grabbed the object, bringing it up above his head as if to cast it away. Something calmed the beast, however, for he stopped and slowly replaced the globe on its stand.

For once acting with intelligent reason, he turned and moved to the window. Had his vision been better, and his self image less majestic, Michaelis would have seen something that night at the horizon out in the sea that would have concerned him greatly. Instead, he saw nothing but the sea. Here trouble for the man had already begun and the ship out at sea was just the first sign of a resistance to come.

THE QUEEN SLOWLY CLOSED THE golden doors quietly with sadness. Her head was lowered, as she stood for a moment in obvious despair. Fordem could be heard climbing the stone staircase behind her, his spurs clicking away on the stone hewn stairs. She lifted her head, her eyes now full of the tears she had tried so hard to hide. Her world seemed to be crumbling. She remembered back to a time of happiness, which seemed so long ago. A family made in heaven, hers had been, now thrown to the wind. Her life had been only for her children, such hopes and dreams; "what of them now?" she thought. They were all gone after arguments and anger. Where were her family now? Could they even be alive? She stopped and forced herself not to consider the negative of that question. Theirs had been a kingdom ruled by kindness and love; it seemed now headed towards hatred and slavery.

And what of her King, she wondered silently to herself? His control had fallen over the last few months and the King was now nowhere to be found. She wondered for the hundredth time, where he was, and by whose hand was he was detained? She suspected the answer but tried to forget. He was sly, the pig man, as she called him. He called himself a boar! He was the origin of the unrest. It seemed so clear now.

Even Fordem who had grown up serving her seemed evil and her trust in him was lapsing of late. She crossed the chamber to her nightstand. She felt so alone that night, so helpless. She must have stood there in thought for hours, for soon she heard spurs striking the staircase as Fordem descended. She heard the kitchen boy on the stairs. Must have been the pig's fifth meal tonight, she thought in disgust.

As if drawn by some magical force, she rose and crossed the chamber to the window to look out over the sea below. The moon was just rising over the horizon. The night was clear but as recently there was foulness in the air. She stared across at the horizon. Something made her heart race. Could that object really be what she hoped? On the horizon, now silhouetted against the moon, was a ship full of sail. Why did she know its occupant? The ship was just a speck across the sea; no insignia was visible at this distance. Only a mother could be so sure, and somehow she was. Somehow the sight gave her a comfort. She knew then that all was not lost.

THE MASSIVE WOODEN SHIP GENTLY twisted in the churning sea. The masts were full with billowing white sails. A flag flew high above the deck, a crest of an unusual Laughing Lion embroidered upon it. The port and starboard banks showed full with cannons. A boy in age but mature beyond his years captained that ship. In the crow's nest he stood, high above the deck. His light brown hair was blowing in the sea breeze. He wore a silken light-colored shirt, open to mid chest. Dark trousers he wore, cut at mid-calf, and his feet were bare. A blue cloth served as a belt tied loosely at his waist. A sword of beautiful carved gold was holstered on his hip. An eyeglass was lifted to his dark brown eyes. The boy's sights were as well across the sea, now inspecting his prior home, castle Alucemet.

He looked for a long while, then replaced the eyeglass. A quiet smile as if accepting a challenge came over him, his dimpled cheeks apparent. He laughed to himself briefly, and then finished with a broad friendly grin. Lifting a clenched hand the boy seemed buoyed with confidence. He swung with agile quickness from the crow's nest. With a leather throng in one hand and legs wrapped upon a guide rope, he slid swiftly to the deck below. He walked with a skip the length of the deck. With a smile he called to his men, each turning with obedience to surround him.

The ship was manned by boys of his age. Several wore bandannas, one a black patch over his left eye. They looked to the boy as he approached. One said to the leader, "it's to be a mighty tough one tonight, eh Nicholas?"

Nicholas smiled broadly. He shook his head as he said, "nothing too tough for the likes of us, mate."

While the group seemed to have allegiance to the boy, there may have been some unrest, for the boy with the patch stepped forward as if in defiance. Silence followed as the group looked on the boy who stood challenging their leader. The boy was tall and thin, with bushy blond hair and a blue un-patched eye. A stray lock of hair seemed always to fall over his forehead and he would brush it back on occasion. Beyond the patch, he was dressed quite like the others. A red striped shirt was worn, the short sleeves rolled tightly to expose his tanned shoulders. The hem of the shirt was tied in a knot over his left hip. He wore black trousers, which like the leader reached only to mid-calf. His shoes were black with a silver buckle.

His eyes seemed focused on his goal though expressed a slight hint of fear. . Despite his height, he went by the name of Little Andy. Once stepping forward the others spread out on the deck to encircle the two apparent adversaries.

"A pirate you are Nicholas the Blue, but your sword is challenged by your servant. Shall I assume that you are reluctant?" The boy spoke loudly to the leader.

A quiet smile came to the lips of Nicholas; he drew his golden sword quickly. The leader spoke, "better than the likes of you have gone down my trusted cabin mate; you best ready yourself, for your words have spoken once too often of late."

Little Andy was tossed a sheathed sword, which he caught in his left hand. He drew the saber slowly and lifted it in challenge to the leader. They circled first to the right and then to the left and the boy lunged forward to engage Nicholas. The leader stopped the boy's sword turning to his left quickly pushing Little Andy past him. The boy returned in a moment and moved to engage Nicholas. The blades flashed in the moonlight as the two dueled on. Little Andy advanced seeming to make progress on Nicholas, forcing him back toward the rear deck. They engaged at the base of a stairway where Nicholas was able to push his adversary backwards. This allowed him to quickly climb to the deck above; he regrouped as Little Andy charged up after him. The fight continued at a furious pace. Nicholas seemed pinned in but at the last moment turned and jumped to safety over the rail to the main deck below.

From the mast a large rope hung lashed to the deck by Little Andy's foot. With a single blow, the boy swung his sword cutting its attachment from the deck. With an enthusiastic grin he eyed his prey on the deck below. With one hand laden with sword, the other on the line, he swung down towards Nicholas. The quickness of this seemed to catch the leader unaware for as he looked up he could see Little Andy now descending upon him at a great pace. Almost off balance Nicholas was able to just avoid the swinging boy's sword. As he went by Andy, Nicholas swung his saber, now behind the swinging boy. He severed the line completely and Little Andy crashed violently on the deck just at the starboard edge of the ship.

In an instant, Nicholas was upon him, his sword flashing. Little Andy had crashed violently and now lay on his face dazed. With his blade now just between the defeated boy's shoulder blades, Nicholas coaxed Little Andy to slowly rise, his back now towards the victor. Nicholas raised his foot, placed it on Little Andy's back and pushed him over the rail into the churning sea. He planted his sword's point briskly into the wooden deck as if at attention, as he climbed to the top of the rail to watch his defeated prey now just surfacing in the cold water far below.

Nicholas smiled for a moment and yelled to Little Andy below, "Well mate, that is three out of the last four duels that you have ended upon in the brink, shan't we have a few more lessons?"

Little Andy rose coughing and sputtering. Like a fountain, he expelled a mouth full of water slowly through pursed lips. His eye patch was slightly ajar. With one hand still clutching his sword, he sank as he quickly repositioned it. He kicked himself back up to the surface again, looked up to Nicholas and smiled. He threw his sword up upon the deck above and shook his head in friendly defiance. A lowered rope was accepted and he climbed back upon the deck. A friendly hand from Nicholas helped him take the last step back on board. The group cheered, laughed, and Little Andy smiled and snickered in a good-natured way. They stood for a moment watching each other, then turned with friendly arms upon the other's shoulder as Nicholas ushered Little Andy to warmer quarters below deck.

Boys they were, and the events of the night suggested that theirs was a life of fun and games. The ship however, laden with canons, swords, muskets, black powder, and supplies of war, predicted otherwise. And while this was just a friendly battle between two friends, the ship though far at sea was in the cross hairs; a Queen was sensing possible destruction of her family and a tyrant oblivious to an eventual adversary, both mother and son viewing the scene from separate venues that dark moonlit night.

CHAPTER 6
Autumn Bienville

> FOR WHOEVER FINDS ME FINDS LIFE
> AND RECEIVES FAVOR FROM THE LORD.
> PROVERBS 15:1

The traveling boy awoke reluctantly from a deep, unsettling sleep. Like a canon respond, the thought blasted through his squishy, still sleepy brain. It asked him the expected question, in various but always delicate manners: "where am I?" Like Dorothy to Toto, his brain responded: "we're not in Temecula, dude!" The fact jarred him fully awake.

Jumping straight up in the still dark room, sweat collected like dew on his screwed up little brow, and panicky thoughts flooded his drowsy, innocent, modern day boy's brain. These thoughts led him quickly to the next several questions, firing in rapid, manner: "its dark, its cold, where's my Magic Johnson comforter, and why am I sleeping on the frick'n rock floor?"

Then he remembered. His rude arrival and fact that this was not a dream, in the real dream sense at all. A real dream ends when you wake up. Chris was awake, but so far, he was still in this unusual world. If it was a dream, it was a real life dream from which he could not awaken. It was a real life dream where real people lived, and these real people just happen to be pirates, scoundrels, and Kings. Chris decided quickly that the only two things he was sure of that first day were that he was not dead, and secondly, he definitely was not at home.

The panic subsided as he looked around the windowless room. "Alone," he realized. When he went to sleep he was with the Pitlings, but he was now alone, and their absence disturbed him. Chris pulled himself out of his bedroll, stood, and wondered what to do.

"That cloud, that stupid cloud! Never argue with a cloud," Chris thought with some remorse. It was cold and wet in the room, and he shuddered recalling the evil from the prior day. Foul air followed those black riders, and who or what was the Boar? Recalling his performance, he laughed to himself; he did not realize he could rap.

Then a promising series of thoughts struck him with some delight. No school, no bus, no teachers. Cool, a world without school, a world without parents!

The boy grabbed his sunglasses from his backpack, pulled his shoes on, and exited the room with laces trailing. Glancing across the chamber, he noticed that Alex's bed showed no sign of use.

"First step: get out of this rocky, freezy, Flintstone-like bedroom. Second: walk to the room with the fireplace."

He noticed extinguished oil lamps as he moved to the main room. Here he realized that the fire in the hearth was gone, leaving burnt embers and a wonderful smell like outdoors.

He stood by the empty hearth and thought. He remembered the boy's medallion. It was shiny and obviously valuable. His gaze led Alex to conceal the pendant. "Cool, it's a key to a secret crystal," he decided.

He paused, his eye adjusting to the dark, and planned a route across the dark unfamiliar room. By feel, he cautiously crossed the floor and walked along the long shadowy hall. He removed the brambles guarding the exit, stepped outside into cool fresh air, and met the beautiful mid-morning sun.

Once outside, muffled sounds became clear voices, which he followed from the camp along the dusty trail. It was a clear and cool morning, the air fresh now, without the red haze seen when the dark riders were present. Birds sang a joyous song to the modern day city boy.

Christopher continued along the trail without a care, dipping through a clearing in the brush, and sliding down a steep incline.

Here Chris paused, emptied a shoe full of dirt, and continued exploring. Following a narrow trail, he moved toward voices, hoping to find his new world friends.

The Pitlings were gathered across a large rocky clearing. Chris paused for a moment, shaded his eyes, and observed the group. The boys were busy with various activities: carrying water jugs, climbing trees, and maintaining the band's arsenal. Michael Shaun was astride, and cleaning vigorously the barrel of a canon. A boy that Chris recognized from last night, James, was sharpening a wicked sword with a foot powered grinding wheel. Those in the trees seemed to be guards on watch. Alexander was sitting with Manzell off to one side in consultation. Laughing and song drifted carelessly through the air.

As with the floor of Alex's cave, the clearing was smooth and flat rock, perfect for the daring wheeled boy. He turned, and in a flash returned from camp with his faithful board. With shades on, Chris rolled out toward his friends. Gradually the group all stopped their activities and watched him approach. Alexander and Manzell stood and walked to meet him. Michael Shaun dropped his ramrod, swung off the canon, and with a grin waved to Chris. The others dropped from trees, stopped their work, and moved to meet the boy as well.

With cultivated guise, the boy approached the group gaining impressive speed. He fancied himself a rock star, rolling with breakneck energy towards a dynamic entry, so dashing, so suave, and just so cool. A tiny, insignificant item penalized his fragile ego that day, for as he gathered speed, the board rolled over a small pebble, locking a wheel, and flinging him, like a foolhardy projectile, onto his face before the startled throng. Chris was quickly up off the tarmac protecting his ego. He rose, brushed off the dust, managing a humiliated smile. His friends eyed him curiously but said nothing.

Alexander broke the awkward silence, disregarding the humorous entry. "Christopher of Temecula, a slumber the depth of which I have seldom seen was upon your brow this morning. I chose to leave you for the present. Your travels have weighed heavily on you my friend. I trust we find you better for the world this day?"

"Me? I crashed like a rock," Chris said forgetting his embarrassment. Recalling the leader's undisturbed bed, he went on to ask: "and what's up with you Alexander? Your bed looked like you didn't sleep?

The Pitlings giggled in response to the question, as if discussion of the subject had occurred before. The answer boomed loudly from the rear of the group. "Why, Alexander sleep?"

Manzell continued. "This would require a very much larger event than the rude arrival of a singing wizard!" The boy finished with a knowing wink, and the group concurred with amusement.

It was Chris' assumption that Alex made up the bed before he woke, or that he slept elsewhere. He got the distinct impression from the group's response however, that the boy was not in the habit of sleeping.

Alexander smiled shyly. He turned to Chris and placed a friendly hand on the boy's shoulder. His countenance betrayed a deep sadness as he responded: "time allows for little sleep in these troubled times, my innocent friend. Be free of cares, at least for now, Christopher of Temecula."

The boy turned and faced the group. His sadness quickly melted away as he addressed them. "Enough of this gloom. We must celebrate the arrival of our wheeled friend."

The boys loudly responded their approval. Alex lifted his hand. "Some quiet for the moment, lads. Now, our noble plan is proceeding. Events must line up. For now, we primarily wait. With our sentry in place, we should be safe from any unwelcome guests for now. So, let the rest of today be just for fun!" Chris sensed that this hypothetical guest would not be a friendly one.

As Alex spoke, he turned and found himself looking directly at the huge boy Scott, the appointed sentry. With Chris' arrival, the boy had moved from his position as a lookout, high above in one of the trees at the edge of the clearing. For the first time Chris saw Alexander puzzled, as he looked at the boy eye to eye. That this was a major infraction was apparent in the sudden expression of fright seen on Scott's face. The group had been very informal until now, but they all realized the significance of this offense. Silence replaced their laughing, and they all stood at attention. Scott hung his head and said nothing.

Manzell was annoyed, and he made his feelings known to the delinquent sentry. "Scott, watch continues till relieved. Being a witness to laughs and fun might be tempting, but in your absence, our backs the enemy might have!"

Manzell moved to approach the frightened boy, but Alexander held up his arm to stop him. Taking the boy aside, the leader and Scott walked away in discussion towards the trees.

Chris was not sure at this point what enemies plagued the Pitlings. However, the sentry's transgression made the reality of opposition obvious. He noticed a sick feeling in his stomach as he remembered the look on the boy's face. It reminded him of that too familiar feeling, a mixture of surprise and fright, when suddenly confronted with the teacher's request to pass forward forgotten homework. Chris watched in silence as the two boys stopped their walk some distance from the group. Alex put his arm on Scott's shoulder. They spoke briefly, after which Alexander returned to the group. Scott jogged away to the tallest tree and climbed to his neglected position.

The boys were quiet as their leader returned. Alexander put a hand on Manzell's shoulder and said. "A trusted friend must be forgiven for being a boy. He will learn and be the better for it. It shan't happen again I assure you Manzell."

Dismissing the event, Alex looked directly at Chris. "I am curious Christopher of Temecula, in your world are the wheeled boards used freely?"

Chris pondered the question and then realized his meaning. "The wheeled boards?" He picked up his board and continued, "Skateboards Alex, we call them skateboards. Nah, they're just for fun." He handed the board to one of the boys who in turn passed it around. "Big people don't use them that much, you know, adults

I mean. Kids, now kids do use them, I guess you would say, freely. Where I come from, the United States...you know, America. Dude, is that near here?"

Blank expressions crossed the majority of the boy's faces. Alexander, as always, gave the slightest hint that he knew of what he spoke.

Chris continued. "Anyways, most people in the US. You know, big people, ah..., adults, that is. No, they don't use skateboards much. They drive cars to get around."

Looking across the audience, Chris realized that automobiles as well meant nothing in this world of horses. He decided to change the subject and ask for some more information. "People in my world fly airplanes for long trips. Like, you might fly to New York. New York's my favorite city, but I haven't been there yet. I wonder, is New York around here?"

Again, he drew only blank stares. Alex had some knowledge of Chris' world, but he was silent, standing and watching the boy with a knowing smile on his face.

Christopher moved on, continuing his typical salvo method of questioning. "Look... dudes; there's something I got to figure out here." He spoke in an animated manner, waving his arms and betraying an era of desperation. "When I left my world, it was like 1994. This can't be the year 1994. It's like ancient or something. Like the Romans, or maybe Napoleon. I mean...you don't even have... well, showers for example. And what's up with the candles, there are no light bulbs here. Do you even have years?" He said with some exasperation. Rethinking his question, he continued. "Well, you got to have years. Okay, I guess I'm asking, dude what year is it here anyway?"

Alex had been observing the boy closely. He admired the traveler boy's energy; his fury of questions amused him. He was a curious person, now that much was certain. He realized that this boy from the future, who had arrived so suddenly, just might be very helpful to their cause. As Chris' frustration mounted, Alex's interested smile became a friendly chuckle. "We live in the year of our Lord, 1000. I trust that 1994 is one 994 years in the future for you, Christopher," responded Alex.

Chris was amazed at his answer, and his surprised expression reflected it. "Woo.......dude, he said!" He was stunned, and his eyes widened, indicating his shock. The modern day boy dropped his gaze to the ground and considered the answer. Now realizing the meaning, the nearly one thousand years distressed him. He had really messed up. "I'll never get home now," he said quietly under his breath.

The Pitlings, however, were impressed with his world. Skateboards, cars, New York, the second millennium, these were new concepts to them. Many of the boys were quietly smiling at Chris, while others whispered to one another. Alexander, on the other hand, took this amazing revelation in stride, appearing to give it scarcely a thought. The leader's gaze returned to the skateboard. "The board to which you call skate....board muddles me. Dare I could ride it?" Alexander looked up at Chris with an excited childish smile.

Adults have fought wars over minor differences, sometimes even just a thought. For some reason kids are just different. Kids are kids the entire the world over, and not just geographically but temporally, over the centuries, as well. For the fun that followed might just as well been seen at any modern skateboard park or playground across the world as in a medieval world.

Chris instructed the boys on the art of riding, and they learned the sport quickly. One after the other, the boys politely took their turn riding, laughing, and performing for their friends. On occasion, one would lose his balance and find the way rudely to the rock surface. Undeterred, true to a kid's nature, they skated on. Bruises and scrapes went without much notice for, as with modern kids, these kids seemed to have no nerve endings when it came to fun. Soon, they were not distinguishable from modern day skateboarders. Laughing and a feel of joy were evident that wonderful spring morning. It was fun; peace prevailed for the time.

Of course, the skateboard was nothing new to Chris, but Alucemet was. Once he had shown the boys the basics, he realized with just the one board that he had time on his hands. He turned and walked to the trees where the Pitlings had been working before his arrival. Scott called down to him as he arrived. "Christopher of Temecula, is there a chance that the wheeled board will survive beyond my watch?"

Chris looked up at the Scott and smiled. He looked out over the valley. Rolling grass-covered hills and not a cloud in the sky stretched out before him. A breeze was blowing just enough to keep it wonderfully cool.

Below him stood the materials on which the boys had labored. Wheeled cannons, recently polished, glistened in the sun. There were piles of cannon balls and barrels of gunpowder. Rows of guns were present as well. They were new and shiny but old in design, at least to the twentieth century boy. "Like the redcoats used, he imagined."

Chris crossed and considered the items of war. Picking up a musket he realized the irony, boys yelling and laughing behind him like the kids they were. He had played at war often, but this was different; this war was all too real. Its relation to the group of friendly boys still seemed out of place to him.

As Chris thought, he wandered away, walking down towards the valley. A traveled path led to his left and he followed it for quite some time. Walking through a clump of trees, he found himself upon a grassy clearing. Flowers, some of the most beautiful that he had ever seen, surrounded it. His mother loved flowers, he remembered, and the memory saddened him.

His mind drifted away as he began to consider his plight. The friendly sounds of boys on boards disappeared, and he returned to his thoughts. The sky was clear, the air crisp and fresh, but Christopher did not notice for he was confused. He wondered again, "Where am I, really?" He knew the answer, but did not trust it.

Distance seemed to make the heart grow fonder. He knew this to be true, for he was beginning to miss his two maniacal brothers. These two monsters of gore, two beings whose sole goal was his torture him, began to look sympathetic! The thought was so bizarre that it frightened him. He found he missed his family as well. Given the events since he last saw them, this would be a Thursday, and his father would be doing urology cases in the operating room. Chris was sad; he guessed his family would not even miss him.

Across the clearing was a densely wooded forest, with scattered rocky areas. A clump of beautiful flowers stood along a dirt path that pushed deep into the woods. As he approached them, their size amazed him. They were all the colors of the rainbow, many with stalks that stood above his head. "Someone feeds them vitamins," Chris thought to himself.

"Would you care for one?"

The question startled the boy, for he was certain he was alone. The words were those of a young girl, apparently directed at him, though their source not obvious. He turned in the general direction of the query, staring down the dirt pathway where it disappeared into the forest. Searching in vain for the voice's origin, he attributed the question to his imagination. He recalled the discussion of evil present in this strange new world. The words were not lost on him, for he had witnessed it himself. Remembering the jaundice-eyed horse, he shuddered and turned to return quickly.

"I'm fond of the red blossoms. Father speaks of me on occasion as his little flower. All fathers say as much I suppose. By what does a father say to a son, odd boy?"

Christopher turned back in surprise. Hearing the small voice a second time allowed him to be sure. There was no mistaking it now; the utterance was real. Chris moved cautiously and stood at the origin of the path. For the first time he realized that while daylight covered the world, this area was oddly dark. He took one careful step forward. As he did so, the figure of a young girl appeared, but slowly, as if someone was turning the light up.

She was standing her tallest, on the tip of her toes, cutting a large red flower from a stalk well above her head. A coarsely woven basket filled with gardening tools and brightly colored flowers sat on the ground, neatly by her feet.

"Dude, I must be in someone's yard," Chris thought to himself, feeling for the moment as if trespassing. Her sudden appearance had startled the boy. While the girl had spoken to him twice, she continued with her gardening, not acknowledging him.

She was a young slight girl, with long straight dark brown hair cut short across her brow. The girl was dressed in a fine lavender dress, with a layered ruffled hem falling to below the knee, and a white lace collar, gathered at her neck. Fancy decorative trim adorned the ends of her long sleeves, her hands covered with delicate white gardening gloves. Cinched at her waist was a wide lavender sash, tied in a billowy bow in the back. Below the hem of the dress, black stretch stockings covered her thin legs.

The girl was shorter than Chris by several inches, and appeared a year or two younger. Her eyes were dark walnut brown that sparkled mischievously. She had a fine straight nose just tipped up on the end, and scattered freckles across an auburn complexion. The girl had a friendly country look, but dressed quite formally in this remote place.

"Girls are so clean, even out here," Chris thought to himself, as he stood watching the girl. He did not have any sisters, just a mom, and he often wondered about them. The boy did not understand girls yet. He decided that girls are just different somehow. He recalled using the phrase, black party shoes with bows, to describe what he thought girls always wore. The thought seemed so far away now, but it drew his attention to her feet. Here she wore ankle height, black leather, pointy-toed shoes, secured with two rows of shiny black buttons.

There was something surreal about the girl, the boy decided. She had appeared out of nowhere and seemed illuminated by her own personal light. Chris still wasn't sure that she was speaking to him, the girl not having acknowledged the boy yet.

Pirates, Scoundrels, and Kings

The girl finished cutting the last of the flowers. Slowly bending to her basket, she arranged them all just right. With this, she stood, pulled her gloves off, dropped them in the basket, and turned to faced Chris. With the gloves off, she wiped her hands together, and looked curiously at the boy.

She had neatly trimmed fingernails, painted with a lavender polish, which was flaking off in several areas. A big friendly smile came to her face as she said. "Are you without speech, odd boy? I love the woods in mid-morning, are you of the same?"

Chris tried to respond, but her questions continued. "Memory does not recall the likes of you sir blond, and knickers of such an orange cast I fail to recall. To what tailor do you subscribe?"

For the first time the girl paused as if expecting an answer. Chris was not sure what a tailor was, but the reference to his shorts was obvious. He looked down at his shorts self-consciously. Pulling at them he responded. "Active, I think my mom got them at Active." Here he referred to a Temecula Skateboard and Ski shop.

The girl dropped her eyes in thought about his answer. "I do not recall the tailor Active? Mind you, I know not all such tradesmen." Proudly she added, "His toil, however, I shall recite to our Queen. An audience can be pursued. How goes that with you? But never more! Only a rude gentleman fails to introduce himself to a lady, but as you seem not to talk, I will tell you that I am Autumn, Autumn Bienville. To what do you answer, odd boy?"

The rate at which this girl talked left even Chris in a blur. She seemed friendly enough though and she certainly seemed intent on making him her friend. While trying not to speak *kingly*, he answered with the name Sir Alexander gave him. "I am Christopher... Christopher of Temecula."

"It is bliss to know of you Christopher of Temecula" She curtsied to the boy and then quickly continued. "Temecula, ...Temecula? It is not in my mind to recall such a place." Autumn smiled again, and took a few careful steps towards him. "Have your travels brought you far?" As was her pattern, she fired another question before he could answer. "Why must you curtain your eyes?" With that question she looked perplexed, and for once paused long enough for Chris to consider an answer.

Her question stumped him, curtained... curtained eyes? Then he realized that she was referring to his sunglasses. He removed them and offered the glasses to the girl. "They're sunglasses. Ah..., shades. Like...people call them shades...sometimes. We wear them in the bright sun that is...where I come from. And bad...I mean cool...I mean they make you look good, I guess. Here..." He said moving a step towards the girl. "Try them on." Chris said, returning her smile.

Autumn took the glasses cautiously and put them on, just as Chris had. The frames were magenta, and the modern day boy concluded that their color went well with her lavender dress.

"Is the sun to be feared in your home, Christopher of Temecula? I care to like the sun here." The girl looked up at the sun overhead. She turned her head first to the right and then to the left, experimenting with what was, to her, an obviously new item. As she realized the lens's function, she added with excitement, "oh... I fathom it now. The sun's brilliance abates. Shades... very inspired. Did Sir Alexander create these?" She said with some suspicion in her voice. "May I partake of them?"

He realized that he did not have any choice in the matter. For as she finished her discourse, Autumn turned and picked up her basket. Silently, the girl walked by Chris into the clearing. After a few steps, she placed her basket gently on the ground. Smoothing the rear of her dress, she sat daintily on one of the boulders and looked through the sunglasses at the boy.

Chris followed and sat next to the girl. The rock was exposed to the rising sun but its temperature surprised him. It was cold where she sat, which he thought was odd. Sitting close to her now, he noticed that the girl was very pale. Not much sun lately or maybe she had been sick, Chris thought to himself.

"Tell me of yourself and of your foreign home, Christopher of Temecula."

He had not thought of himself as foreign until that point, but in fact, she was probably right. Suddenly, he was wondering if he was an alien. An illegal alien? Now he was an illegal, he concluded. The thought was unsettling. "What next?" he wondered to himself.

In his least kingly voice, Chris tried to answer the girl's question. "I really don't know…I…I… think I'm from the future, though."

As he said this, Autumn looked at him over the top of the sunglasses and shook her head yes, as if she already knew.

Surprised, he continued. "I live in Temecula, that's near LA. Is that near here?"

Autumn dropped her head to think, and took a moment to answer. "I know not of it, this LA." She said, shaking her head a resolute no.

Chris had learned to fire his questions quickly before the talkative girl could interrupt. Regaining the initiative, he went on. "New York…what about New York? Is New York around here? That's my favorite place. It has big buildings and a sewer. That's why the Ninja turtles live there. So do the Ghost busters… all superhumans live there," he said stating the irrefutable fact. "I don't much like the Jets or Giants, but still someday I got to go to New York." Shaking his head in the affirmative, he waited for the girl's reply.

"New York! What could ever be new about this York?" she said with some pretense. Not bothering with an answer, Autumn went on. "Now, it strikes me that you refer to across the sea, in the kingdom of Flarion. But odd boy, there are not tall buildings! Castles, me thinks you refer to castles. I know well of turtles, but Ninja they are not. Ghosts, you speak of ghosts. Ghosts exist not. All aristocrats with any semblance of knowledge know this to be true!"

Chris suddenly realized that an argument was brewing, or maybe she had just insulted him! It was nice to meet the girl, she was very friendly, but he really didn't like to argue. He decided quickly to try silence, answering only when questioned; a technique that garnered some success with his Mother.

To his relief, however, Autumn moved on, changing the subject. "I dwell within the Castle Alucemet. My father commands the Royal Guardsman."

"Christopher of Temecula," rang out a voice from across the clearing, interrupting their conversation. Across the way, a lone horseman trailing a second horse was baring down upon them at high speed. As he approached, Chris realized that the rider was Michael Shaun. Time seemed to have disappeared, and the boy's presence reminded him of his predicament. Michael Shaun was waving wildly; obviously, he had been searching for him.

Christopher stood up and waved to the boy. "Yo dude, Michael Shaun, what's up!"

The rider arrived quickly, sliding to a sudden stop in front of Chris. "United States this is not my friend! What brings you to such a place as this? Alexander beckons me to secure your presence. Quickly, we must mount and make haste!"

Chris turned to speak to Autumn, but to his surprise, the girl was gone. He glanced around, expecting to find her; instead, at his feet he found only his sunglasses. Autumn disappeared while he was talking to Michael Shaun. As he picked up the glasses, Chris touched the rock where she had sat, just a moment before. Oddly, in the brilliant morning sunlight, the rock was still icy cold. The boy found that quite strange, completing his befuddled impression of the girl.

Now, there was a dilemma to consider, the horse! Well…Chris had never quite ridden a horse; at least a real horse, that is. It seemed so long ago now, but once at a county fair, Christopher had refused the pony ride. The boy felt horses, like clowns that carried an especially horrific image for the boy, were just a little scary. Add to his humiliation, both younger brothers rode while he watched. The event permanently scared his super-hero heroic, half-pipe pipe-ing, extreme sport touting psyche to this day. His two monster brothers did this, he was sure, just to spite him. Younger brothers, in his experience, imprisoned as they are in their *younger-ness*, always look for an opportunity to repay the older brother's *older-ness*, with just such treacherous ploys. Seeing the two smiling traitors, he wanted to ride but his pride, and a little fear, did not allow him to change his mind. Now the two, while not even present, were tormenting him again. He wished now that he had taken that opportunity. Something told him that Michael Shaun would not understand his clown-horse fears.

The boy seemed in a major hurry, already turning to leave. Chris recalled his atypical abilities in this world. He rapped and rode a skateboard like never before. "Maybe, in this world, I can do anything," he reasoned. Deciding to fake it, with a brave little expression, the modern day boy placed a shaky foot in the stirrup, and mounted the mighty steed, just as if he had done so his entire life. Within a moment, the two were riding away at a harrowing pace, across the clearing and back to the Pitling camp. "Dude, what was I thinking? Horses are nothing like clowns," the boy concluded.

As they rode, Christopher tried to carry on a conversation with Michael Shaun. "Did you see where that girl went Michael Shaun?"

"Girl? To what girl do you speak, Christopher of Temecula?"

"That girl, she was sitting right next to me when you rode up, dude." Christopher replied.

"To other things my mind was upon, but I dare say, you were as alone as when the Pitlings first spied you. Come, our haste is demanded." With that, Michael Shaun sped up and any further conversation was impossible.

As the two boys galloped along, Christopher continued thinking about the girl. "There is something very strange about that Girl. Odd and she calls me odd. He thought to himself. Michael Shaun should have noticed her, he figured. His friend had seen him, from far away, across the grassy clearing, like a hawk. In addition, he could not explain the icy rock. On a day like today? No way, the sun is shining and those rocks should be hot, but where she sat, they were cold, he questioned, struggling to keep up with the more experienced equestrian. As he considered this, he realized that the sky, bright and beautiful just moments before, was now overcast, hazy, and a rust color. The carefree ambiance which accompanied it was gone; seriousness was the new image of the day.

THE HORSE-MOUNTED TRAVELERS GALLOPED ACROSS the grassy meadow. Chris crushed the bridle tightly in his frightened hands, and his legs fought with the bouncing saddle. He hoped just to survive, with some semblance of dignity, this crashing, sweating, phobia generating, legatee of a pony ride.

A murky darkness was growing, the sun seemingly replaced by a gloomy curtain of rust. The destination was not clear to the modern dayboy as they raced through the deserted camp, the gun and cannon arsenal of munitions now absent. Earlier the boys vowed to spend the day skateboarding and carefree, but something had changed that plan.

In the distance was a long, straight, dusty road, outlined by tall trees. To the east in the distance rose black Rocky Mountains, shrouded in the darkening rust. To the west, the road entered a craggy gorge. As they approached, Chris could see the other boys, mounted on horses behind the trees watching the road, an apparent major route. The two arrived in a dust cloud, their horses sliding to attention alongside of Alexander.

The sky continued to darken in its reddish hue, growing dark as sundown. None of the group seemed willing to discuss this curious turn of the day, scarcely acknowledging the two boys' arrival. There was no more laughing, the group deadly serious about something.

A boy named James arrived, galloping along the road from the east. He came to a sudden stop, with a dusty slide in front of the group, and reported to Alexander. "The coach arrives my lord. It is the one to which we speak."

The leader acknowledged him with only a slight nod. He turned to Manzell, and motioned him silently across the road. With him a group of boys moved out quickly crossing to the other side.

In the eastern distance, a small cloud of dust was rapidly approaching from the horizon. As it neared, one could make out a horse-drawn carriage barreling along the tree-lined lane towards the boys. Behind the coach was an open wagon, its contents hidden by a burlap tarp. The coach was a dusty black, pulled by a team of six powerful black horses. Two maniacal men with whips drove the coach from above, and a purple flag with a black insignia flapped in the wind behind them. Tightly drawn purple curtains obscured the passenger windows, as if its occupant had little interest in the world around.

As the carriage blasted past the boys, Alexander led the two groups, one from each side of the road, pursuing their apparent foe with haste. The coach was now some distance in front of the group, and it was nearly a mile before they could over take their quarry.

As the boys closed the distance, approaching the coach from the rear, one of the drivers became aware of them. With caution, the man moved to the rear of the vehicle to observe. Without warning, he hurled a projectile backwards toward the group.

The group screamed in unison, "Imploder," and scattered to avoid it. The device hit the ground with an explosion, casting rocks and dirt upon the boys. It did not dissuade them, for soon they were back upon the road, speeding in pursuit of the rapidly escaping coach.

Chris was sure glad that his horse knew more about horse riding than he did. The stead had taken everything in stride, speeding along without orders from the boy and nimbly avoiding the fall out. He realized, however, that the explosion had delayed their pursuit. It might prove to be significant, for ahead the road disappeared into a rocky gorge just wide enough for the coach. The coachman shook his fist in success, grinning jubilantly, sensing that they had escaped the Pitlings. On the other hand, had they? Outmaneuvering Sir Alexander was a feat rarely accomplished in those days.

The explosion split the horde, with Alexander's group to the left of the escaping coach, and Manzell's to its right. There was a faint suggestion of a small smile upon the leader's young face, as he motioned to Manzell and tossed the boy an end of his rope. The two quickly made their way up opposite sides of the gorge, and soon were above the speeding carriage with a rope dangling between them. They over took their target, lowering the rope to hang in front of the speeding team of horses.

The sight apparently frightened the team, and soon the coach was erratically veering from side to side. Frustration became apparent in the two coachmen, for they shook their fists in futile anger, snapping their whips in desperation. The two boys slowed slightly, bring the dangling rope to within inches of racing horse's front hooves.

Chris could not have imagined what followed. Force is proportional to change in velocity, i.e. stagecoach going very fast then suddenly wedged to a stop, and mass, i.e. heavy bad dudes, coach, and horses. The next event demonstrated this Newtonian principal, much better than any physics classroom could.

Tripping a team of twelve speeding horses results in a violent chain of events. Simultaneously, with uncanny timing, as if signaled by medieval cell phone, the two boys abruptly halted their harrowing pace. They braced for the impact as their horses slid to a stop. As the first horses stumbled, the entire team followed them, in an equestrian mass; with bridles shorn from their mouths, they collapsed in a heap. The front of the carriage was suddenly wedged to the ground; the rear projected over it, like a missile into the air. Launched spinning, the coach struck the ground with an explosive impact. Sliding, rolling, and grinding to a jarring halt, the coach came to a shaky stop on its side, covered in a cloud of dust, wood, leather, and deafening noise. Both coachmen landed unceremoniously, in a heap, on top of one another. The rear wagon tore free, and rolled to a gentle stop ahead.

The Pitlings wasted no time, racing to solidify their position. Four surrounded the coachmen and roughly forced the two to their feet. The men gasped in horror, spit rocks and blood from their mouths, and pulled their bruised bodies and egos to attention, their bloody faces shocked at the turn of events.

The rest surrounded the carriage expectantly. Alexander and Manzell carefully descended the sloping gorge walls and joined the victorious group. Manzell moved to his leader smiling and laughing and they exchanged hand slaps in success. James climbed onto the shattered carriage, and stood next to the passenger door. With a signal from Alexander, he forced the twisted passenger door open.

Meanwhile the sky grew darker, the rusty smog rolling in and descending, covering the area like a shroud. A foul stench surrounded the destroyed scene, suggesting rot and decay. Slowly, a shaky hand emerged from the coach, and grabbed the edge of the opened door. Struggling to climb from within, a disheveled figure dressed in black finally emerged.

"Fordem." Chris recognized him immediately. Here was the man on the jaundiced-eyed horse, the former tyrant, standing unsteadily on the overturned carriage. He had obviously been eating, rudely interrupted, for he wore a brown lumpy meal humorously on his shocked face, a broken wooden spoon still in his left hand. His long black ponytail stood up over the back of his skull, the knot sitting ridiculously atop his head like a quail's crest. His regal purple cape, hung shredded and rotated covering his chest like a babies bib.

Chris, still mounted on his horse at the rear of the crowd of victorious boys, stared at the man who had once been so frightening.. He could not keep from laughing; Alexander had humiliated the man.

Fordem, however, quickly regained control and evil defiance quickly. He tossed his broken spoon at the boys, and jumped to the ground to confront them. With a hideous snarl, the man defiantly faced the boys.

"Another misguided trick, Alexander, your last to be sure." The captive yelled and spit! Before the leader could respond, Fordem whirled and pulled a small knife from within the collar of his cape, and drew back his hand to launch it at Alexander.

As before, with lightening quickness, Manzell fired his crossbow at the man's knife barring hand. The weapon fell harmlessly to the ground; the arrow imbedded in the web between Fordem's first and second finger.

Fordem screeched in agony and dropped to his knees. He forcibly pulled the arrow from his hand, and with hatred covering his face, slowly rose again to his feet. He seemed to measure his odds, glancing for the first time at the surrounding group of boys. Without warning, he took off, yelling profanity and sprinting for the safety of the woods. The man's action startled the others, and he sped past them quickly, trying to escape.

At the rear, only Chris stood between the man and freedom. As he flew past him, the boy dove from his saddle towards the escaping man. Junior Seau, plugging holes, and Dodger dogs, were his only thoughts as he landed on Fordem's back. The boy clung to his neck, kicked, and wrestled the man, who stood nearly two feet his taller. His cautious side was horrified; the man would disembowel the boy given the opportunity. Again, however, he sensed a superhero's ability in this world, and like a NFL linebacker, he drug the fleeing man to the ground. Before he realized the danger, the Pitlings surrounded them with drawn bows and steel. Michael Shaun helped Chris to his feet, and the modern day boy paraded for the group, in his form of an end zone dance.

Manzell angrily pulled the captive to his feet. "Shall you make foolishness again Christopher of Temecula will bring you down," he said.

"And what is a Christopher of Temecula, a citrus-filled fruit bowl? This one's garb is as a clown!" Fordem barked, now glaring at Chris with hatred. The boy had never before been called a clown and ironically, he was just a little proud.

Manzell stood up quickly to the man. He grabbed and tore off the remainder of his shredded cape. "Like a blade of grass you fell! The traveler dropped you like the weak fool you are!"

Fordem raised his hand and rubbed blood on Manzell's shoulder, outlining the cauterized scar. In a vengeful hiss, he said, "weakness your screams of pain revealed. It still humors me to recall. A shame I had not cooked you for the Boar's feast."

Manzell jumped and grabbed the man's hair, yanking the ponytail down over his face. He pushed him away and yelled, "A feast you will soon witness! It is of roast pig! The day of the Boar draws to a close, you twisted rat."

Alexander had been watching this confrontation from the sidelines. He moved on his horse and gently placed his hand on the bloodied shoulder of Manzell, drawing him aside. With this, the leader quietly took center stage again, dismounting his horse.

The boy was just a boy, standing much shorter than the man, but Alexander drew attention from the captive. He stared into his eyes and spoke calmly. "Fordem, how low have you fallen. Doth not you see the evilness that Michaelis has woven over you? Sir, you are lost!"

Alex now turned and walked slowly away from the man. Turning again to him, he continued, "I am afraid your loss goes beyond rescue. Recall now our determination! Your world has little time. Carry this message to the noble imposter, the Boar. Tell him of us. Tell him I shall come for our Kingdom. Alucemet shall shine again." Mounting his horse, he turned away from the man. "Now leave, take your fallen henchmen with you."

Eyes reveal the inner thoughts of men, and Chris studied Fordem's with interest. Throughout this challenge, deviance and confidence were evident. With Alex's last words, they betrayed a flicker of self-doubt, and for just that second suggested defeat. Just as quickly, his former conceit returned. He turned and marched towards the woods, the two disheveled coachmen at hisheel.

Once out of sight a cheer went up from the group. Many of them turned to congratulate Chris. The boy was beaming after his deft open field tackle.

Alexander placed an arm around the adopted Alucemite and quietly whispered to him. "A linebacker such as that I can't recall, Christopher of Temecula."

Surprised again by the leader's knowledge of his world, Chris turned and looked at the boy closely. "A linebacker, a linebacker in such a world?" In *Kingly* style again he said. Alexander's command of his world mystified the boy.

"Thanks dude," was all that Chris could offer. The two friends then walked together toward the recovered wagon.

Scott and Michael Shaun were already removing the tarp from the wagon. Within, they found a stash of hundreds of spherical items, each about six inches in diameter.

"Imploders!" Chris heard Manzell and the boys shout.

The sky was clearing as the group made their way upon horseback, out of the gorge and back towards camp. Relief from the stress of the recent events was obvious in the group. Fun began to return to the group.

Alexander and Manzell stood on their saddles, riding with bridles in hand. At just the exact time, they would leap and simultaneously exchange horses to the delight of the others.

There was singing and laughing as they rode along the dirt road. Scott, as usual, was the loudest. The huge boy sang and laughed, turned in the saddle, head resting on the horse's neck, legs crossed confidently at the knee, and his hands behind his neck.

James suddenly rolled over and dropped from his saddle to the ground. He had one foot still secured in the stirrup, dragging at full speed on his back. Chris thought he had fallen and quickly moved to help the boy. When he arrived, he realized the joke. Chris laughed; he reached down and pulled James's foot out of the stirrup with a jolt. The boy yelled as he found himself on the ground with the group passing him by.

It was nearing sunset now. For the first time since their pursuit of Fordem, they could see the sun, now only slightly obscured by the clearing rust colored smog near the western horizon.

They were returning with overflowing saddlebags full of imploders. Desert storm flooded through Chris's mind; they possessed enough explosives to invade Iraq, he figured. The full bags reminded the boy of his Halloween bag, overflowing with candy. "Would I miss Halloween?" he wondered to himself, sadly.

The thought made him melancholy, something he wished to change. Before he knew what he was doing, he rode his horse to the front of the group, and turned around and sat in his saddle to address the group. With the entire clan's attention, he began an impromptu limerick.

> Their once was an carriage in Alucemet,
> came speeding down a road where the Pitlings lay.
> But Alexander and his men,
> took off to stop them.
> So began pursuit on that famous day.

Smiles and a few cheers from the boys led him on.

> Along that road the horses would run,
> sky became dark and blocked out the sun.
> Fordem thought the Pitling beat,
> he laughed so at his brilliant feat.
> But Alexander had in mind much more fun.

> To a narrow gorge they would come.
> They're wasn't a hope in the world, said some.
> But Alexander had his say,
> it was to be their day.
> With a dangling rope he tripped them on their bum.

With the last word, the group burst into laughter. Chris surprised himself with his creativity. He realized that he used the word bum from Manzell's song, before he remembered the boy's verse. "This world!" he said to himself, thinking how much he was able to do here. He relished the group's acceptance.

Chris turned back around in his saddle. He edged his horse back into the group. As they rode Chris remembered the girl: the flowers, her appearance, and disappearance. He was curious; perhaps the others would know of her. He moved his horse between Manzell and Alexander, and tried to find out.

"My friends, a girl of our age I spied today." He stopped himself. *Kingly* again he realized. "I saw her in the meadow, across the clearing, near our camp. The chick, ah girl, she was cutting these huge flowers, bigger than me! I think she lives there."

Manzell turned to the boy and laughed. He seemed tired, not really interested in his question.

Chris said, "Manzell, who is she?"

"Nary in one hundred leagues doth anyone but a Pitling exist, much less a damsel to which you speak," Manzell responded.

"But Manzell, I saw her myself! I spoke to her!" Chris replied.

"A trip so long from your world doth strangeness to one's mind, Christopher of Temecula. Regard it as such. A being of which you speak would be hard pressed to survive here. And mind you, the stench has long since destroyed flowers in the meadow," Manzell spoke in a certain tone. He appeared unwilling to speak further of the subject. The boy sped up, moving ahead to speak to James.

Troubled, Chris pondered the conversation. He was sure that he was awake, not dreaming. She was as real as he was, but Michael Shaun did not seem to see her as well. At the time, he thought the boy had other things on his mind. Now he was not even sure; was the girl a delusion? He forgot, in his deliberation, that Alexander was riding at his side. He sensed that the leader heard the conversation. "Do you know a Girl like that Alexander?" Chris turned to look at the leader as they rode.

A troubled look came across Alexander's face. The boy did not answer for some time. When he finally broke the silence, he said, almost hesitantly. "By what title doth this damsel go, Christopher?"

"Autumn. She called herself Autumn, Alexander. She said her last name, but I don't remember it." Chris replied.

Alexander said quietly. "Bienville." There was sadness in his voice, and distress etched his face.

Christopher waited, expecting more of an explanation, but none followed. They rode in silence for some time. Now, he really wondered about this girl. Bienville was the name she mentioned. Alexander knew her. She was not a figment, but his response was somewhat spooky. He imagined that Manzell knew her as well, choosing for some reason not to speak of her.

Never leaving an unasked question, Christopher reluctantly continued. "But who is Autumn....what did you say....Bienville? And how can she live way out here?"

"Life is the tragedy; your question bereaves me so. One more casualty of the Boar. Oh, the woe to recall! Just a child. The King, my father's guardsman, his only child." There was a short pause and then he continued. "I shall revenge them!"

"Now I'm really spooked. I thought clowns were scary!" Chris said to himself. "Sorry I asked. Life? Life is what tragedy? Avenge them? They're very serious here! What's up with this Autumn?" He was afraid to think, but now he had a pretty good idea. He recalled her appearance, sudden disappearance, and her own illumination. She sat in the bright sunlight, but the boulder was ice cold.

Alexander quickly regained composure and returned to his controlled way. He seemed to weigh his words before he spoke. "An apparition, she walks in torment, not knowing the state of her soul."

Chris thought for a moment in shock. Under his breath he whispered. "Dude...Autumn's a ghost babe?"

Chapter 7
A Pirate's Life

> THE WICKED MAN FLEES
> THOUGH NO ONE PURSUES,
> BUT THE RIGHTEOUS
> ARE AS BOLD AS A LION
> **PROVERBS 28:1**

"Ahoy on deck, we've a need. Shan't we come aboard?" With hands cupped around his mouth, the young boy shouted frantically, kneeling in the bow of the dingy as it twisted in the churning sea. Behind him, a determined friend rowed frantically, battling the cresting waves that grew increasingly capable of swallowing up and crushing their small craft like a wooden match. The two were exhausted and frightened, for they had now fought the powerful sea for hours, rapidly daunted in their plight and searching beyond hope for a rescuer.

The unforgiving ocean thundered in white tipped squalls, restless and churning, much more so since they first spied the huge sailing ship that now seemed to represent a thready hope. As they approached the massive vessel, the sky became overcast, not long before a brilliant azure blue, and covered with the reddish haze so common of late.

With determined skill, the two paddled the dwarfed craft to flank the mighty sailing craft. The leader boy grabbed frantically for a rope ladder lowered for their ascent and secured the boat, as the two boys scampered for apparent safety of the deck above. The ladder twisted in the howling wind as the last rungs approached, before a strong arm grasped the scruff of their shirts and rudely pulled the boys one by one sprawling to the wooden deck.

Pirates, Scoundrels, and Kings

Whether they expected such a welcome was not obvious from the boys' valiant expressions. Thrown tumbling to the deck in a tangled pile, they looked up with brave but tentative countenances, surrounded quickly by a less than welcoming crew.

The two boys appeared approximately six years of age. They were dressed in simple common garments, clothed in salt-water-drenched, rough-cut, brown, cowhide coatcoats tied loosely at the waist with fraying braided rope. Each seemed to have outgrown their well-worn trousers, stretched and touching to mid-calf, constructed of coarsely woven cloth torn from years of wear, their near frozen feet bare. The boy, who seemed to be the leader, had light brown hair with bleached ends, short and spiked on top with a dab of pine tar. He had dark piercing brown eyes, with the hint of a dimple in his chin. His suntanned shoulders were bare and muscular, and a crude black insignia was smeared upon the left. The second boy carried slightly darker, sun-streaked brown hair with a wisp of hair falling over his brow. The two were cold, wet, and frightened as they looked upon an ominous welcome.

Towering before them stood the buccaneer known as Balaam, captain of the sailing ship and self-proclaimed master of the sea. Seldom mistaken for handsome, the crude man owned a deeply lined face, chiseled and coarsened from years of sun and sea. His left nostril was devoid of its lateral attachment to his cheek or nasal ala, residual gifts from a prior sword fight, and a black bandanna adorned his balding mangy head. He was toothless- a fact only obvious during the rare event of a smile- and black stubble of beard covered his grubby mug. Foreboding in his black frock uniform, an unsheathed dagger dangled ominously from a thick and greasy stained leather belt. A rag tag, filthy, salty crew, neither looking upon the new passengers with any fatherly love, completed the welcoming party.

Out of place on Balaam's greasy being sat a brilliantly colored and manicured parrot, whose radiant appearance seemed to mock the captain's primitive facade. Walking side to side on the pirate's shoulder in a frantic pace, the bird's sharp bill made one wonder whether the story of Balaam's nostril might reside with the beak of this powerful bird.

The man's appearance was frightening for certain, but what distinguished Balaam was a severely diseased respiratory system, his breathing labored and rapid, which the pirate cultivated in almost glee. The coarse man suffered, some would agree enthusiastically, from bronchiectasis, a chronic disease in which there is destruction of parenchyma, leaving large pockets for purulent airway secretions to collect within a chronically infected lung. Bronchiectasis is the result of, rather than the cause of, disease and in this medieval time tuberculosis was its usual etiology. In Balaam's case he seemed well compensated, for he functioned admirably, seeming almost happy for his disability save his continual wheezing and coughing.

Characteristic of the disease, Balaam was an accomplished creator of thick and purulent sputum that he would produce from deep within his diseased lungs. With camel-like ruthlessness, he could launch these projectiles without warning, nailing with pinpoint accuracy whatever or whomever he decided to purge his wrath.

The two boys seemed like baggage before the ruthless group, and they soon questioned their wisdom and choice of this savior. After examining the cowering boys tossed unceremoniously at Balaam's feet, an insincere toothless smile greeted the boys.

"Me... nice... young... laddys," Balaam questioned with sarcastically concerned glee. "What has you'se to say fer you'selfs? What cause has the likes of you'se fer a sea like this?" he said raising two greasy hands. "Passengers, why mighty poorly they do on the Boar's frigate, aye mates!"

With that, the pirate turned to his semblance of a crew, which had quickly gathered to surround the two helpless boys. Tossing a self-serving wave of his hand, he expected and received dull nods of approval and ghoulish laughter, as might a neighborhood bully comforted by a besotted gang.

Quite a tattered group had gathered to support the captain. Most were dressed in plain black knickers. Shirts, when worn, were torn and soiled with sweat and gunpowder. Primitive tattoos, most vile and suggestive, decorated the majority of the filthy sailors. One such person had a wooden peg leg, and carved upon it was a scantily clothed miss for all to worship upon when time allowed. Not a clean-shaven face decorated the crowd, most of the sailors displaying poorly trimmed mustaches or ragged beards.

As Balaam spoke, the parrot squawked, the bird appearing to add punctuation to the captain's tortured words. The bird insisted as well on summarizing the captain at each pause. "Poorly they do-Mates," the parrot repeated.

Each squawk and comment received a grimace of displeasure from the captain. The parrot's last remarks were all that he could stand. In disgust, Balaam turned and using the back of his hand struck the bird, knocking him to the deck in a cloud of feathers.

"Vile creature... interrupt me no more," said the pirate, as if this was a common but intolerable nuisance.

The parrot shook off this insult without a beat. He ruffled his feathers and tossed back his head. Clawing upright, the bird stood, and then rose confidently from the deck. Unfazed, he flew with some caution back to the captain's shoulder.

Balaam paid little attention to the parrot, concentrating now upon the two visitors. The gang closed in upon the boys as the interview continued. The motley crew brandished swords to the boys' dismay, and musket-pistols within their belts suggested that this was not a pleasure cruise. The group drew tighter, encircling the captives as the ship tossed in the rough sea. Staring hungrily at the boys, the crew seemed to expect some response.

The leader boy now rose and stood stiffly at attention. He motioned to his friend and helped the other boy to his feet in deference to the captain. With reluctance, the two beleaguered boys now faced the threatening scene.

"Captain sir," the leader said to Balaam with a hint of fearful hesitation. "To your great ship and capable crew, we are beholding for our lives. Not more than an hour ago, my father's ill-fated ship ran aground and alas, is now helplessly doomed to this thrashing sea."

Dropping his head in obvious anguish, a silent sob came to his lips as the boy continued his saga. "To you sir we beg for assistance. My father may soon be in a watery grave, and as for the ship, its contents must not be lost for the good of the kingdom!" The boy now raised his head bravely to face Balaam with a tearful but determined eye.

Following with interest the course of the boy's sad saga, the pirate seemed to relish their hopeless plight, his increasingly sarcastic grin met by supportive hoots and howls from the sickeningly despotic crew. The parrot squawked in a rhythmic avian pattern, pacing back and forth on the man's shoulder and brandishing his menacing beak. The man deftly caught the boy's trailing remarks, however, and with the suggestion of the ship's precious contents, a benevolent change came over the toothless countenance of Balaam.

The parrot was a quick study, rapidly grasping the statement's significance as well. "Squawk, treasure...Balaam needs treasure," screeched the rainbow colored bird.

The remark again brought quick anger to the pirate, but he controlled himself for the moment and reconsidered the case. With the idea now coursing through Balaam's mind, he tolerated the bird temporarily, silently scrutinizing the boy's account. The pirate smiled and slyly approached the boys placing a gnarled soiled hand on each of the boy's shoulders. "And to what might be on that ship? Oh, such young laddies and in a sea such as this? It saddens me heart it does," Balaam said with his most sincere visage.

"Why gold, silver, and jewels such as I have never seen, master," the leader boy responded. "To Alucemet with haste, we must return, securing our contents within the castle hold against sure and certain pilfering. But sir, our ship now lies in the sea unprotected and my father!" With that, the boy dropped to his knees in respect to the sailor hoping for merciful intervention, bravely quenching back tears.

Pirates, Scoundrels, and Kings

The friend now dropped quickly to the floor to comfort the boy with a gentle hand. Adding quietly in the leader's ear, just audible to the group, he reassured him. "Nicholas, the treasure was lost once. It may be lost again. That is of no import. Your father, he will be saved, of that I am certain!"

Silence followed for a time punctuated only by the bronchiectatic wheezing of the man, as the captain pondered his predicament. The parrot stopped his pacing for the moment, turning an intelligent eye and considering the boys as well. For the pirate, his labored brain was only now totally realizing this fortunate turn of fate. Here was a man who sailed the seas, dedicated to the theft of treasure; could this story possibly be true? Had fate finally cast itself in his deserving direction, dropping into his lap what he so nobly stole at every opportunity? He scratched his half-shaven beard and turned to the crew staring in disbelief, trying to hide his growing excitement.

The boys jumped nervously, as the pirate returned to them suddenly. Without warning, the shabby man produced a purulent sputum, which he expelled with violent force skimming over their heads, dropping harmlessly to the crashing sea below.

The parrot spoke up, for the bird evidently knew this man to be dim-witted, and judging the situation wished secretly to signal a possible windfall. "Balaam loves children, squawk."

The captain grimaced with anger, turning his head toward the bird. He caught himself suddenly now adopting an attitude of agreement, nodding in response to the statement and looking for the first time approvingly upon the bird.

"Yes.... Balaam do. Yes... yes.... Balaam do like children he does. Love... love's children, me do. And, be clear on that, my little ones." Balaam returned his attention once again to the boys with an overly concerned voice and sickening smile. "My dear lad, worry not your head, Balaam will serve you." He turned to the crew expecting a show of support for his newly found benevolence from the motley group.

The crew was neither the brightest nor the quickest group to sail the mighty seas. Their lues-infested minds were even slower than the dull witted captain's, and the bird certainly possessed the only brain capable of tax returns. Slowly, however, even the motley crew began to understand the change in the captain's goal; their menacing scowls melting into concerning smiles of insincere love, punctuated by blackened and missing teeth, exposing a malodorous nightmare to the young boys.

"And where might one search out a ship such as this?" the captain questioned. "Ah, we aims only to help you'se poor shipwrecked father, mind you'se laddys," The crew agreed in unison, nodding their heads in the affirmative supporting their suddenly loving captain.

With rapidity, as if memorized, the boy fired back, "33 degrees north latitude by 118 degrees west longitude! Ah... that be if I'm not mistaken... ah... sir," he added as a second thought looking down now at the deck.

Balaam thought for some time, chewing upon a stubby nub of a finger. The boy's quick response troubled him, and he seemed concerned with its details. Staring down at the captives, he considered in silence the two frightened boys with a questioning frown. The parrot, always the conversationalist, was silent as the bird examined for himself the two refugees, cold and wet, standing before the evil pirate. Perhaps the bird's silence ensured the captain, for after some consideration his toothless smile slowly returned. Now quite confident and delighted in himself, he turned quickly to face the insincerely concerned crew.

With a dismissing wave of his hand, he ordered them to their posts. "We'se a mercy mission we'se do," and with that the captain dispersed his men throughout the ship to their stations.

The sky had grow darker and the sea more ominous during this discourse. The wind was now blowing with gale force and the huge wooden vessel twisted on the restless sea. Thick rusty haze surrounded them blotting out the overhead sun.

Pirates, Scoundrels, and Kings

As the crew spread out along the ship, the leader boy turned and delicately addressed the pirate. "Captain, sir..." he said in a quiet but sure voice. Balaam stopped and turned a questioning eye to the boy. "If I may be so bold my mightiest of captains, as if curtained, the sky darkens with each moment!" Expecting a response, the boy stopped at this point without finishing his thought.

Balaam returned now to the boy's side. Standing closely looking down and wheezing he asked impatiently, "get on with it boy, what be's in you'se minds?"

"Well, forward it is for one such as I to suggest to one of your stature sir... but why must you and your crew go to all ends of this vessel?"

Balaam took delight in what he felt was the boy's ignorance and he laughed at the child fiendishly. Placing a greasy hand upon his shoulder he responded, "a ship has many a job my boy."

Before the captain could continue, the boy spoke again with bravery. "With reluctance kind sir, but may I be so bold? For it strikes me, experience in these matters I have none mind you, but it seems that in a sea such as this more eyes rather than less are worthwhile to locate a ship so small and so precious I might add."

The captain now was bearing down on the boy with impatience. A malodorous bouquet caused the boys to grimace if ever so slightly, as the pirate considered launching his ample supply of sputum. "Babble no more boy, what's you'se to say!"

"It would strike me so honorable captain that just for the moment, if you would, to the foredeck move all of your devoted crew, and with eyes trained at our goal, would we not sight that goal more surely? Instead of breaking up to their usual posts, that is...kind sir. We have no enemy to fear other than visual contact, I would venture to guess."

With an evil twisted smile, the captain pondered the boy's suggestion rubbing his scraggly beard for a long thoughtful moment. He was enjoying his position of intimidation, reeling in it really, playing this point of control as he stared from above at the pitiful boy, whose only hope was to free his beloved father. In truth, the pirate could not have cared less about the youth's predicament, save of course the treasure. On cue, a stridulous roar began as the pirate produced a wad from deep within his rattling lungs. Rolling his tongue around, he examined the result and expressing obvious dissatisfaction, swallowed the tenacious wad of sputum rather than expectorate an inferior product.

Without acknowledgment to the boys, Balaam turned to the crew denouncing them for their mistake. "You foolish brood, he screamed! We'se need more lookout we'se do, see to it." As he yelled, he directed the crew to the forward deck for trained observation upon the source of their rescue attempt. As the captain moved to the helm, Balaam dismissed the boys without a nod. Pointing a greasy finger, he directed the peg-legged crewmember to take the boys below. "For ther'se protection," he added with an insincere snarl. Finally satisfied, a greenish wad of sputum flew across ship dropping to the sea below.

The two boys appreciated the warmth of the hold, if for only a short time. They moved to sit next to a small burning torch, rubbing and blowing upon the bluish hue of their small frozen fingers. The weather had turned for the worst since the sight of the pirate ship, as if the vessel created its own brand of tortured climate to match its evil. The rust-covered haze enveloped the sun as a blinder and an icy blast of chilling air knifed through the body to the bone. From their sojourn within the small craft, both were soaked and exhausted. Huddling together now for warmth, the two boys looked at one another, their two exhausted smiles giving each a modicum of comfort. Dwarfed in the belly of the huge wooden craft, the two eyed with curiosity a latched porthole. Starboard and above their heads, the thick glass window gave a clouded view of the ocean outside, separating the hold from the turning sea. The leader boy nodded in its direction, his friend shaking his head in silent agreement.

It was not to be a long reprieve. They had just begun to warm from their harrowing experience, when they were rudely returned to the deck for a second audience with the captain. Pointing excitedly off starboard bow, the pirate looked to the boys for confirmation that a visibly scuttled ship was the intended prize.

A few hundred yards across the sea stood a stranded sailing vessel apparently runaground, twisting and moaning in the heavy sea. The ship was deserted and wrecked, having journeyed too close to the mainland in a low tide. With lowered sheets, the craft had been obviously laboring in the heavy winds. Seemingly abandoned, the ship's crew, father included, were nowhere in sight. The captain was quite excited and proud of himself when he heard the boy's affirmative reply.

"That is our vessel sir, but my father seems already lost!" Dropping his head in dismay, tears began to form as the boy tried to fight them away. His friend turned to comfort him, placing his arm upon the boy's shoulder.

The captain had another question for the boys. "And to what might all those nets be me lad?"

Balaam was referring to a dense collection of fish netting hanging bow to stern just above the waterline of the shipwrecked craft. On a ship of this sort, their function was not immediately apparent to the wizened old captain. The pirate turned to the boys, towering over them with intimidation, demanding an explanation.

"Why with only those could the treasure be brought to the deck, Sir. Fail you to recall the shipwreck, Bailsmith, scuttled at sea in the year of our Lord, eight hundred and fifty eight? Why just where we stand it was, and in a sea much as today it seems. The noble ship went down to its fate. Loaded with treasure, goes the tale. My father," the boy's words stumbled before he could continue. "A good... and fair man, King William commissioned him to search the bottom to right that tragic loss for glory of our Lord. And right it he did, were it not for this sea." The boy now looked to the pirate for reassurance. "Sir I am troubled though. We must hurry. I see not my father!"

The boy's response lifted the captain's last ray of suspicion. Excitement was building with the good fortune, matched only by the size and consistency of his next sputum wad. With a long rattling wheeze productive of a foul gob of decaying lung, and with violent accuracy, he expelled it flying just by the boys' heads, splashing with ceremony into the sea.

Quite elated with these events, Balaam motioned to the one-legged crewmember. With an evil laugh, he spoke to the leader boy. "You'se shall see that father, straight away, you'se will. Purneshench, me vile and wretched friend. Show me friends a nice swim in the drink will you'se? Me thinks they honor the plank, yes sir, and delightfully, they do." With an aside the Captain laughed, "and of course for the glory of our Lord!"

With that, the captain dismissed the boys to an uncertain fate, moving with quickening steps to the forward deck dreaming of ill-gotten gain and gold. At any other time, the plank would serve the captain with delight, an event he would not miss. However, the pirate was concerned with more important wares ahead, and so wheezing and sputtering the captain was off, smugly directing the crew to their posts. The buccaneer's luck for once matched his misused talents, he surmised, handed as he was a ship for the easy taking. Leaving the two boys to their fate, Balaam moved aft. Grabbing his periscope, he eyed the wrecked ship with anticipation.

The wooden legged pirate jumped forward with glee, turning his every attention to the convicted youngsters. Pruneshench was quick for a peg-legged man, for he took his job seriously and torture was his chosen profession. He pushed the two boys roughly across the craft to starboard, and forced them to their wobbling knees. The crew quickly produced two narrow wooden planks laid just so over the edge of the ship, each counter balanced by the weight of a gleeful sailor.

It seemed all too clear now to the young boys. A foul pirate with one functioning lung had betrayed their fate. The trusting eyes so true of childhood now changed to a countenance of frightened treason and treachery. In stubborn silence, they moved each boy, forced at sword poin,t to the edge of their respective planks and a date with a churning watery precipice. Below the two rolled the

Pirates, Scoundrels, and Kings

unforgiving sea, cold and gray; yes, it seemed bleak, two brave boys betrayed by their trusting faith.

Pruneshench wasted little time. Drawing his sword, he coaxed the two trusting boys out onto their plank. "Say you'se prayers laddies," followed the poor boys as they fell to their fates below. He turned quickly from his beloved task and moved toward the stern on his way to the deck below and his beloved band of canons. Had he been more cautious and studious, the lack of two splashes might have caused curiosity even in his laboring mind.

It seemed as if the parrot had no such pressing assignment for the time. He had observed with interest all of these activities from a nearby mast. The bird now flew and perched upon the ship's edge above the lost boys. Turning his head first one way then the other, he eyed the sea below with each eye. "Well I'll be, squawk", but no one else seemed interested.

Now content with his view from the periscope, Balaam cast it aside quickly. For good luck, he reached deeply, producing a green, blood tinged, foul specimen, quite pleasing to the pirate. With violent force, he launched the projectile over the side of the ship, his package striking the ocean with a proud splash. Expectantly, Balaam moved quickly to the deck's edge to view his canonry bank. With rage, he returned and called through the speaking tube to his head gunman below. "Open the canon doors you dimwit!" Waiting he heard no reply and his anger grew.

Pruneshench had hobbled with amazing speed and reached the captain in a total panic. As he approached, the unfortunate man inadvertently intercepted a flying spit wad from the captain with his face. A common event it seemed for he wiped it away with nary an acknowledgment to the insult. "Captain, the hold's a-locked and jammed shut from inside it seems! We shan't get to those canons fer now."

Like cogs in a nearly unwound clock, questions now floated slowly through the demented gray matter of the captain's irate brain. He had little time to think for from far above he heard his name called. Looking up to the sound above, he saw his two prior captives, beaming free and defiant.

"Balaam," the leader boy spoke proudly. "Little Andy and I wish to thank you for your hospitality. We are beholding to you! Thank you, Sir for your kind, and fair treatment."

High above the deck on the main mast crow's nest, the two boys stood now splendidly. The leader boy, no longer dressed commonly, wore a white silken shirt now blowing in the sea wind. Around the boy's waist was a bright blue sash, tied over his hip as a belt. Within it, a sword holstered without sheath. Confident brown eyes stared down in defiance at the wheezing pirate. Little Andy, his fellow stowaway, reached for a rope secured just below the nest. This boy as well brandished steel, and an odd black patch covered his left eye. The two beamed here-to-fore hidden smiles as they swung without hesitation from the mast. Flying with obvious experience down upon the bewildered captain, the two boys landed with agility at the foot of their apparent prey.

The first cannon ball struck as Balaam fully realized his fateful error; shattering the deck sending crew and wooden fragments flying in a fiery ball of flame. Several more hit their target in rapid succession, and soon the ship and crew were in a frantic condition. The captain turned his attention from the insolent boys and stared in horror out over the sea to his "ship wrecked prey" in disbelief. Baring down upon the pirate was the same ship obviously without disability and sailing now full of sail with canons blasting. The supposed treasure gathering nets swept away, and replacing them just below the deck was a bank of twelve blazing cannons, each rapidly punctuating the circumstances with fire. They had turned a trap on the pirate, with his canon hold locked, ship dead in the water, and the deck braking up blazing in flames.

The captain returned in a frenzy to face the boys. The circumstances had now rapidly changed, and Balaam stared in horror upon them realizing his mistake. The leader boy stepped forward, and he motioned to his friend to see to the boarding. Coughing and sputtering, the angry pirate was now surrounded by enemy canon fire, a sinking splintering ship, and this rogue of a boy with whom he must deal with quickly. Balaam drew his saber standing his ground.

The boy seemed amused at the thought, smiling quietly at the captain. He drew his sword slowly, seeming to savor the moment. With confidence and glee, he moved to engage his prior captor.

The boy's determination was too much for the cowardly pirate. Once the master of the sea, a ship full of booty had almost been his; now his world was splintering and ablaze around him. "How could a boy out smart this seaworthy giant?" the captain thought in horror. Balaam was not about to be run-in by the boy's blade and so he did as he had so often done before: he turned to run. Before he could drop his sword and run, the determined boy was upon him. Grabbing his belt and collar, he hauled the man to the ship's edge, and threw the degenerate captain, wheezing and hacking, into the icy sea below. The barefooted boy jumped to the deck rail and spied with delight the defeated captain now floundering in the rough sea below. He watched the sight for a moment, then turned jumping from the rail to the splintered deck just beginning to breakup from the cannon rounds. The boy reached for a filthy life preserver attached to the burning cabin, lobbing the ring without hesitation over the ship's edge toward his pitiful defeated prey. "That's more than you intended for us! To your good health, mate," he said quietly to himself.

The boy turned his attention now to the burning ship. He rubbed his hands together in anticipation, joyful of his impending capture of an enemy vessel. Before him stood a ship reeling towards its death, seawater rushing in through a shattered hull. The ship was on fire and the main mast was crashing to the splintering deck destroyed in flames.

Little Andy had seen to the ship's boarding with obvious experience. Rapidly directing twelve individuals, the ship was taken by a band of pirate boys. Over the starboard side, they now climbed and with cheers raced to the ship's bow.

When the battle had begun, the entire pirate crew had been above deck and starboard at the insistence of the now defunct captain Balaam. Not only had they been denied access to their cannons, they had been unable to even maneuver their ship from the deadly enemy cannon fire. The crew now stood helpless upon the bow of the ship. They were in disbelief, the ship breaking up in total disarray. Overwhelmed with surprise, their tide changed from one of certain victory in a matter of moments to one of certain defeat, their hopes and dreams now shattered with the first canon ball. With swords and fists the boys made quick work of the dismayed crew who, being cowards, ran from them finding the same fate floating in the brink with their sinking captain.

Little Andy now returned to his leader with a broad smile. They confidently exchanged looks of victory, as the pirate ship began to break up. The ship was taking on water quickly, the deck beginning to roll with each moment.

"Open that hold if you will Little Andy, and make a point of it to hurry my friend," the leader boy instructed. As an afterthought he noticed something on the boy. Stopping his friend for just a moment, he moved his eye patch to the right eye. "There, much better, you hooligan."

"Hooligans we be, and proud of it I should say," Little Andy laughed, straightening the patch. Referring to his previous order the boy followed with, "Aye sir."

The patched boy now scampered for the starboard side of the deck. Without hesitation, he swung over the deck rail where earlier the boys had faced certain death on the plank. Finding his objective, the oval window stood agar just below the deck ledge. Little Andy quickly kicked in the window and entered the sinking ship through a route only one the size of a boy could possibly enter. Once inside he moved to the hold's door, jammed from within, denying the defeated crew access to the canonry bank. A broken post wedged into the runner of the door was now evident in the dim and smoky innards of the ship. Little Andy jumped as high as he could and grabbed the oaken beam with both hands. He swung his legs up to push on the massive door. Using his legs and all of his strength he slowly moved the post free of the runners. Abruptly, the beam came loose with a grunt, and he was thrown by his force to the floor below. Twisted, more surprised than hurt, Little Andy looked up as the hold's door slowly rolled open. The sky was clearing with the victory, for now sunlight beamed and blazed through the opening. Little Andy squinted as he looked up, flat on his back and smiling with embarrassment.

Staring down at the fallen boy, the leader boy smiled and shook his head in jest. "Had you needed a rest you had only to ask, my patched friend! A better way to open a door I have never seen though." The boy bounded down the ladder to his fallen friend. With a strong hand, he helped him to his feet.

As each moment passed, the shipped reeled, its watery resting place seeming to be just moments away. Smoke began to fill below deck as the fires above roared out of control. The two boys moved through the ship quickly, down a narrow hall. "Just a might much from Sam's cannons I would say Little Andy, but we've treasure to find," spoke the leader boy over his shoulder.

The ship was rolling now, making their travel down the hall quite difficult. In front of the boys, water began entering the craft through a broadside canon rent. The blast of water roared in, and the boys quickly ducked it moving toward the ship's stern. The hall floor was quickly filling with water, and Nicholas slipped briefly. "Wow," the boy yelled as he slid on his back. He quickly regained his footing and the two hurried towards a closed door ahead. They were climbing in elevation as they traveled rearward, along the gloomy hall, the ship's bow now completely submerged and the boys now on its stern.

Reaching the vestibule of the passage, a thick heavy door stood, blocking the path into the boy's apparent destination. The leader tried the lock to no avail. He motioned to Little Andy and using shoulders and body they both pushed and strained the door, just budging slightly after quite a struggle. From far above a huge cracking sound roared as one of the large masts, now afire, fell crashing to the deck above. The creak of the tortured vessel did not seem to worry the two, as the ship twisted in agony, sinking by the moment.

The boys persisted despite the reeling ship, determined to gain access to the secured room. Nicholas turned quickly to a rotting banister lining a stairway that led to a deeper portion of the sinking ship. With a kick of his foot, he made quick work of a portion of the rail, breaking loose a large fragment and then ripping it away with force. With Little Andy's help, they wedged the broken end into the door's jam as a lever. Struggling, the two pried the door open just enough to accommodate the boys.

Once inside, it became apparent that they had found the old captain's quarters. Dark, dingy, and thrown in disarray, the stale room reeked of old tobacco, lit only by one still-burning candle and a odd stray beam filtering through partially submerged, grimy portholes. Along one side a broken wicker hammock swung ajar, partially covered with water, its fall indicating the exaggerated draft of the sinking ship. Half-eaten stale crumbs of bread and cheese were cast aside, littering the plank wooden floor. A small circular map table occupied the center of the small cabin, many of its documents now strung out over the deck.

Tucked deep in one corner of the room stood a small-closeted door. Using his blade, Little Andy made quick work of its lock, the door swinging open to reveal the source of their dangerous pursuit, a small wooden cask rolling out by its weight at their feet. Dropping to his knees, Nicholas opened the trunk. The dim light was sufficient to reveal glowing precious contents: gold, silver, and jewel purloin, pinched without permission from the King's navy.

The boys were jubilant, their smiles now from ear to ear. "I knew it Little Andy, ours again. Bet on this, Balaam tells the Boar nothing of these!"

With the ship sinking rapidly, Nicholas closed the cask, and turned with his treasure to their escape. However, as the boy passed the map table he stopped abruptly, startled by the document that had rolled open, still clinging to the map table.

Little Andy was already at the door when he noticed the boy's delay. Turning to his leader with concern he said, "Nicholas, we must make haste sire...or we shall soon be with this ship on the bottom of the sea!" The boy slipped on the soaked floor, grabbed for the door and righted himself. Looking now to his friend with concern, fright for the first time appeared in the eyes of the brave boy who had stood up to such a mighty pirate foe without any doubts.

Nicholas did not respond; something had caught his attention, for he stood holding the treasure chest staring at the parchment with dismay. Again, Little Andy voiced his concern loudly. Nicholas at last lifted his head, silently responding to his devoted friend. Something had a profound effect on the spirited boy, for suddenly he seemed solemn and changed. His complexion had lost all color and he seemed not to breathe. Once one of strength and confidence, he now stood meek and troubled. Glassy-eyed he stared upon his friend for a moment. Obviously troubled, he slowly recovered his composure but did not move. With authority, he firmly instructed his friend. "I want you to go on ahead. I shall follow presently. Little Andy, do as I say."

Something in his tone told his friend that this was not debatable. Little Andy was reluctant. Standing in the door he wrestled with the command silently. Suddenly he turned and was gone.

Nicholas set the cask on the floor and moved to the flickering candle on the wall. The ship cracked in agony again, twisting and filling with cold ocean water, but the boy seemed not to notice. As if in a trance, he removed the candle from its stand and returned to the table. Now with adequate light, Nicholas examined the document, spreading the parchment out, slowly drinking in its content. Here was a printed proclamation, dark gothic letters describing details of great import.

Sir Alexander of Alucemet Slain at the Hand of Nicholas the Blue

The boy stared at the document in disbelief. With an irritable shake of his head in anger, the boy tossed the candle across the room, immediately extinguished by the flooding water covering the entire cabin's floor. Nicholas grabbed the parchment, stuffed it within his open shirt, and moved to the open door dragging his cask.

The situation in the passage had changed for the worse. It was flooded now and the water's depth increased as the boy moved with difficulty along the hallway in search of the open hold door. Soon he was swimming in the icy waters that engulfed the doomed ship. With each moment the water level within rose, with debris and fractured pieces of deck floating and clogging his escape.

In the blackened drowning passage, the boy paddled reaching the hold door now nearly submerged and swallowed by the sea. Nicholas viewed the scene with a sinking dismay. As the ship had reeled, the bow becoming deeper, the fall of the ship was such that the massive oaken hold door had rolled shut again. To lift it against gravity and sea, opening an escape route was now impossible for the boy. The seawater continued to swell into the craft, a head's space of air only remaining in what was left of the darkened passage. Nicholas looked around for an avenue of escape. To return towards the rear of the ship and air would only prolong the inevitable, as he had seen no routes to the outside. He remembered their prior entry to the ship. A porthole had allowed Little Andy's entrance somewhere, if he could find this only route of escape.

Nicholas made several dives in the dark water, each time frantically exploding back to the surface gasping for air. It was black and deep, and the boy was beginning to tire. With one last effort, he was able to feel his objective, the open porthole. Stretching and straining he reached for his treasure chest, dragging it close to the opening. Moving quickly now, Nicholas pulled himself through the open porthole to the open sea. His lungs had nearly burst, as he bobbed to the surface with a gasp. Diving again, returning to the sinking ship, he reached within the porthole. Feeling around feverishly he was at last able to retrieve his treasure chest. One last

Pirates, Scoundrels, and Kings

important quest remained, however. Throwing the chest to the nearly submerged ship's deck, he pulled himself and stood upon the doomed vessel. Quickly he searched the sky for the moment. Then raising his fingers to his mouth he let out a long whistle. "Rainbow!" the boy yelled at the top of his lungs. From the sole remaining mast sticking up just above the sea level, the parrot flew. As if reunited friends the bird landed gently on the pirate boy's shoulder.

"Balaam loves children, squawk," the bird mimicked once again with an ironic bark.

"No longer, I'm afraid, Rainbow," Nicholas said shaking his head and laughing deeply to no one but his irascible bird.

Nicholas now searched the sinking segment of remaining deck. Quickly finding a small piece of deck planking, he loosed it with a deft kick, moved to the edge of the rising water, and dropped it to float alongside in the sea. Just as the ship reeled for the last time, the boy took his sword and placed the blade in his mouth. He dove from the ship into the swirling sea. With strong strokes, the boy made his way towards his ship in the distance dragging his captured treasure chest on the floating wooden plank behind him.

CHAPTER 8
The Laughing Lion

> IF A RULER LISTENS TO LIES,
> ALL HIS OFFICIALS BECOME WICKED.
> **PROVERBS 29:12**

Christopher bolted upright, startled to the world, breathing hard, his brow wet with perspiration. In his sleep he dreamt of Richard of Fordem, mounted upon the jaundiced-eyed horse and pursuing him, without mercy, down a dark, dingy, alley, his escape blocked in a dead-end. In this foreign world now, every morning began the same: awakening from a frightening dream in terror. Yawning and stretching in the cold morning, he realized that he was safe and the fear slowly disappeared.

As always, Alexander's bedroll showed no sign of sleep. Relieved by the disappearance of his dream, the boy sighed and dropped back to his back, staring in the dark light of dawn. His former world now crept into his mind, so far away it seemed, or was it? Worldly distances meant little to him now. Was a mile a mile, a kilometer a kilometer? Who could tell in this world of frightening horses and fighting soldiers?

This world contrasted with his prior home, and he realized he possessed so much. Nostalgia swept over the boy, and he resolved to value his former life if he ever regained it again. He laughed when he noticed his backpack, basketball, and skateboard neatly arranged at his feet. Meager in comparison to his former world, these items were the sum total of his belongings in this newly adopted home.

In many ways, this new world was so simple. It was absent television, telephones, and most of all school. The absence of fast-paced multimedia of his former world produced in this world a slower tempo. While this civilization's pace was much slower, it seemed to Chris that it wasat the cost of much danger. Innocence was difficult in a world of conflict and battle. Intuitively, a world without adults was cool, but how can a child be a child when parents were not around to spoil and protect them? He would find years later that he irreversibly grew up at that moment, and from then on, it would be hard to feel like a child again. Slowly a sense of loneliness overcame the boy. He missed home, "Oh... but for the wrath of a cloud." He thought sadly.

Chris stood up, shivering in the cold morning air. After he wrapped up and buried the evil Fordem, Alexander had presented him local clothes as gifts. At first, Christopher resisted the britches preferring to wear his beloved orange shorts. As the days passed, he began to feel more and more comfortable dressed as an adopted Pitling.

Quickly, the boy pulled the rough-cut coatcoat over his tee shirt, gaining some relief from the cold. With reluctance, he dressed in the dark britches, sadly folding his orange shorts neatly. Alexander had insisted on these, and now Chris realized that in a world of violence, nothing so bright and different made sense. Fordem reminded him of that, making the orange color an issue.

Footwear was different, however. Here, oddly, Alex directed the boy to continue wearing the skateboard shoes of his modern culture. The leader had examined them closely, feeling the sole, inspecting inside, and testing the laces. Had it been possible, Chris sensed, he would have made them standard issue for his band of medieval boys.

With his basketball, the transplanted boy dribbled his way out of the underground hideaway. It was cool and fresh that morning and a fragrant woodsy air greeted him, as he emerged along the dirt path leading from the Pitling's lair. He could tell from the sun that it was still early, but he encountered no Pitlings.

Alone in the world that morning, the quiet gave him some peace in an otherwise all too confusing situation of late. The sun was just peaking above the horizon and songs of happy birds reminded him that it was springtime in Temecula.

He found that he missed so many little things that he had always taken for granted before. As he dribbled his way along the dirt path, he recalled his father waking him on school mornings, much to his dismay, using tickling and crazy songs. Why did school always start so early? Why was seven AM so early on school days, but so late on Saturdays?

In a melancholy moment, Chris found himself longing for a morning bus ride to school! "Dude, snap out of it," he thought, as Hurley's disgusting visage entered his mind. He wondered again, "What had happened to that dreaded pig man that last day?" The beast never missed a day of driving and tormenting Chris before. The thought of the man actually made him sick, as he pondered this for an uncomfortable moment. Pushing this unpleasant vision aside, he soon returned to more pleasant reminiscences.

Things, which in the past were nothing but a bother to the boy, he missed dearly this morning. He barely tolerated his brothers, four and two years younger than him, and therefore, much less worthy. He wondered how his parents could have one child, himself, a boy so awesome, and then the other two...well they were just monsters! Chris shook his head in the affirmative, as he finally realized the answer! "Adoption, of course, they're probably adopted!" Today however, he forgave and even missed the devilish duo.

As the boy walked, he whistled without thought and sang the Pitling's tune.

> The Pitling, the Pitlings;
> The good shan't fear us naught....

"Yes..s..s..s," he said with confidence. Chris was gradually feeling better, and as he dribbled and wandered, the untied laces of his beloved shoes waved with his pace and were in total agreement. The clean smell in the air filled his lungs, and he felt peaceful; the sun's early light warming him wonderfully. The boy climbed a group of boulders, tossing his basketball ahead of him. From this vantage point, the view was breathtaking, looking below to a peaceful valley. He dropped to the sun-warmed rock below his feet to lie for the moment on his belly. He totally pushed the thoughts of home away. For the first time in his life, he sincerely enjoyed nature and just being alive.

Christopher rose and made his way back down to the dirt pathway below. Crossing this, he descended the embankment to the rock-covered clearing where he had skateboarded several days before. Dribbling the ball, he eagerly yearned for his basketball hoop that he spent hours using in the past. Chris looked around the area and thought about his hoop at home. Then the powder kegs bound with metal hoops came to mind. He remembered where they were stored and ran quickly to the hidden cave.

"Will Alexander mind," he wondered? "Oh well." He would replace it, anyway, when he was done. He found an empty keg, and using all his strength pried loose the metal hoop.

The boy quickly moved to the trees at the edge of the clearing. Standing at the base of a one, he wondered how to finish his idea. He had the hoop, and the tree certainly seemed willing. Then he thought of his belt. Now that might just work, he thought. Chris placed the hoop in his mouth, slithered up the tree, and lashed the metal ring to the trunk. Dropping to the ground he admired his handywork.

It took some time to learn the nuances of his new, albeit, primitive basketball court. There was not a true backboard but the tree trunk served the same purpose, much less forgiving than the real thing. Much narrower, any stray shot would fly past the trunk and totally out of the court. If he was to use the trunk to bank the ball into the hoop, its curved surface required him to bounce the ball off its dead center. He began to get the feel, however, making most of his shots with a sweet imagined swish.

It was basketball, however, and soon he lost himself, playing his heroes from the NBA. As always, the game clock was nearly expired. Time was short, and only he could pull out the last game of the NBA's finals in a miracle finish.

"Excitement is in the building! Chick Hearn here and we have a possible heartbreaker tonight! Double overtime. The Lakers have come from behind to tie the game with only seven seconds left on the clock. They have the ball at mid-court. Magic takes the inbound pass from Scott. Dribbles down the lane. Three seconds… two. He pumps, fakes, puts Bird in the popcorn machine…shoots… he SCORES! Magic Johnson sinks one at the buzzer. Heartbreaker! Lakers beat the Celtics. They are the new world champions."

In his head, the crowd's cheering was deafening. The boy pranced around. He shoved his hands in the air with a quiet roar of the crowd coming from his mouth. He was lost in glory, imagining the scene at the Forum, when the voice began.

It was a quiet sound at first, perhaps just the wind, the boy decided. Then he heard it again, annoying and not going away. Chris recalled the recent past. First there was a cloud, and then the girl; now the only object around, a tree, seemed to be yelling at him. "Déjà vu all over again! Un-real things. Just leave me alone!" he said to himself.

When he heard his name, "Christopher of Temecula," blasting through the trees, he knew he was in trouble.

"Oh great! This totally sucks!" Painfully, he remembered the bolt from the cloud. He thought of the dark riders. The boy frantically looked to the sky, turning around and around in a panic, as he searched for his nemesis. Thankfully, there was not a cloud or rider in sight, but his memory of those frightening events would not go away. Clouds, like clowns, could never be trusted.

"Christopher of Temecula," the voice said again.

It was louder now. Again Chris searched the sky, but no sign of the wayward cloud. Chris pondered his choices. Should history be repeating itself, he might soon find himself very sorry!

"Darn, give me a break, can't a cloud forget," he thought, beginning to panic. "Forgiveness is heavenly…, you're in heaven aren't you!" He yelled to no one in particular above him in the sky.

"Christopher of Temecula!"

This time it was unmistakable. It was loud. It was angry, and you don't fool around with clouds. Tossing his pride aside, he gathered up his basketball and began to run, deserting the newly acquired court. It was the laughing that stopped him dead in his tracks. He felt so foolish, as he realized the mistake, and turned around with a red face. "Alexander," he yelled at the top of his lungs, knowing before seeing the responsible boy.

"Ha,ha,ha..." The laughter was now uncontrollable. Chris stood at the base of the tree and looked up. Alexander was high above him and loving his joke.

"Christopher of Temecula, your appearance is as a Ghost pursueth!"

The sun was rising directly behind the tree, and Chris squinted at the boy. "Trees, it is always something," he thought to himself. Chris could now see the green-clad boy, high within the branches of the tree.

"Dude..., you scared me royal!" Chris picked up and flung the basketball as hard as he could, striking the branch just beneath the boy's feet.

"Woo...," came the reply, as Alex's laughing came to a sudden stop. A frightened expression replaced his comedic one. Losing balance, the boy frantically grabbed for any branch with panic. He twisted, lost the battle, and fell, striking branches on his way down, as he rudely fell to the ground at the boy's feet. He looked up at the boy, now with a humiliated grin.

Chris was laughing hysterically by now. "Serves you right, dude," he said, reveling in his revenge.

"Why just innocent merriment, mate!" Alexander bounced to his feet. His confidence returned, he smiled at his new friend and dusted himself off as Chris retrieved his ball. "Again you bound the round orb? I know some of your world, but its title escapes me. By what title goes such a pastime, Christopher of Temecula?"

Chris stared at the boy with a puzzling frown; he pondered the question, dribbling as he thought, the gist of his question stumping the modern day boy. It dawned on him suddenly and with a puzzled look he gazed at the boy. "Oh, you mean this," he said. "It's a basketball." With that the boy stepped into a sharp chest pass, the back-spinning ball surprising Alex, who caught it awkwardly, after it rebounded from his chest.

"Basketball! Yes, but the basket, I see no basket?" Alexander wondered.

The question made Chris think about the phrase basket, used in the word basketball. "No one plays with a basket? Ya…there's no basket! But…well…I guess the hoop with a net. Ya…that's it, sort of a basket. See the hoop, that's why we call it play 'in hoops I guess." He answered the boy's question with a two-step dribble and jump shot that dropped through the hoop with deadly accuracy. "All day…, all day…Alexander," Chris said, now turning to his friend with a prideful grin. "Just like that dude" he said, slowly backing up and savoring his accuracy.

Chris bounced a pass to the boy who smiled with his new discovery. "I recall now your audition to Alucemet, Christopher of Temecula. Bound the ball is what you did that night, if I shan't be mistaken. It seems as if the orb is to be thrust upon the hoop, is it not?" Not waiting for an answer Alex carried the ball to just below the hoop and shot an errant shot.

Chris retrieved the ball. "That's traveling, Alex, and dude that shot sucked. Here you must bound the ball," *Kingly* again he realized. "I mean bounce, no..no..dribble. It's called dribbling, and you can only move when you're dribbling. If you stop your dribble, ya have to pass. Here like this, then you try." As before, he was able to do things with ability unlike anything he possessed at home. He dribbled behind his back through his legs, and finished with a beautiful lay-up in front of his admiring fan.

With a boyish smile and a curious air, the medieval boy learned from watching Chris. However, Alexander was competitive. While he had no concept of the game, he was not going to concede so easily. "Might I have a go of it my friend? It looks to be quite fun."

Chris returned the ball to Alexander with a brisk bounce pass. This time Alex did quite well, copying Chris's every move perfectly. While the ball did not make the hoop, the game had begun.

Christopher found the Pitling a quick learner, and the two began to compete for every shot. He enjoyed showing what was old stuff to himself, but revolutionary to his new friend. The two spent the next hour having a wonderful time. It was a freelance practice at first, Chris the coach and Alex the student. Very quickly the two were playing as if on the same team. The teacher took time at each turn to instruct his student on the finer art of basketball. The rules, at least as Chris understood them, rebounding, and jump shots were taken up all in due course. The shirts came off as the sun began to warm up and they worked up a healthy sweat.

To complete Alexander's basketball education, Chris continued describing all of his favorite players. "You have to choose a player, Alex, you know to pretend like," the boy explained.

"Player,? What's a player?" the pre-NBA boy wondered?

"You know, dude. A player, a guy, a DOG. Famous dudes. Their job is hoops. That's all they do. Well some think they can rap. Awful, it's so funny. Oh, oh, then there are some that fight. They wear big diamonds in their ears."

Alexander stopped his shot with a curious look. "Why? Why ever would one wear diamonds in one's ears?" his friend wondered aloud.

"I...just...don't... know! But dude, they really do. And you know, most of these dudes have no hair, you know, shaved bald heads. Oh, and they sign autographs and have posters; I have Magic Johnson's in my bedroom. And they drive Ferraris and Maseratis."

"Magic Johnson lives in your bedroom? Is that one's sleeping chamber?"

"No, no...Magic's poster is up on my wall in my bedroom, ah sleeping chamber. Oh, oh...I forgot! Tats, ya...they all have tattoos, with girls, or skulls and stuff, which are really cool! DOG, I forgot, this one dude has a psycho evil clown tat! But I hate clowns. Clowns creep me out. Do they have clowns here, Alex?"

Alex responded with just one word. "No." As always however, the boy seemed to know of Chris's world. "But if such a site existed, I too would not like Clowns."

"Me neither, freaky!" Returning to the basketball, Chris realized that he would have to start from scratch, if he was going to have any fun playing the game. Alex would have to know certain basics and some basketball lore as well. He took the ball, and sank a ten foot shot. He directed the boy aside, and they both sat down on the rocky edge of the clearing. "Ah….see, basketball, it's a game, you know, a sport." Spreading out five fingers to illustrate, he continued, "Five players on a team." Then two fingers, "two teams play each other. Where I live we watch them on TV."

"TB? Oh no! People here die of TB, Master Chris!"

The statement shocked the modern day boy, and you could see disbelief in his face as his eyes grew bigger and bluer. "TV? TV? Dude, you can't die from TV! Cause I'd know. You know… cause I watch a lot of TV, and I never died!" This was one concept that Chris was sure of. Television was about the most important thing the boy could imagine. Death from sports shows, MTV, or an X-Box just could not be true. Now cigarettes, now they caused death. He knew this because of all the coughing, danger no smoking signs, and Joe-Chemo ads on MTV. However, death from TV, no it just could not be! The magnitude of it all hit him, and unlike his usual cadence, he even slowed his talking down, but just for the moment.

Now Alexander could hear the difference. "Oh TV, you speak of something called TV, not TB! Christopher, what's this TV?"

"Oh, TB…not TV. You scared me for a minute, dude. Hey, wait, what is TB?"

"Oh, well…coughing, spitting, wasting," Alex responded.

"Yuck, that sounds like chewing tobacco! Does it stink?"

"Me thinks not," answered Alexander. "Death, yes; but chewing, no. Consumption, scrofula, bronchiectasis, dropsy, these are all manifestations of a disease. The disease is Tuberculosis; it goes by the initials T.B. In your world, quite successful treatment is possible. However, query this, Christopher of Temecula, this TV of which you speak, you indicate visualizing such a game? Would TV be a crystal ball of sorts?"

"No usually TV's are square, but they sort of work like a crystal ball. See it's like a box in your house. You can see everything in the world on a TV. Like with a movie, but it doesn't have a start or an end, unless you turn it off."

The technology was foreign to the medieval boy; however, Alexander never seemed just medieval. Chris had doubts; the boy confused him, for somehow he seemed to grasp the concept. Sitting quietly now, like a student in a class, he let Chris go on, wanting, like all kids, to know everything, about everything, especially a game.

Chris stood up and paced as he spoke. He would like to have a blackboard, just then, like his teacher, Mrs. Hanks. Never would he have imagined, but this teaching, well, it was kind of fun. "First, players, they wear uniforms and everything, and sweat...they really sweat."

"Hot from exertion, me thinks," Alexander added quietly.

"Ya, that's it. But, they get to do commercials, and that must be really tight. You know, they even get to have their own shoe!"

"Here too, we all wear our own shoes," Alex answered looking down at his own. This was serious for the medieval boy; he would never wear another's shoes.

Chris followed his eyes to his own feet. "No, no....that's not it. These guys have their own brand of shoe, their own even type of shoes. No, no..., they wouldn't wear each other's shoes! Dude, they have their own type of shoe made just for them. They wear new ones every day. They get to name them! These guys are rich!"

"Such as a King, Christopher of Temecula," the student replied.

"Ya, maybe. Maybe like a King, Sir Alex." Chris pointed to his own shoes. "But not these shoes. They're, skateboard shoes, not basketball."

The medieval boy realized something quickly, and smiled with a big happy grin. "Aye, for the wheeled board! Brilliant, their function is obvious. By what cobbler were such as these created?"

"Cobbler? Cobblers are pies, I think, aren't they? No…these are shoes, they're not pie. There're just all different kinds of shoes. Work shoes, doctor shoes, jumping shoes, beach shoes, flip-flops, party shoes; you know, Sear's repairs man shoes, tiny shoes, funny shoes. Now, girls love shoes! There are rows and rows of girl shoes at the mall. Spiky shoes, clucky shoes on chunks of cork shoes, high-heeled booty shoes, running shoes, slippers, brown shoes, black shoes, red shoes, white shoes. My mom has so many shoes I can't even see in her closet!"

Big wondering eyes showed Alexander's amazement with the concept. The boy continued his examination of Chris's shoes, now with a functional interest. His own shoes were very different, an elf-like slipper without laces, and a leather upper covering a thin leather sole. With a questioning twist of his head, he wondered, "Boots; best one's boot match the task. Dare I query? Those that you speak of, basketball shoes, doth those have such a spongy sole as well?" he wondered, now pointing at Chris's shoe. "For jumping, I dare say, such as the case in your contest of basketball. Basketball shoes, would they be such as this that is with a spongy sole, such as boarding shoes, these shoes for basketball, given the jumping to your fine game of skill?" It seemed to please the boy, grasping the simple concept. It was a different world to him for sure, but kids are kids, games are games, and fun is definitely fun the world around.

"Ya, sort of like these, these are boarding shoes. But I left home sort of quick. You know like lightning quick. Anyways, I left my other shoes at home. Hey, you know what? To really have a lot of fun, ya got to pretend you're your favorite player." Here Chris turned and faced Alexander squarely. He was emphatic, you must chose a player, and then pretend that you are that player, in order to have real fun. "Here you choose. Do you want to be Magic Johnson? Ah no wait, no I'm Magic! Maybe you can be him next time. How about Shaq, or maybe Michael Jordon, maybe Larry Bird? You could be an initial player, like A.I., that's Allen Iverson, or K.G., you know, Kevin Garnett. No, no, no, here, here! I got the perfect guy! Alexander you're Charles Barkley; Sir Charles cause you're a Sir."

"Then that's it! I am to be known in the orbed world as Charles, Sir Charles Barkley of Alucemet. But is this Barkley really a Sir?"

"No, I don't think so, just a great basketballer. But you'll like him."

And so, for a time, Chris a.k.a. Magic Johnson, flying and jumping away, drawing millions of fans and dollars as well, sponsored in fiction, and endorsing his must-have Air-Chris's shoes, played one on one with the Barkley, Sir Charles Barkley;,and as only a kid can, fun prevailed for the time. Forgetting their past, just kid against kid, the game went on, for the time being.

Soon, the noonday sun was high above them, and both of our players became hot, tiring of their game. Chris was the first to slow down and stop, breathing heavily. "Sir Charles, let's take a break. Race you to the boulders!" He took off after grabbing his precious ball and made his way as fast as possible to the dirt path. Once there he climbed to the rocky perch where he had laid in the morning sun. Alexander was soon behind him. Breathing heavily from their fun, the two stood silently viewing the beautiful open skies below.

"Awesome," was Chris's response, as he took a deep breath of the clean cool air. "That smog, where is it today, Sir Alex?"

"Smog? What meaning do you refer to with this word smog, Christopher of Temecula?"

Chris thought for a moment. This was another insightful question from the medieval friend. "You know....that reddish air, haze..... It seems to come and go. It was thick yesterday when we made Fordem."

Alexander sat down slowly, silently pondering his friend's question. Dangling his boot-clad feet over the edge of the boulder, the boy smiled, but his usual carelessness seemed absent. He leaned his head back and gazed up at the clear blue sky. "I take your meaning now; do you speak of the fouled air so often seen of late?"

"I do...it was thick yesterday. It's sort of like Fontana. That's this place in my world where the sky is thick and black. You can't even see through the sky cause of smog in Fontana. I think dudes who live there must make dirt. Maybe they make charcoal or they just burn the entire world's trash or something. You know, Alexander, it's sort of like maybe Hell there really. But your fouled air, it comes and goes. Like today, it's perfectly clear. Then when we were catching that Fordem dude, it just appeared. Evil, I think it appears whenever evil is around."

"Yes evil, you are quite right in your observation. Moreover, your mention of trash is very interesting indeed. You will soon realize that rubbish, refuse that is, emerges as a thesis central to our plight. The air represents evil; we have taken to speaking of it as the Stench. We see this Stench only in our recent times of trouble. I am afraid it doth speak of the sorry state of Alucemet, Christopher."

It was late afternoon, the following day. The sun was just sitting down comfortably, on the distant ridge of blue-tinged mountains. The air was cooler now, and even the first owl hoot echoed somewhere deep in the forest, perhaps in protest to the approaching two rather than the setting sun, for darkness was still hours away.

"Where are we going, Manzell? Come on, you're pulling me, I can keep up!" Manzell had hold of Chris's hand, as he led him deeper into the woods. "Come on, where to dude? We're looking for the bad-guys, right Manzell? How 'bout setting a trap, you know with fire or bombs, or something, like the CIA, or the FBI, or the NYPD! Oh, oh..., how 'bout the DOJ, or the DOD? We can get the DA involved, Manzell. All that cool stuff, I won't tell anybody! You can trust me you know. Look, Michael, my friend down the street, he broke his mom's mirror, and I didn't tell anyone for a whole year," Christopher pleaded.

Pirates, Scoundrels, and Kings

Finally, they arrived, the silent medieval boy leading the loquacious modern day boy braking into a small clearing, lined around its circumference with tall piney trees. "Now, Christopher of Temecula," Manzell said with some relief, "Alexander's wish is for you to learn the crossbow. If you are with us, you must be prepared to fight, he says."

Chris was ecstatic, raising his right arm in a fist. "ALL RIGHT! Alex said I get to fight? Bad...that's so bad, dude. Ya, arrows, bows, I'll be great at it Manzell!"

Manzell handed his trusted crossbow cautiously to the excited boy. "Use mine, and when you master this, another will be provided."

Chris grabbed the bow from his friend, and sited along it, looking at his friend.

"NOOOOO," Manzell yelled as he hit the ground.

"Manzell, sorry dude! But, I wouldn't shoot you! Oh, Oh...I know...don't point it at anyone. Sorry," he said again, dropping the crossbow and helping Manzell to his feet. "Sorry Manzell, I forgot. Like in Young Guns, Pat Garrett, "Don't point that piece at me, unless ya want to eat it!"

"Yes, a very good rule of thumb, my friend." Over the next hour, Chris learned to load, draw, and shoot a crossbow, using Manzell's bow and a tree for a target. He was a quick study, and soon was quite accurate, able to nail small pinecones more often than not.

"Now we go in secret right. Invade the castle. Get that Fordem dude. How about assassins? That Boar, do we assassinate him? What did Alexander want us to do, Manzell?"

"Capture our nightly meal, Christopher of Temecula. We have no mighty assignment at this moment. And we do not assassinate for our ends. Sir Alexander prohibits such actions."

"Oh, but food? I learned this just to shoot food. What kind of food's out here anyway, Manzell?"

"We must search. Mainly rabbits."

"SHOOT A RABBIT! No way! Oh, like before," he said remembering his first day with the boys. "But a bunny, I can't shoot a bunny, Manzell. Come on, something big. A bunny, those eyes, those cute little ears, oh…and that little white tail! No, no way Manzell, can't we shoot something else, dude?" Chris turned and implored the boy.

"Well how about a Hawk," the boy responded.

"No birds, Manzell, I couldn't kill a bird!"

"It's quite unusual to happen upon a fox, sometimes a squirrel, but not much as far as a meal. We must eat, my friend!"

"A fox, you'd shoot a fox? No squirrel either, you know, how could you kill a squirrel, like Rocky the flying squirrel?" Turning now to his friend, Chris put a hand on the boy's shoulder and with a serious tone said, "Can't we just be vegetarians Manzell?"

"A vegetarian, what's a vegetarian? Why, you mean to eat only vegetables?" Manzell now looked at the boy curiously with a small smile.

"Ya, that's not going to make it, vegetables. I forgot. I hate vegetables. Oh, oh here…I got it, frozen food. What about frozen food? Can't we eat just frozen food?"

"Frozen food? Frozen food? What's frozen food? What do you eat, ice?"

"No, ya can't live just on ice, maybe popsicles. Can't we just take food out of the freezer, Manzell?"

"What's a freezer, Christopher of Temecula?"

The statement stopped Chris. He realized again, here were two different worlds, and even in his world, Chris was not a real expert. It dawned on him in fact; he was not even sure just how that food, mostly dead animals of course, got into his Mom's freezer. He decided not to think about it. Luckily, Manzell supplied the solution.

"Christopher, today others will supply the feast." He moved to the edge of the clearing, climbed up on top of some boulders, and laid down in the day's dwindling sun.

Pirates, Scoundrels, and Kings

Chris followed the boy, so glad that he would not have to kill his dinner, at least tonight. He climbed up and lay down on the warm rocks next to his friend. The air was clean, and the two were at total peace. Of course, wondering came naturally to Chris, and this world seemed to bring out the most in him. He began to do so, thinking of question after question for his friend. Queries, they seemed to come rapidly when the mood struck him, which it did so today. He hesitated at first, remembering Alexander's mood and response to his last questions, sensing the trouble his question might cause Manzell. Soon however, as it always did, his curiosity won out, not to be dissuaded. "Does the smog or stench that is, come from the evil Manzell?"

His friend was short with his response. "It seems as such," was his only quiet reply. Again, the boy withdrew inwardly, the subject obviously causing serious thoughts for Chris's new friend.

"Alucemet, the stench, Fordem, I mean, it's confusing! Does it bum you out, Manzell, but why? Also, what is Alucemet anyway: a place... a town... a family...what? And, just how come Alexander is a Sir? Because he's just a kid? Two nights ago, you know, he had this glass thing around his neck, and he didn't want me to see it. What's up with that? Is it like a secret or something, cause you know, I told you, I definitely can keep a secret if it is? I really like secrets, you know. Is it magic, Manzell? Then there's this Boar everyone talks about. In my world a bore is someone you got to listen to, you know, cause you're supposed to be nice, but no one really wants to play with him. And, what's up with this Fordem dude, and that horse he rides? Now that's one bad horse, dude! Of course, I don't know horses, but dude, that horse is scary. I've got to know these things. And this Pitling stuff...come on, the Pitlings? What is this, summer camp? Be straight with me, I mean, where's your parents, dude? I mean you guys are sort of like Peter Pan, but there's no Wendy. But pirates, I bet ya got pirates, huh? Do you have a Captain Hook here, Manzell?"

Christopher fired question after question at the unsuspecting, reluctant boy, with unending pursuit. Short one-phrase responses were all that Manzell could wedge into the conversation. Questions, Chris had a way of pursuing a person with them, and today they bubbled forth with a vengeance.

Manzell bolted up with a start, his hands to his ears during the nonstop cross-examination. As if to rid himself of the harassment, he walked a few steps, turning his back upon the boy

Chris was silent, sitting up and staring at the back of his distressed friend. "I'm sorry Manzell! I...I....only wanted to know." Forlorn, Chris hung his head wanting to know more but realizing that he may have pushed the boy too far. He soon looked up to find Manzell staring at him, and to his relief, his friend wore his usual calm smile. The boy started to laugh quietly while he shook his head in amazement.

"I have never seen the likes of you before, Christopher of Temecula. Alexander wishes to not burden you with our day's troubles, but your curiosity is constantly on the attack. How am I to deny one such as you?" The boy sat down again next to Chris. "I am afraid, however, that a quick return to the world of Temecula is not likely for you, my friend."

"Not a quick return, or do you mean never, Manzell?"

"Alexander states, you shall return to your world, but you are needed here for the time being. You will be back with your two little brothers soon enough."

"How do you know I have two brothers, and are you for sure, will I sometime get home?"

"Alexander knows of your world. All that I know is what our leader tells me. He has spoken about you, and yes, you will return home to Temecula, but you will learn much before that time. It is right, for you to know something of this, your adopted world. Mind you Christopher, much of this world would be best not known. I am not to tell you these things, but you will learn them without my help, no matter. Keep these ideas to yourself, please. Do not let on that it was me that told you of them. Listen now and I will tell you of the predicament Alucemet faces." Slowly, interrupted only on occasion by the curious boy, Manzell told Alucemet's bitter story.

"Our world lacked for order not long ago, Christopher. Strife ruled our world, for there was no rule of law or order. Now mind you, this was long before my time. William of Lion became one who could rally the good, and lead the people from this world of grief. Honest and kind, with a keen sense of leadership, our people rallied around him. He sought not the kingdom, but soon his success was so overwhelming that the people made him their sovereign. He made Patrice his Queen, and between them, Alucemet became girded. They took for their crest the Laughing Lion, for between them strength and good humor flourished. On the cliffs of the great battle of Alucemet, the people built a towering castle in tribute; castle Alucemet and their dominion swept the entire known world with peace and harmony. Soon their first child, Alexander of Alucemet was born. Alexander grew to be a child who never seemed to be a child. A calm intellect was apparent from early in his life. The boy flourished in his studies of the sciences and inventions. The second son Nicholas was as well a most special child. Fiercely confident and athletic, he as well possessed a sharp mind. Happiness was everywhere; the Kingdom and the Royal family seemed of the same mind. Loving their subjects, they developed the land and created fair democratic laws. City elders were elected, and the people's will was expressed in a society of equality. The Royal families' love for their subjects was matched only by the admiration of the people for the good King and his loving family."

"But something got messed up, right Manzell? It must have," Chris questioned for the first time. "Why are you here? I mean, kids where I live stay with their families. And what about this Autumn chick...and imploders? I know! A war broke out and all of the parents killed each other, must of. No, but wait, Fordem he's alive, I think...wasn't he Manzell? Or is he a ghost too?" Chris fired his questions at the boy like a blur.

Manzell turned to him, and motioned for the boy to slow down and quiet. "All in good time my friend...be keeping some patience! Such a story shall be given its due. Quenching such a querulous mind will require time. And mind you, if I am to corrupt your innocence with this story, I must do so with all the details available to myself. You must know what trouble befalls you in this new world."

His seriousness frightened the boy somewhat; quickly however, he was over this. Chris felt himself more frustrated because here was the first opportunity to get all of his important questions answered, and now his friend was doing so very slowly. "Well, it wasn't every day that he popped into a new world," Chris thought. Soon he was doing something so strange and foreign to the curious boy, he sat still and just listened. His father would be proud, he decided.

"What went wrong in due time Christopher," Manzell said. The boy now lay back upon the boulder and looked up to the clear sky. The two turned and lay prone, watching the beautiful setting sun. Manzell reached behind him for his knapsack, and pulled out some treats wrapped in a large leaf. With a happy sigh Manzell ate one and offered another to Chris. He turned to his back again, placed his hands behind his head and restarted his story, basking in the setting Alucemet sun.

Chris gave up, and like his friend, laid back to listen. As he did, he looked closely at the treat. It appeared to be a raw meat item, wrapped in a green leafy like cover. "Hum...Sushi," he said, as he first chewed and then swallowed what was quite a tasty treat!"

Manzell continued his saga. "Unbeknownst to us at the time, a very small event occurred, much to our dismay now, one of future doom. A mortal, closer to a pig than a man, appeared in our beloved Kingdom. To this day his origin is debated. Some say he swam his escape from debtors across the sea from Ateirrum, a distance of over 1000 leagues. Knowing his disdain for the soap bar, me thinks a trek so long within a hated medium such as water unlikely, however. I have always felt spontaneous generation likely, arising from the fouled refuse he came to take charge of. Certainly his appearance would speak loudly of that. From what ever route, it is not of importance now. Of unfortunate fact is that he did appear. Michaelis he answered to, and no more of a scourge and pestilent being has been seen since time began. He sickens me so!

Pirates, Scoundrels, and Kings

Of this I must beg your forgiveness Christopher, but he is one of such foul appearance and detestable grace. He likened himself to a lofty boar, a pig however was superior to his resemblance. How his importance came to be is perplexing, for he is not of a brilliant mind; rather our opponent is shrewd and capable within his favorite vehicle, evil. And with this ability, his influence grew and grew. He managed at first the kingdom's refuse department. Doing a fair job of this I suppose, the title of Minister of Refuse was soon bestowed upon him. With this title came power, which he consolidated with brutality, subjugating those unfortunates who labored under him. It was at this time that his power over our King began. An evil spell I must suspect, for a finer judge of character was seldom seen than in King William. Alexander has said that the Queen was not so taken by Michaelis, sensing his evil, but alas her warnings were heeded naught. By decree he gained control of the castle guard and with it the castle's defense. The fall of one close to our Queen next met with sadness on her part, I'm afraid. He had grown up with the Queen, as if a brother. His trust and swordsmanship brought his rise in the realm of the Laughing Lion. It is credit to this man that the swordsmanship of both Alexander and Nicholas doth stem. Upon him, the Queen's personal trust and safety was bestowed. And deserving at the time it doth so. But a fatal flaw he hath, the one called Richard of Fordem. He soon was the Boar's henchman over much protest and unbelief from our Queen."

"That's the evil guy, Manzell; the Fordem dude, right?" With this Chris jumped to his feet and began gesturing as he spoke. "The one on the horse, and in the carriage. The royal creeps he gives me. He gives me the creeps Manzell," Christopher said. The two boys paused for the moment, both thinking deeply about the subject.

"Why is Alexander a Sir, Manzell," Christopher finally asked?

"Now you speaketh a much happier matter, my friend. Of the events that I hath spoken, Alexander speaks often of. Now mind you, of knighthood, I know of only common knowledge; for Alexander talks naught of himself. I was at that time, you see, a common boy living a good life with my family in the city Alucemet.

The Castle life I know of is only common knowledge. The dubbing of Alexander cannot be separated from the happenings of his family; father, mother, and especially his brother Nicholas of Alucemet."

"Two royal dudes," Christopher added.

"Aughth now you sayeth," laughing loudly, Manzell began. "The love of Alucemet for our King and his family runs deep. That speaks for why recent times weigh heavily on us, Christopher. Both Alexander and his brother Nicholas, grew to be deserving of that love. Royal dudes as you sayeth, but to a commoner they seemed not above us, but rather just like us. At first Alexander would leave the castle and quietly meet all of the kingdom's children, playing as if one of them. When Nicholas was older, he too followed in this practice. A game they taught us, to which we still play today. With a stick and ball....LionBall we Pitlings have named it. We must partake with you of such tomorrow. It was with this that I first had occasion to meet Alexander. Quick of foot and strong of arm, soon all would flock to him, unbeknownst of his position. Fairness, beyond his years, he doth possess. To Alexander we would turn to settle our disputes. It was he who gave us our name as well, the Pitlings. While small of stature, our faith and beliefs matched our leader." At this point Manzell stood at attention, clicking his heels. He then relaxed and returned to his story. "We are commoners, having not much of this world. We learned our worth and earthly priorities from him. You hath noted Michael Shaun, Christopher of Temecula? It is of his disadvantage I speak."

"Yes Manzell...I...I...have," Chris responded.

"Twas a shut-in. Alexander insists on his presence. As plain as one can see, a disadvantage he doth little now. Much he has taught us all. Not one of the Pitlings would question our leader."

"But a Sir, I guess that's a Knight, huh Manzell? Has he fought some bad dudes?" the visitor wondered.

"Of swordsmen, Alexander and Nicholas have no equals, to be sure. But while of kindness and strength me speaks, it is Alexander's wit which is singular, and from where his knighthood springs. To the mysteries of our world Alexander pursueth. Mathematics, physics, much beyond my reason, came to the boy always. I know not of much at this point but of what is spoken. To the event you query, his Knighthood, I will tell of that to which I am privy."

Manzell stood again. He turned after stretching, and sat cross-legged. "The energy of our sun, once captured could do such good, or harm I must sayeth. It is from this idea that his Knighthood sprung. For he hath done so, as I take it, mind you. The Mirrorlass...I shant claim to know of its workings. But of this it is spoken. A globe of glass and perfection, it is reflective within its center. Once focused upon our system's star, a powerful force was found by Alexander. Imagine infinite power, harnessed for our Kingdom's good. To relieve our toils was his purpose, and of this he had begun much. It is upon this feat that Knighthood doth fall upon Sir Alexander."

Chris suddenly recalled that night in Alexander's room. That glass medallion around his neck, he had hidden it so quickly when he realized Chris's interest. He wondered. It certainly was not a globe, but rather an hourglass shaped piece of glass, one side mirror like. Perhaps a piece! "Where is this thing now, Manzell?"

"Alas young friend, therein baits our greatest dilemma. For the evil to which our Kingdom falls, at this very minute, doth possess that which might bind us all? The Boar possesses the Mirrorlass, and if in fact that evil, somewhat dull-witted man I might add, realizes and understands the Mirrorlass' usage!" Manzell did not complete his thought, the idea so unspeakable. He sadly dropped his head as if examining his shoes.

Chris began to understand. "A power such as that, sort of like Saddam Hussein with a Nuc!" Manzell looked up at Chris, shook his head yes, as if somehow knowing this modern day monster. Saturday morning cartoons, Chris lived for them, and now it seemed he lived in one. "The super bad dude has the Mirrorlass ...Manzell? But Manzell, why did he leave it, and I still don't understand why Alexander left the Castle anyway."

"His exit was swift, but the key to it he hath. That is why the Boar must never find him. Michaelis is slow of wit, and to what he searcheth... me thinks he ponders. But to him Alexander is his solution. The medallion to which you doth speak, Christopher of Temecula?"

"That glass thing.....yes Manzell, is that the key?"

"Of these matters, I speaketh too much. No more, you do best to forget that to which was spoken here today. You were to learn the bow today, and you did." With that Manzell leapt up. He quickly climbed down the rock embankment in silence.

Chris watched his troubled friend as he move away. He looked toward the horizon, squinting in the last bright rays of sunlight. Chris ate the last piece of his Alucemet Sushi without thinking about it, for his mind was elsewhere. "Heavy world...way too heavy. What's the big deal in this place? A kid doesn't have to care about such things in my world; it is against the rules, whatever those rules are. Seriousness just isn't fair! Yes, that's more like it. Seriousness is possible in a kid's world, but it wasn't fair, like never getting to play goalie on the roller hockey team even if you suck at it. It wasn't fair. Parents, who controlled the world, always played by the rule of fairness. They probably signed an oath or something when they signed up to be parents. Seriousness then was not fair for kids, and so seriousness was not common in a kid's world because it wasn't fair. What was fair is what was, and what was, was what parents did, at least it seemed that way. It's not fair for kids to have serious things around them all the time. If it was fair, kids would have to work, have their own cell phones, carry briefcases, dress all stuffy in ties and things, and that was obviously not true. But then he could be wrong. Maybe everything in his world was serious, but since he was a kid, he just didn't see it. And then he saw for just a moment that he had changed. In that moment he saw serious problems, and he found himself wanting to help. Somehow he wanted to make things better. He wanted Alex and his Pitlings to not have to be so serious. He didn't want them to have to life in caves and eat raw animals. They should be TigerCubs, play soccer, play video games...and...listen to Green Day or Metallica. He wanted to help them get back to being kids, not worrying about Boars and stuff, but just having fun. He might as well help; it did not seem as if he was going anywhere. Chris stopped philosophizing, stood up, and caught up with Manzell.

"Hath there clean air in your world, Christopher of Temecula?"

Manzell's voice brought the boy back to reality. "What...,air... of course, Manzell, was his reply." He looked up to where the boy now stood, several feet above him and looking out far over the horizon. Chris rose and climbed to his friend's side. Manzell was again peaceful and seemed happy. He was breathing in deeply the fresh air and enjoying the view. Far below them were green rolling hills meeting a peaceful sea. "Is that the beach, Manzell? Temecula is not a beach, but we go to the beach in the summer. Hawaii, the beach is awesome! Have you ever been in Hawaii, Manzell? I guess not, huh. Anyways, lots of sand at the beach, dude... do they surf in Alucemet?"

Manzell thought for a moment before answering. "Unbeknownst to I, good friend. Smurf? To what do you speak?"

Chris broke up laughing. Smurf, the vision of Poppa Smurf standing next to him, and for that matter slightly resembling Manzell came to his mind. Chris glanced down at his friend's feet. Clad as always in elf-like green shoes, the boy fit his vision perfectly. He tried to hide his amusement. Manzell wouldn't understand. "Please Poppa Smurf.... save us from the Boar," Chris said silently to himself as he regained his composure. "Not Smurf, Manzell! Smurfs are little blue dudes in cartoons. There I go, TV again." He emphasized the V in TV, remembering his discussion of pulmonary diseases with Alexander.

Manzell turned to him, smiling with a wondering look.

"Surf not Smurf. They use a board...like a skateboard, only much bigger...and with no wheels. They cruise the waves at the beach, get sunburned, and full of sand. Surfers never go to school and their moms let them wear tattoos and stuff! And chicks, the girls really dig surfers, Manzell."

Manzell thought for the moment then turned again to the sea view. "A board, riding the waves. Alexander will know of this. Ah but the sea, to that Nicholas seemed drawn."

"Is Nicholas a Pitling too, Manzell?" Chris's questions began again.

"It is in some ways true. He would come often with Alexander to the country and he too gained our undying loyalty. They were very close as brothers go. They are very different those two, mind you. While Alexander was a quiet leader, Nicholas was more outwardly. A swordsman I hath never seen his equal. It is to him that our Marshall skills are traced. Fun comes to mind when one fancies Nicholas. He would often play LionBall with us. But he was younger and had his own mates to which he kept as well. Near to the end a falling out the two doth had. We have seldom seen Nicholas of late."

"Where is the dude now?"

"It is rumored that he too doth journey away from the castle and his family. A Pirate the lad has become, one hears."

"A Pirate?" Chris responded with excitement. "You mean with buried treasure, and ships, and.....Pirates are bad, Manzell!"

"Aye it seems as such. I know naught of him of late. Rumors as they are, one hears of bullion and captured ships. Knowing the lad, however, evil I shan't believe. Disillusionment with the kingdom's state, as with Sir Alexander, is more likely what drives Nicholas."

Silence followed as the two thought for the moment. Manzell turned and began climbing down from their outlook.

Chris thought to himself for a moment, then turned, and hurried to catch up with Manzell. As he approached the boy, his mind was spinning full speed, and the questions and comments began once again in earnest. "Manzell, if I was a King, I'd have everything. No school, that would be the first thing, Manzell." As he talked his excitement grew. "Then, I'd get all those trading cards, you know, the ones that are worth a lot of money. Some cards are really worth a lot, Manzell. Especially old guy cards. Like there's this old guy named Willie. You know, hit dat ball Willie? I guess not, but his card's worth miles of Jackson, dude! He must be a really old guy, cause my dad says they have to be old to be worth anything. Yes, that's what I'd do! If I were King, I would have trading cards, no cash in the whole kingdom, just cards. It would be much more fun that way. And that way, no one would have to carry a wallet, not even have to have any pockets! No pickpockets, no credit cards, and for sure no pennies. Pennies, what's up with those anyways, Manzell? Does anyone use pennies here? In Temecula, a penny's got an old president's face."

Manzell thought about the question, but did not answer the boy.

Chris thought for the moment having wandered somewhat from the subject at hand. "Excellent," he said to himself. "Hey Manzell, do they have trading cards here? Cause if they do, ya, well maybe I can like borrow some? Cause when I, if I do go back to my world, in the future they'll be real old." Chris considered his idea, and then answered it himself. "Naw...you all don't have trading cards here, I'm sure of it. No sports heroes, no TV for sure, no gum either I think, and maybe you guys don't even have cardboard, then no trading cards. It's simple. Too bad, Manzell, we could have been rich, maybe."

Once on the ground, the two journeyed along the dirt path towards the Pitling's cave. Gum came to mind. He had some in his backpack, and he had taken one of his precious sticks of gum with him this morning, and now was just a time for it. He took it out of his pocket and began to unwrap it, when he realized to himself, "Be polite...but I don't have many of these!" He stared at the stick of gum thinking about his options. Torn with a huge choice, his better nature won out. "Oh well," he thought, tearing the stick in two. "Manzell, here's some gum for you. Remember, don't swallow!"

The Pitling looked curiously at the torn stick of gum. He stopped walking, watched Chris carefully as the boy opened his piece, placed it in his mouth, and began to chew. The boy followed Chris exactly, and began suspiciously. When he realized the taste however, chewing continued with obvious delight. Manzell turned to his friend and shook his head in the affirmative. Once he had chewing mastered, the two walked along in silent bliss.

An unlucky rabbit crossed their path suddenly. As before an arrow had dropped it before Chris could think. Manzell had his prey and was laughing as Chris caught up with him. "Forget naught. We serve no rabbit soup tonight, my friend," Manzell said, reminding the boy of his inexperience in the medieval world.

Chris was grimacing as he remembered his dietary transgression on his first night in the Pitling's hotel. "Yes feel free to use it as you practice, he remembered the boys laughing and telling him. He was quick to change the subject, however, wishing to ask more questions as he watched the boy clean the night's meal. "But dude, I still don't get it... why did they leave?"

"They?" Manzell was in thought and had forgotten their former subject. "What means you of they?"

"You know. Why did Alexander and Nicholas leave the castle?" Chris wondered. "Oh dude, oh that's so gross Manzell," Chris interjected as his friend began to clean the rabbit. His action shook Chris, but he regained composure and listened intently as Manzell continued his story.

"Ah yes, it seems that as the Boar's influence grew, a web of distrust began to wear between the two inseparable brothers. Just how this distrust began seems unknowable, and Alexander speaks of it naught. There are rumors of possessions found in the other boy's room, broken belongings, accusations, and arguments. The smell of the Boar was at work even at that time!"

Manzell continued his story as he cleaned the rabbit carcass. At this point Chris turned his head in disgust as he split the rabbit's gut in the midline, leaving only the meat for their meal.

Without a thought, the Pitling continued. "I believe the Boar somehow blinded the two brothers to the source of this friction. It is to this trouble in part only that Alexander left the castle. It seemed that as the Boar's strength grew, King William began to appear less and less. No longer was he in attendance at his courtly functions. Decisions of supposed Kingly source seemed not of him. Edicts, rulings, and laws took on an evil flavor. It is rumored that the King has not been seen publicly now in many fortnights. The two princes began to take blame for that which was naught of them. The King supposedly turned against his own blood. Alexander was troubled and lost. He appealed for one last audience with the King, to plead for his father's insight to the source of all these troubles, the Boar himself. But it was naught to be!"

"Why Manzell, why didn't Alexander speak to his father?" Chris asked. "Wait I know, Alexander met the Boar in a duel, and... and...he cut off his ear! Ya, maybe that's it. There was this dude... a painter...named Van Gogh who cut off his own ear. Then you know what? He sent it in the mail to his babe. Seems weird to me!"

Manzell was interested in his friend's story. "Is this true? For what hath the damsel use of such as that?"

"Got me, Manzell. The dude was crazy, I guess. Any crazy dudes in your world Manzell?"

"Ah yes, of that our world suffers as well. A duel, however, the Boar would never submit to such a duel, for it would spell his certain defeat."

So by the dwindling light of afternoon the two friends walked peacefully back to their camp.

Chapter 9
Ambushed

> A TYRANNICAL RULER LACKS JUDGMENT,
> BUT HE WHO HATES ILL-GOTTEN GAIN
> WILL ENJOY A LONG LIFE.
> **Proverbs 28:16**

"Sweat--, they play baseball here," Chris thought as he arrived at the field. The Pitlings rose early that morning, intending to play a game; a game that they referred to as LionBall. Before him stood the grass meadow, where several days before he had met the girl, Autumn. The meadow now was crudely marked in white, not unlike a baseball diamond. In these woeful days of the Boar, recreation provided a rare treat.

In many ways, the game was like the modern day boy's national pastime. A pitcher would deliver a white ball to the hitter all right, and they used a stick, similar to a bat, to hit the ball. However, the first major difference occurred when the hitter made contact, striking the white ball with his stick. At that point, the player would run, not to the right as if going to first base, but passed the pitcher to where Chris would expect to see second base. The Pitlings knew this base as the 'ace'. Safely at the ace, the runner then had the option of advancing either to his right or to left. To the right, first base in modern terms stood the 'deuce.' To the left, the modern third base, was the 'thrice.' Once on the ace, the logic behind choosing to move to the deuce versus the thrice, was not yet clear to Chris.

There were defensive fielders as in baseball, but only five and arranged differently. Two defenders awaited a ground ball. One stood between thrice and the ace, the other between ace and deuce. Similar to baseball, three players resided in the outfield. Before the strike of the ball, however, they would line up three deep in what Chris would call center field. With the crack of the bat, two would run towards and one fielder away from the ball. The object for the hitter was to be on a base when the ball made its way back to an infielder's hand. Once the runner was able to advance three bases, the runner scored a twit. Abbott and Costello's famous routine would require some modification. Who is on ace or who is on deuce would take some adjustment.

Eventually, the differences between American baseball and LionBall were minor. Soon Chris was playing as only kids can, hitting and throwing with the best of them. Sliding in this world was unheard of, a fact which Chris began to use to bolster his base running. Soon the Pitlings had adapted and even improved on his technique, quickly turning in perfect headfirst slides.

He would always remember the event. It occurred during the third inning or round, as the boys would say. Alexander took his practice swings and moved to the plate, or trap in Pitling talk. The boy had managed to score in each of his prior appearances, much to the pitcher Scott's dismay. The pitcher delivered the pitch; Alexander swung and made contact with all his might. The ball traveled a good three hundred feet down the left field line, bouncing and rolling into dense shrubbery. They had a second ball but losing one of their precious possessions did not sit well with Chris.

As anyone who has played in such an informal game knows, only one person chases the foul ball. Once Chris took off, he found himself alone, slipping and sliding off the field and through the trees at the end. He had wandered quite some distance from the group, but he could still hear their laughing and yelling. Just like recess, he remembered.

With the ball safely in hand, Chris hurried to return to the game. Recovering the ball had taken some time, and as he turned around, he realized how far he had traveled to do so. Moving slowly through the dense underbrush and trees, he hoped he had not missed his turn at bat. He was just at the edge of the field when he noticed the change.

Before Chris had run off to retrieve the ball, the sky had been so blue and clear, birds singing their songs of joy, and the soft breeze and cloudless sky seemingly endless. It had been such a beautiful morning, but now upon Chris's return, the change was immediately obvious and striking, as he trudged his way up the incline from the rough below to look out over the playing field

Looking upon the field, Chris whispered fearfully to himself, "The stench!" That red, foul, filthy air was hard to forget, and he remembered that its appearance consistently portended evil. A feeling of fear mixed with anger suddenly washed over the boy, a feeling that was faintly familiar.

It was like when his father would admonish him. "You're in trouble Christopher David!" If he had just used the first name, Chris would have been fine, but the pronunciation of his entire formal name predicted dread. It carried a feeling of dismay, a sickening feeling in the pit of his stomach, and his heart would race. Looking down on the field that morning, clearly seeing the remarkable change and red stench rolling in, Chris felt the same anxious feeling. He dropped the ball to the ground, and quickly climbed the last few steps up the dirt bank to view the meadow below with a sinking resignation.

Standing in full view of his friends, the boy was horrified. "Where did they come from?" he wondered in panic. Surrounding the makeshift field were horses and foot soldiers, appearing in silence without the least warning. Unaware, the Pitlings continued their game, laughing, hitting, and sliding, as their apparent destiny began to dwindle. The enemy advanced with caution, much to the boy's chagrin. He felt helpless as he considered what to do. "This was planned, it must have," Chris thought. For with regimental control an army was methodically surrounding the unsuspecting group. The enemy's numbers could easily overpower the boys. Canons rolled silently into position. Swords were drawn, every escape from the meadow covered. That sickening feeling continued to grow as he all at once realized, They're toast," and he was too late to help. He would gladly take his father's displeasure if he could but switch the situations.

Helpless, he turned in circles stamping his feet, his thoughts flying through his brain quickly. Should he yell out, there was no escape. A warning would cause them to fight, and to their demise, he was sure. Perhaps, if they did not fight, they would be captured but not harmed.

Chris felt obliged to help his friends. He was so upset, torn; quickly he decided. Speaking silently to himself, he said. "I will fight to the death! Death? Oh great, I'm only ten," he lamented. "Why didn't I ride Ghost Rider when I was at Knott's Berry Farm? What about sleepovers, and eating lucas; I've never even had a girlfriend!" Overwhelmed with grief, he knew he had to go to their aid, no matter how fruitless his help would be. The enemy soldiers were in position and all hope was gone. They were outnumbered, outweaponed, and of course the element of surprise made the result known before the first shot. "Was there a Geneva convention here?" Chris wondered. Wait, he realized, "What is the Geneva convention anyway?" These were the thoughts that tumbled through the young boy's mind as he decided to run to the defense of his brave friends.

"Christopher of Temecula," whispered a diminutive but defiant voice, stopping the boy with a start. He remembered that voice, somewhere, but where? Chris turned quickly towards the tiny voice as a small cold hand grabbed the boy and with surprising strength pulled him back down the incline before he could resist.

"It is of no use! Come, it is only alive that you can help our future. Your resources do them no good now! Have you no sense at all, odd boy?"

"Autumn!" Chris yelled at the girl who appeared just as suddenly as she disappeared the other day.

Choking his hand with her grip, she pulled the boy along with strength unusual for such a slight girl.

"I—I-- can't go Autumn! Let go, let go of my hand! Alexander, Manzell...my friends--let go, let go," he said, trying to stop the girl, unsuccessful at pulling his hand from her grip.

"Silence, peculiar boy," she said as she continued pulling the boy along. "You are such a strange boy, why can't you see, their fate is cast...you must survive!"

It occurred so quickly. Before he could resist, the girl pulled him down the slope, through the dense brush, and well towards their escape. The girl was determined and she pulled the boy under and through the brush putting distance between them and the apparent ambush. In the distance behind them, shouts and cannon fire rebounded. Soon, the only sound was that from being whacked in the face by passing brush, and their breathing.

Leaving the scene did nothing to take the horror away from Chris. He was crying now, vigorously trying to return, but the girl was incredibly strong, and she would not give up, dragging the boy farther and farther away. And his hand, she was crushing it, or was it just cold? Her hand was so strangely cold!

The two now were running along an overgrown path with low-slung branches. The girl was pulling him, and he was slapped disrespectfully across his face by a branch as they frantically made their escape.

"Hey, that hurts!" Chris yelled as another branch struck him across his scraped face. While the girl was opaque to the eye and obscured the branches, they seemed to pass right through her without a scratch. He remembered Alex's description of the girl. He said that she was, "an apparition." Well, apparition or not, it did not seem to dissuade the horror grumbling in Chris's stomach. In one last furious attempt, the boy finally wrestled his hand away from the girl and slid to an angry stop. For the first time Autumn turned around to face the boy.

"Hey...who do you think you are Autumn? Dude, you're strong, what are you, Pebbles Flintstone?" Chris yelled at the girl as he shook some feeling into his crushed hand. His mind returned to his friends. "Autumn, it's awful! I mean Alexander...the guys, what can we do? They're history, they're toast!" Wiping his face, the boy noticed some blood from his face on his hand. The horror he had just witnessed returned to the boy and a sense of hopelessness was overcoming him. This world was way too serious for the boy, and now he was alone, well except for this odd girl. Anger was his next feeling as he sought to relieve some of his loss.

"Watch what you sayeth, for I am a lady," the girl responded in her coquette manner. "Nothing, Christopher of Temecula, you can do nothing! Did not you partake of that site! Their numbers overwhelm, and soon, very soon indeed, they will pursue you! Do you not realize? Do you think that the Boar knows not of your presence?" Autumn stamped her foot, grabbed Chris's hand, and turned to pull him away again. The boy wrestled his hand away from the girl. The boy was not going anywhere.

The words tumbled out of him quickly, and in anger. It was one of those statements best left within his mind and unsaid. Had he been in his world, Chris might have done a better job of it, but he was not. Looking now at the girl with displaced fury, mixed with a dash of fright, Chris said something he would come to regret. He wondered later, "Did she think I was swearing at her?"

"What do you know? You're not a lady, you're just a girl, and a weird one too! And—and--you're not even real, you're not even a girl--you're just a ghost!" Christopher yelled at the girl.

Suddenly the girl was upon him, showing no intimidation. *Slap...* she struck him across his abraded face in outrage with an outstretched, very cold, but all too real hand. The strength of the blow and her amazing quickness startled the boy. He fell backwards to the ground roughly, staring up at the girl. He would remember an injured scowl upon her countenance as she choked back her tears. When he was finally aware, like her entrance, she had vanished without a trace. Now lying sprawled upon his back, he pondered this most recent turn of events.

"Oh no--Ya great!" Chris said in frustration, lying in the dirt. Putting his hands to his head in hopelessness he said, "Now what do I do?" He rolled slowly to his side and gradually pulled his aching body to his feet. He was a mess, dirt all over, weeds sticking out of his shoes, and his face scratched red and bleeding. The boy looked around desperately. Chris hoped that the girl was still around, maybe just hiding.

He soon discovered that he was very alone, however, now without a clue to his location. Reorienting himself, Chris tried not to panic. "Come on dude, think," he said as he looked around hoping to recognize something. "It's not as bad as it could be," he told himself as he pulled pieces of brush from his shoes. He could have been lost in his own world. At least then he would know in general where he was. However, now he was just lost in a world that he was lost in anyway. In a twisted sort of way, the thought gave the boy some comfort.

Chris decided that Autumn had dragged him to the heart of nowhere, with anywhere surely a better place to be. The boy looked around frantically, trying to recognize where he was. He found himself within a deep-forested area, every direction looking identical, and no route familiar or inviting. He remembered again his friends, and that sick feeling returned to the pit of his stomach. He thought of retracing his steps, but which way? Unfortunately there was no sign. He chose a direction, for better or worse, and began walking, thinking it was generally where Autumn had been leading him. When you do not know which way or where to go, the direction is probably unimportant, he decided.

Much to his surprise, he did seem to make some quick progress. While still unfamiliar, the surroundings gradually began to clear. Ahead, a footpath became apparent. Taking this he reached a small dirty road quickly.

"Food, I'm starving, dude… when did I eat last?" he thought as his empty stomach reminded him of its lack of attention. Some of Manzell's sushi would have been great right then, Chris decided. The sad memory of his now lost friends returned to his hungry brain, but he shook off the thought and tried to forget.

The road was narrow, dusty, and twisted; it seemed well traveled, however, an observation that was not necessarily comforting. While the social boy welcomed the thought of people, he had come to understand that in these troubled times, fellow travelers might not be so desirable. The road was not only narrow, it was nearly impossible to see ahead, for any distance, for it wound first right, and then sharply to the left, lined by dense underbrush, with tall trees obscuring his vision. From a world where he never considered his safety to one of violence, terrible thoughts raced in his sheltered mind. "I am probably walking into another trap! No knife, no sword, no piece, no nine-millimeter. I don't even have a pellet gun. This sucks, dude," he lamented as he wandered on.

Suddenly, a creepy feeling came over the boy, a feeling that made him stop. Now not talking to himself, he listened to overwhelming silence. His heart pounded and sweat began to appear on his brow. Chris listened closely and realized that in the distance he could hear approaching horses. They were behind him, he was sure, and he moved quickly to the side of the road and the brush for cover. Just around the bend came a horse drawn wagon driven by an old man and pulling a load of hay.

Chris whispered to himself. "An old dude with hay!" Innocent enough, he thought, but he still was suspicious. "What to do?" Chris wondered. This might just be the only person he would see today. Thinking with his life on the line was new to the modern day boy, and he frantically searched his mind for what superheroes would do in a similar situation. MacGyver, Hunter, Michelangelo, Dick Tracey... like an encyclopedia he searched his mind. With horror he realized that he recalled no relevant episode! He was panicking now, and all that seemed to be running in his mind was not all that settling. He fought it, but each time in an empty spot within his boyish brain the same line would pop in uninvited.

"What would Bart Simpson do?"

"Oh man, ya got to be kidding!" In his mind, hidden on the side of the road, Chris had to do something. "Pull yourself together, pull yourself together, dude. Bart? I've got to have a better idea than what that dude would do?" He finally gave in and let the nonsensical idea develop. The thought of turning to Bart Simpson for advice was frightening, but it was all he could come up with on such short notice. "A tree...I'll climb the tree!" It had always worked for his spiky haired friend from television, Bart, when his dull-witted father, Homer, was after him. So before he could think further, he snaked up the nearest tree and onto a large branch which hung over the road. From his vantage point, he could see the approaching wagon, pulled by a broken-down, dapple-grey horse, and commanded by an old farmer who seemed quite unconcerned about getting anywhere fast.

"Now what do I do?" he wondered. Another decision, maybe he should call out, hey old farmer dude! Maybe honesty was not the best policy. Bart never used honesty; that was definitely true. He only had a moment to think, for the wagon was now just passing below him. For better or worse Christopher, complete with Bart's best wishes, dropped down in to the rear of the wagon, the fall softened by a nice bed of hay.

The smell of a fresh pasture engulfed the boy. Laying in silence, he tried to sense whether the wagon's movement had stopped. Hearing the clip-clop of the horses' hooves and the gentle bounce of the wagon, he was relieved to have arrived undetected. He would listen to Bart more often, he decided.

Chris made his way in silence to the top of the pile of hay. Moving forward on the wagon he could just make out its driver. He was sad when he realized the poor old driver was even older than his Dad. They live a long time in this world, he thought, as he quietly watched the man driving the horse-drawn wagon slowly down the road. The boy lay back, happy with the ride and stealth arrival. While he wondered where they were going, that thought could wait.

After all the excitement of the day, Christopher felt an incredible fatigue descend upon him. Laying in the hay and looking towards the blue sky, his thoughts returned to the events of the day. He was safe now. In his excitement he had forgotten, but now that sick feeling of loss returned to the pit of his stomach. His friends were gone now certainly. They were outnumbered and caught off guard.

Pirates, Scoundrels, and Kings

Chris was sure that Fordem was behind the ambush. He was so angry, he could have helped, he could have fought, but that strange girl grabbed him and pulled him away. Sir Alexander, he could not have survived, of that he was sure. He tried to put the Pitling band of boys out of his mind, but it was hard, for they were all he knew in this world.

Chris did not know where he was, scared and alone he realized again his incredible hunger. He sank into hiding within the hay not sure of what to do. The wagon continued on slowly, the wooden wheels bumping over the dirt road. As the wagon moved on he began to slowly feel better. The hay was soft and comforting. The gentle monotonous movements of the wagon were so soothing. He always fell asleep on a long car ride he remembered. He was almost asleep when peace was shattered, and he heard his name again.

"C.R.I.S.O.F.E.R..." his name ran out in a peculiar way. The boy was quite sure that he did not want to respond, but he heard it again. "C.R.I.S.O.F.E.R..." There was no forgetting it now. He had heard the voice distinctly and the accent was unmistakable and very familiar. Tentatively the boy lifted his head and parted the hay to get a look at the source of this voice. Next to him was standing a tall man cloaked in armor. It took just one look at his hat to confirm his worst suspicion.

Aluminum cans and the asian voice supported his fear. His hat always reminded him of aluminum cans, sharp ones arranged on what looked like a funnel. Could it be? This world was really full of surprises, but please not him!

"Oh, great-- just perfect," he said with dread as he realized. The *Shredder*-- he was sure of it now. But how did he know, and why was he here, and why me?

Yes the comic strip bad guy, the nemesis of the Ninja turtles had somehow found him. He knew who Chris was, and worse yet, he had found the boy and was set on death. He was frightening enough on the screen, but there were always the four Ninja turtles battling him. He wondered what else could happen to him during this now almost perfectly dreadful day.

Glaring at him through the hay stood the turtle's nemesis, that Ninja warrior, kick boxing, mutant controlling, nonperishable, and devil man: Orukai Sokki. He was better known to all who lived for Ninja turtle lore, as the dreaded *Shredder*. He appeared as the same monster man that Chris had loved to hate. Decked out in his splendor, Chris could now make out those hated almond shaped eyes under his coke factory helmet. Beneath it, the boy knew, resided the face of a Japanese master criminal, irreparably scarred by the claws of a hero rat, and leader of the turtles... *Splinter*.

He was his usual vicious self, and for some reason quite unhappy with the innocent boy at this time. Quite frankly, Chris was not concerned with his motivation, for this bottle capped creep reached through the hay, grabbed the boy and pulled him to the ground in front of him. As Chris looked up, there stood the *Shredder* glaring down at the boy and speaking his favorite intimidating saying: "UGGGH."

Chris stood face to face with the monster from his worst dreams. It was then that he noticed the nunchakus in the distance to his right. "Quick, it's Michelangelo," he said, trying to convince his adversary of his impending ambush. For just the briefest moment the Shredder turned to check on the situation. Through the monster's legs the boy scampered making it to the weapon just as the can-clad demon was upon him.

"You won't escape me again," the *Shredder* yelled at Chris who now rose with the paired chained weapon in hand.

"*CAN* I offer you some Campbell's cream of chicken?" Chris said with an air of suddenly defiant humor, an emotion so important when fighting superhero fiends.

His adversary said little, but he registered distaste by a serious and confused scowl.

"I...didn't think so. Not my favorite choice either, my metal-brained friend," Chris responded. Here it was very important to distract the giant, just as his heroes did with their quips. The Shredder stood a good two feet taller than Chris, and the boy used this to his advantage. Crawling again quickly between his legs, he blindly swung his nunchakus against the only nonarmor-clad portion of his adversary's anatomy: his buttocks.

"Ahhhhhhhhhh," shrieked the *Shredder* in pain and surprise!

Another quip, that's what the turtles would do. The boy bounced up behind the character, now in obvious agony. "I see that you have reconsidered your lunch time menu." A second blow with the weapon across the back of the head dropped the villain to his knees.

"YESSSSS, SWEAT!" Chris raised his clenched hand in victory. It was so much fun to be a superhero, saving the world, clobbering all evil, and doing it with such cool-ish-ous and bad-ish-ous manner.

A sharp stab of pain in his gut was the first sign that this glorious adventure was over. Awaking, he was not standing in victory at all, but unceremoniously buried in fresh hay, with a sharp pitchfork probing his belly.

"Get up, ya little rat, you worthless rogue!" the old man yelled, angrily spitting at the frightened boy. "No little, lazy, worthless, scoundrel rides in my wagon, ya cretin, ya bumpkin! Get yer self's up now, ya hear?" The man was quite angry, yelling at the top of his lungs, and threatening him with his pitchfork. "What's wrong with ya? Can't ya hear, or ya's just stupid?"

The boy could very well hear him, as he shook his head trying to wake up. What a nightmare, a nightmare he had to wake up to experience. The man was serious, and he kept shoving his pitchfork, threatening to skewer him right there. "Think," Chris said to himself, as he rolled away through the hay, trying to free himself from this crazy foe. The boy shook his dreaming head. It was one thing after another he thought. Quickly, he realized that Orukai Sokki had been but another dream.

Glaring down at him was the old man who had been driving the wagon. He had looked so nice before, so harmless, and here was the man threatening him like an insane person. He did not like Chris trespassing, and he showed him as much brandishing his pitchfork.

The man was all red and mad, threatening the boy and spitting as he yelled at him. Chris glanced at the darkening sky, the now familiar red hazy sky reflecting back. The old man continued his tirade, prodding Chris and forcing him to jump from the cart.

"You'se a nasty villain," the man said, "and ya's gonna hang fer it! Hang fer it? Ha ha; if yer lucky ya's gonna hang fer it, that is! No, the Boar's gonna eat ya. That's it, ya…I'll throw ya's to the Boar. He'll eat ya's in one bite, that he will, and I'm gonna help. Now, gets ya's lazy butt up, and I'm gonna to march you yonder. Ya, that's it, quite an audience fer-yer, it is, for an audience before the Boar. Ya won't last nothing at all. I can taste ya already, ya's fried, almost worthless vittles washed down with Ale. Out of my hay now," the old man said to Chris as he prodded him with the biggest and most devilish instrument the boy had ever seen

Once on the ground, Chris turned to confront the man. "Hey, that hurts, and stop spitting on me, you creepy old freak, you! Dude, I didn't do anything!"

The man backed up, giving Chris some confidence.

"What's your problem, you old fart. And quit hitting me with that fork-shovel like thing."

The man regained his control. Once again he was yelling and threatening the boy with his pitchfork. "Get a move on you freak. Stop your winning and sniffling! What's ya one of those baby boys, can't hold their water. Now ya's gonna pay. Off with ya's now!" The man grabbed the boy by the collar, spun him around and pushed him to the ground. With the pitchfork prodding him, Chris stood slowly and began walking as the man threatened.

Now a prisoner, encouraged along by the man's pitchfork, he examined his surroundings. After crossing a wooden-planked drawbridge, spanning an oily moat, he had come into the central courtyard of what appeared to be a huge castle. The castle consisted of four massive circular towers, rising skyward in the four corners of the square, each of four towers covered with a slanted cylindrical stone roof. The walls and towers surrounded a large cobblestone courtyard, which housed many tradesmen and shops, most of which began closing for the day. Built of beautiful, smooth sawn, rose colored stones, the structure had seen better times.

"That hurts dude, ya old bat," Chris said, in response to one vigorous probe. "I got bones inside me, ya know. Aren't you too old to be doing this, dude?" At this point, Chris stopped in rebellion, and looked over his left shoulder to assess the man's response. It did not speak of early reconciliation. The man was still very angry, and he spit as he grumbled to himself. He had horrible dentition, and the flagrant bouquet of infrequent baths, old cheese, and doubtful bi-annual dental exams. What was most distinctive about the man, however, were his ears; his quick glance suggesting a pointed, even pig-like appearance. "This man was getting spookier by the moment," Chris decided.

"Get movin," he yelled and spit at the interloper. "He'll be of nice and poor cheer, right and hungry; just fer you, ya little brat! Get up, ya twisted cretin, freaky garland; have you no ears boy, get going!" the man yelled.

There was little choice in the matter, for the man stuck the boy repeatedly with his great pitchfork, all the while ordering him to march across the courtyard. As Chris marched along, his thoughts turned again to the man's ears. The man had said, "Have you no ears boy?" Chris now wondered about the old man's choice of words. Ears, what is with this dude's ears, he wondered in silence? Chris turned his head and looked over his shoulder once again, taking a long inquisitive look at the man.

It was the first time that he had seen the Mark of the Boar, but it would unfortunately not be his last. The man's ears had been sharply filleted; sliced longitudinally from top to bottom, missing the entire rear piece of each auricle; giving his ears a strange and pointed appearance. The posterior half of both auricles were then actually missing, the free rear edge heaped up with a dense and irregular scar. This mark gave them a pointed, pig-like appearance as if they were crudely clipped and healed with rough cautery. The fact that this process affected not one but both ears suggested a premeditated motive to their appearance. A glazed crazy look crossed the eyes of the man. Chris's examination of him was evidently now over for he angrily pushed the boy ahead. The man motioned with a grunt and a flick of the pitchfork for Chris to move on in front of him towards the huge stone tower in the distance.

The man marched his captive in silence for the next few moments. As he passed, people would just drop their heads and move about their business. They were obviously frightened, just trying to live their lives and did not want to help the boy. With this, Chris realized he was in trouble.

The boy slid to a dead stop. He turned once again to face the old man. He would probably suffer for stating the obvious, but political correctness was never his forte. He made stupid statements so many times during this journey. As before, without thinking, and with that confident wit, the words were out of his mouth before he could measure the consequences.

Loudly, he yelled at the man with an agitator's smile, "Hey dude, nice ears!" A swift blow to his head with the wooden end of the pitchfork was all he would remember.

Chapter 10
Prisoner

> Wealth is worthless in the day of wrath,
> but righteousness delivers from death.
> **Proverbs 11:4**

At any other time, in his Xbox type life, an ancient dungeon would have thrilled the modern day boy. The finality of a rusty turn of tumblers, and the friendless force used in his capture, spoiled what would have been a fun haunted house experience like Halloween, and left only an empty quivering fear. Rudely tossed, without Miranda rights, (yes without Miranda rights), Christopher now found himself within a dark, dingy, and evil dungeon!

Incessantly and without mercy, Chris had badgered his parents to visit the modern day equivalent many times. Earnest goes to Jail; it had all seemed such fun at the time. In one of his favorite movies, the court wrongly placed the hero, Earnest, in a dirty, terrifying prison. To the boy, the movie created a belief that incarceration was like summer camp with professional wrestlers.

"Ya, I want to see the CHAIR." He remembered now his prior foolish thoughts. The boy felt a good deal different sitting in a real dungeon, however. A sharp stab of fright overcame him as the mental picture of an electric chair flashed before Chris. Thankfully the thought: no electricity in this world A relief washed over him briefly. The boy remembered his foolish desires of days gone by sadly. Those were simpler times: fun, games, and Hollywood hoodlums; he never appreciated them before.

The jarring crash of the heavy cell door closing sounded very permanent. Chris moved to the door's small iron-barred window. He felt hopeless as he watched the old man hurrying away down the stone-walled corridor. He was cold, lonely, and frightened. Sort of touchy about those ears, old CODGER, he thought with remorse.

Chris turned and assayed his surroundings with regret. Slowly he sat cross-legged, taking in the present state of affairs as his eyes slowly accommodated to the overwhelming blackness. Covering the dungeon floor were the remains of other unfortunate fellows who, with little choice, left their bleached bones behind. While it was dark and cold, the smell was most bothersome.

Blessed with a sensitive nose, he reinforced that to his mother several years earlier. A preschool field trip to a farm, complete with barnyard animals, had been the scene. Much to his mother's remorse, and with all her peer group's silent disapproval, he insisted on yelling at the top of his lungs repeatedly, "It stinks! Why does it stink here?" Alas, there was no similar audience present to voice those same complaints now.

The boy decided to pursue other matters and forced his mind away from the disgusting odor of imprisonment, as a rat crossed his path, hopping gracefully over his foot. The boy shook his lowered head. He was even too tired and hungry to cry. "Sir Alex will show us how!" That lively jingle now seemed so far off; certainly, if there was still a Sir Alexander, he would never show him how again.

"No one will ever come to visit me," Christopher realized sadly. "Dude, I didn't even get my one phone call," he repeated to himself in anger. "I know my rights...oh, but the others guys didn't get their rights. Ya sure... rights," he realized in despair. Chris struck the old wooden door with both hands and turned to look across the almost total darkness of the cell. Left to rot within a foul smelling dungeon, to never see or hear of anyone again was a fate he would rather avoid. The thought of starving was too cruel.

"Hey, this is child abuse," he figured indignantly in silence. "Pizza, oh...for just one piece," he closed his eyes and dreamed of his favorite food. The thought panicked him, as he realized it was unlikely he would ever see his beloved pizza again. Here was the ultimate insult, dying in this filthy dungeon, never to see a beloved slice of pizza!

Time passed ever so slowly for the reflective and discouraged captive. He began reviewing the unfortunate set of events that had brought him to such a predicament. Chris took his imprisonment hard, and he despondently resigned to waste away within his cell.

The sound of heavy boots marching on the stone floor of the corridor interrupted his dejection, their source stopping before the prison door. Chris jumped up in expectation as he heard the jiggling of a set of iron, clanking, keys. With a rusty squeak, the ancient lock turned slowly, and the huge oaken door opened. In his solitary confinement, the boy's eyes had become accustomed to the darkened cell. The invading bright light of an oil lamp, now shining through the doorway, caused him to squint and turn his head. When his eyes accommodated to the light, he turned back to see the dark shadows of two men, standing before him forebodingly. One of them silently moved towards him, grabbed his wrist, and twisted the arm behind him brutally. The guards secured his wrists with a leather thong, and they were off immediately, rudely escorting the frightened boy away from the cell.

As they pushed the prisoner along, through dingy corridors, hands bound behind him, the thought of his eventual destination frightened the young boy. A stairway loomed ahead, and a rude shove started him up the rough-hewn stone steps, ascending in darkness, the tower, or donjon, which seemed to climb forever.

To anyone but the first time visitor, the changes in the Kingdom of Alucemet would be apparent immediately. The kingdom had once been proud and happy, but now in its place stood a rusted, disused, foul, and evil realm. Formerly, the royal family ruled the kingdom with love. King William, once moving freely within the dominion, now seldom appeared to his adoring subjects. The beautiful Queen Patrice, tirelessly tried to direct Alucemet in his absence, but her power was slipping. A tragic breakup of the royal family had occurred as well. Many citizens heard rumors of royal son pitted against royal son.

Many would ask: "And what could have happened to such a fine kingdom?" To this question, one would get varying opinions. "Like the fall of Rome," some would say it was "inevitable." To others, however, there was just one certain cause or culprit in the kingdom's rapid demise, and they suspected that he was not human, but rather created with a porcine genome.

The kingdom of Alucemet was, or perhaps had been, well beyond its time. Democracy was the King's vision and hope. Town meetings within the castle had grown to be a loosely organized forum, the forum intended to lead to a citizen elected republic. Weekly meetings allowed the town leaders contact and dialogue with the royal family. Lately, however, this tolerant atmosphere was rapidly disappearing.

The two men continued in silence, pushing the frightened boy ahead of them as they climbed the narrow stairway at a frantic pace. At the summit the trio pushed through a large doorway and into an overwhelmingly bright flood of candle light. While the light and the end of an exhaustive climb gave some relief for the boy, it also revealed, as he had feared, the worrisome appearance of the two men, who until that moment had remained behind and not visible to the boy.

"Like that crazy dude, Van Gogh," he thought to himself, glancing with caution at the ears of his captors. Chris quickly diverted his eyes away from the men whose ears had met the same fate as the old man, clipped from behind in a cruel fashion. He was not going to make the same mistake again. People with ears such as these were very sensitive he realized.

They boy now found himself at the rear of a large room constructed like an auditorium, with wooden benches cascading down to a central foreground where people milled around nervously. The jailers turned Chris around roughly, and forced him to stand with his back to the wall as if presenting him to the gathering crowd below. As he stood at attention, other similar unfortunates arrived as well, all bound and forced to stand in a similar military fashion beside the boy. His fellow prisoners were men, each much older than Chris. Their captors made it clear to all that they were to remain silent. A look of uncertainty and fright was common to the men's faces as they stood against the wall with wrists secured behind their backs, as if awaiting harsh punishment, perhaps execution.

Anticipating the beginning of the assembly, the crowd began to sit on the benches arranged in a semicircular fashion around a raised platform or dais. Upon that dais was an empty stone-hewn chair, one as if constructed for a King. To the right of the dais, a hardwood fire roared within an enormous hearth. To the left a balcony, the rear enclosed with velvet curtains, suggesting a route of entry.

It was incredibly warm in the room, and with the roaring fire along with lighting supplied by oil-burning torches, smoke choked the unventilated space as the boy stood at forced attention. A bead of sweat formed on his brow and he longed for a free hand to wipe it clean. Regaining some composure after his rough treatment, Chris scanned the audience below. To his right, standing alone near the fireplace, one man in particular caught the boy's eye. He was a filthy-clad man in a tattered outfit. Leaning his large frame against the wall, the hulk of a man stood in grizzled silence, interacting with no one. While from the distance the details could not be certain, his nose seemed odd, as if scarred and twisted. Upon his head, as might a pirate, he wore a tight black bandanna. What most marked his presence, however, was a severe respiratory malady, for he continually wheezed and sputtered, coughing and frequently wiping his unshaven face. Periodically he would reach deep down to bring up a loose wad of sputum, which he emptied with a skilled hawk into the brass spittoon at his foot.

Chris continued, scanning the crowd gathering before him. Fearsome men stood scattered throughout the throng each dressed in black tunics, tied loosely at the waist. Their intimidating presence seemed to indicate members of the castle guard, each rough, crude, and like Chris's jailers, reveling in their menacing manner. One such man in particular stood out from the others as their apparent leader.

His name was Ogelby de Openhowfffffler; his name to those brave enough to speak it, however, was the Ogre of O. He was one of the up-and-coming in the Kingdom, just recently named the Royal Guard Grand-Am.

The man's appointment was the latest in a series of odd events that had become commonplace in the Kingdom, since the Minister of Refuse, a pork-like man named Michaelis's meteoric rise in influence. He had swept to a formidable position of power, from a lowly laborer in the Kingdom's waste collection division, to a swaggering being, demanding and receiving the impressive title, the Minster of Refuse. Viewing the kingdom lately, commending those individuals involved in refuse would certainly seem a ruse. It was odd then when first this Michaelis, and then his assistant Ogelby, received lofty positions, rising to powerful status from the bureaucracy involved in waste management. The promotions did occur, however, and so suddenly as well, "as if staged," some said, but only in privacy.

Such rumors of corruption flourished recently in the Kingdom, fed by the oddest of all events, the death of Louis Bienville. Louis Bienville had played a pivotal role in the founding of the kingdom, and had commanded the Royal Guard as Grand Am and trusted assistant to the beloved King. Truly dedicated and honest, the recent changes in the Kingdom had troubled the man very deeply. In the King's final public appearance, he had expressed his dissatisfaction vigorously. Reports of his suspicious demise circulated the very next day. An accident they claimed, but to those who knew the man they could not explain his trampled body, surrounded by cloven hoof marks, within the isolated Devil's Pass. Further, rumors associated with the subsequent disappearance of his daughter, Autumn, gave fire to questions of conspiracy.

The new Grand Am, Ogelby, was quite a contrast to the former, and his rise to such a lofty position truly confusing. Born a fief of a poor fiefdom, the disadvantages of his youth left deeply hidden scars. While he tried to hide his background, there was something about the man that betrayed him. Perhaps it was his manner, crude and vulgar, supported by his less than successful attempts to hide his rough exterior with gaudy medals and pendants. He was as well a man who seldom made eye contact when he spoke, preferring to imagine some important object drawing his eyes across the room. When by chance eye contact occurred, it seemed by mistake, as if his empty gaze might betray to another the masquerade of his life.

While one could not imagine a grander story of poor boy made good, even his success could not erase the deeply ingrained sense of inferiority that lived and guided his every decision daily. His deeply pock-marked face, the result of a bout of the devastating vulgarian plague, did little to build his inner image. It clouded his judgment on occasion, a fact that his superiors had realized and used to their advantage. If one summarized the man's being, here was the perfectly corruptible man, disadvantaged by his incompetent upbringing and brilliantly incompetent mind.

It was perplexing that a person cultivating the friendship of no one, and receiving respect from even fewer, could claim such a lofty position such as the Grand Am; his promotion was baffling to those without any devious political shrewdness. However, his sponsor, Michaelis, read the foolish man as if illustrated within a book. Here was a man that would lead the guard with ruthless intensity. Ogelby was a man that if crossed would quietly cross the crossed. Here was a man whose brilliant incompetence allowed manipulation with ease. The question then might be how to control such a man? Why only to have him feel that his ideas were his own would be enough. Once skillfully planted within his simple mind as his own, the new Grand Am would pursue it right, or more commonly wrong, until the very end. Yes, Michaelis had read him, and while he detested Ogelby, as all who knew the man did, his fraudulent needs outweighed his repulsion of the man.

In contrast to Ogelby, it would not be so simple to control another participant in attendance that day. A man of honor, the events of recent times deeply troubled Robyn of Hobinsiefken. The tall man stood alone below the balcony, quietly watching the proceedings with his arms folded. He had grown up during the early times of the Kingdom and had made the public welfare his only desire. The man appreciated all citizens, from the rich property owner to the most unassuming child selling apples upon the street corner. It was his habit to search out the downtrodden and discouraged individuals, offering a few words of spirited encouragement. Robyn's only reward would generally be just a grateful smile from the now lifted-up spirit of the soul, whose life would be better off just for the simple recognition of that person's worth.

Beyond his love for his fellow citizen, the public of Alucemet recognized an outstanding leader who nearly always would make the right decision. He was the right person, in the right place, at the right time, and so his unanimous election to a powerful position came without surprise. Occupying the single most influential position, apart from those in the King's court, Robyn of Hobinsiefken was the mayor of the city of Alucemet.

Robyn worked within his city with public dedication, admired by all. While the royal family had supplied the structure to build the society, the mayor had rallied the people and supplied hours upon hours of detailed planning upon which this framework could succeed. He was selfless in his dedication; however, deep within his soul Robyn longed for royal acknowledgment of his contribution. With the knighting of Alexander, the ceremony and image it created had obsessed him. It was common knowledge that the King, given his fine judgment of character, sincerely appreciated the man. It was odd then, when along with the sweeping changes in the Kingdom of late, a royal decry would make such Knightly titles a matter of porcine birthright only. Unlike usual edicts that grew from healthy and open discourse, this decision had come as an unannounced statute, posted without warning within the town center. That the document was issued by the King was without question, for affixed to the parchment was the royal seal depicting the Laughing Lion and giving it officious authority. While shocked, Robyn displayed his betrayal to no one. The mayor was only now just appreciating what this meant to his ultimate goal, the ruling dashing the Mayor's innermost desires for Knighthood in a swift and viscous manner.

Another individual entered the meeting hall, his appearance causing immediate silence to spread across the room. He was tall and gaunt in profile, and moved with an arrogant swagger, drawing fearful attention from others within the gathering crowd. He held himself in a manner consistent with a belief in his superior superiority, giving very little regard to others in attendance. Glancing now at the cast of prisoners across the back of the crowded auditorium, Fordem eyed each, one by one, with unhidden disdain, pausing to scowl at each as if calculating their fate.

As the roaring fire illuminated his face for the first time, Christopher gasped in horror as he realized he had met the man twice before. "Fordem...," the boy spit out the word under his breath. Their last meeting left the boy realizing that the man probably did not like him. If not quite certain of his fate before Fordem's entry, Chris now had a greasy feeling in his gut.

While Chris recognized the man, he tried for a neutral 'I am not here' kind of stare. With his blue eyes widening, and his mouth stretched in a tight grimace, the boy tried his best to be unremarkable.

Fordem could sense the boy's growing tension. As the imposing man scanned across the prisoners, a special scowl crossed his face, and his eyes rested for the longest time when his gaze came to Chris. As he did so the boy was certain that a menacing twitch actually came over Fordem's left eye.

Chris decided, this was not good! He tried to avoid Fordem's burning gaze and melt into the stony wall behind him. It would have worked, he thought, but he could feel his beloved skateboard shoes shining for the entire world to see, as if the stupid shoes were on fire and betraying him.

Fordem dismissed himself without much courtesy to the group. He climbed the stairs, slowly keeping his threatening eyes upon the boy. Chris lowered his head, but the man's stare seemed to burn his scalp. Soon Fordem was directly in front of him, towering down upon the boy, his muddy black boots just touching the boy's rubber-clad toes. Unable to resist, the boy slowly raised his head making reluctant eye contact with his adversary. He tried an, "I am so surprised," type of smile with a playful twist of his head that worked so well on his Mom when she caught him eating green starbursts instead of broccoli at lunch. Unfortunately, Fordem neither believed in his sweet innocence nor cared.

The evil person whom Chris had so happily sacked in linebacker style looked down upon the boy, breathing in and out loudly, for quite some time. Chris stood in silence, afraid himself to breathe. He was so close now that the boy could only see the golden buttons upon Fordem's black silk tunic. Engraved upon them were the words, "I Hate You, Twirp." Startled by the revelation, his eyes became even bigger, and he regarded his recent perfect tackle now with a heavy remorse. The boy hoped for mercy, but expected none.

It was a welcome surprise then, when Fordem failed to acknowledge the boy any further, turning without a word from the intimidated boy. Chris sighed in relief and took a severely overdue breath. Fordem left him with a silent message, however, using a casually stretched elbow, brutally striking the boy's jaw, as the man, in military style, rotated upon his boots to return to the group. This insult confirmed the boy's fear of detection. He knew and recognized him, of that Chris was sure! "Embarrassed... the dude's embarrassed," he thought, with some consolation as he longed to rub his battered jaw with one of his still secured hands.

Fordem returned to the group in a dejected silence. Subdued and almost troubled, the proud Fordem walked away slowly, less like the earlier arrogant rogue. Sitting alone upon an empty bench, he glanced over his shoulder at the boy with one last angry scowl. Placing a hand upon the bridge of his nose, he dropped his head in revengeful thought. With his free hand, he began thoughtlessly cleaning the mud from his riding boots.

A dusty barrel of a man now made his appearance, entering the hall with little acknowledgment to the group. He was short and greatly overweight, approaching the gathering with an air of regal indifference. His prominence with the gathering was apparent, for silence again fell over the hall, and those standing took obediently to their seats. The man's nose ended abruptly in a turned-up snout, separating two black, lifeless, beady eyes. He had a balding head with pink shiny skin, appearing pork-like, but on the other hand strangely familiar to the boy. Except for his shoe apparel, which was brilliant, he seemed to dress quite carelessly for one of such apparent regard. He wore wrinkled, stained britches, and a dirty tunic, the latter tucked within one side of his belt, but carelessly loose on the other. However, the boots, now here was something that this person obviously valued. In contrast to his unkempt attire, the boots were a shiny black finish, gleaming brilliantly in the fire light. He stood on exaggerated high heels, which while giving him some height, just seemed to emphasize his lack of it. In addition, he walked gingerly on those heels, seeming to be unsure of his gait. It reminded Chris of his little brother walking in his father's shoes, ones that his little feet did not completely fill.

The man walked to the rear of the auditorium and approached the group with an uninterested scowl on his face. He stopped before them, eyeing each with disgusted disdain. With a click of his heels, he turned sharply, returning to the front of the room. As he did so, his leading foot followed this quick turn nicely, while the trailing foot did not. With his leading boot pointing forward, the trailing boot remained for just a moment still pointing rearward. With this split like stance, the man stumbled slightly, but as if faced with this situation before, the oaf-like person quickly righted himself, flipping that wayward rear boot around to quickly point forward without delay.

At the room's front, the rotund man attempted to park his quite prodigious rump on the huge, stone, throne-like chair. The chair dwarfed the man. It was humorous as he climbed up on the throne; it obviously designed for one of much larger, king-like stature.

A few choked laughs came from the group. They seemed to consider the lumbering entrance of their apparent leader, as he literally climbed, albeit awkwardly, into his oversized seat.

A productive cough came continually from the emphysematous buccaneer, still standing for more efficient chest physiotherapy, off to the right of the meeting hall room.

"Silence you pestilent fools," the man on the throne growled in a hideous, high-pitched, rasping voice and made wide vigorous movements with his hands. "It pities me that such a lofty and superior being such as ...**THE BOAR**, must be saddled with the likes of you dim witted laborious idiots! All of you be seated at once," he yelled with such fury that spit flew from his mouth!

Complete silence overcame the hall, and the gathering began to inspect one another questioningly. Glancing around with confused fright, all in attendance realized simultaneously that they were in fact sitting, a fact that had not changed since his entrance. The men returned their attention again to their obviously near-blind leader with a curious expression. Many seemed to expect another outburst.

This bumbling man's appearance and manner began to trouble the boy. Had he seen him before, or was Manzell's reference to the *Boar* enough to give him a familiar feeling? That hateful way, that top-heavy physique, those empty brainless eyes! "Hard to forget someone like that," he thought. He had experienced similar feelings of past familiarity many times before. Chris had often arrived somewhere or seen someone when he felt that he had seen the person before. This feeling if wrong was always brief, leaving him quickly, and after such an episode, he would not be able to reproduce the feeling. This scene was different, and the feeling of familiarity, of meeting this man who tormented him repeatedly, by this inverted bowling pin of a pinhead man would not leave his mind. Chris began to search his memory for why.

Then he remembered where he had seen him! *"Hurley!"* There was no other loathsome scum like him. Could it be that his long and gone bus driver was alive in this medieval world, reappearing to torment Chris? He doubted the existence of more than one such creature in all of eternity. It was just typical of his prior nemesis to follow him. "Can't you stay away? Find someone else to bug," the boy steamed in silence. He recalled that last day at school. Strangely, Hurley was absent from the bus that day. He had never missed a day before, never before wanting to allow the boy to ride home in peace. He would never miss a day, for the beast could not resist the opportunity it gave him to abuse Chris. At the time, he had taken it as a good sign. In retrospect, however, he was not so sure. A hideous voice brought the boy back to the present scene.

"Silence... you reptilian-minded sausages!" The Boar screamed.

"Yep, that's the dude," Chris realized in horror. Suddenly feeling angry he thought, My day just keeps getting worse and worse."

The Boar rose from his chair, stomping his boots and roaring in anger out of control. Those in attendance were obviously uncomfortable, slouching as they sat, attempting to escape this misplaced wrath. They had all been and were completely silent since his entrance. The reference to noise had no founding, as there really had not been any. The boy was certain of one thing. The hall could not have been more silent. No one dared utter a single word since the tyrant's entrance. Even the pirate guy was not coughing. Chris soon realized that the Boar, like Hurley at home, needed little to incite his violent tirades.

Fordem seemed unaffected by the man's outburst. "Was it because of bravery? Could there be a cunning reason or strategy behind his temperament?" Chris wondered. Perhaps they had planned his entrance to intimidate the gathering. For whatever reason, Fordem alone gave little acknowledgment to his superior. He continued to sit as before, cleaning the mud from his boots with a large rusty nail and glancing occasionally at Chris.

As the Boar's tirade continued, a woman of royal stature silently entered through the curtained door of the balcony and sat quietly. Dressed exquisitely in a velvet-trimmed, rose-colored, silken gown, her dark hair rested tightly behind her in a silver embossed chignon.

She scanned the crowd as she sat. Examining the scene below, her piercing green eyes fell upon Chris with a curious expression. She seemed so sad and she twisted her head for a moment as if wondering about the boy.

The woman's entrance caught the attention of Fordem as well. He stopped the maintenance of his boots and looked to the balcony. For just that brief moment, before he could again regain his composure, the stern individual betrayed a small breach in his otherwise impenetrable fabric. As a child discovered doing wrong, his countenance revealed a discomfort with the presence of the woman. As sudden as the change he caught himself, forced away his apparent guilt, regained his evil appearance, and returned to cleaning his boots.

The Boar's outburst was done by now. His hearing was better than his sight, and he realized that he based his tirade on a mistake, for no one in the hall was either standing or talking. For just the briefest moment, an expression of embarrassment crossed his foul fat face; the Boar quickly corrected this, however, and rose to address the crowd.

"Business is at hand here. Master Fordem...With interest I turn to you. Recant for the people the imploder situation to us." The Boar turned, stumbling in his boots briefly, but as one experienced with the situation, he quickly regained his posture. He stood now leaning upon the stone chair, awaiting his military officer's response.

Fordem forced his long frame slowly out of his chair to speak reluctantly to the group. He glanced at Chris for a brief moment, displaying some discomfort with his presence. He soon regained his arrogant, confident self, and began to address the meeting hall.

His voice was deep and calculated as he spoke of a wagonload of implosives that he had successfully secured within the Castle Alucemet. Concluding he added, "The Boar's Hoof may safely count on our largest supply of imploders, to the defense of our fortress, armed and deployed upon the periphery of our castle." As he finished the man looked hatefully at Chris.

"And of the oldest boy?" The Boar questioned.

Turning now to the Boar, Fordem's frown exposed his turmoil. He glanced briefly at Chris before he pondered his answer. Righting himself quickly, he addressed the leader as he responded, "The briefest of contact, his cowardice caused him to retreat. Had our burden been less precious our pursuit would have routed him. Future events will make this moot, however."

"But whom do we defend against?" A brave citizen yelled anonymously, expecting and receiving no answer.

"Ya, where are the Royal Princes?" another citizen yelled.

A scowl quieted the group, as Fordem returned to his seat. He did not bother to answer the group's rhetorical questions, though as a child caught in a lie, almost involuntarily, he gazed again at the balcony. He then sat returning to his mud-caked boots.

Only someone examining Fordem with suspicion would have noticed the slight hesitation in his answers. A carefully scripted scene, few in attendance that day suspected the truth. Chris, however, had been at the scene, and though an adequate acting job, the man's lies were apparent to the boy. Fordem's deception made complete sense. The defeat had come as quite a blow to the arrogant man.

The visitor within the balcony had noticed Fordem's discomfort and attention to the prisoner boy as well. She glanced at Fordem with a questioning stare, influencing this fearsome man. The woman looked again over the balcony edge, staring at the boy, and wondering about his presence.

A silence now shrouded the room, the Boar shuffling back and climbing onto his oversized chair. He seemed quite pleased with his military might.

With the temporary quiet, the Mayor rose politely to address the audience. "Tis at this point that I must speak." He said as he moved to the front of the room. "The changes that are apparent within our Kingdom trouble me deeply." Pausing for a moment he looked down. Returning to his speech, he continued in an animated manner. "Recently one hears rumors concerning our noble royal family! Cowardice--? I say, never! The boy's bravery, and honesty

I might add, have been proven time after time. Such rumors are nonsense," he said, staring intensely at the Boar.

Robyn of Hobinsiefken appeared troubled to anyone who was familiar with him. An individual of few words, he spoke seldom in these meetings, preferring to sit at the rear and read the minds and inner thoughts of those around him. When Robyn spoke he did so always to make an important point, and he did so with brevity and insight quite uncommon of a man with little formal schooling. In the past, the man would always capture the attention of his audience, and reduce any problems to a simple and understandable plan. It was his custom to hold the audience's attention with intense eye contact. Speaking to a large group, he referred in turn to each person, if only for a brief moment. This personalized his point for each, and gathered tremendous respect and support.

Robyn of Hobinsiefken was quite different today. There was no such communality in his manner. Deeply troubled, his hunched posture reflected the serious change. He spoke disjointed, his head hanging low as if defeated. He seemed angry, and he jumped from one complaint to another.

"And what of King William? His absence sits sourly." He turned now with anger away from the group and walked to address the Boar. "And what of the younger boy? We hear such rumors of son against son, of an ambush---And what have become of the Bienville's, both patriot and daughter? That one of such suspect fiber, sits as his replacement, is an affront to the kingdom and to Louis Bienville's memory!"

Some quiet growls of agreement began to take over the crowd. A rare brave individual here and there slowly stood in frightened support of the good Mayor.

Michaelis had heard enough. He jumped from his throne, spit flying from his mouth with a vengeful shout. As his weight hit the floor, each boot rolled and collapsed laterally, and he found himself standing on their outer walls. Not seeming to care about his awkward stance, he used a single wave of his raised sweaty hand, signaled silently to his security force, and destroyed the mayor's momentum.

"My good mayor," he said with a calming pause. "As you know the judgment of our King has been—ah--yes, a bit clouded of late. Now, your trusted servant has tried to right these wrong decisions, but alas not before that necessary dictum concerning our distinguished mayor's worthy recognition."

The Boar flipped first his right and then his left foot, standing now correctly on the sole of the boots. "Yes, the Porcine Reconciliation Act is unfortunate for the minority, but necessary to support the people's rights. Of that, even you I am sure would agree." With this, the myopic Boar moved to stand just inches in front of the Mayor. Perhaps from lack of conditioning, perhaps for intimidation, he stood inhaling and exhaling as if winded.

It was all that the Mayor could do to tolerate his fetid breath. As it was his nature, he tried being polite, but with the odor he managed just a twisted scowl.

That the Boar detested all that was good was apparent to even the casual observer. He tried to hide his disgust, but he managed just an insincere smile, just a sneer that exposed his rotten teeth. The beady black eyes now focused upon the mayor, trying to muster, though unsuccessfully, some semblance of concern. "Tis quite the pity, and you so deserving," he said, rubbing his hands together hungrily and turning to return to his throne.

The statement brought several chuckles from the crowd. The loudest chuckler of them all was the Royal Guard Grand Am, Ogelby, who roared exposing his enormous ignorance, enjoying the embarrassment of a former enemy to its fullest. With one look of disapproval from the Boar, however, he quickly silenced himself.

The Mayor now resigned himself sadly, turning and walking to his bench in apparent defeat. His face had become brightly flushed with the mention of his desire of royal recognition, and he returned slowly to his seat without further resistance. He was a person of little selfish desires. The despot revealed Robyn's hidden thoughts of Knighthood for the briefest of moments, and it embarrassed his noble humility. Had he continued his attack on the happenings of this rapidly deteriorating Kingdom, those responsible would reveal the degree of his passionate desires of knighthood. It must have been one of several recent defeats for the Mayor, for he appeared helpless and resigned to his seat in despair. So common of late, the Boar controlled challenges, cutting ruthlessly to the heart of any potential adversary.

Without the Mayor's challenge, Michaelis returned to his condescending tone as he summarized his views on the "tragic" fall of the kingdom. Standing again, and with a sarcastic bow, he ended his reference to the mayor and was off again pacing, snarling, and stumbling, manufacturing words in his arrogant manner.

"Even such nobility as our beloved King must inevitably with time fail. When such as this occurs, only with swift action can the failure of a Kingdom be **_prebossquillated_**." With a dismissing wave of his arm to the Mayor, the Boar continued. "I assure you, my just and proper Mayor, that I truly speak for our temporarily weakened, King. I have just honorable and sincere **_ignorations_** to be sure. Now, if it is possible for such a noble King's judgment to fail, why not his two insolent offspring?"

The Boar paused to emphasize his gibberish. "The Boar predicted as much long ago. With the failing of their King, those within the bloodline would begin to feel for their power. Such petty infighting as we all have witnessed. Why, their absence from the castle now allows us to continue with the royal destiny of our kingdom. And, of the oldest one's bravery--Ha! His cowardice was always apparent. The two insolent brats have now disappeared. It is so apparent that this is to our betterment."

As he spoke, the Boar became increasingly animated, pacing madly across the front of the hall, his shiny boots flipping around sometimes pointing forward other times rearward. His love of his voice and thoughts were obvious. He often spoke of himself in the third person, as one of royal nobility might speak. As the Boar's excitement would grow, his mind could not keep up with his speech. He was in the habit of creating twisted versions of certain words and grammar for his particular needs. Commonly, one heard lines such as, "Might could," or "flustratable, and he often completely manufactured words when needed, such as prebossquillated or ignorations. As he spoke, he paced, and as he paced he stumbled, righting himself expertly and continuing on his irrational discourse without interruption. He was in command, and his arrogant pride bubbled forth as he spoke of his favorite subject: the fall of the royal family.

"And the Mirrorlass, that foolish boy's project! Why only the Boar could unlock its secret energy and power." With this, his heightened frenzy came to a stop. He calmed himself quickly, as if catching himself for the briefest of moments. Michaelis then quickly amended his words with a twisted facade of a smile. "Mind you," he said quietly. "Civil pride will certainly direct its infinite power towards only proper perspectives."

The announcement cast a grim pallor upon the gathering, while those of the Boar's sentiment such as Ogelby laughed quietly with evil glee. Horrified citizens sat stunned, weighing the impact of infinite power unleashed for devilish purposes.

There were rumors of such a device, one with limitless power. The Knighthood of Alexander had stemmed from its development. Most were under the impression that the key to its use had disappeared to safety when the older boy disappeared. The Boar's reference now suggested a frightening possibility; that the mirrorlass's power was now available to the evil that held it. The mayor's supporters sat in horrified silence, unable to respond. The mayor deepened farther into his gloom, hanging his head in resignation as his worst fears neared realization.

With their discouragement palpable, the Boar gathered energy as he began to dominate the mood of the meeting hall. Wishing to release his next announcement with discretion, he waited until a silence filled the room and all eyes were upon him. He scanned the crowd with obvious disgust. Quietly he returned to the stone throne. Under his breath, and in his usual butchered manner, he whispered, "and of the younger brat boy, why just now he has **decupidated** his worthless Knighted brother." With his announcement, the Boar leaned upon the edge of the throne and allowed the silence to sink into those in attendance. He was quite proud of himself, and a cruel sneer acknowledged his complete disgust for the citizenry.

The audience sat in stunned silence weighing the Boar's last statement. Many wondered in silence, others asked questions quietly. "How could this betrayal of Royal boy against royal boy really be true?" A gloomy time enveloped the room.

"Had there really been an ambush of Alexander by his brother?" the mayor wondered to himself. Rumors suggesting this ambush were widespread of late, bad gossip spreading so quickly. Hushed whispers had spoken of this event for weeks, but the loyal mayor had until now refused to believe them. Robyn was indignant. Speaking to himself he said, "Such a tragic event should be announced officially in the town center to demonstrate substance and respect for the kingdom!" That alas, had been in another time, a time of honest sustenance, a time that seemed so distant now to the dutybound mayor. If there had been such an ambush, then what became of the ambush loser? "Decupidated," was the bungled word the Boar used. What was its meaning? For that word sounded like "dead," and shocked him! If he believed the Boar, the ambusher would be Alexander's loving brother Nicholas! Sure, there may have been troubles between the boys, but if true, the act was diabolic. The kingdom had so decayed, however, that the mayor could no longer count upon the morays of those he had come to know and trust.

The acoustics of the immense hall were quite exceptional, for the whispered statement was audible to Christopher who remained a bound prisoner and witness to the Boar's commentary. He was an eyewitness to this apparent ambush, at least its beginning. The boy was not aware of its perpetrator or the outcome, however. Here, the girl Autumn had made sure of that. It was certain that Alexander had been hopelessly outnumbered. The girl had concluded this as well. Ambushed by Alexander's brother, and "decupidated." That sounded like "dead dude," the boy concluded. What had he learned of this Nicholas, known as Nicholas the Blue? Alexander had seemed so sullen about his brother. Manzell had referred to disagreements between the two royal dudes as Chris referred to them. However, ambushing his brother? If true, Nicholas was one bad dude that Chris would rather not meet.

The Boar arrogantly leaned upon his throne and snarled with delight, reinforcing the magnitude of the statement. It was important to him at this point to allow an overwhelming silence to fill the meeting room with wondrous agony. Those who did not hear or comprehend his consequential declaration heard it again by whispering neighbors. All of noteworthy importance eventually understood; all that was the kingdom was now in abject turmoil. Their Sir Alexander had been decupidated, and the culprit it seemed, the second hero of the kingdom, Nicholas.

One could almost acquit the Boar of the next series of events, for the agonal hacking of the pulmonically crippled pirate prematurely interrupted this silence. His outbursts had been brief each time before, but now the man's trouble continued with one bronchiectatic productive cough followed by another. With each cough, the pirate struggled for air, and accomplishing this gasp would lead to the next deep and rattling hack. The Boar would reward this disrespectful interruption with cruel incredulity. The Boar acted amused, or perhaps he was just mocking the poor man. Had the pirate not been hacking so consistently, the nearly blind beast could not have located him. He moved, however, with a sickening smile, led by the rattling noise to stand next to the hacking pirate.

Michaelis addressed the buccaneer, who was just gradually controlling his paroxysmal cough. "Captain Baalam, our supreme Maritime commander?" the Boar questioned with sarcastic respect.

The Boar's inquiry took Balaam by surprise. The disheveled pirate, caught inattentive and unaware until now, stood quickly at attention gazing upon his superior with a skeptical face. The sailor's violent cough began to calm and he tried his best to respond to the Boar. The captain straightened his wrinkled tunic nervously as he spoke. While quite pleased with the Boar's unexpected attention, and certainly he deserved the respected reference, the leader's attention surprised the roughened mariner. Wiping the last remains of sputum from his scarred face, a proud smile broke his lips, exposing his toothless gums. In between labored breaths he answered, "Aye sir, to what question might your servant speak?"

"Rumors would have it, that younger ***bratnifian*** boy- I believe they call him Nicholas- now rests for eternity upon the bottom of the high sea in response to your superior naval skills. Recant these victorious events for this prestigious group, Captain Baalam. And mind you, spare not any of the captain's nautical ***geniality***, for which your success depended!" Michaelis now insincerely glared at the proud Captain, awaiting his reply.

The commander of the Alucemet's navy worried about his response. While the Boar's question was somewhat unintelligible, he understood its gist and thought it might even have included a hidden complement! Understandably, he had not advertised the truth about the conflict with that brat pirate boy Nicholas, the total loss of his ship, nor the lost treasure. However, he deftly circulated rumors that Nicholas drowned when the Captain expertly sacrificed the craft for the cause. Rubbing his stubble of a beard, he remained silent for the moment, thinking. Was it now his time to shine in this constructed story?

Michaelis became impatient with the Captain's silence. A tapping sound came from his right foot, and while the movement of the ankle was apparent, movement of the boot was not. "Come now Captain, speak up." the Boar said curtly. "Tell these honored citizens of your recent conquest!"

The Captain continued to be hesitant. Honesty or dishonesty, between these two options the lues-infested pirate brain debated? Before addressing the crowd, he spat a particularly thick and foul spittle with deadly accuracy into the brass spittoon at his foot. Being of such fine color and texture, the Captain concluded it spoke of good luck. Suddenly he calculated his response. "Okay, dishonesty," he concluded silently to himself with growing confidence.

"Aye sir," he said with a forced smile. "The brat, or bratnifican as be your saying, met an untimely fate high upon the merciless sea. Me tried me best to save him, but alas he suffered a watery grave he did."

An audible gasp came over the meeting hall, which pleased the pirate immensely. He had begun his discourse with hesitation. Bolstered now by their response, the pirate decided that he was finally receiving his due respect. The man knew Michaelis, and never trusted the grotesque leader, always suspecting a trap. However, the Boar just smiled giving the pirate the courage to continue with his lie. He concluded happily that the Boar was buying his story! Further placating Michaelis, he attempted to use the Boar's butchered speech. "Ignorations aside, the Boar's Hoof stands free of the geniality of the boy."

Until this moment, the Boar appeared to support Balaam's version of victory with an enthusiastic silence. His smile, while sarcastic, seemed to show support for the pirate. With lightening quickness, however, he was upon the unsuspecting captain using the pirate's weakness as the Boar's strength. With his stubby fingers, he forced a hidden apple deep into the pulmonary cripple's mouth, and then quickly pulled his bandanna down past the man's ears, obstructing his sole remaining port of air, his distorted nose.

The captain lived on the edge of suffocation daily, and while able to tolerate the day's brief hypoxic moments, he had little reserve in this present condition. A horrified shudder came over the hall as the dreaded Captain fought violently for air. Panicking, he tried to rid himself of the apple by taking a bite, but the loose fragment more than complicated the situation. Balaam flogged himself in stridorous agony, falling to the floor, and thrashing like a fish out of water. The Boar showed no concern for his asphyxiating colleague. Turning from the scene with boredom, he motioned to Ogelby.

Laughing ghoulishly at Balaam's misfortune, the Ogre grabbed the suffocating man by his boots. Pulling his legs out from under him, he dropped the man without ceremony to the ground. Howling with glee, the Ogre stood over the man laughing foolishly.

A fear swept over the citizens. After hearing of Alexander's and Nicholas's demise and then witnessing such a brutal act, each stood silently and filed passed the gasping man, leaving the hall. The mayor stopped and kneeled by the wheezing captain. A laughing guard attempted to usher him away. Robyn brushed the man away angrily. He stood and before leaving, planted a well-placed foot into the pirate's epigastria, expelling the foreign body from his mouth.

Ogelby returned and looked with disgust at the cyanotic man trapped beneath his bandanna and lying moaning on the floor. He motioned roughly to one of the black tunic guards. The sentinels grabbed the man by his boots, drug him to the door, and flung him into the hallway. With the door now closed and visitors gone, the session would continue in private.

"Cool Heimlich maneuver, dude!" Chris thought as he watched the scene in silence. Distracted by all the action, the boy had lost track of the woman in the balcony. Returning his attention to her now, he noticed that she no longer remained in the box. The woman interested him, but he had no idea of her identity. "Why had she left?" the boy wondered. Had she heard the described downfall of the kingdom and the purported death of the two boys, or had Michaelis's cruelty and the resulting spectacle precipitated her exit? At sometime during the events, however, the royal appearing woman had disappeared.

With the exit of the citizenry, Michaelis, Fordem, and accomplices moved now to the helpless group of prisoners bound at the rear of the meeting hall. One by one, a gleeful henchman recanted each prisoner's offense with scant detail to the indifferent Michaelis. The accusation leveled was always the same. To each the charge: "guilty of excessiveness," rang out with ghoulish delight. To this baseless allegation, Michaelis would respond, "Mark him as mine," and the fate of the next prisoner would then be considered.

It was obvious that marking was a fearful sentence. Many hostages would yell, "No...Have mercy!" All the prisoners struggled to escape when summarily escorted away and led to their punishment.

Chris was sure what the sentence *mark as mine* referenced. He recalled with fright the clipped ears of the old man. His belly churned with anxiety. Hunger pains became replaced with a sickened feeling in the pit of his gut. Measuring his options, he decided to expose Fordem's lie when the judge and jury came to confront him. Perhaps he could divert attention from himself.

He was unable to use his knowledge of deception however, for Fordem with deft swiftness forced a gag into his open mouth. Now Chris had had it. Bound and gagged he was the next prisoner to receive his verdict.

When the group turned to Christopher, Fordem was quick to speak. "This dangerous criminal has extensive charges, sire."

The Boar stopped his pacing suddenly and stood in front of the shackled boy, examining him with unusual interest, as he awaited Fordem's accusations. The boy tried desperately to avoid the gaze of the too familiar Boar.

Fordem began his series of charges. "My attention comes direct from those who have experienced the boy. A wizard he seems, for his dress in times past has suggested as such. He speaks of magical turtles, and fancies himself the destroyer of a foe named Shredder, when no foe exists. His entry to the castle was as well an evil event, for concealed as a thief he entered Alucemet hidden within the hay of a loyal fief's horse cart."

It was hopeless, Chris realized, for his charges were overwhelming, and now bound and gagged, the boy could not defend himself. In addition, why was Fordem all of the sudden Perry Mason? Certain punishment awaited him, the boy was certain.

In deliberant fashion, and in great detail, the Boar inspected the frightened boy. Chris hoped that his poor vision would preclude the recognition that he feared the most. He prayed that pseudo-Hurley would not recall him from the bus days of Temecula. Perhaps the Boar possessed olfactory senses superior to his sight, for his nostrils flared in rhythm with each morbidly tainted breath. The fetid breath of Michaelis enveloped the boy, and he thought for a time that he would faint.

Then the Boar suddenly seemed to lose all interest in the boy, for he precipitously turned away, his back now to the captor. In another setting, the Boar's exit would have been humorous, for while his body made the turn with flawless agility, his boots, as usual, did not. Facing now away from the boy, his boots still pointed towards him. It seemed a common event, for as if magnetized, each boot turned magically around meeting its calf with a snapping sound.

The boy sighed in relief as the Boar now began to turn away from him. Quick thoughts of escape flooded his panicked mind. However, for the second time that day his relief was premature. As his tormentor turned with a violent flurry, an outstretched elbow caught the boy on the chin, rendering him thoughtless. As the Boar marched away from the scene, he whispered, "Extinguish this pestilent maggot!"

Chris descended the donjon and was well along the stone corridor before his wits returned. While still dazed, he recalled the events that he had just witnessed. Somehow, he had heard his sentence, and appreciated its grievous consequence. As before, his journey in the corridor leading to and from his dungeon was with haste, and complete with constant pushing and prodding from less than jovial individuals. He stumbled from time to time, once falling on his face. The guards yanked him upright and led him along towards his fate. The group reached the dungeon door. One guard held him up against the wall as the other unlocked it. Once again, his captors rudely threw the boy to the dungeon floor, and left him to his own, in total blackness.

There was a brief moment of relief, now being alone and temporarily safe. Chris sighed with relief as he heard the two pig-eared henchmen disappearing down the hall laughing like fools. Soon however, the brutal reality of a desperate situation began to flood-in, overwhelming the young boy. Once again, Chris found himself within the black, impenetrable, dark, foul, and stinking dungeon.

Sitting alone in the dark, the boy began to talk to himself. "Extinguish, did that dude say extinguish? That's not good! I'm gonna be liquidated!" the boy screamed to his rat infested cell. The deep dark emptiness did not respond in the slightest. "Do they extinguish dudes here?" he said, lying on his back in the dark and yelling at himself. "How do they extinguish dude's here?" he wondered in panic. While in the dark one could not appreciate his cartoon-like appearance. His blue eyes were wide open, almost popping out of his head with dread. Pinocchio eyes, his mom called them, but his mother was unfortunately not present to comfort him. Chris jumped from the dirt floor, banged his head on the door, and ran around in circles hysterically.

Pacing and thinking he repeated, "I crashed and burned dude... I crashed and burned..." With a sudden reflection, he struck the rocky wall behind him with his hand and shrieked, "Oh, why am I alive?" Realizing the answer instantly, he continued, "Wait a minute..., I am going to be dead! This sucks! No..., I'm done for, that Hurley, that frick'n pig! This world... oh I'm gone!" In a gloom, the boy sat down dejectedly in front of his cell door with a thoughtless thud. He hung his head shortly, overcome with a deepening despair.

Chris began to think aloud. "No electricity, so no chair...good." He was certain of that. "Of course no gas...so no gas chamber... good." He shook his head vigorously yes with each affirmative conclusion, a gesture that comforted him momentarily. The boy took solace in the absence of modern day technology, which had elevated the art of execution to a sport in his world, until he realized, reaching for his throat: "the guillotine, no...no...not my head!" It was getting too serious for the fun-loving boy. The harsh reality of this world made him long for his salmon-colored, stucco, and very cozy warm house.

Time allowed the boy to calm down. The silence in the hallway outside of his cell, for the moment, was comforting. "No one coming, no one to extinguish me," he thought with a relief. Chris quickly reviewed his knowledge of the medieval world. *Robin Hood*, and *The Prince's Bride*, both movies that summarized the sum total of his experience. "I got nothing in my head, how can I even fight? Dude, I'm over," he concluded with remorse.

Christopher had not studied world history, but he remembered some American history from school. In his mind, he thought about this subject searching for something, anything that might help in this desperate situation.

"George Washington, Red Coats... ya... Red Coats, they were from England, and this is England right? I think its England, sounds like it."

The very distant relationship to these Red Coated soldiers and their glorious defeat by the 'good guys' gave him another moment of relief. However, the absence of anyone dressed in a red coat abruptly returned the boy to reality.

Christopher thought he remembered stretching; they stretched people to death! The thought of being tall by such as the rack did not comfort him. The boy sat despondently, not sure how he could escape this horrible predicament.

As his eyes began to accommodate to the dark he was surprised to realize that an object lay on the floor in front of his cell door. "What's that," he thought as he jumped to his feet. Just at the edge of the door lay what appeared to be a small parchment scroll. Chris picked up the item, unable to read anything in the dark. "Great, an old newspaper," he concluded, and with that he carelessly tossed it away into the darkness. As he did so, fright immediately flashed through his desperate mind. "Newspapers, paperboys, news, what's up with that," he asked himself frantically. Suddenly, the possibility that he had just discarded a clue rushed into his panicked brain.

It was so very dark within the dungeon cell, only a wisp of light coming from the crack under the cell door. Chris looked across the black void and tried to imagine where the scroll might have landed. At the time, he had recoiled in anger, reacting to his desperate situation and tossing the paper harshly over his shoulder. While he recalled the general direction of his careless toss, its exact location was uncertain. Imagining its position, Chris ran in the dark across the foul room and dropped to the dirt floor to search. Groping along the floor in ever widening circles, the boy was unsuccessful

Pirates, Scoundrels, and Kings

in his hunt. Giving up for the moment, he sat alone in the center of the black cell, trying to think.

"Dude, I'll never find it, probably nothing anyway," he said to himself as he felt along the filthy floor. "But now... bones, there were bones here before." He remembered now the skeleton that he noted during his first non-chaperoned visit to this lovely paradise of a room. Not knowing why, he began groping for the bones in their general direction. Rubbing his hand blindly over the floor of a rat infested prison cell did not sit well with the boy, but times were tough. His playhouse castle at home had black widow spiders each spring. If monsters, like spiders, could infest a playhouse, imagination ran wild concerning what awaited him in a real life castle dungeon. All he could think of was what his hand might unwittingly touch next. "Tough times call for tough dudes," he concluded with a new conviction.

His search of the ground covered ever widening circles. He hoped the bones were human and not attached to anything that still wanted them. The first bone he first touched was solid, a long bone, leg or arm he decided, and he traced it to its insertion in the subject's lost pelvis.

Perhaps he could use this as a weapon. Cavemen used bones for spears all the time, he reasoned hopefully. On the other hand, thinking of combat with a sword toting knight, himself armed with only a bone, seemed almost pitiful to the innocent boy. The thought interrupted what had given him some encouragement.

He sat dejectedly, wondering about his predicament, alone and cold in the dark. The enthusiasm upon finding the object was now replaced with reality as he realized he had no clued what to do with a bone. However, Christopher was not dissuaded; so as any hero from his century would do, he turned to his generous reservoir of knowledge: television.

MacGyver snapped immediately into the boy's forebrain. "What would *MacGyver* do?" he wondered of the ingenious creative hero. MacGyver was in US intelligence. A secret agent, MacGyver always tackled the toughest situations and succeeded. His specialty was using small unimportant items, turning them into the perfect weapon or device and saving the day. "MacGyver, dude, MacGyver would know what to do with these bones! For sure MacGyver would find that newspaper. MacGyver, dude why can't you be here or why can't I be MacGyver?" the boy lamented in silence. "That newspaper, or whatever," he spoke, wondering to himself. "That newspaper, that newspaper would get me out of here! I could have burnt it or something. I could a blown through it like a poison dart, maybe."

A tear of desperation came to Christopher's eye as he thought of the hostage who had met his fate within this same room years before. The dead captive's bones indicated that he had not been particularly successful in escape, so what about himself? There were deteriorating articles of clothing clinging to the dead man's torso. This indicated to the boy that the man died within them, not dropped into the cell after his death, stripped of all his possession to decompose. The tears continue to flow as he loosened a small tattered piece of cloth to wipe his eye.

His arm dropped with resignation to his side, touching a square metallic object centered upon the dead man's belly. A belt, Chris decided that the hostage had died with his belt! Now that might be an object of merit, something to use in escape. "But how?" he wondered. Encouragement returned, and the boy decided to be more thoughtful before casting away other objects so carelessly.

Again, the ingenious MacGyver dominated his thoughts. He knew that the television hero would use bones, the belt, and perhaps the newspaperand make the perfect escape. The boy was certain that MacGyver would think of the perfect gimmick. As he thought, he ripped the belt from the corpse. The leather strap of the belt was rotten, but the large metal buckle was still intact. In the dark, he could not be sure of its surface's appearance, but it was large, flat and smooth. He remembered the episode where MacGyver used a buckle to focus sunlight and burn something. The details were not clear, but he remembered the principle. Chris turned to the door. A thin line of light swam under the heavy dungeon door and lit the adjacent floor dimly. "What if I could reflect light across this cell with the buckle?" the boy questioned.

Chris moved to the door and then stopped. He was not sure that he could find the body in the dark again. Returning to the corpse, he grabbed hold of the sturdiest portion of the corpse and dragged it with him across the dark floor to the door, reminding himself to not discard anything again.

At the door, he dropped to his knees, and with the small beam of light examined his newfound treasure. Tarnish covered the buckle, not shiny, he realized disappointedly. If he were to polish it, he decided, he would have a reflective surface. Chris tried first a scrap of the dead man's tunic, but the tarnish would not budge. Rubbing the metal buckle on the bones however, met with excellent success. With some effort, he was able to polish away the tarnish and leave a smooth, brilliant, silver surface.

The polished metal buckle reflected the doorway light directionally like a weak flashlight. With just the right angle, he could spot the light tangentially across the floor, illuminating items that lay in the shadows. Christopher saw things that gave him little comfort. Animals, insects, and various debris lit up in the path of the light, each jumping out of sight when the beam fell upon them. After sometime his makeshift light came across what appeared to be the newspaper, well out of the area he had supposed. He held the buckle tight and tried to fix the paper's location in his head. Dropping the buckle, he quickly moved to the area, hoping that the image within his eyes would last that brief time until he could make his way to the object of his desire. He kneeled on the floor at the intended spot. With some groping he felt a paper object rolled as a scroll. He had retrieved the object of his search!

"Yes," Chris said excitedly, thinking MacGyver thoughts.

Returning with the object, Chris moved quickly to view his precious treasure with the weak light of the door. The object consisted of a single piece of thick, coarse paper. Rolled tightly, it had been sealed with a single waxy spot. Once uncoiled, the boy realized that here was scroll Rocky might read in *The Rocky and*

Bullwinkle Show. Had its appearance predated his imprisonment, or had just someone placed it under his door for him?

The dark pale light made the scroll's examination difficult. With the parchment open on the floor, Chris used the buckle to focus the light on its contents. To the boy's surprise, once illuminated, a hand written message appeared. The letters were odd with wide sweeping brush strokes. He recognized the penmanship as old fashioned, like in *Indiana Jones, the Temple of Doom*, he concluded. In the center of the document was a single penned line. "No way dude!" he said to himself, as he began to understand the document's message.

Open the Door

"Open the door?" the puzzled boy repeated the phrase. "Open the door?" Chris considered discarding the note in disappointment. "After all this work," he concluded sadly, "the note's for the other guy, and the dude's dead!"

Chris sat in the dark considering all this silently and then he realized his mistake. The boy had not excluded the simplest of possibilities. Chris had not checked the door! His mind returned to his rude arrival. The thug brothers had locked the cell door. At least that rusty turning sound that had sounded so final before their exit suggested as much. Recalling that moment again, Chris was sure they had secured the door. The message, however, was clear and simple, and if marked for the boy, he might realize his escape.

"A trap, what if a trap?" the boy worried as he calculated his next move. If the door was unsecured, was the hallway empty? The passage remained silent since the guards had left the boy to rot alone.

Chris placed his head on the floor and strained to view the limited perspective of the hallway visible through the small crack under the door. The passage seemed to be empty, at least as far as he could see. If the door was open, and there was a guard within the hallway, Chris could imagine a tragic end to a relatively short but promising life. He wondered, however, can you die in a world you don't really live in?

The answer was not forthcoming and so the boy continued. Pushing on the heavy door he found that even if not locked, just moving the door would take all of his efforts. He grunted and strained for a moment, and then the heavy wooden door gave way. "YESSSS," Chris celebrated.

Silently, like a cat, Christopher slipped through the partially-opened door and escaped out into the hallway. The muffled thud of the closing door was startling to the boy who anticipated discovery at any moment. "Now where dude," he wondered, as he eyed the long corridor? The hallway was dark, lit by several oil lamps, casting foreboding shadows along a passage that seemed to go forever. He thought that he entered his cell from the right, however his sense of direction failed him, and surprisingly he could not be sure. If he followed the corridor to the right, retracing his recent steps, he might be seen. On the other hand, to the right would be the most likely exit. Oh the strain of decisions, the boy thought, realizing that in his world he made only a few of his own.

He was beginning to hope for parental guidance, a thought of last resort, when out of the corner of his eye a brief movement caught his attention down the corridor to the left. Chris quickly turned and stared in the dim light. For the longest time, he could not see anything, and he began to feel that it might have been his imagination. Then it happened again, a definite appearance of something white flashing for a brief moment from the opposite wall, down the passage to his left, some distance away. Chris took two cautious steps in its direction, and as he moved, the white flash appeared again, and now that he saw it, he realized that he was seeing a waving cloth, here one moment and then gone, appearing from the opposite wall signaling to him. Could it be a fellow prisoner signaling through a barred window in his cell? He slowly made his way down the corridor, hesitantly, all the while keeping his gaze focused on the spot. Again the object appeared and as he approached it did seem to be a flag signaling to him. Turning and looking behind him, Chris decided that he was alone, and now running down the passage, made his way to the waving flag.

He was beyond the opening to an intersecting corridor before he realized it, and he stopped suddenly, sliding to a stop. In the shadows, deep within the hall someone was standing. The torch was out, and the corridor was very black. With no warning, a hand appeared, and grabbing his upper arm, it twisted him around, pulling him with a jerk into the darkened hallway. He stumbled when pulled and his forward motion caused him to fall on the origin of that arm. With a shout, they both fell tumbling upon each other in the dark, rolling to a stop.

"Unburden me!" A woman's voiced said to the unbalanced boy as she struggled to free herself. "We ought not dally, release me, thy freedom hangs on it," the woman whispered, pushing the boy off of her. She was up and moving deeper into the corridor before the boy could right himself. Beginning to run she had second thoughts, and turning to the terrorized boy grabbed his hand and pulled him deeper into the shadowy passage. As she pulled she ran, and it was all Chris could do to keep up with the woman. Remembering Autumn, he thought to himself, "Do all girls travel like this?"

They ran hand in hand at full pace down the darkened hallway. Without a break in her gait, she grabbed the torch from its wall-mounted moor, and holding it aloft, lit their harried path. With this light for the first time Chris could just make out his accomplice. "The woman from the balcony!" he said quietly to himself.

"Stairs," the woman warned the boy behind her. They ascended the staircase with the same exhaustive rate, Chris behind, and the woman pulling him from the front. Two flights of stairs later, they were within another passage, running hand in hand.

From behind the boy, unintelligible shouts of alarm began to echo through the corridor. The woman picked up their pace in response, the two running for their lives as the shouts became louder and closer. With a sudden twist he was violently pulled into a blackened doorway. She snuffed the torch and flattened herself up against the wood door trying to disappear. Placing her hand across the boy's mouth she signaled to the boy to do as well. It was dark again within the shadows of the entree, and he could feel the woman's heaving deep inspirations suggesting that she was near exhaustion from their blistering journey.

The shouts grew louder as the two stood paralyzed, hoping for safety. A number of angry black-dressed men, raced passed them without detection. Once gone, the woman cautiously looked into the hallway with deliberation. When satisfied of their absence, she lit the torch and dragged the boy at a harried pace along the darkened passage away from the men.

Soon they rounded a corner only to be confronted by several black-dressed men. It was too late for concealment and their momentum carried them along as they tried to stop. With an underhand cast, the lighted torch became a tossed projectile, exploding on impact and hurling fiery debris at the startled group. Wasting no time she retraced her last few steps back into the corridor. Again the two were off and racing, running quickly away in the opposite direction. As they ran, the woman deftly dislodged each wall-mounted torch behind them, casting them and creating fiery obstacles to the pursuing mob.

Their actions created some distance, and the woman halted, dragging the boy to a stop. She released his hand and turned to a closed heavy wooden door. Producing a large iron key from her bust, the woman looked behind them. With no pursuit, she unlocked the door and pulled the boy within a shadowy chamber, the door secured behind them.

Gasping for air, the woman turned to the boy and addressed him for the first time. "Have you word of my boys?" she asked, a panted pause punctuating each word. Before he could respond, she added, "Show haste young master, we are lost for time, what says you of Alexander and Nicholas?"

Shouts began again within the hallway outside of their chamber, as Chris realized her identity. "You're the Queen," he said excitedly. Before answering her question, images of the surrounded Pitlings flashed into his mind. Deciding not to burden the woman further he mumbled, "I saw Alexander—I don't know what happened to him."

Their harried conversation ended as sounds outside the chamber door began to grow. Opening and slamming of doors during an organized search of the corridor was growing closer and closer with each moment. Shouts within the corridor betrayed the pursuing guards bearing down on the two with a congealing anger, and it was certain that soon these persons would reach their hiding place. The Queen looked at the door and their conversation quickly ended. She turned and scanned the room in desperation, looking for weapons or anything that might prove useful in their defense as the two dug in, ready for battle.

The boy did as well, and spying an open window at the room's edge asked of the Queen, "What about the window?"

The Queen turned and stared at the boy. Dismissing his impossible solution she answered him, "It is of frightening height, to be sure! Your bones would be all that survived."

Soon men were outside the door accompanied by shouts. "Tis locked! They are here, of that it is certain!" a bristly voice yelled outside their room. Thrusting against the thick door, the angry men violently attempted to break it down.

Soon others arrived in support with jeering shouts of anger, and rattling heavy iron keys as the men scrambled to unlock the door that protected the boy and Queen.

Chris glanced at the torch now burning brightly along the chamber door. The Queen signaled for help from the boy as she desperately jumped to their defense, moving everything and anything from the room to block the entrance of their antagonists. The pounding on the door continued and despite her determination it was unlikely that anything would interfere with the men's entrance.

The Queen's determination distracted Chris for the moment. Like a mighty ant, the slight woman moved piece after piece of heavy furniture, blocking the door. Returning again to the torch,

Chris searched his memory for something. "*Home Alone!*" He yelled with excitement, as he pulled the torch from the wall.

The Queen by now had moved nearly the entire room in front of the pounding door. She was exhausted and wiped a bead of sweat from her brow. With Chris's shout, the woman looked at him with a curious expression.

"*Home Alone,*" he repeated to the woman, expecting the medieval Queen to understand his phrase from one of his favorite movies. The Christmas video boomed into his memory, and the boy realized now why he had watched that stupid movie repeatedly; it was just for times like this. Kevin, the protagonist in the successful movie, uses ingenious schemes to undermine the attempts of two bungling thieves to gain entrance to his beloved home. Chris realized now that one of these schemes was perfect for their present situation.

Outside, the shouts continued. The crowd seemed to grow with angry yells, pounding on the locked door. Now hearing rattling outside, Chris quickly moved to put his plan in place. He began by holding the flames from the torch directly on the iron latch and keyhole. Conducted through the door latch, the metal quickly heated and waited invitingly to satisfy the curiosity of the rabid mob outside.

The Queen quickly understood his plan, and she moved to secure the torch resting delicately on a flower vase with the flame just touching the metal of the door latch. "Young master?" the Queen questioned. "When home alone, hast though occasion to bar your portal in this manner?"

It was humorous question for the boy and for the first time since their meeting, a brief feeling of relief came over him. Chris began to laugh as the Queen began to understand his plan.

"Remind me never to open a door that you wished secured most odd boy," she joked as the two waited for their foils to painfully discover their trap.

Simultaneously their two smiles melted in the face of reality, and they returned to the job of escape. Turning to the window, they quickly moved to the sole unguarded route of freedom. It was dark outside, and Chris could not make out what would await him if he were to jump. On the window ledge stood a small, clay, potted plant. Chris picked the object up and asked her permission. "How far down Queen?" the boy questioned.

The Queen understood his purpose and nodded affirmatively. Dropping the object out of the window it was dangerously long before a splash from the moat below indicated a formidable height awaiting any attempt to escape by this route.

The sounds from across the room behind the thermally sealed door had quieted for the moment. One of the guards thrust his hand within deep pockets and searched for a key. He shook out a large iron ring, and selecting the correct one placed it in the lock deploying the now fiery weapon. As he tried the key, the man screamed in pain as he realized too late the trap frying his hand. Yelling continued as he stepped away from the door, launching expletives as a drunk in a bar, the man shaking his branded hand in agony. Before he could warn the others, another grabbed a hold of the burning key, testing it with similar agonizing results. The man jumped back violently knocking the group to the floor by the door. They all began to yell and scream in anger as the hallway changed to a confused conflagration.

Chris realized that the distraction he had created would not last for long. The drop out of the window was dangerous at best, but it began to look like his only route of escape. He frantically looked around the room for some sort of rope, hoping to climb securely out of the window and away. The Queen did as well, but between them, they only found a three or four feet of linen curtains. While the Queen began to rip these into sections, Chris realized that it just would not do.

It was for the right reasons that the boy remembered stories and movies like a videocassette recorder, and not for the last time this talent jumped to his rescue. "Repunzzal!" the boy yelled. With this he looked with excitement at the Queen, noticing her hair, tightly pulled back and secured in a silver chignon.

Pirates, Scoundrels, and Kings

"Repunnzzal?" the Queen repeated to him. "She lives down the way in her own castle! To what need of her have you?"

"Your hair, your hair!" Chris repeated moving now behind her and examining the beautifully coffered hair with delight. The boy had always wanted to be a shining knight, and a descent to the moat below upon the golden or in this case brunette stair would eventually cure him of this childlike desire forever. It was the only way, however, and as the shouts from his pursuers began anew he questioned her concerning her hopefully stair-like tresses.

"How long is the doo, Queen?" he yelled in exasperation.

It seemed that such a personal question as Chris's did not conform in any manner with the Kingdom's royal etiquette, for the Queen stared at the boy in disbelief as if the question was an affront. The longer she thought though, the less insulted she felt, and a mischievous smile came to her lips. Reaching her hand to the encircled hair, she thought in her mind of the possibilities. Being practical, her conclusion pardoned the boy from his insolent statement. A sudden pull on the hair's snare, resulted in the longest locks the boy had ever seen. Immediately, the Queen magnanimously swung her precious tresses through the window to dangle along the castle wall below.

While it had seemed a great idea at first, a fairy tale dream come true, when presented with an open window and a black watery landing below, the looming task looked less inviting and chivalrous to the boy. The growing disturbance outside the door changed his perception. The screams of agony had stopped, replaced with revengeful shouts of anger and brutal bashing of the door.

Chris looked upon the Queen as she knelt below the window, her beautiful locks now hanging through the window for his descent. She smiled at him as he lifted a leg through the window. "May the Lord see us through," she said.

The boy was quickly alone, descending down the Queen's hair. To himself he whispered, "May the Lord grant you strong roots, Queeny."

"Young master," the Queen shouted down to him through the window, "to what may I name you?"

It was out of his mouth before he could calculate his response, and he had to admit it had that air of Camelot. "Christopher of Temecula," were his last words to the brave Monarch.

The Queen had forgotten her sensitive scalp. She wore the chignon to support the weight of her long hair, which even by itself, without the help of a growing boy, wore heavily upon her Queenly brow. The boy was well down the wall and just beginning to see the icy moat below when he realized that the Queen could stand it no more. Above she moaned in pain, wishing for alopecia.

"Christopher of Temecula, I beg of you, turn loose thy locks!" Screams of agony continued from castle above. "Jump odd boy!" the Queen yelled.

Neither of the two, in their noble plight had weighed the effect of weight upon the royal scalp. The scheme had worked much better in the fairy tale stories, and Chris realized his predicament as screams of torture came from the window above. The hair was now moving and the Queen began to shift with the excruciating discomfort. A good twenty feet remained between the boy and his destination. Having little alternative, the boy released the hair and dove into the icy moat below. The thought of an alligator, snake, moat monster or worse were the last thoughts on his mind as he entered the water. He nearly made the shore before he was wet, and jumping to dry land turned and looked to the window above.

"What a MOM!" the boy whispered to himself. Turning, he took off, running like the wind to the forest protection surrounding the eastern end of the castle, just avoiding barking dogs and pursuing guard.

Chapter 11
A City Alucemet

> AN ANXIOUS HEART WEIGHS A MAN DOWN,
> BUT A KIND WORD CHEERS HIM UP.
> PROVERBS 12:25

Robyn of Hobinsiefken had spent a restless night considering the disastrous town hall meeting. True to habit, he arose that morning greeting the early morning dawn. Traditionally the new day brought joy, and he would awake refreshed, ready for a new challenge. The act of governing this fair city, however, and his zest for life at this point seemed but a distant and irretrievable memory. Of late, the new day brought a sickening feeling deep within his gut, and though the day wore on and events came and went, their distraction did nothing to relieve him of it. A dread, a fear, a hopelessness: in times past these emotions were foreign to Robyn, a man who would attack the world with joy and excitement, anticipating the challenge of each new day. It seemed that *the Pygmalion plagues* as he called it secretly and only to himself, were beginning to wear upon and threaten his lofty dreams.

He found this morning an extreme effort to prepare for the day. Shaving at such a time of distraction can be dangerous, for the straight razor is unforgiving to the wandering mind. While cuts and nicks were becoming more common to this once steady-handed man, the painful discomfort could still not distract him from his desperate thoughts.

His mind returned to events and trends that he wished to forget. Times so obviously crucial with the retrospective mind, he wondered whether timely action could have diverted this present predicament. The comfortable mind seldom sees crucial change at the time, for the perception of success cloud and breed contentment for things as they are.

As he shaved, Robin replayed the sad turn of events repeatedly within his tormented mind. He was hard upon himself as no one else and lamented decisive action that might have changed the condition of things. His mind returned painfully to his disjointed tirade expressed the night before and the unforgivable vulnerability that the Boar had used to perfection with him. The memory was embarrassing, resulting in a sour grimace and another nick to his poorly kept profile. "For what purpose?" he said to himself shaking his head. An official end to his grooming arrived as he tossed his razor down and wiped his face with a dry towel.

His walk along the quarter mile to his office was automatic, the to and from journey traveled as clock work each day since the man was unanimously elected Mayor of the city of Alucemet, some ten years prior. In the past, the Mayor would pass secure and happy cottages of citizens. Along his route, people would wave to the man, but now most kept to themselves. The streets and front yards were empty this morning, for the citizens seldom journeyed outside anymore; any trip was accomplished quickly and for only mandatory chores. The dejected man imagined them sitting within shadows of their homes eyeing him with accusatory looks. Today the absence of citizens along his route further reinforced the Mayor's isolation and self-inflicted blame.

The thatch-roofed cottages and brightly painted homes along the lane were in disrepair, unlike ever before. In times past, wide inviting windows and doors beckoned the traveler to stop for welcome and friendly conversation. More often than not, those same citizens would be minding their beautiful gardens in the peaceful beauty of the Alucemet morning. Many jolly men and women would greet this most respected citizen with open homes, for this single Mayor was married in practice to the good of their city, and the citizens loved the man. They would offer fresh baked goods and friendly hellos. Wonderful fragrances from cooling pastries and ovens would engulf him as he made his way to the center of town. These fond recollections disappeared as he recalled that they were from a past world with little resemblance to the dispirited and run down humanity of late. As he continued his journey, the Mayor defensively pushed his surroundings from his mind; today he wished not to dwell upon this demented spectacle again. His desire was unsuccessful, however, for he could not forget these problems so easily.

As he continued walking to the center of town, the Mayor wondered how things had unraveled so quickly. One day his world was secure and the next so out of control. Who was the culprit behind this evil decline? Why to the Mayor there could only be one suspect! Could that foul, porcine, corpulent creature, whose ignorance conflicted ironically with his power over people, one whose rank, fetid, and foul appearance matched only the rusty stained sky that had gradually enveloped this once beautiful country be responsible? Yes, the answer was so obvious and simple. He had sensed as much when he first became aware of the oily, pestilent, carunculous nemesis. The Boar, whose vanity now insisted on the title, was the guilty one. The creature orchestrated an evil, precipitous decline, and now heaven help the people of Alucemet.

The night's meeting confirmed many of his worst fears. King William was absent, his presence sourly missed and so important. It appeared superficially that the King supported the Boar's actions in absentia, a troubling conclusion. The Queen's disapproval was obvious, her disgust made apparent by her quiet entrance and sudden disappearance, but her power to change the country's course seemed feeble. Rumors of the disappearance of the eldest son, Alexander, were confirmed. The Mirrorlass, with its promise of unlimited power, evidently was not in the boy's possession, but rather in the enemies' hands. While created for good, in evil custody the worst nightmare became a definite possibility. In addition, what was he to conclude about references to the boy's cowardice? It sat poorly in the mind of the Mayor, for strength and bravery always characterized this royal son.

Disturbing as well was the fate of the younger son, Nicholas. Rumors of piracy on the high seas had circulated. While a free spirit of sorts, with unmatched skills upon the sea, criminal behavior was out of character for the boy. And with his kingdom's demise, his betrayal of good could only suggest hopelessness in this once royal and quite proper prince. To believe as well that Alexander had in fact met his fate at the hands of his once loving and loyal brother just served to reinforce the despondency of the Mayor's situation.

His walk to town was nearing completion. It was cool that morning, but the foul rust color was already rising in the usually blue Alucemet sky. The streets were near empty this dawn. Those walking past the Mayor did so without friendly acknowledgement, representing a lost and troubled persona. These good citizens relied upon him, but this morning his troubles distracted his mind, and their questioning glances received little more than a disgruntled nod.

A small crowd gathered within the town center as the Mayor entered the city. Posted upon the town's withering central stage, a public decry garnered silent attention of those who could read, and many who did not. Those who posted it had just completed their errand, nailing the parchment to the timber that rose from the raised wooden platform in the center of the town's central courtyard. The towns' folk came to expect the worst these days, and they stood in silence expecting the same.

This decry was shocking, even in this time of hopelessness. During the proceeding days, rumors of treachery were rampant, and now the document officially confirmed the worst fears. Robyn slowly crossed the dirt road, standing upon the dying grass at the rear of the stunned crowd and read the notice sadly.

<u>**Sir Alexander of Alucemet**</u>
Slain by the traitor,
Nicholas the Blue

Pirates, Scoundrels, and Kings

To the town's folk, the seal of the Laughing Lion in the corner of the document proved its authenticity. Offering a reward for his capture, the announcement went on to detail the outlaw's sentence of death. Those who could read did so in hushed whispers to others. Those who showed any emotion just shook their lowered heads in defeat, while most walked away returning sadly to their various livelihoods.

One of the braver residents stared blankly at the Mayor as he turned and returned to the day's tasks. His sadden gaze communicated the tragedy that they all felt. He stopped on his way passed him, almost as an afterthought. He stood now looking at his boots for a moment not knowing what to say. "When shall it stop Mayor?" the man did not bother to wait for the answer that the Mayor did not have.

It was just another of those all too common disappointing days for the city and its devoted Mayor. Announcements such of these, they had come to expect. People slowly resigned to this siege as their happy and once secure world began to tear apart. Privileges and freedoms slowly eroded, and the citizens lived in fear of what awaited them next.

An offhand remark of another citizen did little to change the dreaded atmosphere that plagued the mental spirit of his city. "And just a score ago, that writ forbidding pork partaking, why Mayor how shall it prejudice our Ladies Feast?" The man referred sadly to the Queen's yearly celebration at which tradition would have roast pig served at the people's table, a food recently ruled unlawful by similar decry. Robyn of Hobinsiefken turned, dropped his head with sadness, and resignedly shuffled slowly to his office across the town square.

The Mayor felt burdened; he hoped for some relief, but expected none. The pig-eared ones, those marked by the Boar, became an increasingly common sight. Treason, laws outlawing roast pork, rumors of required slop pits on each street corner, and many other changes supporting porcine privileges, were now everyday occurrences.

As Robyn left the town center, deeply resigned to the truth of the royal boy's treachery and fatal conflict, and walking in oblivion towards his office, he passed an odd boy without a glance. Such an observer as Robyn would not have missed such a visitor in days past. Missed he was however, and by everyone else as well, as the town center cleared. A wet and dirty boy, shivering and dressed in skateboard shoes, his laces today surprisingly placed just so, walked alone through the town.

CHRISTOPHER SPENT A COLD, LONELY, frightening night, wandering without direction through the woods, after his narrow escape and drenching in the royal moat. His experience in this uncomfortably real world so far dashed his childlike dreams of castles, battle, knights, and prisons, one after the other, and he found himself now quite discouraged. **B**y chance he came upon an obvious city that morning and now stood off to the side of the town-square observing some type of public gathering. The square slowly cleared of citizens as the first ray of sun light appeared, giving a modicum of warmth to the wet and starving stranger.

From his perspective, the boy recognized many men as castle guards from the night before. Each was a shabbily dressed hooligan, with bland affect, idiotic grin, and pig-like ears. They had nailed some document to a wooden stage, attracting a crowd. Without apology they roughly brushed aside the citizens, plodding through the crowd, arrogantly expecting them to step away or face trampling under their shiny black boats.

Their leader remained mounted, sitting proudly on his horse off to the side of the crowd, eyeing his accomplices as they returned and mounted their horses. He too was familiar to Christopher, for the Ogre was a hard individual to forget. He had impressed the boy, with all his gaudy medallions upon his chest, and obvious delight in other's misfortune. He wore an ignorant grin and a gleeful howl, seeming to laugh continuously to himself.

The man seemed a blundering buffoon, but the Ogre's horse was quite a different matter. Always superior in intellect to his rider, the stead stared across the square at Chris, leaving a feeling of doom upon the already frightened and cold visitor.

Christopher recognized the Mayor as well, disheveled, a seemingly fallen hero, so out of control of the situation. The boy watched sadly as the man turned dejectedly with head hung low, and walked alone across the town center right past the boy.

The informal gathering was just ending. The Ogre and his men turned and raced away. Sufficiently convinced of the writ's distraught meaning, the people scattered, most disappearing into shops that lined the town square.

Chris stood off to the side until the square was empty. Feeling safe now, he crossed to the posted writ. The boy had a premonition of the document's content and moved slowly, hoping to be wrong. Standing in front of the wooden platform the boy tried to decipher the news. Posted here was a thick paper document covered with a flowing script, something you might see in an old Bible, the young boy decided. He recalled the day of LionBall, and his brief view of the eminent and overwhelming ambush. At the time of the conflict, the enemies were faceless people in the distance. The ghost girl saved him from a similar fate, pulling him away before he could witness the completion of the evil deed. The odds that day seemed overwhelming, and he never doubted the outcome, Alexander hopelessly outnumbered, and surprise on the stalker's side. Standing alone, Christopher read the text confirming his suspicion, the official appearing document confirming his friend's recent demise and supporting the references of tragedy heard in the town meeting. But was he really killed by his brother? It was difficult to believe.

"Poor dude," Chris winced to himself as he recalled that scene. Shaking his head the boy whispered, "Blown away by your little brother!"

He wondered what must have gone wrong in that family. Fights with his brothers were common, but certainly not fatal. Ambush and demise, it was so foreign to the boy whose only contact with such brutality was in video games. Even the Gulf War against Iraq was not real, rather an exciting series of television images fought out in Nintendo like machines, and sprawled out, without reality across the television screen. Here he had nearly witnessed a slaughter in real life, or was there such a thing as real life in this peculiar and illusionary world? Such brutal behavior was foreign to the boy. This rogue of a boy, Nicholas the Blue, was frightening. He decided that like a return to the castle, like another visit to a prison, meeting the boy was something he would rather avoid. The boy put his hand within his britches pocket, deep in thought, staring up at the document.

"Belief in such rot leaves little hope for the gullible," spoke a voice from behind the boy.

Chris turned with a start, expecting to be towered over and driven from the city by one of the citizens, angered by his presence. To his surprise, however, standing behind him was not an irate adult, but rather a confident young boy distinguished by a black eye-patch over his left eye. The boy wore an open necked white shirt and torn trousers that reached to his mid-calf. He had sun bleached light-brown hair visible only in the back, covered in front by a black bandanna tied with a large knot over his right temple. In addition to his patch, his shoes left an impression on Chris as well. *Hook, Captain Hook.* Like the pirate captain of fantasy, this boy stood in black shoes with square buckles of polished silver. With a ring in his left ear lobe and this garb, Chris decided that this could only be a pirate-boy.

Chris might just have well not been there, for the boy stood gazing past Chris with his one uncovered right eye staring with disgust and obvious anger at the posted document. He jumped to the wooden platform and quickly wiggled his way up the timber. Grabbing the writ with a flourish, he tore it from the post and dropped to the ground. The pirate-boy grimaced angrily as he read the announcement, silently ignoring Chris. Crumbling it violently, he dashed it to the ground and crushed the paper with his buckled shoes into the dusty street.

Pirates, Scoundrels, and Kings

As with his appearance and without another word, the boy swaggered confidently away. With an open surprised mouth, Chris watched the boy saunter away in silence.

"Hey, boy-- I'm lost—wait—dude!" Chris yelled as the pirate-boy disappeared into a shop at the edge of the square, quickly moving through swinging doors which shut behind him with a thump. Once again, Chris was alone.

The town square stood surrounded by shops, which in the past were bustling with commerce. Not a friendly place now, the town square stood deserted, each shop closed shut, windows tightly shuttered and their doors secured against entry. The morning was warming quickly as the sun made its way higher into the rust-colored sky. A foul and stale smell became apparent as well as whenever evil was present in this world.

Now he was alone again, knowing no one, not knowing where to turn or where to get his next meal. Faced with this abandoned feeling, he wondered if anyone cared where he might spend the rest of his life in this troubled world.

Strangers were the only option for the moment. The Mayor looked pitiful, and Chris feared that he might recognize him from the castle. Hunger and loneliness dominated his emotions; the pirate-boy was his same size, he looked like the best bet. Chris now stuck out to find him, Del Taco dominating his mind.

The town square was the center of this deserted and sad little town. It stood at the crossing of two wide, dusty, cobblestoned roads that stretched off into the distance. Around the square and along these roads stood shops with a common wall between their neighbors, each closed tightly and without any sign of habitation. An eerie quiet surrounded the place, replacing the activity and muffled dissatisfaction that earlier filled the square. It was as if the people feared the worst, perhaps seeing too much of that lately and disappearing for their safety.

To his left, the road led out of the commercial area of the town, leading eventually to homes with quaint cottage visages, thatched roofs and ginger bread details obvious in the distance. The homes were shut up as well by the same frightened group whose defeated attitude was apparent in the cracked and weathered rainbow colors that once gave a fairy tale feel to a proud town. Disuse and decay now sat before him, rutted streets with pools of mud stretched in each direction.

These pools of mud seemed out of place and caught Christopher's eye. It was quite odd, for they seemed to be the only maintained aspect of the town. Each street corner had its own sunken pool of orderly arranged muck. If not filled with mud, they could have served as civic wading pools. Jacuzzi jets would serve them well if electricity existed. The irony of a well-tended mud hole in a decaying dying city was curiously apparent to this observant modern day boy.

"Where is the MacDonald's?" the boy sighed with remorse as he crossed the street to the boarded-up shops before him.

Chris first encountered the town cobbler's shop. Stepping up to the wooden walkway running parallel to the town businesses, he stopped for the moment to examine the cobbler's products displayed in a dirty bay window. Unlike the modern day shoe stores, in which rows of nearly identical shoes are on display, the cobbler's shop seemed to be one of a craftsman. Here was essentially the only open window in the town, and within it were displayed an array of partially constructed leather footwear, all in various degrees of construction and repair. Shoes of all sizes filled the window. Shoes with worn soles, torn leather uppers, and an occasional completed and expertly repaired cousin of their worn counterpart, filled the shop's bay, most not in the cobbler's shop for their first repair. The majority of these shoes in Chris's world, if shoes of this sort existed at all, arrived in the trash, their disposal much more economical than their repair. However, shoes with this leather and artisanship were marked a different value in the medieval world of Alucemet.

In a dark rear corner of the window, a particularly unusual pair of shoes caught the boy's attention. While newness seemed a rare commodity in the shop's display, these were shoes recently sewn and cut of fresh material. They were fashioned in light-colored leather, something not seen in any other pair before him. Streaked upon one heel was a test splotch of navy blue dye, a color certainly out of place for the time. The shoes were of low top construction, and pierced eyes for future laces began just above the toe and continued well up the front of the shoe. The sole was flat with no heel, unusually thick, soft, and spongy. The interior of the shoe was lined with soft layers of cloth unlike the simple construction of the unlined leather medieval shoe. A tongue had been fashioned as well, and while some of the other shoes within the window did as well lace up their front, this structure separating the front halves of the shoe was unique.

Glancing down at his own shoes, Chris realized that here was a lovingly crafted product resembling his own beloved skateboard shoes. It struck him as odd, for certainly the tennis shoe would wait centuries to be historically correct, and the tennis court from which its name was taken did not exist in a world where jousting in knight's armor was in style.

As Chris considered the shoes, a knurled and stained hand appeared from behind the curtain, quickly grabbing the same partially finished shoes, and whisking them away from his view. He had thought that he was alone, and the move startled the boy. It suggested that here was a prototypical secret, the revealing of which might turn the tides of some hidden economic or political revolution. A bearded, deeply-lined face with big bushy eyebrows attached to a scowling patron appeared at the window.

"Oh—" the frightened boy yelled, jumping back from the window.

"And for what brings such as you, odd boy?" the man yelled through the glass pane. "These are not for the likes of you, now shoo!" The man snarled, punctuating his fury by pounding viciously upon the glass pane.

It seemed as if these shoes were secret, hidden innocently in the window corner, meant not for viewing especially by a strange foreign boy. As quickly as he appeared the man was gone, and the wooden shudders covering the window closed shut with a pointed thud. The shop again appeared deserted, and once more the boy was alone.

Chris looked intensely at the closed shop window with startled widely open eyes. He hyperventilated briefly and his heart raced in his chest. Taking one slow deep breath, he turned and sat with anger upon the raised wooden walkway that ran in front of each shop forgetting his hunger. He hung his head in both hands for the moment. He was alone.

"Odd boy, I'm always the odd boy! That dude scared me." Thinking for the moment he lifted his head and yelled at the top of his lungs, "What's up with the shoes, you--, you—old--shoemaker! He's probably a little girl shoe freak!" Chris thought to himself. I wish I was home, no more fighting with my brothers vowed the lamenting boy. Chris regained his composure. He stood and walked down towards the doors through which the pirate-boy disappeared.

The pirate-boy had disappeared across the square into one of the shops ahead. Arriving at the door where he had entered, Chris found himself in front of a tavern. With double swinging doors like the cowboy saloon, Chris thought immediately: no children admitted without parent or guardian. The thought brought a smile to his face as he realized the absurdity of that statement in his situation, and he wished for once that he was with whatever a guardian was.

Stepping back he looked to a sign above the door identifying the shop. The Boisterous Boar, Ye Old Pub was written in chiseled letters on a splintery sign hanging from the edge of the roof, the boisterous portion partially blackened with tar. The sign then actually read: The Boar, Ye Old Pub, the tar an obvious attempt to remove the less than complimentary, but ironically descriptive adjective. This adjective was in the climate of the time, politically incorrect. The sign, as everything else in sight, was treated with neglect and hung agar.

"A pub--what's a pub?" Chris asked silently to himself? He chewed on his lower lip as he searched his memory. The term pub was foreign to him, but the resemblance to a saloon worried the boy. He certainly was not old enough to enter a saloon, he thought. Considering his plight, Christopher convinced himself that pub referred to public, a term that was less threatening. It was to this pub, or public that he decided his best chance for food and friendship might lie.

The double-hung doors to The Boisterous Boar were as well in disrepair and neglect, sagging in their middle and seriously needing a coat of varnish. One door had almost fallen away from its hinges and opened with great difficulty. Chris entered the tavern; the saloon doors creaked closed behind him, leaving him alone in a dark foreboding place.

Standing in the entry of the tavern, Chris blinked rapidly as his eyes began to adjust to the darkness. In front of the boy stood rough-cut wooden tables and matching stools, scattered carelessly across the room. There was a rank odor and a gritty feeling to the wooden floor below him, suggesting months of debris tossed and left to rot. The plank floor was uneven with many of the dato joints broken and lacking proper care. Some crude saloon-like paintings hung on the wall to his left, drooping, discarded, and needing adjustment. Across the room Chris could just make out a waist-high counter top spanning the opposite wall. Behind it, a hallway lit with a single hanging yellow candle disappeared in the distance.

Christopher crossed the floor heading towards the candlelight. He tripped in the dark on a raised floorboard, falling to his hands and knees. Embarrassed, he quickly jumped to his feet, and by habit looked around to assure himself that no one was witness to his graceless fall. "Ya right, dude, nobody here," he chuckled, reassuring and mumbling to himself.

Carefully now, Chris continued across the room. As he neared the bar, he stopped, suddenly aware for the first time of a hulk-like profile standing behind the counter.

"Wow, ah--" he screamed, stopping in his tracks.

The man was standing silently behind the bar, his profile lit from behind by the pale light of the hallway, watching Chris cross the room, hidden menacingly deep in the shadows. A blink of two threatening yellow eyes were all that betrayed him as a living being.

"Hey dude, you scared me," the boy blurted out with a nervous laugh. Approaching the man for help was the only alternative that Chris could see. He was deep within the tavern, and to turn and run would betray him as an intruder. The air hung dead and stifling, and sweat dripped from the brow of the frightened boy. Hoping for a friendly gesture, Chris stretched out his hand in friendship and forced a silly smile.

The man was not interested in friendly discourse with Chris, however. He stood in silence, gnawing a stubby finger, and watching the boy without sympathy.

Chris tried to calm himself, taking several deep breaths in succession. His heart stopped pounding, and he wiped his brow of sweat. He needed help, and this man, unfortunately, looked to be his only chance. The boy was alone, cold, hungry, and tired. He was the survivor of a trip to a dark locked dungeon, drug through the brush by a ghost, shocked into this world by a cloud, and a visit to the restroom was sorely in need. With resignation, he approached the counter. Finding a barstool missing one leg, Chris sat down carefully with both elbows on the counter top, head supported between his hands, and a fearless facade upon his face.

"You, ah--got any food?" the young boy asked, opening a conversation hesitantly with the silent hulk. Chris had never been one to mince words. His style was to end unanswered question with another, especially when anxious.

"Well sure you do—ha--this is a restaurant, isn't it? I mean—a—tavern--I mean a tub, no--pub. Ha, Ha--Ya, that's what I mean, a pub, this is a pub isn't it?"

The man stared coldly at the boy, his only response an occasional blink.

"Ya sure--it is," Chris said, completing the question for the man. "Anything would be good dude—but—but--oh ya, I don't have any money." Looking down at the bar, Chris began thinking rapidly. Glancing up again at the man and trying to smile his most likeable smile, he continued, "I know! Could I charge it? You know—plastic--American Express." He said trying to hide the fact that he did not carry one. Then it struck him; he really did not know what American Express was! A quick review brought only the saying: never leave home without it, and he could not be any farther away from home. In addition, the boy never understood why one could purchase as much as you wanted with a plastic card. Truthfully, he had never really paid for anything in his life, much less a meal. On second thought, he had paid for video games, however, these machines guzzled his father's coins up so fast, were coins really money? "What's up with a penny anyway?" he wondered to himself. Could you really use the copper coin, or was it just an item to fill empty bottles and drawers? Yes, money certainly was a perplexing issue for the young boy, an issue he rapidly wished he understood better.

To add to his confusion, he must deal with the intimidating hulk behind the counter. "React, say something please, don't just blink," Chris yelled to himself in frustration!

Then unexpectedly, the beginning of a small smile began to turn up from one corner of the man's mouth. As it broadened, broken decayed teeth became visible within a stubbly, unshaven face, betraying a glimmer of humor within a hard heart. The tavern-minder turned slowly without a word and made his way toward the lighted hall behind him.

"Hello, sweet!" The boy whispered to himself excitedly.

Hunger forced him to see progress in the grizzly man's response. Maybe cash did not matter in this world.

"Yess--" Chris whispered again, slapping a closed fist on the bar top in starving victory, smiling and shaking his head in excitement. The man was preparing a meal for the boy; he was sure of it. A wonderful salivary reflex began with dreams of a Big Mac. "How about a delicious Taco Supreme Grande! No, no...wait, a Carl's Junior Bacon Western Double Cheeseburger, sloppy style, oh please," he begged in anticipatory silence.

Thinking now of dessert, his mind went to Mom at Nordstrom's, and he pictured himself ordering: "one half short espresso mocha decaf cappuccino blizzard, and oh, ya--forget the white junk, ya that's it!"

Chris was so hungry; his dog Gidget's bowl began to appear in his mind as a fine restaurant. "Horse meat would fine," he thought to himself.

"Well, wait a minute," he said, recalling the jaundice-eyed horse. "A rat would be great, that is, like—well-cooked, maybe burned-like, and tons of catsup." He did not need to know the rodent's origin, just serve it, and don't tell me, he thought with acceptance in his mind. The boy sat very excited, brushing off the dusty tavern bar, expectantly preparing a place for what certainly would be an appreciated meal.

The man appeared again abruptly. He rudely tossed a wooden bowl filled with warmed muck, floating chunks of just what, the boy was afraid to ask. Consistent with its uncertain origin, the foulest smell anyone who hated leftovers could have imagined rose from the bowl, rising in steam and filling the boy's sensitive nose.

"Garbage?" the boy said, gazing in disgust at this culinary atrocity. "He cooked me a bowl of garbage?" Lamenting to himself, as dreams of fast food delicacies disappeared, Chris looked up from the bowl hoping that the man was just joking with him. The tavern-minder was laughing alright; his affect suggested, however, that he was doing so at the boy's expense. Saddened, Chris stared down at the bowl as the man walked slowly away.

"Gruel--and of a taste more worthy than its aroma," A small voice said from the shadows.

The voice startled Chris. Beside the tavern-minder, who now leaned on the wall staring at him with a satisfied smile, he thought he was alone. Sitting in the shadows, however, sat the pirate-boy, who trying to hide his amusement, rose and walked to the modern day boy's side.

"Come now lad, eat up! You will be wanting for less if you pass up Mac's famous gruel. You shan't worry; the beast died a noble death, just a few moments ago." The pirate-boy laughed loudly, Chris's disgusted reaction amusing him greatly. He picked up the steaming bowl of broth and tossed a golden coin down on the bar top. With a hand on his shoulder, the boy led Chris to a candlelit table at the rear of the pub. The pirate-boy retrieved two chairs tossed to the floor, pulled them upright to the table. He set the bowl on the table, sat in one of the chairs, and signaled for Chris to do likewise.

"Mac's not the bad chap. Mind you, there's one not to be trusted," he added after further thought. "You best eat up," he said, pointing to the bowl. "Meals are rare and friends few in the time of the Boar." Reaching for the bowl, the boy pushed it slowly towards him.

The pirate-boy looked slightly older in the dim yellow light, perhaps a year or two younger than Chris. A mischievous grin and a twinkle from his unpatched left eye encouraged the modern day boy. "It ain't half bad, go on now, eat up," he said, rising from his chair and returning for a moment to the bar.

With hesitation, Chris tasted a drop of the putrid liquid. He found to his surprise that the gruel tasted much better than he imagined, hunger most likely switching off his very selective palate. Soon he was gulping down the entire bowl and licking the bottom with enthusiasm.

The pirate-boy returned to the table with a loaf of coarse black bread. At home of course, Chris and his brothers were all very certain, no bread but white bread ever. Here, however, the boy ate the bread and every last crumb with glee.

With his meal finished, Chris pushed the bowl aside and smiled with gracious satisfaction at the boy. Realizing that his face betrayed his last meal, he laughed and wiped his mouth with his hand. As he looked across the table at the pirate-boy, something about his appearance struck him as different. Chris replayed in his mind the morning's scene involving the writ's announcement and the pirate-boy's appearance. The left eye wore the patch this morning, he thought to himself. He was sure of this, and now the patch sat covering his right eye. Chris did not want to call attention to the boy's disability, but it bothered him. Hunger could have affected his memory, however, the more he thought, the more he looked, the more sure he was. This boy had worn the eye patch over the left eye this morning, and now it covered his right.

"By what title goes you?" the pirate-boy asked.

The question broke his chain of thought, and Chris realized that he had been staring at him quite intensely. Certainly any pirate he was familiar with was cruel and vicious. A pirate may not take staring as polite. Would he draw his sword and run him in, the boy worried? Chris glanced away and tried to focus elsewhere.

"My title goes Christopher—ah--Christopher of Temecula," he added, again dropping effortlessly into kingly jargon.

"Ah yes, Christopher, a good and strong name," the pirate-boy said, glancing down at his new friend's waist.

Alexander had told Chris that one should not be without a piece of stout rope in this world, and he had taken to wearing a strip of rope for a belt immediately ever since. The pirate-boy's attention, however, now made Chris a little uncomfortable. "You like my belt?" he wondered, looking up at the boy.

"I have seen such advice before," said the pirate-boy quite seriously. "A certain prince councils his men on its importance." Looking up at Chris, the pirate-boy stared with a questioning look.

Chris looked down at the floor, not knowing what to say. The boy was a pirate, a pirate-boy but a pirate all the same. He had been quite upset over the accusatory document that denounced Nicholas as a traitor and Alexander's murderer. Was he now in danger? Chris looked up at the boy with a forced smile; he found himself afraid to answer the boy.

While waiting for his reply, the pirate-boy turned his attention to the bar across the floor. Something had caught his attention, and he began to scowl, seeming to forget the question.

Christopher tended to forget that in this world danger was always around the corner. The pirate-boy, however, did not forget, and drawing his dagger he stood quickly looking over the boy's shoulder and across the tavern. A child in appearance but with adult-like awareness, the pirate-boy was both and something troubled him.

Chris pushed back his chair and stood. "What's wrong dude?" he said quietly to the boy, turning and looking over his shoulder at the bar. Mac was gone, the candle lighting the back hallway out, and a rear door was closing shut with a thud. Chris's heart began to race again, his relaxing meal now a piece of history.

"Mind you, there's one not to be trusted." The pirate-boy repeated deliberately to himself in an irritated tone. "Oh, such a witless fool!" he said loudly. "And what did I think, the show of a doubloon! On return it'll be wrath for me in camp!" he spoke with a frenzy. The pirate-boy grabbed Chris's hand, pulled him around, and led him quickly across the darkened floor. "We must leave at once. They'll be at us soon!" The excited boy yelled over his shoulder to Chris.

They crossed the floor with abandon, tripping in the dark over strewn, broken chairs, and the loose planked floor. A troubling, all too familiar pattern was developing here, pulled with abandon through escape after escape. Chris now followed the pirate-boy, his hand strangled within the boy's, as he ran for his life.

They moved quickly to the rear of the tavern, burst through a tiny rear door, and turned into a darkened alley. Run-down buildings overhung the narrow roadway and their bulky shadows and a rust-colored haze darkened their path.

The alley was cold, wet, and the smell of decaying garbage overwhelmed the modern day boy's sensitive nose. Rats would love the place he decided as the two made their escape, barreling for their lives along the narrow alley. Chris stumbled as he ran, trash and debris scattered across their path at random places along the way making their escape difficult.

Just ahead the alley ended, crossed by a cobblestone street. Sensing danger at this point the pirate-boy dove and rolled into the shadows of the adjacent building. Pulling Chris behind him, they now sprawled on one another cowering in the shadows. Recovering quickly, they sat upon their knees viewing the intersection. Chris was about to question the boy when he lifted a finger to his mouth and whispered, "silence my friend," and then leaving nothing to chance, he raised his open hand and covered Chris's gasping mouth.

Sitting silently within the shadows, they heard the sound of an iron-shod horse approaching from their right, quickly bearing down upon the two hiding boys. The rider slid to a stop in front of them and stared for a long while in each direction. It was the Ogre of 'O' sitting in front of the boys on his much more intelligent horse. The man did not detect the two frightened boys as they pushed themselves into the wall, but as they held their breath and prayed in the shadows, the horse seemed to.

Even an average person gains wisdom by knowing his limitations and using superior minds to his advantage. However, the 'O' was not an average man, rather much less so. So while sitting upon a wise stallion, a horse so much more than the mind of the man, the 'O' was not sensitive to the whims of his horse. The beast pawed the ground, whinnied in equine language, and tried in vain to turn his bridled neck in the fugitives' direction. Not heading the horse's warning, the man rode away against his beast's most sincere objections.

With each day, it seemed the modern day boy was growing accustomed to events such as this. Accustomed did not imply enjoyment, however, and while in the past Chris longed for such a chase, he was now becoming weary, the consequences of capture outweighing the excitement.

Chris was aware roughly of his pursuant, but the motive behind his interest in him still eluded the frightened boy. His heroes, who made up the bulk of his prior life, seemed always decisive when faced with situations such as this. Chris wondered if he would do honor to those buffed cartoon characters that always succeeded and fought for the good of the world.

Chris and the pirate-boy remained in the shadows, huddling against the building. To Chris he seemed to be a boy hardened by the streets and wise beyond his years. As an action film critic, he was impressed. For while the other paths seemed more obvious, without delay he moved out, following their assailant's path from the rear, with distance and silence protecting them.

Confidently the young leader spoke to Chris over his shoulder as they ran. "Be of haste Christopher of Temecula. Luck shines well upon you...forth the spilith runs!" he said, pointing ahead.

"The *spilith* runs? Dude, that doesn't sound good," Chris said under his breath, running for his life, committed to following the pirate-boy. One should not count upon luck, for luck is a passing fancy, and pass it did once more.

He appeared out of the shadows, along the right wall of shops that lined their route of escape, one hundred meters or so ahead. Inching slowly into their path, he waited, knowing their location all the time. This time it was Fordem, the man on the jaundice-eyed horse.

Fright gripped the boy once again. "Fordem--that dude's bad!" Chris whispered to his friend.

Chris had information the man wished to suppress. Fordem had deliberately used his incompetent associate to set this well-thought-out trap. He used Ogelby to flush the two into running, knowing the incompetent would neither grasp the identity of their prey nor capture them. The 'O' given all his faults was valuable to Fordem here, for he would never report something that he did not understand, and he never understood anything that he could report.

The two boys slid to a crashing halt in front of their enemy. Before them stood a huge, towering, evil horse, staring at the two boys with disdain. The animal snorted at the boys, his jaundiced, slightly-crossed eyes penetrating their psyche with evil intent. The horse's powerful hooves pawed the ground in delight as the two stood with hands clasped, their confidence quickly shattered. Fordem sat upon his horse, cloaked in a black hood, and covered with deep shadows.

Chris whispered again, "Fordem."

The man's whip was soon to follow, clear and deafening, the snap so close to their heads that Chris could smell the leather. Fordem raised his whip for a second pass. Quickly, the pirate-boy pulled Chris to the side and rolled on the cobblestone street avoiding the tyrant's lash. As they rolled clear of the menace they found themselves in a heap, each now rising and scampering away to avoid the next assault.

The whip snapped, and Fordem directed his powerful steed ahead to intercept the boys. They had a small jump on their pursuer, and quickly turned down the alley, finding some safety in the darkness. Behind them, the whip snapped again, and their pursuer followed quickly after the two.

A wooden awning, designed to house refuse cans and attached to the back of a broken-down shop, backed up to their alley prison. The boys sped around the corner and into the alley, dropped to the ground, falling and rolling under the covering. It was their only chance, for their hunter and equine partner were quickly upon them, and the man did not seem inclined to take prisoners.

They leaped beneath the lean-to in desperation. Here the two boys hoped that the rotting wooden structure would give them at least a moment to collect their thoughts. Once within the shaky shelter, the pirate-boy turned to Chris, his face for the first time showing fright. "And whom might you be, Christopher of Temecula?" The pirate-boy gasped between labored breaths. Beads of sweat had formed upon his brow and were flowing down his scraped and abraded cheek. The pirate-boy was angry with Chris, realizing that the boy was a major deterrent to his continued survival. "Fordem... and why such an interest in the likes of you?"

Chris was not sure how to answer the boy. "Me?" he said. "Dude, I--I'm just a kid like you, but I saw things, and at the castle."

"Of course, I knew as much." The pirate-boy said with a spit. "Not the doubloon; your countenance tipped them off." The pirate-boy knew their assailant as well, and from the man's position of power a young boy would never cause such an interest unless he had or knew something.

The man roared down on them again, cracking his whip with snapping percussion. The pirate-boy quickly dropped his concern and put these thoughts aside; survival was now the priority. The man whipped their shelter, shattering pieces of roof as he lashed. Intermittently, the dogged villain cast the whip under the covering, bouncing the leather tentacles and grasping for the two boys.

When Fordem's whip did not succeed in getting to the two boys, he followed with his devil horse. The beast was coaxed, more likely allowed, to bash repeatedly the wooden cover which now was the only thing separating them from their aggressor. The hooves crashed down in perfect rhythm, casting a deafening sound echoing in the alley. The splinters flew, and the roof began to collapse under an overwhelming assault. It was only a matter of time before the horse would finish the shelter and crush the two hiding boys. Flight now was certainly out of the question, for between the boys and freedom was the horse and the closed end of the foul smelling alley. Trapped again.

Chris found himself removing his rope belt without thought. He was beginning to develop insight into these troubled matters, a trait that even MacGyver would have saluted. Chris fashioned the middle portion of the fraying hemp braids into a quick noose. Tossing one end to the pirate-boy, he directed him to secure it. His colleague completed his duty by knotting the end and wedging it securely between two of the twisted upright frames supporting the now nearly collapsed roof. The powerful hooves continued to crash down on the splintering shelter, and the whip cracked in rhythm as the angry man continued to pummel the boys mercilessly. From below, it became obvious to the two that the horse would soon split the roof and crush them. Their foe was succeeding, for with each lunge from the huge animal, the splinters were flying, and the center of the roof flexed down towards the prisoners, beginning to crack, an obvious prelude to a total collapse.

It was just a matter of time; a few more horse hoof blows, and their precarious shelter would tumble down on them. Chris held the noose to the roof, centering it upon the expected entry site of the hoof. The pirate-boy sensed the plan without speaking. With one end of the noose now wedged tightly, he quickly moved around the boy and held the free end of the rope, ready to close their trap at just the right instant.

With the horse's last kick, the splintered cover gave way. Cracking and tearing away a small section of the awning, the hoof appeared suddenly, blasting through the awning. Christopher quickly slipped the noose over the horse's hoof and the pirate-boy pulled the free end of the rope, tightening the noose down on the horse's shank. With their entire weight and strength applied to the free end of the rope, they cinched the noose down on the horse's powerful forefoot, trapping their prey securely. Quickly, the boys lashed the rope to the supports, securing and gaining a brief reprieve from attack. While it could not last given the beast's incredible power, it served a purpose of disrupting and trapping the evil pair for the moment.

The horseman realized instantly that he had fallen into the boys' snare. His beast was frightened, frustrated, and unable to release its trapped forefoot. Recoiling violently, the black horse snorted and whinnied angrily, bucking and pulling, attempting to release itself. Fordem yelled hysterically at the horse. He was furious and began to direct his whip to the rear haunches of the trapped beast.

The pirate-boy emerged cautiously from the wooden shelter. He admired the site of the trapped assailants humorously, and their plight greatly pleased the boy. Loud sputtering and cussing came from the horseman who clung tenaciously to the bucking and fuming horse as the beast tried hysterically to free his noosed hoof. The boy measured the situation, realizing that between them and freedom stood Fordem and the bucking beast. The alley was narrow, and the recoiling of the horse's back hooves dashed any hope of escaping around the beast's rear. Dropping to the ground he quickly rolled under the violent horse's mid-section, and was up on the other side running for freedom.

Fordem was not so easily distracted. While being tossed to and fro he saw the boy roll beneath him. He reached down grabbing his collar as the pirate-boy rose from the ground. The boy yelled and reached back desperately for the man's arm.

"Turn me loose you grunt!" the boy yelled as Fordem began to pull the boy off the ground and onto his horse. The boy was heavy and struggling violently, fighting off the man's attempt to capture him. Fordem leaned over from the saddle, placed his free arm around the boy's neck, and began to lift him off the ground.

Chris finished securing the noose. He emerged from the shelter to witness his friend dangling in the air, kicking, and struggling, the stronger man attempting to drag his prey by his neck up onto his horse. Chris needed the pirate-boy, for he knew no one else and had little idea of his direction of escape. He weighed his chances and made a split second decision, with little time to consider possible consequences. It is times like this when instinct alone determines fate, for to consider ahead your options inhibits heroic actions. Chris sprang up towards Fordem with no thought for his own safety. Grabbing the man's cape, he climbed upwards, scaling the horse's flank, and pulling himself up hand over hand. Gaining a foothold, the boy sprang with all his might, landing squarely on the man's back.

Fordem was wrestling desperately with the pirate-boy and now was trying to fend off this new arrival as well. Chris climbed up his back, and hung from the man's neck, trying desperately to drag him and his friend off the hysterical horse. He gave a brisk kick into the horse's mid-section, and the man and two boys were thrown off the angry steed, rolling into a pile of kicking, swinging, and tangled arms and legs onto the cobblestone alley.

Now a boy cannot match a man in a physical exchange. However, with two boys scratching, pulling, and biting if needed, with the off balance man pulled to the ground from a bucking horse, the kids win, but just for the moment. Chris jumped to his feet. He pulled Fordem's cape up over his head as the man thrashed on the ground in comic book manner.

With Fordem temporarily incapacitated, the two boys were up and running the instant they hit the ground, scurrying for their lives, and not looking back. The pirate-boy took the lead. Coming to the intersecting road, he veered left in full flight running like the wind. With a friendship cemented by such harrowing circumstances, Chris raced after the boy. As he sped along, he found himself laughing at the sight forever cemented in his mind, of the noosed hoof and the flogged evil man who had hated him before this latest defeat. As he ran, he hoped that Fordem would never have his revenge.

"Make for the spilith Christopher of Temecula!" the leader yelled over his shoulder as they ran for their lives, turning the corner down another darkened alley.

"What's a spilith?" Chris questioned between deep breaths, running full speed behind the boy? The pirate-boy glanced back briefly at the boy and just smiled; it was a curious smile.

Chris knew that their efforts would only delay Fordem's angry pursuit. He took a chance and looked behind briefly; they were alone for the moment. Looking forward again he continued on their harried pace. The timing of this glance turned out to be poor, for when Chris turned his head back he saw that his guide was dropping to his knees, lowering himself through an opening in the alley street. The pirate-boy had just entered the breach when Chris crashed on top of him. Without being able to stop, Chris went sprawling over the boy, unable to avoid a collision. Down, head over heels in a jumbled mass, both boys now fell through the alley opening, down with a splat into a hard, cold, and wet passage running deep to the street. Chris knew within a split second the origin of the term spilith. If forewarned properly, he would have easily taken his chances, battling the evil Fordem unarmed, with his teeth if necessary.

They were now seven or eight feet below the street level, rolling over one another, in a bundle of bruised and tangled limbs. Their fall landed the two in a wet and vile chamber with a disgusting smell. Rolling finally to a stop, Chris sat up yelling, Aa sewer, dude, we fell into the sewer! Ah...dude, it's all over me!" Chris raised himself in the low chamber, and brushed imaginary and real debris off his chest and legs. "Oh dude," he said suddenly very panicky. "Dude it's rank...what a smell!" He spit now, hyperventilating. "Dude I got to split...why'd ya drop us in here?"

"Without the likes of you, we would not have fallen," said the pirate-boy angrily, as he spit grime from his mouth and shook his soiled sleeve. "Quiet yourself, Fordem's above." He whispered pointing over his head. "He'll be upon us for sure!"

The medieval town of Alucemet was far ahead of its time, constructed with an eye to the future over a complicated system of subterranean tunnels. The system constituted an open sewage system, flowing deep to the city, and dealing with the refuse problem hampering life in other cities. The spilith consisted of blackened tunnels, stretching for miles within the bowels of the medieval town. The floor of each tunnel slanted down from the side, creating a central funnel shape, allowing the liquefied sewage to flow, driven by gravity to a distant disposal. Blessed at this time by the dry season, the spilith was nearly empty. This allowed the higher edges of the tunnel to be above water level, and relatively dry. Foul or not, the spilith now offered a source of possible escape from their brutal pursuant.

"Dude...there're logs floating down here." Chris yelled repulsed by the thought of buoyant refuse hidden in the dark and perhaps even touching him.

"SILENCE...to what other path have we? Perhaps a trip in Fordem's dungeon is more to your liking! And you shoved me down straight away. You're an odd one," The pirate-boy whispered, covering his disgusted friend's mouth with his open hand. He moved quickly to his feet, a finger raised indicating silence, and brushed off as best he could. Pulling Christopher to his feet, he led him to the edge of the tunnel wall, away from the floating sewage. "No time for talk, Christopher, we shan't be alone for long, make haste."

Flying along the wall of the spilith, trying to keep dry, the two boys ran for escape. As they ran semi-upright in the low tunnel, the boy easily forgot the pain and bruises. However, as for the smell, it was overwhelming, a real test for the sensitive nosed boy. Moving as quickly as possible, the modern day boy tried his best to keep up with his rugged friend.

They arrived quickly at a cross in the road. Here the pirate-boy stopped, and with an outstretched hand signaled Chris to do likewise. Above them a grated cover sat as a possible escape route to the fresh air. Breathing hard, the two listened for any sound of pursuit from the street above.

When one runs hard, wind rushes by moving ears, and the heart is pumping and pounding with fright. It takes then a moment or two before these rushing sounds subside to an audible level. For that moment then, the two escaping boys heard nothing, happily indicating they might have eluded capture. Chris recalled his brief rearward glance just before their high-speed collision and rude fall to the spilith below. There had been no pursuit at the time. Therefore, before their hearing returned all was silent, giving the two encouragements.

When their hearing cleared, however, a snort, an expired puff of air, a shift in weight, one hoof to the other, quietly gave way the presence of the enemy. Worst of all, visible through the iron grate above, yellow equine eyes could be seen searching frantically for prey. The pirate-boy looked at Chris. Chris looked at the boy, and both stood holding their breath with mouths wide open. While neither horse nor rider had seen them at this point, Chris thought that while Fordem might miss them, somehow the horse would not.

"Glue factory…hear me? Glue factory," Christopher whispered threatening the beast under his breath. What horses could possibly have to do with a glue factory was unknown to the boy, but it made an excellent and timely expletive, and he wished the horse to disappear to one immediately. The beast was just a horse certainly, but it seemed human, especially in its hatred and uncanny perception. The jaundiced eyes glared now, and Chris became certain that the horse could see the two fearful boys, standing and trembling within the shadows.

Pirates, Scoundrels, and Kings

The two trapped boys saw few options. To the left, a passage led off into darkness. Rightward a similar passageway led with a pale light entering a grated hatch on the roof of the tunnel a good twenty yards away. To run was discouraging for it was a repeat, and Fordem had intercepted their every move.

In his world, Chris would never try such a stunt, but he was learning, realizing that in this world, the impossible was possible. The feat would require a deadeye throw at just the right angle and with perfect velocity. His goal was to ring the heavy iron grate down the passage to their right, distracting their foe while the two boys scurried in the opposite direction. King David's shot at Goliath came to his mind, and he found himself believing like David that anything was possible with God. Without time to think or second-guess, Chris grabbed just the right rock, wound up, closed his eyes and then threw. The perfect clang as the rock struck the iron grate echoed loudly in the confined spaces of the spilith.

"Woo--" sang the pirate-boy, staggering and holding his ears from the deafening ring that echoed along the spilith. Chris was more surprised at his success as he too plugged his ears protecting them from the loud reverberation.

The throw had the desired effect, the echoing sound ringing loudly through the grate of the street above. The horse turned immediately to the sound, and Fordem quickly dug his spurs into the horse's flank, galloping down the alley, and leaving the boys alone.

Hearing Fordem gallop off, the boys did not waste a moment, sprinting and disappearing down the unguarded passage to their left. Now with new confidence, Chris laughed to himself, wishing he could see Fordem's reaction when he realized their ploy. The pirate-boy led as before, running in a half-stooped manner and making turns here and there within the maze of the spilith system.

They had put some distance between themselves and Fordem when simultaneously the two boys slowed, relaxing and sensing their successful escape. Breathing heavily and dripping sweat, Chris and the pirate-boy began to laugh uncontrollably, bending over and supporting their exhaustion with their hands on their knees.

They felt an overwhelming sense of relief and pride at their ingenuity. Standing now, as their breathing normalized, their tension released as the two had escaped from Fordem so narrowly. Chris began laughing, and soon the two were hysterically slapping each other with outstretched hands in friendship.

"Such a throw I've never seen Christopher of Temecula." The pirate-boy said, finally catching his breath, wiping the tears of laughter from his one uncovered right eye, the left eye now patched.

Chris had stopped trying to remember which eye the poor pirate-boy kept covered and accepted the respect his lucky throw had brought. "That's nothing. Dude—one time I got my ball off the top of our house? I threw it like this." Chris closed his eyes and made a tossing motion, backwards, over his head. Looking directly into the boy's eyes for effect, he continued, "It nailed my Mom right in the head while she was picking weeds. She conked out for an hour. I told her something fell from a military secret plane, you know, from the Pentagon or something. And you know what?" he said, laughing again. "She wasn't thinking very well, so she bought it!"

They laughed for some time, satisfied now that they had saved their skin. Here was the explosion of happiness and joy so unqualified that moments like this come only in our youth. Adults lose something when they grow up, child-like innocence that once gone, never returns. It bridges the difference in all at times when only friendliness can survive, and hate just never had a chance.

"Dude, that horse is bad!" Chris spoke between gasps as they both began to regain their calm.

"Bad it is Christopher of Temecula, and upon it rides badness as well. And why does Fordem pursue you so my friend?" The pirate-boy sat, sliding down the wall to sit with his back to the sidewall of the spilith. The boy drew in a deep breath, relieved with this moment of rest. As he recovered, he looked to Chris for an answer.

"Me? I thought he was after you dude!" Chris laughed, looking at his friend. He knew perfectly who Fordem was after, but this was a pirate, and given Alexander's fate with buccaneers, he worried about the boy's response. Besides, he had not established whether here sat Nicholas the Blue himself. Chris decided he would rather not know.

The pirate-boy jumped to his feet. "Well I'm off cracking. Good times to you Christopher of Temecula." As in the town's square, the boy walked quickly away with no further remark, leaving Chris in the dark and alone.

"Hey dude." Chris said, quickly following the pirate-boy. "Hey where am I anyway?"

The boy turned, smiled at him, but did not slow his pace. "Any of these covers above us will return you to Alucemet. And from there, well I couldn't guess—a-where doth Temecula lie, Christopher?"

"Got me dude. I don't know where, or if, I ever lived there, or whether I'm really here or what." Chris put a hand on the boy's shoulder. "I'm so lost. I've been stepped on, lost then found, in prison, jumped out of a castle; I've hardly eaten for maybe a week--I drank rabbit urine. I just don't know."

Turning to the boy, the pirate-boy said, "no place for you it seems. Well come along. Mind you, I perceived some danger around you. No problem, Nicholas will know the route." The pirate-boy picked up the pace. He was off jogging down one leg of the spilith, turning right here and left there, obviously in a hurry to get somewhere.

Chris kept up with the boy determinedly as he silently debated his friend's last remark. The pirate-boy was rushing. While friendly he certainly was not waiting for further talk. He had dropped the name of Nicholas so casually that Chris was not sure that he heard the boy correctly. The name Nicholas worried the boy for the only Nicholas known to him in this world was a ruthless rogue, a true pirate of the high seas, a murderer, and traitor to the kingdom.

Nicholas the Blue he recalled, and to whether the blue referred to his color or mood was not clear to the boy.

Picking up his speed, Chris drew even with the boy. "Say—dude." Chris said breathing rapidly, the quick pace beginning to wind him. "I can't remember your name."

"I never gave it," responded the pirate-boy, glancing in Chris's direction with a sly wink of his one now uncovered left eye.

"Ah, does it begin with an N?" Christopher wondered.

"It has one," The pirate-boy said proudly, continuing to walk, staring now straight ahead.

The tunnels were becoming taller. Fresh ground water entered the spilith through drains in the ceiling, cleaning the river of sewage and improving the foul odor. Along their route, grated openings above were again visible, and there began to be some sunlight filtering through to light their way.

Chris would be clever with this name thing. Nicholas would not give out his name, a wanted boy on the run. He would ask brilliant peripheral questions of the boy and deduce his identity. He would tell Chris who he was, and the boy would not know he had done so. Yes, Chris was bound for the CIA.

"Does it have an A?" Chris asked, betraying little interest.

"What?" the pirate-boy returned, casting a confused glance at his curious mate.

Coming to a halt, Christopher grabbed the boy's shoulder, inquiring in his subtle manner. "NAME--dude! Does it have an I, or a C? How about an H, or O? What about an L? Oh...and how about an S? NAME, what's your name?"

The pirate-boy was stunned. Staring at the boy a smile slowly came to his face. Slowly, he repeated a prior statement. "Belief in such rot leaves little hope for the gullible. Do you remember my friend?"

Thinking for the moment Christopher responded with, "Ya, what's up with that?"

"Nicholas I am not, I go by Andy. Now we must move on or Nicholas will surely slay us both. He might just for fun in any event." With a loud laugh, Andy quickly turned and continued down the tunnel.

The two walked sometime in silence. A large overhead grate appeared ahead. An iron ladder climbed the wall to the opening, and bright sunlight peeked through. Coming upon this, Andy stopped eyeing the above grate with escape in mind.

"We best make our escape here, Christopher of Temecula," the boy said over his shoulder. "Give a lift," he said, turning to Chris. He placed his hands upon the boy's shoulder and lifting his buckle-shoed foot indicated that Chris should boost him aloft. "Straight away now," he said, nodding his head, pointing to the lowest rung of the ladder.

Chris quickly made a saddle with his hands and with all his muscle boosted Andy to the ladder. The boy was quickly up the ladder to the overhead grate. Straining, he cautiously lifted one edge of the heavy iron covering. Eyeing every sign available, he assured himself that they had chosen a safe site to free themselves.

The grate was quite heavy, made of thick iron. It was wet and moss had overgrown, giving a slippery surface. Once satisfied with their safety, the pirate-boy set the edge of the grate gently down. Climbing down the ladder, he offered his outstretched hand to Chris. Lifting as Chris jumped he was just able to pull the boy to the lowest rung of the ladder.

"Now, here stands our next obstacle," the boy whispered to his friend who was now just below him. "Climb, Christopher of Temecula. We must both lift the grate and move it." With some difficulty Chris climbed to the same rung. It was crowded but the two boys were able to climb and eventually stand together on the higher rungs of the ladder. Straining, the two could just lift the grate from its recessed seat and with a grunt move it a few inches at a time.

They soon created a space large enough for the boys, and with the pirate-boy leading, they scrambled to the sunlight and clear rust-free sky above. Andy fell to his knees. Straining and pushing, he replaced the grate to its former position camouflaging their site of escape.

It was wonderful outside after their long subterranean journey. The sunlight and clear blue sky was a welcome relief to the two boys, and the absence of rust reassured Christopher. The warmth comforted their wet persona, and once their eyes accommodated to the sunlight, a beautiful day abounded.

The two boys emerged by design upon an isolated area of the countryside, rich with dense foliage. Trees with leaves of beautiful colors surrounded them, and dense underbrush easily hid their tracks. The air smelled so clean and fresh, and there was just a hint of the salty sea. The world sparkled, and the boys welcomed wholehearted the change from the putrid halls of the spilith, the rusty sky, and the persistent evil pursuit.

It was time now to sit and rest themselves from a journey full of anxiety and stress, the toll not measured until they could finally feel safe. Andy sat against a large tree trunk and without a word began to dose, closing his one uncovered left eye.

Christopher watched the sleeping boy for a moment. He could not remember when he had slept last. It was ironic, for it seemed so welcomed. The only other time he had desired sleep like this was from the early morning bed when missing school or Sunday school seemed so delicious. He understood at that moment why his father claimed that the worst decisions of his father's life arose while awakening in the early morning.

Being lost now seemed home to the boy. He began to realize different degrees of the condition, the dungeon being really lost, and right now just lost a little. He felt blessed if only for the brief moment of safety, and the warm sunlight soon comforted his own deep sleep.

So often, it seems that when troubled that full-length dreams accompany sleep. He was home now, and a secure peace conformed to familiar surroundings. His family wished to be together, which of late had been less and less desirable for the fiercely independent maturing boy. Dreams, however, are so different, and he longed for family company, support, and especially their love. A friend tempted him to leave the house; however, the boy longed to stay. His brothers played across the yard, calling to them. They did not seem to hear, or perhaps care. While they were so close, his attempts to join them were frustrated and unsuccessful. He struggled with all his might, but he could not reach his brothers as they laughed and rode their skateboards on the driveway.

THE DREAM DREAMED ON FOR the longest time. When he awoke, the early morning sun showed well into afternoon. Lying on his back in high grass, the boy remembered where he was and grimaced. Remembering pirates, ambushes, and dungeons, he closed his eyes trying to return to his dream of home and family. Failing this, he realized he was alone again, and his pirate friend now nowhere to be seen. It was a recurring pattern in this world, safe and then alone again. Had he not smelled of sewage, he would attribute running, escaping, and evil mounted horses to the dream itself. There was, however, no denying it; the escape through the sewer system was no dream.

Chris was a social boy, very popular at school. Most coveted the boy's friendship. His father claimed that such ease around others and popularity were blessings. Without a foreign perspective, however, it is difficult to see one's own talent. In his former world, he was seldom alone. A friend was a friend; hanging was hanging. He did not miss those casual acquaintances anymore, those necessary hellos and interactions making little difference in his life. Chris decided that he missed true friends, those who really cared about him. He missed only those who could be counted on, those that offered comfort. True friends are rare, he realized, but who were his true friends? Dejectedly he realized that few measured up, but his family did, yes his family was like that. Would he ever return to them? It looked doubtful given his present situation.

The day was now glorious; complete with clear blue sky, absence of rust, tall handsome trees, and colorful flowers blowing in a slight breeze. Breathing deeply, Christopher thought he appreciated the salty smell of the sea. Listening closely, he heard the faint sound of crashing surf and the caw of sea gulls in the distance. Christopher was a Californian, a state blessed with miles of white sandy shores and the bright blue Pacific Ocean. To him the word beach replaced the term sea. His compatriots did not travel to the sea; Brits did. He traveled to the beach. He listened quietly, the sounds and smell removing some of his loneliness.

"A beach, dude there's a beach!" Chris said suddenly. The boy rose, determined to make his way in search of a sandy beach. With visions of the boardwalk, roller blading, and body surfing, he decided that the beach was a wonderful destination.

Chris noticed a bright reflection after taking just the first few steps, a sparkly, brief flicker, lying in the deep grass next to where he had slept. If not shiny, he would have missed it, for it appeared to be a small object tossed careless at his feet. The boy dropped to his knees to see more clearly, parting the blades of the moist grass. Before him stood twenty neatly stacked golden coins, obviously arranged with a purpose. Chris picked up one of the coins. He had seen this golden money before. In the pub, the pirate-boy had paid for his grub with a coin just like this. A "gold doubloon," he said. Chris recalled that later Andy had regretted showing this coin to Mac. It seemed to precipitate their quick exit and fanatical pursuit by the evil Fordem. He assumed at the time that Fordem pursued Chris. More likely, he realized now looking closely at his treasure, that here was coin that suggested a very valuable owner.

Now in the modern world, a golden coin is an oddity. The boy had never seen one, and only knew of them in cartoons and movies. To the young boy money was paper. While an adult might guess that these coins were pure gold and valuable, to a boy of ten golden coins meant one thing. "Video tokens," he thought to himself, and stuffed the stack into his pocket, hoping to find an arcade soon.

Chris continued walking, heading towards two stands of trees. Within a few steps, however, he saw another coin, this time a single doubloon tossed next to a beaten dirt path. Then ahead a yard or so another, and then another, all retrieved with amusement and placed one by one within the boy's pocket.

The coins were familiar from the pub; their deliberate path described an unavoidable conclusion. "Andy left me a trail!" Chris decided as he continued finding coin after coin. Could he have a hole in his pocket, or was he leading the boy somewhere? It seemed more likely the latter, the trail so deliberate in its making. The problem was should he follow a trail left by a pirate? Chris stopped for a moment; he would think this over before going any further.

Chris was certain that Andy had deliberately marked a trail for him. If followed to its conclusion, he would probably find the boy. What worried him was who else might he find? Was this a path to help Chris, or was this a trap? He still feared this Nicholas, who being a pirate as well might certainly be with Andy. Andy knew the name of Nicholas, here the boy was certain. He had destroyed the town square announcement in anger. Did he do this as friend, foe, or neither? Accused of killing his brother, all spoke of Nicholas as a rogue and a traitor.

The boy continued along the path, finding a golden track and pondering his predicament. He wasn't in the position to reject this trail, he decided. Alexander was such a nice sort. Why would his brother be any different, he rationalized. "At least he knew Andy," he thought, and a kid in this world was better than an adult. The decision came to following something known or going elsewhere, and he did not know any elsewhere around here. For better or worse Chris would follow Andy's trail.

Chris walked on following the coin-marked trail. After passing the stand of trees, he found another neatly stacked pile of coins, and to its left, a single coin. A signal to turn was his conclusion; with growing curiosity the boy followed the path leftward, finding again single coins to mark the way. The pattern continued every few steps, a single golden token and the occasional turn marked with a neatly stacked pile of the same. As he continued, the grassy slopes and tall trees fell away in favor of rocky ground forming the base of a mountainous obstacle ahead.

Chris climbed the rocky terrain for some time, always careful to follow the coin-marked path. The ascent was tiring, and the boy worked up a sweat in the effort. He stopped, took some deep breaths, and measured his progress. Ahead was a sheer stony ledge with some meager growth struggling for a foothold. Behind him stood a city off in the distance, and cloaked in a haze of rusty smoke.

With a deep breath, Chris returned to the task at hand. He scaled the rocky ledge and dropped behind into a jagged crag. The opening to a mountainous cave now stood in front of the boy, concealed well and not visible from below. Stepping within the opening, he found himself in a dark and humid tunnel leading off into darkness. At his foot, a stack of golden tokens sat beckoning his entry. Chris was uncertain now, but he had few options. Remembering his super-hero friends, he boldly continued on, finding himself in a slowly rising tunnel, which grew darker with each step. Chris moved slowly now, feeling along the wall to direct him. Finding a rightward turn in the tunnel, he saw ahead a welcome light, provided by the flame of a wall-mounted scallion.

As he passed the torch, the boy found himself within a tall rocky chamber across which stood three exits, neither marked with coins. Looking behind, he wondered if he could even retrace his steps. Certain that moving on without direction was folly, Chris sat timidly, wondering his next move, and pondering another disappointing turn in his fate.

They were upon him like lightning, three huge dogs pawing and growling with jaws full of maloccluded crooked teeth, sharp and gleaming. Growling with tongues hanging, they tossed their heads back and forth, throwing thickened drool everywhere. Chris was their obvious prey, and he feared being a dog's small meal, lapped up at any moment.

"Bulldogs!" he yelled in fright, jumping to his feet. Chris stepped back quickly, retreating in terror. Forcing himself to the wall, he tried to be as unobtrusive as possible. What a pitiful end to a short life this pirate's trail had led him.

"N.N.N....ice doggies." Chris said in his most sincere voice. Before him stood the three largest, meanest bulldogs, complete with sharply studded neck and forefoot collars. They did not like the boy at all he decided, as they growled in unison appearing to want for his skin.

A high-pitched whistle echoed in the cavern. In lockstep, they retreated a few steps, sitting stiff and proud as if in a military review. This single whistle had saved Chris from certain death.

"Spike, Nails, Smasher! To the ready boys!" a quiet authoritative command rang out behind the boy.

Chris turned expecting to see Andy, the pirate boy, laughing at his frightened predicament. Instead, he could see no one, the darkness of the chamber concealing the source of such a welcomed command. Returning to his three sentries, Chris was amazed at the change in their behavior. The trio sat at notice, down on their haunches, with tails coiled neatly behind. With heads held high, the three tensed in military-like attention. These monster dogs, so vicious before, were now examples of the most well-behaved canine citizens. The dog closest to the boy dared an occasional disapproving glance at Chris; otherwise, the trio sat at attention with nonblinking eyes staring into the darkness. A dog's tongue has its own mind, their weakest part, forced by nature to dangle from their mouths, panting to an internal musical rhythm of their own. These bulldogs had tongues as well, big, wet, and drooly, tongues that did not have free reign anymore.

"Worry not, he looks to me but a measly meal. I'd wager just one swallow for you, Spike," he voice said with just the hint of amusement.

Chris looked again with fright at his captors. He did not welcome the reference to a meal, and he was afraid he detected a hungry smile on their lips. The chamber was solid stone, rising in the dark to an invisible roof above. Chris turned again and scanned across the dark, in vain, for the voice's source. The boy pressed himself into the wall and squinted across the black space looking in vain for the source of the timely command.

"Watch closely, his look is not comely boys," the voice was heard to say.

His eyes has accommodated to the low light, and with this second phrase, Chris could just make out the source. On the opposite wall, high above the floor was an opening. Darkened and just barely visible, here stood a boy poised, ready to push off on a thick rope whose end disappeared in the roof of the chamber.

Suddenly the boy was off, flying towards the boy with grace and power. At the top of his arch the boy released the rope, and with a nimble flip, landed silently before the frightened boy.

A boy a few years younger than Chris now stood examining him. He possessed piercing, wide-set, brown eyes, and a dimpled chin with small creases next to his mouth, emphasizing a mischievous broad smile. A few brown locks escaped a black bandana and fell across his forehead. The boy was barefooted, dressed in black britches reaching to his calf. He wore a black loose sleeveless shirt revealing tanned muscular shoulders, the left tattooed with the skull and crossbones. Around his waist, tied as a belt, was as a weathered blue fabric sash. He had a slight build with a wiry strength that exuded energy.

The boy took a few steps towards Chris as he examined him up and down, from head to foot. Before him stood a younger version of Alexander, not identical, but the family resemblance was obvious. While Alexander carried himself with quiet dignity, this boy looked ready for a fight or fun, preferring either equally. Alexander was an unassuming leader, while this boy commanded the room in an outgoing manner. The pirate garb, the blue belt, he was unmistakable; before Chris stood the infamous Nicholas the Blue.

"How do you take to dogs?" the boy asked, startling Chris.

Chris returned his attention to the three intimidating dogs. One was now crushing his left foot with a heavy paw and another flipped a wad of drool onto his chest. "I can't say," Chris replied reluctantly, refocusing his thought to the question. "Those dogs are big, you know, and a--teeth. I don't think your dogs really like me."

With a small wave of his hand, Nicholas dismissed his trusted dogs. Silently they retreated, each to one of the three tunnels.

"Quick now, to the cascades!" he said turning to Chris. With a shrug of his shoulder, the boy signaled to follow as he bounded off into one of the three tunnels not waiting for a response.

Chris had his worries, but decided quickly to follow. Running again, he followed as best he could in the dark and cold. As Chris ran behind the boy, he wondered whether they were off for danger or towards something else.

Chris thought about Nicholas as he struggled to keep up. The stories of piracy and treachery did not seem to fit this character. Perhaps he was not such a ruthless rascal, for he seemed friendly enough. Chris decided to be wary of the boy, but hoped that he would be safe with him.

"Oh dude, what are cascades?" Chris yelled ahead to the boy.

He was in midair before he realized that the tunnel floor had ended. As he fell, the sound of rushing water roared and kicked up at his feet. In the total darkness, he thought of spinal cord injuries. "Gotta land feet first," was his last thought as he hit the watery bottom. His feet went out beneath him, and he found himself speeding on the seat of his pants, surrounded by foaming roaring water and flying at a breakneck speed. Chris was in a stone-floored shoot, rubbed smooth by years of rushing water. He raced along realizing that a cascade was a waterslide in the modern vernacular.

Nicholas shot past him on his left, sliding like a bullet with legs in the air and screaming in fun. Now in front of Chris, the boy tucked his feet, and spun on his back as he raced down the cascade. Chris lay back, pulling his hands into his sides and lifting his feet, picking up speed and chasing the boy. The cascade circled to the left lifting him up on the right sidewall and showering icy water as he slid along. Rounding the corner, Chris could see Nicholas ahead.

Nicholas flew along the cascade with his arms tucked, back arched, and a rooster tail of spray behind. As the cascade twisted and turned, he rode high along the wall then streaked down picking up speed. Spinning on his back, he looked like a top in a vortex of water. Occasionally, Nicholas would dig in his heels and using his momentum, launch himself head over heels landing on his rear with a nimble flip.

If this was what a pirate did, Chris thought, it was a boy's dream, pirating, living a life full of danger, complete with his own water park. Chris felt at home, having hit the water slides of his former life before. He forgot himself, sliding and bouncing with icy water spraying all around. He now relaxed, arching his back and flying like a jet. Sliding and twirling with confidence, he was not yet ready for any front flips like the experienced pirate, however. Racing at full speed, Chris screamed loudly, his voice echoing and reverberating within the cave-enclosed fun park.

They had now descended some three hundred feet within the chicanes of the cascade. Chris lifted his neck straining to see Nicholas ahead. The boy came to the end of the cascade and disappeared off the edge of the slide. Climbing high into the air, Nicholas dove into a pool of water in perfect pike position twenty feet below.

"Woo--" Chris yelled as he launched off the end of the shoot speeding high into the air with blinding speed. Once gravity got hold, he crashed with surprise into the water below. With a satisfied smile, he dropped deep underwater, and for the first time remembered he was fully dressed. Kicking to the surface, his feet felt oddly free in his waterlogged board shoes.

Bursting up to the surface, Chris imagined a huge crowd applauding his efforts. Instead, sitting quietly on the pool edge were the three bulldogs watching him with canine suspicion. The three had beaten the two boys somehow, rushing down by another route. They now sat in perfect attention on the edge of the underground pool, tongues panting and slobbery lips drooling. Chris watched the dogs carefully.

"Christopher of Temecula," Nicholas said from behind him. "You'll have no trouble from them. They take poorly to intruders. They haven't killed you though, and I think they have taken to you, my friend!"

Pirates, Scoundrels, and Kings

Chris turned and swam to the boy. He was still unsure of the dogs' intentions, for those were certainly the largest and meanest looking animals that Chris had ever seen. Chris filled his mouth with water and expelled it in a stream towards the pirate. He turned and looked again at the dogs. They were well behaved, and maybe just a little cute. He concluded that if Nicholas's best interests were his, these four footed bodyguards would tolerate him. He would still keep a wary eye upon them for now.

Nicholas swam to the side with long powerful strokes. With one hand he swung himself up on the side, turned, and lowered his hand for Chris. Pulling Chris up next to him, the boy had a chance to look around at his surroundings.

The boys were standing on the edge of a large freshwater pool, surrounded by high, smooth, stone walls which coalesced into a dome of rock above. High on the opposite wall, a jet of water continually roared from the exit of the cascade, the falling water creating deafening echoes within the chamber. The two boys had descended from high within the mountain, dropping them into a rock-enclosed pool. Across the way, Chris could see recessed foot holdings climbing from water level to a small ledge at the top of the wall. While he could not see the outside sea, the sounds and smell of the air seemed to suggest that it was nearby.

Turing to Christopher, Nicholas pointed to the stony ladder and said, "Across thusly." Without further word, he dove into the water and with strong strokes, crossed the pool quickly, and began to ascend the wall. Chris dove after the boy. When he reached the foot of the wall, Nicholas was high above. He grabbed the first foothold and followed quickly to the top. Reaching the ledge, he pulled himself to stand next to his friend.

On the opposite side of the ledge and through a small opening was a deep drop to another pool below. Without a word, Nicholas was off with a twisting flip, landing without a splash.

Chris considered carefully his next move. Here was a drop of significant height, and while ejected successfully into the first pool, he had little choice in the matter. Thinking interferes with having fun and thinking of alternatives magnifies possible negative consequences. The boy saw negative consequences. "Always know what you are diving into," whispered in his ear. He could see his mom frightened at his situation.

Nicholas surfaced, his soaked black bandana still clinging to his head, and looked to the wary boy above. A big smile and a wave of his hand encouraged Chris. To his surprise the aggressive boy yelled for him to come, but in fact to jump feet first. "Tumble on down, Christopher of Temecula. Mind you, feetfirst is best the first time."

Chris looked down at his new friend with frightened concern. Somehow the conservative dive and entry did not dissuade his anxiety. Nicholas just smiled back, waving silently for the boy to follow.

Now Chris was older than Nicholas and tried to hide his concern. "Feetfirst, feetfirst," he said to himself. "I can't die in this world, I can't die in this world," the boy repeated over and over. Without further thought, he shut his eyes tightly, jumped and splashed into the pool below, feetfirst. He knew immediately that he would survive. What a rush he thought, as he kicked to the surface.

"Bad--" he yelled with joy as his head came up. Shaking his head free of water, he turned to Nicholas, both boys with smiles and laughing only a kid could know.

Adults have forgotten the pure joy of childhood; it is a rite reserved only for the young. To become an adult, one must forgo what you wish, and fun is no longer the same. The name remains, but the feeling is never to be had again. The two boys claimed different centuries, but fun spans the years.

Nicholas floated on his back, spraying water from his mouth and relaxing. Chris lay back as well; he had forgotten his problems, all his fears disappearing with fun.

"Is bad good in your world, Christopher of Temecula?" Nicholas asked, still floating on his back and looking up.

It was the first time he had been asked that question. He now realized the ironic twist. "Ah ya, good is bad. Like this place is bad."

"What is not bad, Christopher?" Nicholas queried.

"Ah, let's see, like vegetables. You know boiled at dinner, they're not bad, but they taste bad, dude," Chris responded, now looking up and examining his surroundings. "Hey, where's your dogs, dude?"

"Spike, Nails, and Smasher?" Nicholas responded. He turned now and splashed some water over at his friend. "They are good at bad," he said with a smile. "But bad at bad with water, I am afraid." Pausing for a moment, he continued. "They safeguard us above, for that is their nature. Say, how shall we exit this chamber, Christopher of Temecula?"

It was just then that Christopher noticed something about their pool. Glancing to the roof above, his smile turned quickly to a questioning frown.

To Nicholas this was all fun. The boy floated on his back, again spraying water from his mouth. He began smiling, glancing on occasion at his friend. Chris slowly began to be aware of a problem.

The two boys were floating in a narrow deep basin, filled by a continuous crashing wall of icy water, spilling over a rocky ledge high up on the wall. The pool's surface churned from the force of the falling water, but its level remained stable. As the level was constant, volume in must equal volume out in this situation, implying a drainage port hidden somewhere. Glassy smooth stone walls enclosed them, rising from the water's edge to rocky ceiling above. A smile slowly disappeared from Chris's face; without footholds or crevices in the wall, climbing out of this pool would be impossible. Christopher turned to the pirate-boy with fright and his blue Pinocchio eyes bursting from their sockets.

Nicholas loved to fool his friends, and Christopher was perfect for such a ploy. A smile crossed the boy's mischievous face revealing a mouthful of white teeth, his boyish brown eyes and dimpled face expressing pure delight as he silently returned the boy's stare. He began laughing loudly, took a large mouthful of water, and expelled it in the air. It was fair to say that Nicholas had been here before and he shared none of the boy's concern. Grabbing Chris's hand, he dove below the water pulling his reluctant friend along.

Swimming toward the waterfall, they surfaced at its base for air. Nicholas then pulled Chris down under the crashing water, its power buffeting them around, the crashing sounds blasting in their ears. Nicholas surfaced behind the wall of water. Reaching under the water, he grabbed a hand of hair, pulling Chris to the surface, coughing and spitting. He then pointed to the wall of rock in front of them. Just at the surface was a small opening too small for a boy to squeeze through. Here in front of them was the drain site for the cave. The water entered the cavern from the waterfall, collected within the pool, and then rolled out through the opening. Their escape, however, was still a puzzle.

"Crazy dude," Christopher said shaking his head free of water and brushing his hair out of his face. "No way, we can't get out through there." He turned to the boy demanding a much better answer.

With a chuckle, Nicholas was quick to respond. The pirate-boy paddled to the wall and grabbed the end of a rope secured to the opening. Pulling on the rope, he reeled up a short segment of wood attached to its sunken end. He then forced this into the opening, sealing the only outlet of the pool. Nicholas then tied the other end of the rope to his foot. With a sly wink, he dove below the waterfall and surfaced within the pool.

"Christopher of Temecula!" He yelled cupping his hands and yelling through the waterfall.

When Chris surfaced, he found Nicholas floating on his back; the water logged rope tied to his ankle, a satisfied look upon his smiling face. With the drain now sealed, the water level rose quickly. Chris now realized how they were to escape this water prison. As they rose, Chris laid back and floated, now content to rise on this ingenious water elevator. He began to trust this new friend.

The unchecked flooding of the chamber lifted the water level and the boys promptly. After rising some twenty feet, an arched opening became visible within the rock wall, a route of escape now obvious. Nicholas scrambled over the edge and signaled Chris to follow. Untying the rope from his ankle, Nichols pulled and dislodged the wooden plug below. With that, the water level began quickly to fall away to its former level.

"Follow me. It's warm," Nicholas said.

Chris hesitated, looking at the dropping water level. He had begun to shiver, a breeze blowing through the caves through unseen vents.

"Come, fun awaits us." Nicholas turned and was off.

Christopher followed closely. They climbed along a short corridor, and then descended several hewn-stone stairs into a darkened vast sanctum. Nicholas struck a flame and lit two oil-soaked torches revealing an expansive compartment carved of stone, the walls merging high above into a pointed vault.

"Awesome, dude!" Chris gasped at the site before him.

They stood at the entrance of an oubliette, a dungeon chamber of horde with only one entrance. The floor some ten feet below could not be seen, covered as it were with priceless collections of gold, jewels, gems, trinkets, a bedazzling panache of riches beyond imagination.

Nicholas stepped down the small stairs and stood along the shimmering surface below. Like into a reflecting pool, Nicholas dove, entering the treasure with a splash of golden coins. He surfaced quickly, in the process tossing opals, bullion, topaz-covered gimlets, and necklaces like confetti.

"Come, Christopher, warm yourself," he said swimming as if immersed in an ocean horde of jewels. Pulling himself up on the stone lip of the room, he started a roaring fire enclosed in a massive hearth.

"Swimming and diving in cash," Chris whispered to himself. Staring below him at the wealth, he searched his memory.

Ducktails, he said now laughing and looking at the boy.

A Disney cartoon featuring Hewey, Dewey, and Lewey McDuck. They were adopted sons of their eccentric millionaire uncle, Scrooge McDuck. Scrooge had a cartoon vault of riches, and would use his horde in the same manner as Nicholas. Swimming and diving in ecstasy, the duck did not allow his nephews the same right. Though not Disneyland, Chris decided to follow his friend. Jumping into the cache, but feet first, he found wealth a superior medium to water.

The two boys now lay within the treasure troth, warming themselves with satisfaction before the blazing fire. Chris imagined the peace a pirate might have felt after a day of hard work upon the open sea, robbing and pillaging, then appreciating their take. Yes, the life of a pirate was something he was growing to appreciate.

"Nicholas, is this all yours? What up with all this gold, dude?" Christopher asked as he looked around. Reaching around himself he could pick up coins, jewels, silver ingots, golden globets, anything in his imagination just for the taking.

Nicholas looked at the boy seriously, shrugging his shoulders as if riches meant nothing to him. He added somberly, "A kingdom's wealth is the property of its citizens. We have taken all this, battling foes on the high seas, from vessels carrying royal treasure stolen from Alucemet. I have vowed to return it someday, and that day dawns soon, Christopher of Temecula."

The boy looked quietly at his modern day friend. Watching him, Nicholas sensed how impressive the wealth was to the boy.

"But Satan now is wiser than of yore, and tempts by making rich, not by making poor." Nicholas smiled knowingly at the boy. He continued. "Alexander Pope, Epistle to Lord Bathurst" Nicholas left the quote for Chris to ponder. Lying back again, he closed his eyes. Suddenly the boy seemed drained and melancholic.

Chris thought about his remarks for a moment. Moving on he asked, "Dude, how did you know my name?"

Nicholas quickly regained his smile as he turned to Chris. "You are known here and there, Christopher of Temecula."

Pirates, Scoundrels, and Kings

Christopher considered this perplexing answer. The pirate-boy appeared as one with a complex character. He was full of fun but solemn, carefree but resolute, and while one of amusement, something within spoke of a sober determination. Chris wondered if there was evil as well? The boy's intuition said no, but he had little experience in matters of the heart. While he guessed that Andy had innocently mentioned Chris to the boy, there were other disturbing possibilities. Was Nicholas informed of him by evil elements from the castle, or worse yet, those responsible for Alexander's apparent demise?

Serious questions pass quickly when ten, and so did this issue for Christopher. As was his nature, he continued his machine-gun interview of the boy. "And who are you anyway. Are you really a pirate? You must be Alexander's brother. And why do they call you Nicholas the Blue, dude?"

Imagine speaking ill of someone and as you speak, finding that person next to you. A warm feeling flushed through Chris's face, lighting his ears aflame. He wished he had not spoken of Alexander, given the rumor that here was the cause of his demise. "The dude's probably sensitive about that, being called a traitor and all," Chris thought to himself.

"Hahahaha.... Slow yon self, my curious friend. I am Nicholas, others speak as such, this blue title." He tossed a delicately facetted ruby high into the air as he spoke and caught it in a jewel encrusted goblet. "You speaketh of Alexander? You last partook of him, when...Christopher of Temecula?" he added slowly.

Now he had done it! Once again something best left unsaid had spewed from his mouth. Truthfully, the last time he saw Sir Alexander, the boy was getting himself ambushed. Even worse, Nicholas was accused of his ruthless death. How clever Chris thought, the assassin now quietly inquiring as to the last time the sole witness had seen the assassinated. This was a trap, and one into which he would rather not fall deeper. He had just met Nicholas; however, the rumor did seem out of character. He would be careful from here on, watch every word, and deftly avoid the issue.

He looked at the room's sole exit, and swallowing deeply he responded, "OKAY, I'll tell you! Did you have to kill him, Nicholas?"

Chris shot a glance at the boy out of the corner of his eye. He was hotter now, his forehead burning with the sudden feeling of pursuit.

Nicholas jumped to his feet in anger, legs covered to his knees in treasure. He kicked his way through the golden coins and trinkets, and clinched his fists. The pirate-boy now stood threateningly over Chris, and drew his dagger without remorse. "You speak of before he met his final reward!"

Christopher smiled bravely at the boy and glanced again briefly towards the chamber's exit.

"Ah yes," Nicholas said, answering his own question. "I recall your visage now, along the side of the battlefield! Did he not die an honorable death, Christopher of Temecula?"

Chris wanted to disappear under the treasure and hide from this intimidating medieval boy. Having turned red and scared, it was like finding oneself alone with Jason from the *Halloween* movies, or worse the insane Chucky. He closed his eyes for a brief moment to think, but he had no ideas.

Chris opened his eyes expecting it to be his last look before death. The smile that he saw though washed away all his fears.

"It is never as it seems Christopher of Temecula," Nicholas said. With one sudden flip of his wrist his dagger was off, twisting over Chris's head striking dead a rat in its tracks. Turning now to the surprised modern day boy he continued, "Do you take me for a slayer? That is, if in fact, Alexander ceases to be, a rumor that me thinks of little substance."

"No, no---I didn't think that, really dude, really I never thought that!" Chris assured the boy, beginning to feel an overwhelming relief. His thoughts turned to Alexander and Manzell's diet of pierced rabbit. Reviewing this he thought about the rat that Nicholas had just slain. "Nicholas...you wouldn't! PLEASE don't eat that rat?"

Pirates, Scoundrels, and Kings

Nicholas was now laughing hysterically. "Never!" He returned gasping between giggles and falling to his knees. "Neither does our custom include drinking rat urine. I don't think it bane, however. Feel free to use it as is your custom!"

Jumping into the air he dove into the horde and surfaced alongside the boy. Chris could not help but laugh at himself. "How could Alexander tell him about the rabbit bladder episode?" he thought silently.

The two boys now rolled on the jewel floor, laughing together hysterically. The nature of kids easily spans centuries. The modern day boy would never again suspect evil in the pirate-boy's nature.

In Christopher's well-tested opinion, a better cure than gum for the stress of the day did not exist. It was of course controversial. There were proponents of MTV, a frozen Geno's pizza hot from the oven, tickling a defenseless younger brother to tears, or hiding mom's sanitary napkins, but none had proven superior to the well-versed boy. He had just two sticks of that precious commodity left, and he reached now into his pocket for them. Handing one to Nicholas, Chris removed the wrapper from his last stick, put it in his mouth, and began chewing vigorously. It was gum time.

A curious look came upon Nicholas. The boy held the stick before him wrapped in silvery paper up to the light and then watched his friend's actions carefully.

"Here," Chris said taking the stick of gum from the boy. Demonstrating for the inexperienced gum consumer he continued. "You un-wrap it, as you would say: thusly. Then you chew like this." He illustrated with exaggerated mastication. Finishing his lecture he added one small but very important fact. "But dude, never, ever swallow!"

Nicholas followed the instructions with careful devoted attention to his task. The moment gum touched his mouth he knew he would never be the same. It was a revelation, a realization of something so basic and earth shattering, forever etched within his mind. He was speechless. Chewing slowly, his eyes opened widely as he grinned from ear to ear. Nicholas was sure that he had just discovered the answer to all this world's ills. For some a rare event occurs, which so profoundly changes one's life that the exact moment, the surroundings, even the time of day will be etched indelibly never to fade. The revelation of gum marked such an event for the pirate-boy.

Turning now and wading across the jewel bedecked floor, Nicholas waved his hand over his shoulder to Chris. "Time awaits us, Christopher of Temecula." he said impatiently. "Hurry my friend, fun awaits us," he added, turning to his friend. Nicholas was chewing now as an old gum pro. "Mind you, in time I will learn to grow this chew."

When old and faded and the story told, Nicholas would insist that this one moment was the equinox; gum changing his life and his world's future forever.

Chapter 12
A Precipitous Quandary

> When the righteous triumph, there is great elation:
> But when the wicked rise to power, men go into hiding.
> **Proverbs 28:12**

Nicholas tossed and turned before dropping into a dream filled, unsettling sleep. He saw strife within his family, reliving the events that had turned his world inside out. They were dreams referable to a time not that distant, a time of uncertainty, dispute, and loss.

It was difficult for the uninvolved observer to grasp the magnitude and consequences of strife within the castle walls. All was not right, however; it was the how, what, and why that were controversial details, particulars that most would rather not deal with. While the inaugurate's culpability and identity was uncertain, the damage became irreparable; the royal family was never to be the same.

For one so young, Nicholas was solemn when considering the fate of his world. He was unsettled when he awoke from his dream. The images during the night returned him to the past, inside the castle, within his royal chamber. He stood at his window and stared blankly high in the western parapet of castle Alucemet. His beloved harbor lay before him, and with the early morning breeze the boy's eyes saw, but did not register, the sailing vessels drifting slowly out to sea. Nicholas played the series of events within his mind that seemed to spell eventual disaster.

His role in the arguments troubled him deeply. He accepted his portion of guilt squarely and wished that he had reacted differently.

He literally had never before fought with his older brother Alexander. Slowly however, a few disagreements became fights, which increased in frequency to something like war and a dulling of a brotherly love, the reactions now so obviously immature.

Strange events began to occur, events in retrospect so clearly clever ploys. Precious possessions lost and given up for stolen appeared, mysteriously implicating the other. Senseless destruction of belongings, inexcusable at the time, seemed foisted and in retrospect trivial. Messengers appeared with messages proven ultimately to be bizarre misinformation and mysterious. These unusual events began to be common and frustrating to the royal family.

The death of the Louis Bienville, the king's royal guard Grand Am, and the circumstances surrounding the event were disturbing. The man's daughter Autumn disappeared as well, vanished after the discovery of her father's trampled body in Devil's Pass. The man was a consummate and professional soldier, and his lone presence within the pass unthinkable.

Nicholas lifted his fist and struck the wall in frustration. His world was cracking, and the once bright future looking so very tarnished. "Little Autumn, sweat and innocent, Lord please take not her as well!" Something smelled of conspiracy, the fetid source evident but impossible to substantiate.

Thoughts of the dead girl brought a tinge of remorse to the boy. He remembered a recent event with a strand of guilt. Nicholas tried unsuccessfully to push the image from his mind.

The crossing shot had drifted wide, bounding into the right corner. The pass was to be for the right wing Nicholas, and the boy would have little trouble catching up with the soccer ball. He was unassuming and so far anonymous to the defender who had not yet given the respect necessary when defending this athletic boy. Nicholas cultivated anonymity to his advantage. Teammates knew that they were never to use his name on an opponent's field.

Nicholas drove over the ball, tipping it backwards as he passed with his left foot. The fullback careened along, passing the boy, unable to stop in time. With a strong right foot, Nicholas drove the ball into the right, outer, high corner of the goal. The ball drew net just over the diving attempt by the frustrated keeper.

Nicholas was jogging back to midfield when he heard a pesky little voice behind him. "You did so well Nick, could I just play for a moment, please?"

Looking over his shoulder, he knew what to expect before he saw the girl. She always wanted to play, he thought with just a bit of annoyance. Nicholas turned to the sideline and addressed the girl backpedaling. He hoped to rid himself of this nuisance, begin on defense and continue the game.

"Autumn, he said quietly, you are but a girl! Girls must not play soccer."

"Oh Nick, I'll pull my hair up into a cap, no one to be wiser. I know that I could play good! You watch, please."

"Autumn, you're wearing a bloody dress girl, you fool no one!"

The girl stood resolutely upon the sideline, looking down upon her lavender dress tied just so with a sash. Looking up again to the boy, she said nothing.

Nicholas's thoughts returned to the present. Closing his eyes, he looked up at the ceiling of his chamber choking back tears. He was so glad that he had taken the girl to field side that day. With her long brown hair pulled into a cap, an old shirt, and shorts, no one had suspected the truth. He had placed her as a defender, and made a point of getting back on defense to cover any possible score off this newly substituted fullback. She made good work, learning quickly, however. She had played "good," the boy recalled. It was the last time that Nicholas was with the girl.

The Bienville name would never be propagated. The death of Autumn's mother during labor was the first tragic event in the doomed family. This dreadful event began, and the little girl's apparent death completed the demise of the valiant Bienville family tree, one of such devotion to the kingdom.

The king's behavior continued this sad saga. King William was rarely visible of late, and when present his political decisions were imprudent and unlike the wise monarch. His mother was distraught as she struggled to contain the downward spiral of the once invincible and proud family. Her efforts slowed this implosion, only to delay what seemed inevitable.

The departure of Alexander had a profound effect upon his younger brother. While fighting and unrest had come upon them, Nicholas took solace in the boy. Why had Alexander deserted his home? Nicholas did not believe the generic story of eldest son packing his bags in the dead of night and leaving his home and responsibilities behind in humiliation. Superficially the story fit; he was present one day and gone the next, but the departure's motivation was not explained. It was not in Alexander's character to shirk his responsibility and escape for better times. Nicholas knew a ruse, and he would die before believing his sibling's cowardly retreat.

Alexander had become a leader. He was a quiet determined consummate representative of the royal family that could never tolerate disrepute. It was true that the two royal sons have disagreed angrily of late. Nicholas blamed himself for much of this, but their blood was common, and his brother would never desert him without even a word. He sensed something had coerced his brother and forced his sudden departure. Frenzied rumors then circulated wildly, created and designed for a deliberate purpose, to conceal truth from responsible citizens. Without effective and timely denial, spin makes the lie powerful and the unopposed deceit accepted as fact.

Alexander's absence left a void in the failing royal family and underscored the serious fate awaiting the kingdom. It was discouraging to see, but Nicholas was an optimist and one of great determination. While he felt unaided for the moment, these lonely troubles girded his resolve. Without a precipitous quandary, greatness becomes futile eluding even the bold.

Nicholas turned from the window. Staring at the stonewall, draped with a velvet tapestry, his thoughts wafted leagues away. The boy considered his own life as his focus penetrated deep within the thick masonry. His boyish image gradually appeared as if reflected from a deeply hidden mirror. Eventually the boy saw the blessings from God that made his life so cherished, illuminating his life, as Nicholas had never witnessed before. It reflected the boy surrounded with blessings so obvious but subtle.

Nicholas saw meadows full of blooming poppies, his dog's curly tail which made him laugh, and the joy of awakening to a beautiful morning sun. Had he truly been thankful for these, and were they now in jeopardy? He decided that he had been thankless more often than not. He had taken his life, the world, and God's blessing for granted. He had everything, but did not appreciate it.

As time continued, his reflection began to illustrate his sins and faults. The image revealed the boy full of imperfections and carved roughly. Before him the disagreements, selfish desires, and ego-driven actions drifted along one by one as Nicholas stood in silent introspection. Turning an eye from the poor, a sarcastic thought, impatient actions, the images ceaselessly flooded over him and a tear began to well from his eyes. A lone rooster appeared in the background and with a single crow; the boy was suddenly awash in shame. With that, blood flooded the image, and Nicholas then realized the meaning of the reflection. A loving God had sent his only Son to die, the death of the savior allowing blood to wash free the chains of sin. The prison of that mirror fled, cracking and crumbling as Nicholas returned to his present time. Nicholas now knew his fate. He needed to take back his life and would have faith about its outcome.

It was obvious to the boy that the Boar, as he fancied himself, was central to this quandary. Nicholas wished to confront him using a quick blade to pry loose the truth and settle the matter. The Boar was a coward, however, a most unwilling duelist unless trapped.

Nicholas measured the risks of such a confrontation. The Boar was a man, the boy, well—a boy. His opponent's daily diet outweighed him by a good stone or two, and he would tower over the boy even if cast upon his knees. Boars are fierce fighters using stout tusks and stubborn tenacity, skewering and torturing their prey without mercy.

Nicholas began to laugh uncontrollably. "You shall fall disgusting being. You lose. Why even use a blade? Prepare for pain Michaelis!" he yelled, gasping between breaths.

The plan took form as he quickly unlocked his chamber cabinet. Hoisting his sword, he wondered if the coward would even fight. "I must not allow him to hide." He decided with determination. The image of the terrified and cornered pig revived his spirit as he began to ache for a brawl.

Nicholas felt relief knowing action as always would rule the day. Having finished the foul beast, he planned to seek out his beleaguered mother. She would know how best to reason with his confused father. Together he trusted they would rekindle the basic character of the man. The key, however, was to remove the evil presence which so unexpectedly had contaminated him.

He was comfortable with the offensive tact, confronting the problem with success or losing his family and kingdom forever. Nicholas thrust his sword within its sheath. Offering a short prayer, he realized that faith was required to carry the day. While his family could not be witness, he was certain to honor the family's crest of the Laughing Lion.

It is quaint living within a castle; donjon and turrets, parapet and battlement, bulwark, moat, and such. Not a medieval tract home, rather a monstrous dwelling the scale of an entire enclosed city. His task was to search, and within such a fortress, the mission often becomes a daunting one.

The first charge that morning for Nicholas was to seek out and reason with his misguided father. He hoped for his blessing and guidance, before slashing to the bone the foul and evil menace, Michaelis.

The boy questioned everyone that morning, but responses to queries were reluctant, with conflicting and misleading information. When queried, smiles of respect turned fearful, their owners wishing to continue about their own business. Nicholas requested servants to call upon the king. They bowed with respect promising to deliver an urgent message. Asking leave, however, they scurried away never returning with information for the impatient prince.

It was midday when Nicholas could no longer tolerate this frustration. He had searched at a frenzied pace, but still no king. While the castle was spacious, the man's absence brought a sinking feeling to his youngest son. Pushing aside his fears, Nicholas turned to his most sincere reflex: action and the Boar beware.

Can the loathsome be found if a loved one cannot? Nicholas knew he would have much more success in venture number two. Remember that the sun burned directly overhead; being lunchtime all one had to do was follow the smell. The pig would be consuming a feast. In addition, he would be alone, for no one dared to distract the man when partaking in his life's ambition.

Like a column of ants, a trail of despairing individuals told a story of sycophant excess. Streaming from the northern kitchen, pensive servants sweating with tension, carrying heavily loaded trays and heaping carts, concentrated upon the culinary desires of a tyrant. Not one dared delay his work for the unassuming boy, who keeping to the shadows followed in silence the coordinated activity.

Nicholas slipped into the kitchen and moved quickly, hiding behind a large hanging carcass that would be prepared and devoured within the hour. From the kitchen, he followed the entourage leading him to the central stairway.

Standing at the base of the stairs, the boy fumed with anger. These small stairs led to the private living quarters of the royal family and staff. It was dreadful who now inhabited this corner of the fortress grounds. The castle meant sacrifice and nobility to the boy. His father had freed all of Alucemet, the citizens then building a towering mansion to shelter their beloved monarch. In response to those awed by the beauty of the castle, his father would quote scripture: He who is least will be first, was the usual response of King William, who always treated these stone walls as being on loan, available to the royal family only by God's good graces. The present interloper had no such respect for the institution.

Nicholas decided to follow one tortured servant ascending the stairs. Upon his shoulder was a golden tray, laden with a volume of food that could sustain a small army. Gripped between his teeth hung the handle of a full pot of steaming soup. The servant looked harried, as if he was a precious moment late delivering an order to an intolerable tyrant. Making his way up the narrow staircase the man hurried, attempting to make up for prior delays. He would grimace but never stop when a drop of the boiling broth splattered and burned, rolling down his face. It was easy for the boy to slip quietly behind, following the distracted man as he ascended the stairs floor after floor. Once at the correct chamber door, Nicholas flew by him.

The boy beheld a disgusting site. Standing now at the foot of a long dining table, Nicholas observed the decadent Boar and grew silently angry. At the opposite end of the room, unaware of his entry, sat a greasy shabby man, who was conducting and drooling over a huge, greedy, and solitary feast. He had a large soiled napkin stuffed crookedly within his shirt neck, which fell over a dirty frock coat. Eating with both hands, the Boar was just beginning to gain momentum. Before him lay an entire roast turkey with ironically neat booties, tied over the stub ends of both legs. Partially eaten bowls of delicacies tossed carelessly, lay scattered on the floor. Remaining plates and saucers covered the table. Taken together, the volume of food appeared suited for a peck of patrons, all of which seemed to have simultaneously defaulted on their invitations.

Nicholas had seen enough. He launched himself across the room jumping up on the table. "Prepare to die you miserable excuse, you nimrod…gristle eating pig!" Nicholas had his sword drawn as he moved across the table after the man, scattering before him bread, fruit, and fodder.

The Boar looked up startled from his feast, his huge mouth open in fright. Grease was running down his chin unnoticed, and a huge ripped chunk of meat dangled from one crooked fang. The pitiful site would be humorous in other settings, but Nicholas was not laughing.

The servant was concentrating intensely upon his delivery. Entering the chamber, the man hurried to the head of the table, never acknowledging the boy's presence. Exhausted after lugging his huge load up the flights of stairs, the man arrived at his master's side. Glancing over his shoulder, the boy's presence startled the man. As the boy approached the Boar, kicking and tossing food from his path, the servant let loose of his tray and pot of soup with a gasp, both cascading unceremoniously upon the generous lap of his patron.

The Boar roared in furious agony, his eyes fixed in horror upon his generously sloping belly as his prized and precious victuals oozed down its slope like an advancing avalanche.

"Vittles for brains, you dim witted fool," the Boar screamed at the apologetic man.

He looked in anger at the servant, to the boy in fear, and then returned his attention to his priceless dripping meal now fully adorning his gravid belly. This trilogy of conflicting problems threatened, looming before the Boar for his dispatch.

Firstly, efficient discipline demanded a fair and measured response to failure committed by those of the servant class. The Boar wished to flog the servant immediately and dangle him as an example from the standard by a hook piercing his scrotal skin. Secondly, his meal was now in disarray, an event that horrified the man. Thirdly, standing upon his dining table was the brat boy, with his disgustingly confident smile and shining drawn blade. Processing this trilogy, inherent cowardice won the day.

Michaelis jumped to his feet pushing away from the table and dropping mounds of food splattering on the floor. He quickly backed away from the table. Tripping and sputtering, he stared horrified with wide-open eyes and debris filled mouth. Standing precariously on the high heels of his shiny black boots; his ankles gave way dropping the man to rest upon the folded boot shanks facing his tormentor.

Nicholas walked the length of the table, kicking and throwing food items littering his path. Reaching for a bowl of bouillabaisse, he launched it down the table dowsing the frightened Boar. With the tip of his sword, he skewered a half-eaten fowl and tossed it where it violently careened off the side of the Boar's head.

Here was Nicholas in his prime, a boy full of energy, outaged, outheightened and certainly outweighed, but ready to defend his family and kingdom from this shameful sack. His face showed determination, and his broad grin betrayed his delight. Nicholas launched himself from the table, with sword drawn, landing and challenging at the boar's feet.

"What brings you here young sir...the boar spit out in fright," as he slithered away, his back now to a wall, hoping to beat the boy to the door of the room.

"I come for your miserable carcass. I shan't leave with nothing less, you brainless excuse for a peasant." Yelling with fright, the boar slipped by the boy still running on the shanks of his boots.

Nicholas grabbed a huge soup tureen from the scattered debris on the floor and in one quick motion threw the projectile with deadly accuracy, thumping the retreating boar's head forward as if on a spring. The deadly blow dropped the man to the floor and he began rolling for his life, yelling for mercy, hoping as well to attract the attention of his guard. Nicholas kept the pressure on the man launching chairs, curtains, and cantaloupes in quick succession, each crashing down on his prey.

"Just as I suspected, like your god Satan, a coward really, you forgot this!" With this, Nicholas tipped the entire table, scattering glasses, candles, and splintering wood across the embattled room. Reaching for the stained tablecloth, he rolled it into a tight ball, and threw a strike at the cowering man's hefty buttocks.

Michaleis looked up briefly, his face covered with the violent remains of his loving meal. Horror was in his face as he began to shuffle across the room on his knees heading for the room door. Covering his head with his hands, he scooted for his pitiful life.

Pirates, Scoundrels, and Kings

"Your world is twisted Michaelis. I claim it back for my father. Prepare for your flames; the pit draws near." Nicholas was in no hurry to complete his work. A quiet boy, he had pent-up anger, and before him its source.

Above the fallen man, hanging from the high cathedral ceiling, was a golden chandelier, supported and lowered by an embossed velveteen rope. The huge light source consisted of oil-burning lanterns placed radially on an engraved, shiny, gold-plated hoop supported by ornate spokes from a central hub. The support rope wound around a crank mounted on the wall. Nicholas looked up at the chandelier and then to his prey crawling for the door. He cut the rope with a single slash of his sword and the light came crashing down.

Michaelis sensed the falling object before he saw it, looking helplessly up at the last second. Closing his eyes, the chandelier fell upon him, entrapping the man between two of the spokes. Sitting on his knees, his arms pinned at his side, he struggled to free himself but could not. Realizing his predicament he squealed in anger as he tried unsuccessfully to move the chandelier and himself away from the boy and towards the door.

"You shan't get through that door now. You are much too wide. Oh, such tragedy. Here, I will offer you some help foul beast!"

Nicholas was upon him quickly. He lifted the man's legs, turning him up on the side of the chandelier like a wheelbarrow. With the boar as the axle, Nicholas rolled him toward the exit. Arriving at the door, the nose to foot length was wider than the opening. Nicholas pushed and pushed, repeatedly striking the man's head on the door jam with the butt of his hand. He quickly wedged the apex of the head and feet of the whining man into opposite sides of the door jam. Kicking at the empty shank of his boots he flexed the man at his ankles, and drove him rudely through the door and crashing onto the stair landing.

Standing at the top of the long stairway Nicholas smiled as he looked at his helpless prey poised for a quick ride down. The boy asked, "'Twas this your desired destination, ignoble master of trash?

Oh, and your leave is granted, services are thusly terminated!" Nicholas booted the now defeated foe down the stairs. Bouncing and rolling, the boar crashed into a heap at the bottom of the stairs.

Quite a good time, the boy thought as he rubbed his hands together anticipating more action.

OGLEBY DE OPPENHOFFFFFFFER, THE FEARED ogre of 'O', was concerned when he heard his master's frantic and cowardly calls. As the royal guard Grand Am, it was his responsibility to protect the castle and its overseer. This position of power rightfully elicited his most distinguishing and perhaps only characteristic: guffawing in thoughtless prolonged outbursts.

As one of unquestioned bravery, the ogre's first reaction was swift and cutting. He hid himself in the closest drawing room. It was to his misfortune that he chose to dive under the bed, for his girth allowed only a fractional covering of his cowering body. With his head and upper torso covered as the ostrich, Ogleby felt himself well-hidden.

He knew what awaited him if he chose to come to the Boar's defense. He had seen the actions of Nicholas in the past. While just a boy standing to the level of his herniating umbilicus, the man measured his chances of overpowering him as poor at best, and next to none at worst. Neither option served the purposes of his pea sized brain. However, the Boar was his literal meal ticket and he needed the beast for his lifestyle. For who would have anything to do with such a man? Why only a master who was even more miserable and stupid than himself.

The Queen heard the disturbance as well. While the shouts and screams were distant and not identifiable to the average ear, as a mother she recognized instantly the voice of her youngest son. Replacing her hand mirror on the armoire, the Queen bolted from her chamber and flew along the hallway towards the excitement. In flight, she prayed for her son's success, as the royal hound Gidget followed barking at her heels.

Pirates, Scoundrels, and Kings

THE ROYAL HOUND APPEARED SAD that day as she lay at her Queen's feet. While the wrinkles of the Shar Pei's face always suggest sadness, in reality she seldom was so, her treatment commensurate as always to her royal heritage and obvious brilliance. She liked the fact that her facial expression led many to the wrong conclusion, as the scraps from the table seemed to depend upon the human's perception of her mood. Today, however, she was truly sad. Alexander had left the castle, a noble loved playfellow. While Nicholas remained, he was distracted, and of late would seldom toss her stuffed toys for her retrieval. However, it was the Queen's dismay that troubled Gidget the most. She took her position seriously, and felt bound in blood to her royal owner. It was to her excited surprise then, when her master responded to the sound so obvious to a dog's ear and ran to support her son. The royal hound quickly followed, nipping for action upon her heels.

THE OGRE HAD CHOSEN TO hide within the chamber adjacent to the stairwell where screams and whining now indicated the location of the continuing battle. He had left the door agar, opening into the hallway within which the Queen now hurried along.

The Queen sped along the hallway and passed the partially open door without thought, hurrying to defend her son. A loud bark from the royal hound stopped her abruptly. Turning to the entry, she saw her trusted dog barking and jumping crazily; something was in that room. Opening the door, she could not help but laugh to herself. Halfway under, halfway out, lay the ogre cowering under the bed settee for his life.

The Queen quickly considered her options. To her left, she could hear the growing scuffle on the stairs just one flight below. From the audible drift of crying and whining, Nicholas seemed to need little assistance at this time. The thought brought a smile to her for her two children had needed little help during their lives, both so independent. Alexander was introspective and with an intense maturity beyond his years. Nicholas was quiet but a boy of action, on the offensive attacking problems when necessary.

She choose to torment the parlor prey, that disgusting Grand Am whose buried head at this very moment felt concealed and falsely secure. A smile crossed her face as she planned her attack.

Since a little girl, the Queen had not had such fun. Jumping up and down on the overstuff mattress brought fond remembrances flooding back. Up and down, up and down, and with each drop, she would bang the ogre's head and trap him more securely as the man cried mercy and guiltless drivel. Gidget was upon the man like a lioness. She began to rip and tear at the man's clothes, dislodging shreds of material from his filthy garment-covered rear.

The Ogre's trousers lit well that day. Continuing to bounce, the Queen grabbed the oil lamp above the bed, and like a Roman candle the blaze took off. The grease stains on his clothing made a perfect fire fodder, for as the boar, here was a man who liked his food and invested little in cleanliness. pretended no cleanliness.

"Wooooo--" the Ogre yelled from beneath the bed. His tail end was now flaming, suggesting to the man a growing problem. Reflexively, he lifted his head, cracking the base of his skull on the underside of the bed while the Queen continued her acrobatics on top of the man. He tried unsuccessfully to back out from under the bed, his girth now wedged tightly. Hysterically he screamed, twisting, fanning, and brushing the growing flames of his burning rear-end. He found little success as the room filled with smoke and the smells of burning flesh.

With one last deep bounce, the Queen sprung from the bed and dropped to the floor. Turning, she watched her handiwork, the man's struggling and misfortune bringing a well-earned smile to her face. While not one to enjoy the distress of others, in times of national security she felt sacrifices were necessary. Frustrated by the recent direction of the kingdom, here was a chance for retribution.

It was an easy matter for the Queen to direct the distracted ogre across the room, out the door, along the hallway to the stair landing. With a determined push, the ogre rolled down the falling treads, crashing into the boar in a fiery ball. Gidget barked as he rolled and then sat quietly at her Queen's feet. Her tail curled neatly behind her back, and black tongue panted in canine ventilation. The Queen was certain that within her facial wrinkles lay a satisfied smile.

NICHOLAS HAD JUST REACHED THE foot of the stairway when the ogre crashed at his feet, packaged and flaming with unceremonious disrespect. High above on the landing stood his mother, jumping, laughing, and waving in motherly pride and excitement.

His first impression was a common one. "Mother, you're embarrassing me!"

How ironic is it that children need and psychologically long for parental approval but at the same time shun this, striving to be mature and independent? Nicholas caught himself in the emotion, for he needed to be an adult now, insight allowing him to realize the love in her elation.

"Mother!" Nicholas thought with pride, realizing that she had just deposited another victim for his disposal in his grips. He turned to her with his most bashful smile, bowed, and signaled his happiness to her.

Nicholas grabbed the two villains by the scruff of their necks. The arrogance, which followed these two preening peacocks, disappeared. They were pitiful, crying, whining creatures with little prior resemblance. Pulling both of the smoking beings to their feet, the boy moved them roughly through the closest exit and into the central courtyard of the castle.

IN RESPONSE TO THE DISTURBANCE, a large crowd gathered to meet the boy in the courtyard, most quietly cheering and laughing in total sympathy to his cause. Despotic regimes directed by evil tyrants have more enemies than friends. Fear is the common keeper of peace and continuing power. Showing successful opposition to repressive rulers liberates this majority, giving the average man confidence in his open resistance. If not met with sudden, swift, and certain discipline, the movement grows and turning down a rebellion becomes more difficult. As Nicholas continued his lone campaign, citizens began to vocalize their support. Picking up his two hostages he pushed and shoved them rudely towards the drawbridge gate.

Brave rebellion opposing evil regimes may suffer for timing and strength. While noble and his cause popular, Nicholas's time had not come.

The deadly dart tracked silently, swooshing downward upon the boy with mortal accuracy. The archer had appeared without warning, posing in military formation upon catwalks recessed into the massive stone walls that surrounded the castle courtyard. At its launch, Nicholas was busy, his back exposed to his assailants, struggling with determination to rid the kingdom of two most disgusting citizens. With uncanny insight, the boy turned suddenly with drawn sword and sliced the speeding arrow mid-shaft, dashing the shattered projectile harmlessly to the ground.

The deadly appearance and swift retort brought a disappointed silence to the crowd of onlookers. Swelling insurgence put down quickly scatters infant rebellion. While fallen short of its mark, the arrow represented this to the Alucemet citizenry much to their chagrin.

Nicholas stood alone with bared sword glaring up in defiance at a multitude of bowsman. Just before noon, the sun shone in brilliance, blinding the boy. It took a few moments for his eyes to become accustomed, having just exited the shadowy confines of the castle tower. Longbow after longbow lined the wall, prepared to unleash fury on the boy as he readied himself in defense. Shading his eyes, Nicholas measured his opposition, realizing its overwhelming nature. Two gross archers before him had bows loaded, ready to rain down certain death upon the lone rebel.

Fordem pushed his way roughly through the battery of archers. With a raised hand, he signaled the bowsman temporarily to hold fire. His cape ruffled in the mid-day breeze and his gaunt malevolent appearance secured the evil change in the day's momentum. The man stood with rigid posture, an angry grimace upon his countenance, examining the boy's quarry. The gradual rise of a subtle crooked smile gave away the amusement that Nicholas's dispatch of the two individuals brought him.

The whining and begging of the disheveled mass at the boy's feet ceased. The Ogre uttered his senseless drivel. He began laughing like the fool he was as he rolled over, came to his knees, and then stood. Still laughing he looked at the boy. "Oh...that was a warm one, almost needed a fireman, Ha Ha Ha. You're time to fry little brat," the man said between chortles.

The Boar struggled to his feet, stood upon his twisted boot shanks, shook off a layer of dirt, and tried to compose himself. He looked a wreck with food clinging to every inch of his obese body. Stuffed into the corner of his collar was his soiled napkin, the free end falling haphazardly over one filthy shoulder. While he looked ridiculous, he quickly tried to regain his superior obnoxious self.

"Shut the gates, flog this most miserable maniac, and do so quickly you fool!" said the boar, spitting as he yelled. His eyes were bulging, and he swung his hands up and down in violent anger.

With a single swipe, Nicholas swung his sword slicing the Boar's belt and dropping his trousers in a heap around his feet. The citizenry had one last chance to feel hopeful as a cheer went up in unison. The Boar looked down at his jumbled britches and stomped in anger. "Flog him, I demand as such," he ranted, steeped up in fury.

Fordem signaled to the gatesman, and the man began the arduous process of closing the huge drawbridge. The heavy mechanical sounds of meshing gears and lifting chain could be heard as the mechanism began to lift the wooden bridge and drop the iron grate, completely closing off the only route of possible escape to the boy.

Nicholas glanced at the closing grate, biting his lower lip in thought. He took in the situation calmly with determination though hopelessly outmatched and his avenues quickly reduced.

The Queen watched the proceedings unfold in anxious silence several floors above the castle grounds. Nicholas looked to her window and sensed her fright. He lifted a hand and threw a loving kiss to the beleaguered monarch. With a broad smile and a wink, the twinkle in his eyes assured the Queen that all would soon be all right.

He was then off, as shot from a slingshot, running like the wind across the courtyard towards the closing gate. A cheer went up from the crowd, proud and sponsoring his safety. The archers followed along the catwalk, launching arrows at the running boy. Nicholas continued running, dodging, and rolling; nimbly he avoided each dart. As he reached the castle portal, the wooden drawbridge was nearly up, and the iron grate was dropping rapidly.

Nicholas lunged to the ground and rolled under the spear like stakes of the grate, as it continued on its path down. He had cleared the grate, but one of the spears tore and trapped a piece of his blue tunic. Taking his sword the boy quickly cut himself clear, leaving a small piece of blue fragment attached to the grate as it crashed close.

Taking his sword and jumping as high as he could, he drove its point into the closing drawbridge gate. Using the sword he swung his body up and stood up on the lifting bridge, soon to crash closed on the castle wall.

The Boar was roaring with anger, blaming everyone for Nicholas's escape. Nicholas turned, staring down the beast. He yelled his name, bringing silence to the courtyard. The Boar looked up at the boy with hate.

"You are rescued for the moment," Nicholas said, pointing at the beast. "Remember my words Michaelis, Satan's bride awaits a lesser fate than you!"

As the gate closed, the boy dropped to the moat below with a nimble back flip, entering the water with nary a splash.

The Queen stared at the scene silently. She knew that for the time her youngest son was safe. She would miss the boy terribly, and she felt so alone now. A tear came to her eye as she turned slowly in thought and walked to her chamber to pray.

Gidget stood upon her rear paws and watched Nicholas disappear. Gone was her last play-friend, her family lying in ruins.

She knew something that no one else in the entire kingdom knew and in King William's absence, her coming part in the drama would be irreplaceable. As she witnessed Nicholas escaping over the closing drawbridge, the royal dog in waiting was sad, her wrinkled face belaying her troubles.

Chapter 13
No Gum till I'm Three

> He who leads the upright along an evil path
> Will fall into his own trap,
> But the blameless will receive a good inheritance.
> Proverbs 28:4

The sun burst over the eastern horizon, painting brilliant colors where the sky met distant lands, yielding a new day. A light sea breeze wafted over the camp, bringing the fresh smell of the salty sea. Seagulls cawed, seemingly happily in the distance, and the breeze gently rustled the surrounding trees. For now, peace found this portion of Alucemet that Nicholas the Blue temporarily called home.

The pirate-boys inhabited a well-hidden and inaccessible rocky bluff overlooking the western coast of the country. Here, sheer cliffs crashed to pummel the rocky shore below. To the east rose stands of tall pine trees whose blackened silhouettes became green with the rising sun.

The bluff formed a natural shelter for pirates, stolen booty and all. The rocky outcropping encircled a deep water cove, closed to the sea except for the narrow portal on its southwest corner. Further concealment from ocean view consisted of a strategically placed boot-shaped knuckle of land just off coast, densely covered with trees and spanning the portal to the cove. For any large hulled ship of the time, entry to the cove was even at high tide perilous, for navigating the hidden inlet risked dashing a deep draw on the fearsome rocks which formed it.

To approach the cove with a deep hulled man-of-war required skill, a very high tide, and a good measure of luck. Here, entry would require skillful navigation of the thin strait between island and mainland, and then a hard, quick, nearly perpendicular turn into the cove through the narrow shallow inlet. The camp then was nearly invisible from the seaward eye, shrouded in rocky cliffs, the cove's inlet hidden by that tactically placed atoll. For an enemy to approach then, they must either scale the rocky terrain leading to the bluff, or navigate the narrow strait and portal to the cove. Nicholas had chosen his pirate hideaway well.

Sleep had fallen quickly over the modern day boy from Temecula. It was his first night of sleep after meeting Alucemet's youngest royal son. Entry to that dream world was simple that night; however, his sleep was fitful, punctuated by disturbing scenes and evil omens. In his dreams, worldly possessions abounded but heartfelt contentment was elusive. He possessed all the of his wishes: video's, rock concerts, long and short skateboards, board shorts, Arnette sunglasses, Etnie's board shoes, and any other desire of his heart. Strangely, however, the satisfaction he longed for was absent. In these dreams, ownership was myriad but happiness was obscure. Loving comfort and true security were distant and inaccessible. It was similar to a subtle feeling that had pursued the boy since entering this strange world: loneliness, and the feeling of loss. In his dreams family, security, true friends, and peace appeared separated and unobtainable. True treasures such as these were distant, and as hard as he tried, he never could acquire peace.

Water played a very important role in these dreams as well, the liquid punctuating them in unusual manners. At one point, he was skimboarding on a sandy beach when a large shorebreaker drenched him. Later, the boy was in a Metallica mosh pit while a darkened figure, with face in shadows, selected out Chris from the huge crowd and used a pump squirt gun to soak him. At another time, he was blessed with heavenly guitar skills, throwing down a killer guitar riff on his *Fender Stratocaster* in a large steamy shower.

How are dreams constructed, what sets the content and length, and what are the purposes of dreams? Answers to these questions known by God, escape understanding in the world. To be sure, however, the origin of his watery dreams was obvious to the boy the next morning.

Christopher awoke startled, aware that something was observing him, something with eyes, something with hot breath, and something with a large tongue. Brushing the corner of his eye and trying to focus he realized overwhelming intimidation. Blinking, panting, and drooling with his tongue hanging from one side of his jaw sat one of Nick's huge bulldogs. Chris was still suspicious of canines, and the bulldog's presence panicked the young boy. He would never confess aloud the racist statement, but all bulldogs do look alike. Whether this was Spike, Nails, or Smasher was not clear but insignificant, for each was formidable. Watching the dog at his bedside, he soon realized the origin of the water in his dreams: doggy drool.

The bulldog was eyeing him with only a tolerable suspicion, sitting back on his huge haunches, his tail curiously not moving this morning. From the boy's supine position, the dog towered above the boy, supporting his weight with one large paw placed painfully on the center of the boy's hand. From the corner of the dog's drooping lips rolled a continuous supply of thick drool spattering on Chris's face. Periodically, the dog vigorously shook his head, arranging his lips just so, in the process cascading salivary products over the entire length of the boy.

Chris was afraid to anger this menacing beast. He lay still and very quiet with eyes wide open staring up at the dog, his hand still pinned by the canine paw. Given the alternative, he felt lucky to accept the dog's dribble as an unwelcome gift.

"Okay, dog...good dog," he said with fright as another drop of drool caught the boy in the face.

"And your drool is bad, ah...ah...I mean good," Chris continued, carefully wiping his forehead with his one free hand. The dog understood humans, he decided, but probably not that ironic choice of words for now. "And dude, I mean dog, a good idea! Ya, good way to wake me up. Silly, I slept too long right? Ya, that's it, ya want me up, right now? And, I'll just wash the drool,

I mean spit, I mean saliva off later. No problem. I like drool... ah, ah, especially on my face. Ha, Ha...maybe it's good for zits. Hey, we could make a million dollars if it was!" The dog turned his head just slightly, his deep brown eyes making serious eye contact with the boy. "Oh well, ah...you don't want a million bucks, I'm sure... right? Ah, I like you, puppy. I mean, ha...ha...silly, I mean...dog. I like you a lot, at least better than clowns."

With that, the bulldog shook his head repetitively back and forth shaking thick drool all over Chris' face and body. Chris shuddered, thinking to himself that the beast might be insulted. It was impossible, but could the beast know his dislike of all things clown? But how could the dog know? he wondered. Well he could not know, the boy decided. The bulldog's size made him question even this simple, well reasoned conclusion, however.

"Nice one, dog. I'll just need to do laundry now. I mean its fine, really."

Time passed slowly as the dog watching Chris closely, the boy trying to appease his apparent sentinel. The dog lifted his paw for a brief moment redistributing his weight, but brought it down again on the boy's palm. Chris slowly moved his arm and rolled the paw off him very carefully. The dog looked down at the boy's hand and quickly lifted the paw and replaced it again on Chris's palm. He moved his hand again, but much more slowly. He hoped that he could do this in such a gentle matter that the dog might not notice. However, again the dog slowly moved his paw and stood on the boy's hand. A quick shake of his head punctuated this, dousing Chris again.

The boy began to realize that the dog's presence was not coincidence. As he lay looking up at the dog, the boy began to question his intentions. Sliding away from the dog, his hand still securely held in place, he stood slowly, coming to his feet and hoping to still appease the dog with a big fake grin. He had used this technique before, presuming that dogs sense the tone rather than content of your voice.

"Nice ugly dog." Chris said, trying to keep his tone friendly and hoping to slip his words by the dog, assuming he would not understand.

"GRRRRRRR--" was the beast's reply, reinforcing the animal's knowledge of the English language.

Chris quickly decided to stop his insults. "I mean, ah, ah… nice… pretty dog."

"GRRRRRRR--" Was heard again.

"Ah—ah--I mean nice handsome dog," Chris corrected the gender error, hoping his new four-footed friend would forgive his mistake.

To Chris's relief, the bulldog now pulled his paw from Chris's grip. Looking for a friendly massage, the dog ducked his head under the boy's out stretched hand. As he appeased the beast, he was able to wipe the spittle off his forehead. Chris began to almost like the dog now. He had never had a dog of his own at home, and up until now had not trusted most of them. Yes, Chris concluded that perhaps dogs were man's best friend. Chris stood in front of the dog rubbing his head. "Good dog," he said, giving him one last pat on the head.

As if by silent signal the dog suddenly took off. Within a few steps he had circled behind the boy. Before the boy could turn the dog ducked his head between the boy's knees. Chris fell backward, sprawling over the dog's muscular back, reaching and grabbing a handful of brush coat for security, as the canine sped away. Pulling himself upright, he found himself straddling the dog; holding on determinedly to the dog's studded collar, and riding the beast in horselike fashion. Slowly, he regained balance. Sitting now on the beast's back, Chris realized he was riding a bulldog bareback.

The boy riding the bulldog shot out of the chamber along a dirt path and through a stand of fir trees along the southern edge of the bluff. The sun was just appearing to the east, and a cool breeze was blowing in from the ocean. As soon as Chris began to enjoy his ride, the dog slowed to a trot, stopped and dropped to his rear haunches, unceremoniously dumping the boy to the ground. Once dismounted, the dog turned and looked at Chris over his shoulder. Looking back, the beast stood and slowly began to walk away. The boy had no other option but to follow.

The bulldog led Chris along a dirt path through a sparse forest and towards the bluff. Still with a suspicion, he walked several yards behind, checking for ambush everywhere. Soon, the roar of crashing surf became louder and the trees began to thin out.

Ahead Christopher noted someone around a bend, crouching down with his back towards him. The boy thought that he was alone, save his canine friend, and it concerned him. Coming to the last tree, however, he was relieved when he recognized Nicholas. He started to call for him but stopped, standing instead behind the last tree and watching the boy.

The dog moved now from Chris's side, and came to sit obediently next to his master. Nicholas seemed to be lost in his thoughts and did not look up. Humming to himself with his back toward the boy, he seemed totally unaware of Chris's presence and preoccupied with his toil. He stood on his knees busy pushing and smoothing the dirt before him. At his side was his trusted sword, standing with its tip driven into the ground as a sentry.

Chris continued to watch the boy, standing behind him and looking over Nicholas's shoulder with curiosity. He was dressed much like the prior day. Absent a bandana, his brown locks blew gently in the sea breeze. He was barefooted and dressed in black mid-cut trousers. Around his waist again was the blue sash tied loosely over his hip. He was chewing and blowing large bubbles with the gum Chris had given to him the day before.

Nicholas was busy excavating a small crater. He would turn to his blade, digging with its tip, loosening dirt in a shovel like manner. Returning the sword as before, the pirate-boy would lift dirt loosened with his blade from the hole with his hands. He then would turn to lifting dirt out of the hole, piling it alongside as if for future use.

Nice bubble, Chris thought to himself. The boy was a quick learner, for Chris had spent little time covering bubble gum etiquette and actions.

Nicholas blew a last large bubble, popped it with his teeth, and removed the gum from his mouth. Deeply in thought, he examined the clump closely within the palm of his hand. Replacing the chewing gum and giving it one last essential chomp, the boy then dropped the wad from his mouth into the dirt hole with great care. Nick supported himself over the opening on his hands and knees and stared judiciously for some time. He then reached down and moved the piece just slightly. Satisfied, he closed his eyes and said a silent prayer.

The bulldog, whose identity was in fact Spike, sat quietly at his master's side during this process. Watching closely, he seemed to miss no salient detail. As was his nature, he was panting vigorously. However, he carefully directed any drop of drool away from the dirt hole. The dog seemed to approve of his master's pursuit, for his tail wagged vigorously as he eyed the hole obediently.

Chris wondered what Nicholas could possibly be doing with an old spent chewed piece of gum. Was it a living being requiring a funeral? Was he disposing of the gum, thinking it ripe and ready to rot? Having stepped on casually disposed gum Chris could understand this. Was he using the gum to test his dog's ability to find buried treasures? Chris felt horrified. Maybe he intended to dig it up later and chew it!

"Dude-- I'll give you another piece, just don't dig it up and eat it again." he said silently to himself.

As Chris continued in his thoughts, he began to feel that he was violating the boy's trust, watching him in silence. Justifying espionage he reasoned it was the bulldog's fault.

The dog brought me here without choice, he reasoned silently. Catching himself he thought, "Oh to what depths have I sunk as to indict a canine for my own deceitful actions?" Laughing at himself, he realized how kingly even his thoughts had become. He would force himself to think as a Temeculian once more.

While Chris thought, Nicholas continued his work. He lifted a clay pot and poured a measure of water into the hole, then swept dirt from the edge down on top of the gum. After another measure of water, the boy gently patted the soil with his hands. Until the hole was full, Nicholas repeated this process. Taking the pot, Nicholas emptied the rest of the water drenching the site. When done he stood and rubbed his hands clean.

Chris took a step towards the boy. He expected to surprise Nicholas but without turning the boy said, "Good morning Christopher of Temecula." Turning now to the boy, he wiped his hand on his tunic and addressed his new friend with a broad confident smile.

Chris walked to the boy's side. He had decided the purpose of this exercise when he had seen Nicholas give the site its last and final soaking. The boy was planting the gum. Chris looked down at the filled hole trying not to give away the humor he felt at this point.

Turning now to address the boy, he said as seriously as he could, "Hey dude, you can't grow gum! You know—it--its not--you know--its not a plant dude." Laughing to himself, he bit his lip trying not to disappoint his confused friend.

To Nicholas, Chris's revelation did not ebb his determination or poise. With a mischievous twist to his smile, Nicholas looked down and reexamined his project. Turning again to Christopher, who at this time could not hide the amused look, he just shrugged his shoulders reached down and rubbed Spike behind the ear.

The boy either knew something more about the science of gum growing or did not really care about Chris's knowledge base. Knowing Nicholas, his reaction was probably some of each.

Some people do things as they see fit, not wavering from their ideas or waiting for the opinion of others. They are polite, they listen and measure contrary views, and if they offer an advantage, they do not hesitate to adopt these. Individuals like this often have a spark, an ability to see what others do not, and the confidence to continue with their ideas and dreams in the face of challenge or initial disappointment. Chris had learned that Alexander was like that, and would learn in time that Nicholas was in this manner very much the same.

Experiencing gum was mystical to Nicholas. From his earliest remembrance, Chris had a similar respect for this chewy substance

No gum till I'm three, no gum till I'm three! He heard this statement over and over in his pre-three years. It had been the rule for this oldest of three boys. It was his parent's attempt at junk food discipline, not allowing gum chewing until he was three years old. Children are quite literal, and Chris had thought that was then a universal law, applying to all Americans. He believed this rule so much that when he met a little girl who was several months older than him, and therefore three years old, careful to speak quietly away from his mother asked frantically, "Do you have gum?"

"Squawk...no gum in a tree? Squawk--we shall see!" a brilliantly multicolored parrot said from a branch of one of the trees.

Looking up Nicholas was already off walking briskly away. A single whistle and the Chris's dog friend moved to follow. Quickly the other two bulldogs appeared from nowhere and obediently filled in behind the boy's heel. The bird flew off trailing the boy as well.

"You, can't grow gum dude!" Chris repeated. By now, he was not so sure.

CHAPTER 14
A Boy in the Sea

> THE WICKED MAN FLEES THOUGH NO ONE PURSUES,
> BUT THE RIGHTEOUS ARE AS BOLD AS A LION
> **PROVERBS 28:1**

The following days rolled along like thunder, night after dawn and dawn after night. Through them all Nicholas showed himself a pirate in all that he did, from head to foot, through and through. For it seems as if a pirate has responsibilities that are myriad, involving much more than roaming the high seas, preying on ships with dreadful boarding and collecting treasure in troves. While this is an exciting and certainly necessary portion of pirate repertoire, a well-rounded pirate involves much more, and to that end, Nicholas certainly succeeded.

Piracy is an obdurate and enduring institution. Etched upon the retinal cones and neuronal networks of children universally, Pirates of the Caribbean serves as a model of pirate-dom, Disney style. Nicholas was a pirate who served this institution well.

Examining the buccaneer life in detail, you find that a pirate lives a life full of danger and excitement, with a relentless search for land-based escapades and sagas sailing swiftly on the maritime sea. A pirate lives each day to the full with a serious pursuit of life's substance for each day may be his last, given the occupational hazards of the trade. A pirate then moves from one stirring episode to the next, not reflecting on the past, but moving forward with a swashbuckling swagger.

Like Alexander, Nicholas was surrounded with a crew of dedicated boys. They were pirate-boys as well, tough but friendly, and devoted to their royal leader. For reasons which escaped Chris, Andy went by the moniker of Little Andy, which was odd for he was as tall as the next. He wore his eye patch with regularity. He was the best swordsman of the group and perhaps throughout the Kingdom, sans Nicholas himself. Sam had a head of bristly red hair, disorganized and in need of a comb, a freckled face, and warming smile punctuated with a missing front tooth. Instructed in maritime things by Nicholas, he became an exceptional seaman and would spend his time repairing and sailing the pirate fleet. When on deck, Nicholas was in command, Sam his first mate.

Tyler was a tall boy with blond hair and blue eyes. He wore a big bright smile and had a liking for the wet life, first into the surf when the occasion allowed. Jonny was a tall brown-haired boy with a quiet, brown-eyed countenance. Spike, Nails, and Smasher continued their patrol activities, only warming to the modern day boy as time went on. All of the troop, canines included, accepted Chris quickly, including him in every facet of buccaneer life.

After a time, Christopher began to appreciate Nicholas's objective. It was clear to him that in addition to the accumulation of treasure, the capture of intact ships and arsenal was equally important. They designated certain of these captured ships for salvage, filling the deep water of the pirate cove. With these additions, gradually a small navy took shape, readied and lashed to their quay. These were his majesties' ships, flying the dreaded Boar's Hoof, and borrowed back for the duration. The armada grew, sailing ships taken on high sea, stripped and repaired to seaworthy status for a future raging storm, whose danger and complexity seemed known to Nicholas alone. The boy lived by faith, however, for the exile led to this buccaneer life, and he accepted God's promise without doubt, even to a renegade brigand.

Nicholas garnered a deep loyalty from those surrounding him. With a roaring estuary of sodden water shoots, darkened mysterious caves, treasure-filled caches, white sunny beaches, brilliant bulldogs, sea jaunts, and a parrot reconnoiter, fun filled the long barefooted sunny days. Christopher came to see Nicholas as vivacious and high-spirited, who led by his actions rather than words, fair to all. He was sure in his way with judgment and bravery drawing people to him like a magnet. They were a close group, doing as Nicholas directed, often without spoken commands. To be the big gun, one seldom uses bullets; to be great, you have to want the ball. As time passed, Christopher observed that these idioms described the pirate-boy leader precisely. Camp discipline was as military as fun would allow. Nicholas was the leader. Sam and Little Andy and the others took their orders from Nicholas, and would do so even to the death.

As with his observations of Alexander, as the days passed Christopher was aware of a dark burden, hidden well but present in the pirate-boy as well. Moments of far off glances, lonely introspection, and times of solitary prayer separated Nicholas from the others. From his perspective of castle dungeons, slain knighted brother, evil tyrants, and a beautiful Queen within high towers, the modern day boy sensed that the onus for a future lay with his new friends.

Little Andy was a diligent boy who longed to wield the steel blade in armed battle. He honed his swordsman skills by continually instigating mock sword combat with Nicholas. While his defeat was inevitable, he never gave up and counted himself better for each opportunity. As with Nicholas, the boy stood a half a head taller than most of the other boys. He wore sun-bleached blond hair spiked with a dab of pitch. A black banded eye patch dominated his countenance. Little Andy looked to Nicholas with enduring respect, the degree to which on occasion extended beyond reason.

Christopher had watched the boy carefully since their first meeting. He concluded right off that his eye patch had little to do with a malady of the eye. The right eye could be patched one moment, the left the next. Perhaps he meant to cover both eyes, but had only one patch. It seemed that Nicholas had encouraged its use, for he had a large influence upon its position. With a silent nod he would direct the boy to reposition his patch throughout the day. Like a bugger hanging from the pupil's nose, the eye patch became an unspoken irritation to the boy. Chris wished to inquire of its purpose but dared not to call attention to a possible disability. It bothered him like an inaccessible itch. One day when alone with the boy he drew himself up. "What's up with the patch dude?" The question seemed to have no affect on Little Andy, and he returned it with a silent shrug.

Now that Chris had broached the subject, he pushed on. "Why wear it, I mean you look cool and everything, but your eye, you can see can't you? Dude, you're not even cross-eyed!"

"Nicholas tells me so. It will improve my sword fighting," he insisted.

Frustrated by his answer Christopher added, "Oh, ya, and by the way, you always lose."

With this Little Andy began laughing, looking at the boy. "Defeat Nicholas with the blade, no one has or ever will!" He paused a moment and looked to the ground. Little Andy became serious and examined the boy carefully. "I am ready, however. And mind you, swordsmanship will play a role," the boy said, slowly shaking his head in the affirmative. "For when the moment comes, I plan to strike down those who have robbed, and those who have defied my kingdom, and especially my Queen!"

Little Andy emphasized his point by reaching and gently grabbing a handful of Chris's hair. The response startled the boy. Drawing deeply, Chris held his breath in silence. With his eyes wide and bursting open, he slowly lifted Little Andy's hand from his head. Chris dropped his eyes slowly to the boy's scabbard as he wondered why he had to insult the boy's sword fighting. It was another instance of talking himself into trouble. He stared ahead, blankly trying to betray himself innocent of the accusation. Inside he panicked and thoughts flew along quickly. The boy took his Queen seriously. Could he have pulled the Queen's hair out from her scalp? Memories of the event flooded his mind, his escape over the moat climbing down upon royal locks. She had screamed and he had released! Oh no, I scalped her, he thought hysterically.

Pirates, Scoundrels, and Kings

Christopher blurted out a confession. "Dude, I'm sorry, I—I--just didn't mean it. I saw it once in a fairy tale book. Oh please, does Nicholas know?"

Little Andy looked to the boy with a curious twist of his head. Thinking for a moment, he responded. "Nicholas knoweth," he said, shaking his head slowly.

Christopher now dropped his head into his hands and began to sob. "She was so nice. I didn't mean it; it seemed right at the time. We were trapped dude, guards, knights, and rats in the freak'n prison! They had me in a prison! It was black, cold, you know there was some dude's bones in there! Are you hearing me? Oh, it was so fast, it was her--" Christopher hung his head, his countenance resigned to his fate. "No it was my idea. Forgive me, please."

Little Andy began laughing hysterically at the boy. "I know not of what you are speaking, but guilt overrides yourself. A court jester could not tell such a story! Christopher of Temecula, an odd one you are." The boy turned and walked slowly away, then tossed a glance behind him. "Only God may forgive, Christopher."

Left to ponder alone, Chris dropped his clenched fists and began a long sigh of relief.

THE DEEP-WATER COVE WAS SO completely hidden that the pirate boy had come upon it only by chance. Named Pirate's bay for its veiled character, the cliffs above its northern edge became the concealed home to the buccaneers. It was an appropriate name, for while visually hidden, sailing access to it as well was obscure.

A densely wooded forest rolled gently to white sandy seashore, protecting the southeastern edge of the deep-water bay. High rocky cliffs crashed as an impenetrable barrier on its northern edge, above which camp was made. To the west, the relentless sea ruled, separated from the bay by two rocky fingers of land nearly meeting and forming a narrow portal. Thick stands of oak trees shot above the western horizon arising from a long leg shaped island called Pirate's boot, the toe of which pointed into the sea.

The eastern edge of the island formed a narrow strait protecting the cove's entry. This was aptly called the Pirate's strait. Within the strait lay a rocky bottom, penetrable for deep draft ships only at peak tide. Entry to the bay then required a coastal approach, dangerous sailing along the strait, and then a sharp bend through the portal to the deep water of the bay. The bay served as a sheltered harbor for masted sailing vessels dashed to a wooden quay, hidden from the seafaring eye and treacherous to approach by sea. Travel to and from Pirate's bay required experience and bemoaned the cautious. Yes, the bay was a perilous area, and Nicholas loved it.

A DAY TO REMEMBER BEGAN innocently one cool overcast morning. Arising early, Nicholas led his troop to his favorite ship, a stout and nimble, two-masted, square-rigged vessel, which he began calling Chewy just that same day. Looking at Chris the pirate boy gave him a sly wink after announcing the ship's name and set sail with furled foresail, slowly across Pirate's bay.

Other than the light spirited reference, Nicholas was unusually quiet that day, pacing on deck and giving the occasional order to his first mate Sam. At peak high tide, they made the bay's portal, turned south along Pirate's Boot, and navigated out to the open sea.

The ocean was rough and harsh once they had passed the protection of the coast. Unfurling the mizzenmast, they tacked directly into a southern wind making for open sea. With their course set, Nicholas left the deck, climbing to the forward crow's nest, looking upon the sea and scanning the horizon with his eyeglass.

Chris's function on such a voyage was still unclear to the boy. He came to this pursuit with no knowledge of sailing and ships, and while he had learned quite a bit, he still felt uncomfortably useless. Looking above to Nicholas, he decided to climb the mast and quickly came to stand next to the leader. He was not sure that Nicholas was aware of his presence when the boy handed him the glass. Nicholas pointed to what seemed a speck on the distant horizon across the choppy sea. He seemed to be expecting its presence all along.

Chris stared across the water. The sun was rising over the eastern horizon, and he squinted, shading his eyes with his hand.

"What do you see?" Chris wondered.

Lifting the eyeglass, he saw the object of their pursuit, a sailing vessel baring a route which would intercept their ship off in the distance. It was a large ship with sails furled and ocean spray cut high into the air by its heaving bow. The ship barred down upon them with velocity, for even in the short time that Chris observed, the ship's image grew and the distance separating the two ships narrowed.

Chris returned the lens. A contented countenance had appeared on the pirate boy's face. Nicholas was keenly looking at the approaching ship knowing, and perhaps expecting the scene, as a small closed-mouth smile came upon him.

"What is it you see, Christopher of Temecula?" Nicholas said, turning to Chris.

"A ship," Chris replied.

"And doth sheets does she run?" Nicholas asked.

Chris thought for the moment, eyeing the ship a distance off. The language needed some translation for the boy, but he took the eyeglass again and closely examined the ship.

"It doth—a--you know," Chris responded looking for the word and spying the ship through the telescope. "It has three—ya--three, up things--you know masts," he finally said proudly, turning to the boy.

Nicholas nodded in the affirmative. He motioned to the deck below and asked, "And what of us?"

Chris now realized that the ship on which they stood was a much smaller vessel, having but two main masts to the other ship's three. "Two masts. Chewy has two masts. So?" he questioned.

Nicholas smiled and turned to the boy. "They aught grander, fleeter, and their guns much out-man ours." With a chuckle he looked into Chris's eyes directly and winked. "It is to our liking!" And with that, he was up over the side of the crow's nest sliding along the lashing and dropping quickly to the deck below.

Chris thought for the moment. He could easily see the approaching ship now as it bore down upon them, gaining ground quickly with the wind in its favor. It was much larger, and having the beginnings of the nautical mind, he calculated that it was as well a much superior vessel. Had he known he would have realized that the ship was a man-o-war, a huge sailing warship found only in the king's navy.

He became aware of the rusty stained sky after the first canon blast crashed into the sea, exploding and sending a massive wave of cold seawater up and over the starboard bow. Drenched, Chris now realized the beginnings of an assault. With little thought to his safety, he was quickly over the nest's side sliding and eventually falling awkwardly to the deck below.

Nicholas was shouting out commands as he ran to stern. The crew had scattered to their battle positions manning sails and lines as tested seafarers. A second explosion flooded and rocked the ship as the navy vessel closed upon them, turning port and letting fly a full volley of shot from its bank of canons.

Nicholas was watching the opposing ship closely. He stood upon the wooden rail, his sword in his hand raised as if triumphant. He had anticipated such a maneuver for a square-rigged man-o-war needs a broadside approach to maximize the bank of side-firing canons. "Hard tiller to port (left)," Nicholas yelled, now standing upon the deck side banister.

Chewy chugged briefly to a stop then creaked and rattled in the wind as it rapidly turned, picking up speed as it became aligned with the prevailing southerly wind. They were now turning away from their pursuit, putting some distance between the two ships. The next volley told of this for it fell further off the bow with only spray as a reward.

Nicholas quickly made his way along the length of the ship from port to starboard (right), viewing and guiding their hopeful escape. Chris hoped they were quick at it, for the intensities of their foe were not in question. Behind them loomed a huge sailing warship intent upon blowing their little ship out of the water.

Pirates, Scoundrels, and Kings

Chewy was now retracing its path, sailing with the wind in a southerly direction. They had gotten a small jump on their foe for the warship having turned port was now making a huge starboard arch, trying to intercept the pirate boy's fleeing ship. Racing now at full speed, Nicholas set their course for the southern tip of Pirate's Island. Tide had receded during their maneuvers, but their draft was light and they might just be able to navigate.

THE CAPTAIN WAS A FOREBODING hulk of a man complete with black bandanna, a scarred nasal ala, and a weathered stubbly face. He wheezed and lumbered to the port side with a concerned grimace and inspected their position relative to the coast. He had sailed the ocean for a lifetime but had little experience sailing about these shores. He was concerned and rightfully so, for with the depth of the sea at this point a fully laden man-o-war could easily run aground.

History has shown the vulnerability of large sailing ships to shallow waters. The Captain's Cloud ran aground in 1658 England, sinking with all the crew drowning in just six minutes. The captain, eventually found washed up on the coast, had survived only to die in his escape. Such was the risk of reckless sailing so close to shore in a deep drafted hull.

The captain was not aware of history, but experience told him of the danger. He launched a purulent wad of spittle over the side using this self-designed method to sound distances and depth. It would be close he calculated, but the reward he pursued mandated abandon, reckless if needed.

He had sensed as much from the moment he sighted the ship, and immediately knew he would risk it all. It was that brat of a boy, the same precocious monster who dared duel him on the high seas. His best and newest ship lay upon the bottom of the sea, sunk by that yet weaned juvenile monster. His purulent pride could not let this insult stand. Here providence seemed shining for once upon the tortured man.

The captain found little room for failure in a totalitarian regime, especially if that failure happened to be a pig. He had tried the honorable route, lying. Just when he thought he had succeeded in covering up the brat's victory and his failure, the Boar had turned upon him knowing all the time of his defeat. The Boar had struck at his weakness; with functionally less than one lung, he could not survive many more anoxic insults. "A spy must have told him, aye, the bird 'twas the bird!" he thought, tormenting himself.

The captain was elated. He had come across the ship by chance and he now bore down within artillery range before the brat boy even realized his predicament. Turning hard to port he brought his starboard canon bank in range. The man yelled for test volleys and gauging their trajectory, the captain launched the entire bank. Canons exploded from their holds with blistering fire punching back the ship with mighty recoil. They hit the water just off distance blasting seawater for miles in the air and spraying his foe with exploding water and billowing smoke.

The captain knew that the boy would run. He was not surprised then when his foe turned port and picked up the prevailing wind pulling away from the captain for the time. Because of the discrepant size, the boy could turn much quicker and soon he was out of canon range. Ordering a sweep to starboard, the captain set a northerly arch to cut off his foe. When the brat boy's ship stopped dead in the water ahead of him, he could not believe his luck. His hatred was building. He had the boy, and throwing caution away the captain now ordered their approach alongside, expecting to blast and then board the wind-loosed ship. "More rounds," he shouted to his crew as he moved forward commanding cannon blasts and railing with delight.

Chris left Nicholas's side, moving to the ship's bow and staring ahead across the sea. They were sailing like the wind now, and judging speeds and distances he thought that they might just make the protection of Pirate's Island. Looking back over the portside, he hoped that the size of the warship would preclude them from the same sanctuary. The ship's violent lurch threw him to deck on his face. Getting up to his knees, he turned. Seeing Nicholas he said, "What the heck!"

Just when escape seemed likely and the crashing shells fell on empty sea, the ship shivered to a sudden and frightening stop. Dead in the sea with a moaning grunt, the wooden hulled ship ground to a halt with only its momentum to slowly push them along. The foresail, those billowing sheets that translated the prevailing wind into power now, bristled back and forth in a useless waste of energy. Nicholas was upon that mast, loosening the line and letting it go, zapping all power from their ship and placing their escape in jeopardy.

"He's crazy," Chris said in desperation as he tried to understand the pirate boy's move.

Nicholas dropped from the mast to deck. Tossing the mast line to a bewildered Sam, he ran to the ship's aft, passing crewmembers that seemed as well unsure of his purpose. Nicholas arrived rearward, and eyed the ship behind. Taking his eyeglass, he quickly measured up the warship. He raised his fist in triumphant as the naval ship responded with a hard starboard tiller now making directly for his stalled vessel. Another volley of canon fire exploded into the sea now but a few meters away from Chewy. The warship had changed course and now steamed full ahead on a track to broadside the ship. The sails were full, the canons blasted and fiery smoke emanated from the gun holds.

THE CAPTAIN VIEWED THE BRAT boy's ship now with satisfaction. That boy is a fool, he thought, as he spied the flailing sheets rustling in the stiff ocean wind. Satisfaction brought salivation as always and with a deep hawk he launched a wonderful wad of spittle overboard as he calculated his revenge. His present course was a large sweeping arch aimed at intercepting the brat boy's vessel near shore cutting off his escape. Now, that the vessel lay dead in the water, Balaam wiped his mouth victoriously with his backhand and howled in satisfying glee. Yelling his commands from the bridge with new vigor, he shortened the arch curl, and drove the warship full speed; he would ram that wretched ship broadside.

NICHOLAS NOW WAS OFF RUNNING along the deck, beaming with a huge smile upon his face. Grabbing the loosened main sail line, he ran to the port side and stood upon the rail. Watching his foe approaching, and when satisfied that the single moment had passed, he swung down from his perch flying on the line across the deck. His mates met him mid-ship, and with the mass of several boys now understanding his idea and without an extra ounce among them, they were just able to tighten the sail and engage it again.

With a sudden jolt the craft shuddered, the sail now fully furled, filled with wind, setting the drifting vessel speeding along once more. The maneuver had bought time, putting precious sea between them and the warship. Having tempted their foe, the vessel had taken the bait, changing course and crossing their stern harmlessly as Chewy accelerated away.

BALAAM CURSED AND SPAT AS he sped harmlessly across the brat boy's wake. "Pruneshench!" he yelled, hurling particularly putrid spittle at his helmsman, striking the man on the side of the head. Without so much as a grimace or a blink, the man reached and wiped his face free of sputum, dropping it unceremoniously to the deck having received worse many times before.

"Hard tiller to port you vile fool!" The captain bellowed and spit at the top of his diseased lungs.

With a tight port spiral, the man-o-war turned with the wind to chase the smaller vessel once more. They had lost precious time, however, now trailing the boy's ship by a good distance. No longer would he be able to cut the boy off, having now moved so close to shore. The captain's pride was boiling as he paced, figuring his next move. He would blast that ship out of the water or ram it into kindling wood, he thought. Anger was boiling over as his ears became a brilliant crimson color, and with that anger, his judgment became clouded.

The captain had sailed these seas many a time, but the coast was foreign to him. What always appeared as a long unbroken shoreline when viewed from the sea, was now obviously an island close to shore sheltering a long narrow inlet. It was obvious that the boy was sailing for this, hoping to make the strait and avoid his canons. However, the boy was quickly losing his precious lead, and before he could make this sanctuary, the captain was nearly upon him. Dashing his fears, he ordered his wary crew to cruise on, full of sail, and hard to port. He planned to follow his prey and crush it like the bug it was.

THE WIND WAS BLOWING FROM the north at gale force as Chewy entered the Pirate's strait. They navigated the inlet, trimmed the necessary sails, and continued at full speed into the channel. Moving north, the island was to the port (left) side, mainland starboard (right), and the portal to their hidden cove ahead.

Behind them their foe pursued aggressively, making the inlet and racing along. The huge sailing warship filled the strait, just clearing overhanging trees from the mainland, and shortening the lead moment by moment. Blasts from their canon bank roared, blowing trees out of their way as smoke filled the rusty sky.

It was at this point that Nicholas for the first time seemed concerned. He made his way to the stern, his confident smile waning as he stared at his reckless foe. The warship was now hard upon the stern (rear) of his craft and closing on the lead. Soon they would run them, the larger ship making fodder of the pirate boy's vessel.

The truth was that Nicholas never figured the vessel to follow him into the strait, but to rather retreat or better yet run aground on the rocky shores surrounding the inlet. The tide was disappointedly holding, the waters surrounding the strait much deeper than he had figured. His plan included the stalling maneuver to build a precious lead and tempt the captain to chase him with a frenzied and careless pace. Subsequently, they would enter the channel, trim the sails to slow the pace, and watch the deeper draft vessel run a ground. A grounded ship of that size had little other options than to be abandoned, and the ship would be Nicholas's!

Nicholas had not prepared for this turn of events. He knew that ship, the crew, and most of all, the captain. Had he over estimated that fool's judgment? Why would he sail at full speed into uncharted waters? No matter the answer, the captain was doing so and would run the boy's ship in a matter of minutes.

Chewy's crew stood helpless surrounding their leader with little to do but watch the unfolding disaster with helpless looks and worry. Nicholas seldom showed his emotions; however, even their leader showed beads of sweat from his brow as he watched disaster unfold in silence. Sam was busy manning the tiller and would periodically look back at their foe yelling, "You'll run aground, fools, desist!" Chris and Little Andy began pushing away overhanging branches on the mainland side with oars hoping to speed up their escape. The chase had been fun, but its finish seemed an overwhelming rout.

The canon ball hit with devastating force, bursting the mizzendeck, showering flaming wooden fragments, and jolting the ship's stern in the air. A quick bucket brigade was formed attempting to quench the burning deck. From deep below a haunting scrapping sound began, soon deepening and becoming continuous as their hull ground upon the rocky terrain of the ocean bottom. While they feared running aground, the evil ship pursued on.

The crew began to divest of ballast, throwing cannonballs, cargo, and barrels over the side. If they ran aground here, their foe would ram them and blast their ship from the sea with powerful canons. And still the evil ship pursued on.

Nicholas could wait no longer with his ship and crew's survival so tenuous. Inaction predicted disaster, a conclusion he would not let come to fruition. Nicholas was unsure of his purpose when he turned, grabbed Chris by his arm, and ran to the foredeck. Stopping, he muscled down a heavy coiled rope that hung from the wall of the forecabin. With Chris's help, they drug it along deck to the foremast.

The ship was now well in view of the bay's portal. On the mainland stood thick oak trees, which slipped by one after the other as they raced on with a harrowing pace. Below, the sound of the dragging keel intensified and grew more continuous. Canon fire from the bow galley roared and the crew's shouting could be heard from the stern as they continued battle damage and fire control. The last blast had ripped a hole in the lower whale just above water line, and Little Andy and the others began bailing with a frantic pace.

Grabbing the rope's free end, Nicholas moved to stand upon the deck rail, watching the shoreline trees speed by as he calculated his next move.

"Feed me the rope, Christopher," Nicholas said over his shoulder as he ran along the rail to the bow. Placing one free end in his mouth, the boy reached an overhanging branch and swung himself up. Shimmying along the branch, he quickly came to the thick trunk. With a square knot and half hitches he secured the rope around the tree, stood on the branch, and returned jumping to the deck. Returning to the foredeck, he threw several turns around the base of the mast. They now fed the line out as the boat advanced.

Another blast from behind shook Chris to the bone. A sickening sound and shudder could be felt as wooden fragments exploded and fire began jumping from the stern galley. Yelling and frantic running was everywhere. A thick and foul air hung over the vessel and began to choke the boy.

"Now!" Nicholas yelled to no one but himself. Turning he threw his dagger, cutting the mizzenmast clew and unfurling its sail. He quickly removed his sword from its scabbard, cut the mainmast clew and the sail unfurled as well. Now the ship was left with only momentum driving it northward in Pirate's Strait.

The tip of the ship's bow was nearly past the cove's entry when Nicholas lashed the line. Throwing several more loops and a half hitch around the mast, Nicholas took hold of the free end of the rope and walked up the mast to hold the line with his entire weight. "Help me, Christopher," he yelled to his friend. Chris grabbed the rope behind the boy and dug his heels into the deck with all his might.

As the ship continued to advance, slack in the rope was quickly taken up. Once tight, a creaking sound could be heard as the mast flexed and the ship began to yawl starboard (right). For a moment the ship shuddered, slowing to a stop until the bow began cranking to the right. As the momentum continued moving the ship, the rope now acted like a spoke of a wheel. Pivoting along this axis, the vessel quickly made the turn into the protected water of Obscure Bay. Like a miraculous rescue from a storm, the silence was deafening. As the crew realized their happy fate cheers and screams filled the air. Nicholas grabbed his sword and sliced through his line, releasing the ship whose momentum carried the craft in to Pirate's Bay.

THE CAPTAIN TOOK WRETCHED JOY in other's misfortune; for more than anyone who had trod a plank, misery was his first love. He had thrown caution to the wind and pursued the brat boy where most would not, and he loved himself for this. He had ordered the bulkheads knocked away and the bow guns released from their confinement. There were only two 12-pound canons in the head galley, but he loved to see other decks splinter and the gloom that was the result. He loved to see the enemy crew torn by his shells, jumping here and there, putting out fire and bailing water in hopeless desperation. He laughed deeply as his craft approached the stern of the enemy. Soon he would run that wretched brat's ship.

When his foe's sails were unfurled, he relished a quick end to the pursuit. It would be sooner that he could ram the vessel, and he planned to slice it from stern to head. He did not notice his loss until Chewy made a quick starboard (right) turn into the quiet safety of the protected Pirate's Bay.

THE CREW NOW SURROUNDED NICHOLAS and Chris as they watched the naval ship's fate. Racing full of sail in Pirate's Strait is a dangerous pursuit, and their foe quickly ran aground. There was a deafening squeal as their keel dug into the rocky bottom of the strait. The enemy crew was off, now diving for their lives into the surrounding water and swimming for shore, the last remaining man, the dark brooding captain, again foiled by that boy. And with little lung to spare, the man jumped overboard to safety. The captain does not always go down with the ship.

THE BOYS WERE AS WELL over the side. They swam towards the wrecked ship with strong strokes and the hope of salvage. On board Chewy, Chris and Nicholas were left to ponder. Chris could not believe what he had just witnessed. Jumping up and down he was laughing and shaking his head.

Nicholas walked up slowly to Chris. Staring out over the water, he could see the grounded ship and his crew. He had cut this one too close, however, and their escape just too narrow. The boy realized that he had snatched victory from the jaws of almost certain total loss. Nicholas loved the challenge but something worrisome had happened. His bay known to no one but himself had now been seen by the enemy. Warship clouds were now possibly on the horizon.

Nicholas smiled sadly and said, "Balaam--times lie with us no longer my friend, Christopher of Temecula."

Chapter 15
The Straits of Abaddon

> I AM SENDING YOU OUT LIKE SHEEP AMONG WOLVES.
> THEREFORE BE AS SHREWD AS SNAKES,
> AND AS INNOCENT AS DOVES.
> MATTHEW 10:16

While technically victorious in battle, the near disaster at Pirate's Island left its mark. The boys salvaged the warship and as repairs continued, a three-masted flagship would soon lead the Laughing Lion's rebel navy. Inside, however, Nicholas thought himself careless. The boy lived on the edge and in his mind that edge had taken a deadly character. Prior to this, the pirate-boys enjoyed a protective isolation from the rising political storm, and now that isolation was in question. Had he not led the Boar's Hoof into his hideaway, the site would still be uncharted. While a pirate takes pride in victory, the boy wondered whether the sacrifice outweighed the prize.

There was a change in attitude in the camp for they were now on the map. The bulldogs illustrated this change. If it was possible, they seemed even more diligent in their duties. While the camp and their master's fate was always their focal point, these dogs took to their positions with military attention to duty.

Spike would not leave his master's side, while Nails and Crusher secured the periphery of the camp. Canine slumber occurred with one eye asleep, while the other mistrusting eye stood open, scanning and ready for any trouble. No one would approach Nicholas without a passing sniff of sanction. They did not tolerate visitors, and Christopher's recent approval seemed to have been revoked.

They watched him closely, and for now, placed the boy on guarded probation.

The parrot's duties intensified in response to the recent event as well. Rainbow spent much more time aloft, swooping here and there, and reporting in secret verse understood by Nicholas alone. There were whispered rumors of a bounty placed on the bird's head by the Boar's Hoof. This rumor did nothing but increase the parrot's standing with the group.

Outings on the sea became much more military in their significance. Nicholas always considered a possible ambush. He was very aware of who observed his Navy maneuvers. Pillaging now, he was focused less on treasure, and more on necessary items of war.

They gathered explosive devices from several ships at sea using their quickness and deception. The boys snatched kegs of gunpowder under the cover of dark from the enemy's ship's magazine.

They obstructed refurbishment of one of the Boar's Hoof naval ships right under the watchful eye of the yard's master. The vessel was in dry dock for repairs. A few well-placed imploders dislodged the ship, crushing its keel. The damage was such that the scrap heap became its new home.

Each day was dedicated to repairing and fitting their navy; ready was the keyword. They looked upon camp security much more seriously now. The band collected hundreds of boulders and placed them upon the cliffs of Pirate's bay, for use upon any unwanted entry.

While a smile marked Nicholas's countenance, his heart saw his world slipping away. He had an enduring desire to rid the world of the evil stench. How to accomplish this was a question deep in the personal folds of the boy's psychic. After all, he was a boy of not more than eight years, still with his primary teeth. His nuclear family was in ruins. No one had seen or heard from his father for some time. Rumor was that he succumbed to the evil that the boy opposed. His mother was lost to him as well, for she was essentially captive within the castle. And of his older brother Alexander, well their strife was known, his end certain, and Nicholas stood accused of his unthinkable demise!

In finer times, these two princely boys had been inseparable. Alexander was the eldest son in line for the throne, and in such manner was a guiding force in the younger boy's life. Together, the world was a benevolent kingdom that they would inherit. He was alone now, and the times became unclear and disturbing.

Nicholas would do his best and the future he knew would sort out. The best, for now, was protecting his boys. His location was known, and he wondered when the worst would come bounding down upon them. He would add a little sabotage here and there, and when treasure presented, he would welcome it. However, Nicholas realized that the peace would not last forever. Still with all this, there was tranquility in the boy. He had an air of quiet confidence, a manner that drew allies to him but poisoned opponents with a jealous rage.

Only a living plant can grow and nothing chewed can be alive, or could it? While nearly certain that gum would never grow, something about Nicholas made the modern day boy question this basic tenet. Christopher came upon him that afternoon, quietly tending the site with enduring love. As Chris approached, he stopped, thinking it sad. Nicholas was devoutly attentive to the site each day and would eventually be disappointed. Nicholas kneeled quietly and gently watered, without the slightest evidence of burgeoning growth.

Watching the boy, gum issues ran through his mind. Chris could relate to an interest in the substance. Nicholas tended the site with the care and love of a person who was new to the idea that the world was better because of gum. It seemed so unreasonable, however; this inanimate material chewed to a pulp would not grow. Whether gum had ever been a plant was not clear to Chris, but he doubted it. Rubber, which shared some of gum's properties, came from a tree; at least he thought so. The idea, however, of gum balls, gum sticks, or wads of the same growing on a tree; trees specific for big, red, juicy fruit, or big league chew did not seem reasonable to the boy.

Pirates, Scoundrels, and Kings

Nicholas, however, was a person who would make you question the most basic of facts. He had uncanny insight, and his beliefs were infectious. Chris scoffed to himself when the boy planted the gum like a rose bulb. However, as the days of watering and caring quietly went by, the question of 'what if...' began to enter the visitor's mind.

Others' opinions affected Nicholas very little for it changed his confident mind minimally. Gum demonstrated this issue well. Here Chris would tell the boy daily, "You can't grow gum, dude." However, as the days went on Chris found himself adding, "It can't, can it?" the question betraying his conviction. Nicholas just looked at the boy and smiled, and with a shrug of the shoulders betrayed little to reassure the wondering boy either way.

The boy was alone in his thoughts when Chris came upon him. The day was drawing to a close, the sun just at the horizon. It was cool and peaceful, and a sea breeze wafted through the adjacent trees. Nicholas sat on the rocks of the western edge of their camp, looking over the cliffs that crashed to the sea below. Spike watched his master, lying and panting beneath the closest tree. When Chris walked up, the dog eyed Chris with that tolerant suspicion. After rising to his feet for a closer look, he dropped again alongside his master and shut one eye to sleep, the other mistrusting eye open and alert as always.

"Hay...dude," Chris said, climbing and sitting on the rocks next to his friend.

Nick had been deep in thought, thinking of things and places in a serious manner. He was staring straight ahead, and tossing a pebble here and there without much thought as to its direction. "Hello, Christopher of Temecula," he said as always in the formal tongue of the day.

Christopher noticed the skull and crossbones tattoo on his right shoulder again. In the modern day world, the tattoo was a lifelong and permanent mark, a sign of rebellion. His parents were completely opposed to these, but secretly they fascinated the boy. He noticed for the first time, however, that the blackened image of the skull was smeared. Christopher realized then that Nicholas applied this pattern daily with natural inks. He chose the symbol as any pirate would.

To the modern day boy, the life of a pirate was an exciting one. Ships with boarding and looting, canons, and swords filled his head and dreams; could he ask for more? The boy was lost, however, and that nagging feeling of loneliness began again. He hid it well, distracted and busy from morning to sunset, fear having a role as well. Fun and excitement went far to divert the boy from his predicament. However, as the weeks passed one after the other that feeling resurfaced and like that persistent itch he could not avoid it

As only males can understand, their friendship involved few words. They sat silently for a time, each rubbing and drawing in the dirt, an occasional pebble tossed over the cliffs and falling alone to the shore below. Chris leaned back against the rocks. He was troubled with loneliness, and he sensed that Nicholas too felt the same aching feeling, being away from home as well.

Nicholas sensed his thoughts, for he lifted his head and turned to the boy. Before speaking, he signaled to his trusted guard Spike who was up and off quickly on some unspoken task.

"Do you miss your home, Christopher of Temecula," the boy said. He rose and stepped forward, staring out over the cliffs and the horizon. Turning to the boy, he knelt down on his knees and then sat with crossed legs in front of the boy. The melancholy lasted shortly, for Nicholas looked at him with that infectious boyish grin, from cheek to cheek.

"Ya, I'm, I guess, lonely," Chris said. He was glad for a simple phrase to capture a complex feeling, and one that it was all right for men to feel. Chris looked at Nicholas who had turned again to the horizon. He realized that here too was a boy who should be lonesome. He felt ashamed when he compared their stories. Nicholas was accused of the death of his brother, had lost his family, was hiding from an evil regime, and was responsible for a band of boys who looked to him for their very existence. "How do you do it, Nicholas?" he asked quietly of the boy.

The dog had returned by now and dropped a wrapped package at his master's feet. Sitting on his haunches next to Nicholas the bulldog sat and stared at Chris, panting and drooling as was his custom. Chris was now certain that the dog had a human brain; he knew everything and even seemed to express concern over the recent conversation. Cocking his head to the right, the dog looked deeply into the boy's eyes with concern. Chris had to laugh and he looked back at the dog. Reaching now with some concern and deliberation, the boy petted the appreciative canine on his huge head. The dog panted an loving pant.

Nicholas chuckled, picking up the package dropped at his side by the dog. He wiped the drool off, tore open the package, broke off a wad, and handed it to the boy. Breaking off another wad, Nicholas placed the same in his mouth and began to chew vigorously, looking curiously at his friend.

Chris rose from the ground chewing and thinking. He turned to Nick again as they began to stroll slowly to higher ground. "Dude you know...what's up with you? Don't you miss them; I mean your Mom, ahh--the Queen I mean. And the King--your home--the castle. Your home, I was there dude--it's sic--I mean good. It's all gone man. How do you stand it?"

Nicholas considered his friend's questions. Chewing away, he blew a huge bubble, popped it, and retracted the wad into his mouth. The boy brushed aside a lock of hair from his forehead. "Yes, it is true. You are long removed from your home as well. When will you be home? How does one arrive at your home? And what of your family? What of your friends? I am certain that a camp such as ours," he said, gesturing towards the camp, "lacks much for a modern day boy such as yourself. Of these needs and thoughts, I too am trouble as well, Christopher of Temecula."

"But dude! Forget me--why can you take it all?" Chris said, now with his hands on the boy's shoulders and staring into his eyes.

"Faith," was all Nicholas said. Just that one word was enough, he thought. It went without comment as far as he was concerned. He accepted it and more importantly lived by it.

"Faith?" Chris repeated, now more confused than before. He turned away from the boy and thought. He had heard of the word before, God's will and all that. However, that was for church. It worked only in church on Sundays, didn't it? What about the other 167 hours of the week, he found himself thinking? In addition, come to think of it, even in church, what did it mean? He had to think, he had to want, he had to try to get what he wanted. However, this faith, well--well, what about video games, what about squirt guns, what about friends, what about being popular, what about pogs, the boy yelled in his mind. "Faith? Dude, I know what you mean, but how?" he wondered now staring at his friend.

"Trials and tribulations are necessary my friend, for without them where can one show his faith?" Nicholas sat again and continued. "If life is how we wish, when would we look for strength and guidance? Consider these burdens as chances, Christopher of Temecula. We do not get many chances my friend. It is written: Cast your cares on the Lord, and he will sustain you," he said, quoting the scriptures. Nicholas looked at Chris, and smiled. He did not wait for a response. Nicholas stood and looked down at the sitting Christopher. "Follow me, he added."

"Follow me?" Chris thought.

Nicholas turned and walked briskly to the edge of the cliff and without hesitation he was over the side jumping and gone. The cliff dropped hundreds of feet to the rocky shore below. Spike quickly followed and sat on the edge of the cliff barking, wondering if he should obediently follow his master over the side.

"Noooooo--" Chris yelled, jumping to his feet. "I didn't mean it!" he said, his eyes wide in disbelief! He hung his head in his hands with shock. What did he say to precipitate this? Did he jump? Had the boy led him to it? Maybe he slipped; no, no way, the boy jumped, he decided. He should not have talked about his family; it was too much for the boy. Had reminding him of his past caused intolerable despair? "Oh no, oh no." His location was now known, and he wondered when the worst would come bounding down upon them. "Oh no--" he spoke to himself and the dog. "Nicholas, why?" he yelled, looking at the sky with a tear in his eye. "Don't listen to me!" he pleaded to no one but himself.

Chris descended the rocky incline quickly. At its bottom, he fell to his belly and slid to the edge. Hanging his fingers over the rim, the boy pulled forward and directed one eye cautiously over the side.

Nicholas looked up at him with a smile standing on a small rocky ledge some ten feet below. The stunt had its effect. Covered with sweat and panting, Chris breathed a sigh of relief as his heart began to slow down. Faith, here was a true example.

Looking up at the boy, he laughed. "Do not always believe the worst Christopher! Come now." He motioned for him with his hand. "We have a job to do, the sun is setting and we must hurry. Faith will come to you in pieces, but we shan't forget fun!"

Looking past the boy, Chris watched seagulls soaring, and saw the crashing sea below. Closing his eyes, he took a deep breath of relief. For a moment, he could not forgive the boy, but looking on him smiling, Christopher began to laugh. He wiped his brow and yelled at Nicholas, "Don't do that!" He pushed some dirt and rocks down on the boy in mock anger.

"Hey," Nicholas said as he raised his hands to stop the downfall. "Please, come now Christopher, we must hurry. Show him Spike."

Spike quickly obeyed his master. Without another thought, the dog jumped down on the ledge and sat quietly, staring up at the boy.

The ledge was very narrow and quite a jump. Even with Chris's legs dangling, he would still be several feet above it. He would have to jump. Sitting carefully along the edge he slid off, the force of the fall quickly throwing him to his knees. Nicholas grabbed the boy and pulled him to his feet. Chris looked over the edge and pushed himself back up against the rocky wall for protection. From the edge, it was a precipitous drop to crashing sea below.

"Off now, time is short!" Nicholas said.

With that, the three companions made their way along the ledge. From here they entered a dark cave. Chris followed Nicholas; Spike was at their rear. They wove around in a darkened tunnel, making steady progress downwards. Around one more corner and the darkness of the tunnel began to lighten, the crashing of the sea and the caw of seagulls becoming more audible.

They exited hundreds of feet below the ledge near sea level. Winding their way down a rocky slope, Chris could see the ocean water stretching now to the western horizon. They had exited from the cave on the western edge of the world as Christopher knew it. No quiet beaches here for the sea crashed with force on a rocky and unprotected shore. Nicholas moved quickly, obviously leading Chris to some destination.

The dog passed them quickly, sniffing and running along the rocky coast that he seemed to know very well. A close bird would occasionally distract Spike for a moment. Soon, however, he was up and running ahead of the two boys, the destination evidently known to him.

They had moved along some distance when Chris could wait no longer. "Where we heading dude?" Chris said, pulling up next to Nicholas.

"To a Boar's trap," he said, pausing for just a moment, wiping his brow. He turned to his friend and smiled. Then he was off again, leading his two colleagues somewhere.

The terrain was quite shear now, the boys a quick slip away from the sea. Around one more bend and their destination became visible.

Nicholas now stopped and pulled Chris behind a tree and brush cover some fifteen feet above the water. He signaled with a raised finger to his mouth for silence.

Their journey had led them along the western coast of Alucemet. Ahead, a long rocky finger of land stretched into the open choppy sea. Dense stands of evergreen trees lined its shore. At its tip, a treacherous strait lay separated from the coast of Ateirrum by just one league of churning, perilous water. It was here, where the narrowest point between these two landmasses lay, that they had come. Blowing gale force winds continually whipped through the strait, churning a turbulent wild sea within this narrow passage.

The strait had bested many unwary ships. It was shallow strait with a perilous rocky bottom, continually covered with agitating winds and crashing waves. It was this reputation, which gave the strait its name: the Strait of Abaddon. Any sea voyage along the western coast of Alucemet would sail this passage.

Nicholas pointed across the water of the strait. "Our trap awaits us, Christopher of Temecula," he said.

"Where are we Nicholas?" Chris questioned.

"The Straits of Abaddon. See how all must pass through in route to anywhere," the boy responded.

Not waiting for a response, Nicholas moved from behind the trees to the water's edge. Here a small sandy landing stood. Quickly, he began dragging out a small skiff, hidden until now in the reeds at the water's edge. Deliberately beached and concealed, a small sailing dinghy lay hidden for their use. Spike took this opportunity to bark as if he alone knew the destination for their craft.

"Shush boy." Nicholas whispered to the dog. Without a moment's delay, the dog did not debate and stopped his show of enthusiasm.

Nicholas quickly recruited the boy to his task. With Nicholas tugging on the bow, Christopher pushed the stern to the water's edge. Spike backed off to the tree line protecting their rear. Nicholas held the boat for Chris to board and pushed the craft out into the water. At the last minute, Nicholas leapt on the skiff. He moved quickly to mid-ship and hoisted the sail. Dropping down to sit on the floor of the boat, he skillfully navigated the craft out onto the rough waters of the strait. Looking back, an obedient but lonely dog sat on his haunches and watched his master disappear in the darkness.

As they approached the strait, Nicholas turned the craft towards the peninsula, seeking out some shelter from the wind. He then downed the sail and dropped a small anchor. Moving to the bow, he uncovered a tarp, which covered a hidden cargo.

Before him were dozens of collapsed leather balls with protruding metal spikes sharpened to deadly points. A short rope was attached to each leather ball with a thick iron pin with a large open eye. A burlap bag was attached to its other end of the rope, open on one side and closed with a drawstring.

Nicholas grabbed a leather ball and tossed it rearward to his curious friend. "Our trap at last my friend," Nicholas said, grabbing a second. "Watch and do likewise."

Reaching into his tunic, the pirate-boy recovered the package given to him by Spike. Opening the package, the boy broke off a piece, put it in his mouth, and began chewing what appeared to be chewing gum. Christopher looked at the wad of gum curiously. Between chews, Nicholas turned his attention to the leather object. Taking deep breaths, he forced air into the globe through an opening. With each breath, the object began to take on its globular shape, the spikes uniformly radiating in a menacing manner as weapons from the globe. Once happy with its state of inflation, Nicholas shoved the chewed mass inside and sealed the port.

"It just took Nick's chew to finish Alexander's idea. Still no faith, my friend?" Nicholas queried.

Then Chris realized what had begun as a single stick of gum had been multiplied, somehow. The boy laughed at his new friend's determination. From the moment Nicholas's first partake of gum, he knew the material was perfect. Not only was gum to change Nicholas's culinary life forever, he realized that here was the substance for an unfinished idea, an idea lacking but one piece, a wad of Gum making an airtight seal of these pneumatic items of war. Not only was gum the perfect chew, it was a fine material for certain inventions.

"Alexander has calculated the ballast to be three stones," Nicholas said, looking at the boy as he worked. With this he grabbed three rocks from the bottom of the boat, placed them in the bag, and secured them with the drawstring. Pointing now to the inflated leather sphere he continued, "Inflated, buoyancy results in lost tonnage." He continued pointing to the burlap sack. "Alexander speaks of three such stones, and depth as an ally. The line is the key," he said. With this, the boy attached a small woven line to the eye of the pin where the ballast line attached to the bottom of the globe. On the free end of the line was a small piece of cork with sharp metal hooks. He tested it with a sharp tug on the line; the ballast bag disconnected and fell to the deck.

Chris watched all this with a sharp and curious eye. Here was the beginning of a crude ocean mine! The inflated globe's buoyancy, created by the trapped air, would be pulled deep into the water by the ballast, a rock filled sack. Then the sphere would float at a predetermined depth, when the upward pull of the air filled globe's buoyancy was equally opposed by the downward gravitational pull affected by the stones in the burlap bag. The free end of the trip wire would float innocently on the surface, until the slightest tug from a passing ship would release the bag. The unopposed upward pull of the buoyant globe would then send it racing upward to break the surface with amazing force; any unsuspecting wooden-hulled ship would be impaled and sunk.

"Awesome, this is totally awesome, dude!" Chris understood, smiling widely. The boy moved to examine the completed item in Nicholas's hand. He lost his balance briefly in the swaying skiff, kneeled down, and held the globe. The spikes were deadly, nearly one foot in length and razor sharp. "We can drop these in the strait," he said with enthusiasm. Chris realized that here was the ideal strategic site. Any ship moving along the western coast of Alucemet must navigate the strait. With relatively few devices, they could control this traffic.

"What do you call these, dude?" Chris wondered asking Nicholas.

Nicholas now frowned, biting his lip as he thought. Turning to Chris he asked, "No name has come to me as yet. What name comes to mind, Christopher of Temecula?"

Chris immediately said a name from the world of pogs. "Slammers," he said emphatically, after the heavy object used to dislodge opposing pogs. "Slammers, dude, they're slammers," he said, proud of himself.

"Slammers they will be," Nicholas said. "A finer name there is not."

With that, the two began to prepare their cargo. With eagerness, they inflated the slammers, secured the inflation ports with a well-chewed wad, and loaded the sack with ballast. Once completed, Nicholas pulled up anchor. He righted the sail, and moved out into deeper areas of the deserted strait.

It took nearly an hour to finish. When completed, the two boys sat within the skiff and admired their handy work. Along the strait, deployed slammers spread across the choppy stretch of water. A test would come just the next day when traffic would again frequent the strait. At this time in the turbulent history of Alucemet, only the enemy would be using the seas. Commercial shipping, other than for the evil purposes of the Boar, had for all purposes ceased. Hope was that all naval activity would become much more difficult for the enemy.

Nicholas looked calmly at his friend, and signaled a job well done with a silent nod of his head. A playful smile broke the boy's face. Quietly he asked Chris, "And now, how goes your swimming abilities, Christopher of Temecula?"

"What?" Chris asked of his friend.

Nicholas did not answer. Grabbing a paddle from the deck of the skiff, he gently nudged a trip wire floating on the surface next to them. Looking back at Chris, a mischievous smile crossed his face as the slammer pounded into the hull below their feet. Blasts of icy seawater spewed through the rents, filling the boat.

"WOOOOOOOO--dude, are you nuts?" Christopher yelled, looking with disbelief at his hysterically laughing friend. Chris looked to the shore, a good two hundred yards off over a very cold and rough sea. Turning back to Nicholas, he just shook his head and laughed. A perfect demonstration of their handy work, he realized. "Dude, " he yelled as the small boat filled rapidly with icy water. "Lucky for you, I can swim. Race you," he said, as he burst over the side and swam with strong strokes to the safety of the shore.

CHAPTER 16
A Fine Mess

THEY WILL PURSUE US UNTIL WE HAVE LURED THEM AWAY FROM THE CITY,
FOR THEY WILL SAY,
"THEY ARE RUNNING AWAY FROM US AS THEY DID BEFORE."
SO WHEN WE FLEE FROM THEM,
YOU ARE TO RISE UP FROM AMBUSH AND TAKE THE CITY.
THE LORD YOUR GOD WILL GIVE IT INTO YOUR HAND.
JOSHUA 8: 6-7

The plan worked and more successfully than anyone could imagine. Over the next several days, the Strait of Abaddon became a burial ground for those who wished to challenge it. While several ships by chance succeeded in navigating the strait, a definite liability of sea travel was established. It was a singular idea at the time, for this was the era of hand-to-hand combat where foes were obvious and the enemy within sight. The concept of a sub-surface concealed weapon, which would fire on contact with a ship's hull, became an unwonted success.

There was no warning, no enemy to confront, no one to claim responsibility, and no foe to aim a counterinsurgency. The stricken ships would often sail leagues with leaking hulls before the calamity was apparent. Even the simple correlation that sinking vessels had all been wounded within the Abaddon strait, took some time and insight to arrive at. Yes, for the time the boys had easy pickings, needing only to wait upon the enemy and wreck havoc, allowing the disabled ships to be of no further service, save to the bottom dwelling community of the icy ocean.

Between waterslide frolics and maintenance of their bursting treasure-laden coffers, the boys watched their handiwork hidden on the Abaddon cape. Nighttime saw maintenance and replacement of the slammers, preserving the effective maritime blockade. Nicholas's reputation preceded him, but with each sunken and crippled enemy ship, the pride and admiration for their leader grew quietly. It seemed as if they could protect the south sea access to the continent indefinitely with this simple but effective obstacle.

In a game of chess, one move begets another; an action here and adjustments made there. While their foe might be slow of wit, brain dead they were not.

Chris was patrolling the western edge of the strait with Trevor when a chink in the plan was noted. Trevor was a dark-skinned boy with a Buddha-like physique. He had bristly dark hair that he spiked with pitch. He wore an ear-to-ear smile continuously, even while asleep. The boy had an infectious high-pitched laugh that reminded Chris of the cartoon chipmunk Alvin. Smasher was leading the convoy today with intense anticipation and a snout full of drool.

It was the end of an exceedingly beautiful day, full of fun and activity, as was the rule in the life of the pirate-boys. They left camp in late afternoon, and as they made their way northward along the rocky shore, the sun was starting its brilliant descent dousing the western sea. A gentle sea breeze met them as they picked their way down the rocky wall.

Appearing to the north was the ominous cape of Abaddon, jutting out from the western coast of the Alucemet and forming the strait. South of the peninsula, the western mainland coastline was treacherous and rocky, with little shelter from the prevailing southerly sea winds. This rocky shoreline continued along the southern edge of the cape, crumbled and changed over the ages by crashing waves. Inaccessible by sea, the southern coast of Abaddon lacked a harbor or even short stretches of protected beach. At the edge of this rocky coast stood a dense expanse of evergreen trees whose trunks pushed skyward with powerful majesty. On the northern edge of the peninsula was a more peaceful shoreline, protected from the southerly torrential winds by this protective windbreak. Here there could be sea access with protected deep harbors and areas of spreading sandy beaches.

A late afternoon patrol would go daily to the strait by covered route of land, hidden from all seagoing traffic by the forest, which covered the peninsula. The pirate band would then conduct seaboard maintenance within the strait under the cover of dark, based upon their findings.

The two boys, accompanied by Smasher, made their way along the peninsula, keeping to the cover of the forest. The peninsula narrowed as they moved along, and trees became less dense. Soon the soil became rocky as they approached the windy tip of the cape. He had been here many times before, but Chris still felt excitement approaching the strait. As they made the last of the protective trees, they stopped and kneeled, assessing the situation. A single sailing vessel had just entered the water of the strait.

"Dude—look!" Chris whispered to his companion pointing to the ship. The two dropped down to the ground, kneeling by the last stand of trees. "You want to bet? I bet you we sink that ship?"

Without response Trevor crawled ahead on hands and knees, all the while watching the ship as it made its way through the passage. Chris followed as the two boys wove their way forward, staying out of site behind the rocky terrain. As they moved to the icy waters, it became obvious that the ship would make the strait safely. At the water's edge, the companions watched the vessel sail slowly away.

"What do you make of this, Christopher of Temecula?" Trevor whispered all the while laying low. He looked troubled, his brow furrowed and eyes squinting as he quietly watched the progress of their prey.

Chris did not respond for the moment as he thought in silence. He looked at the disappearing ship as it sailed away hoping, unsuccessfully, for some sign of damage. Could this vessel by chance have traversed the slammer-laden lane unharmed? Could a slammer been tripped only to miss the intended target? They had witnessed this before, the slammer rising so quickly to the surface and missing the hull that it would launch into the air visible to anyone who was watching. However, here there was no damage and no failed slammers.

"Over there dude, what's that?" Chris exclaimed. His eyes dropped to the rocky edge of the strait. Here the stony coast was sheer, overhanging the water's edge. Trapped and bobbing up and down was an ensnared slammer. A loud bark by the dog behind them confirmed their suspicions as he quickly went to the edge and began pawing at the nodding globe.

"They've washed up on the shore. Dude, they've never done that before!" cried Chris in whispers to his concerned companion.

Nodding his head affirmatively, Trevor moved silently climbing down to the water's edge. Chris followed closely behind, watching the strait carefully as they exposed themselves to possible detection. At the water's edge, bobbing harmlessly under the edge of rock, were four slammers. Each was identical, still inflated with intact spikes, undamaged release pin, and a shortened rope missing the dangling burlap ballast bag.

There was little time for talk in the open. The boys grabbed the four slammers. With a whistle for Smasher, they were off with their cargo returning to their camp.

That night, the pirate boys huddled around and examined the retrieved slammers. A fire roared in a pit before them. The bulldogs lay by Nick's side, observing their master and wagging their tails.

"Upon which shore were these found?" Nicholas asked, eyeing the ballast line of one of the four slammers with an inquisitive eye.

"The tip of the peninsula Nicholas. All four were the same, bobbing against the rocky shore. Save the sharp eye of Christopher of Temecula I'd have missed them completely."

A cheer went up in support from the pirates, and Chris shyly lowered his head briefly, smiling with pride.

"They were lodged under an outcropping of rocks, but he spied as such".

"Nick," Chris addressed the boy, moving now forward and pointing to the severed cord. "The ballast lines have been cut dude!"

"I see as much my friend," Nick responded, rubbing one cut cord within his hand as he thought.

The ballast lines held the inflated slammer below the surface by its attachment to the stone-laden burlap sack. The four retrieved slammers were identical, the line still affixed to the release pin at the bottom of the leather globe with the ballast sack gone.

"Sam, what thinks you of this cord?" Nicholas said, turning and handing a slammer to the maritime expert boy. Sam looked carefully at the free end of the cord. "Cut, not hacked, not bitten, not a ragged edge as one might see over time when worn by the water and tension. No, definitely cut sharply, Nicholas." The boy now moved forward and looked at the three other slammers. "The same, each cut by a diver me thinks."

Chris added, "And all four found at the same place. I thought that was odd. If only four were cut, would each one land at the same place? The chances are slim, Trevor," he said, turning to his partner. "Remember that ship blew through the strait like nothing! I think all of the slammers, the whole strait; I think they were all cut, Nicholas!"

"My belief as well, Christopher of Temecula. How could it be otherwise? Several score slammers deployed in the deep of the strait, slashed free to bob without effect upon the surface and to drift with the current. The strait has a northerly drift," Nicholas continued, now standing in front of the fire. "Wherefore these slammers," he said, pointing to their retrieved slammers. "These four slammers could not by chance be the only such freed ones. If we capture four, many more so must have drifted northward and out of our sight."

Pyle now moved to the front. He was a thin young boy with short sun-bleached blond hair, piercing blue eyes, and two short upper teeth. He was one of the quieter boys, but he had a determination to his nature and always spoke his mind. "Nicholas," he said, quietly gaining the boys' attention. "A diver in the strait by chance? NEVER!" he finished with certainty, surprising even Nicholas.

The group agreed unanimously with that, for a treacherous body of turbulent water such as the strait of Abaddon was not a sight for a carefree dive or swim. They decided that the diver then knew of the slammers and came for a single purpose: to rid the strait of them.

Nicholas now moved to the front of the group. "I obtained one piece of information. Rainbow returned tonight and tells me not one ship sunk today. Methinks that the evidence strong, the strait no longer remains protected."

Therefore, a theory and an action plan grew. It was certain that sometime after the prior night's maintenance that a deliberate cutting of slammer ballast lines occurred. It was likely that a diver had slashed the entire strait's supply. Nicholas felt that the entire strait was now open, leaving this critical passage unprotected.

The boys deployed over one hundred slammers over several nights. With the location of their camp possibly known, an unprotected waterway put the boys at great risk. Nicholas proposed to redeploy their entire supply in one night. With this concerted effort, they could recapture the surprise and reestablish the strategic blockade.

"It troubles me however," said Nicholas as the plans were finalized. "For we may be expected to do as such. Waiting gives the enemy time to prepare. I see little option than to deploy all tonight."

They could only transport this number of slammers by land over the Abaddon cape. Once upon the tip of the peninsula their small sailing skiffs could deploy the slammers, several at a time until complete. It would take the entire night, but they were defenseless without them.

Soon the procession began. Jonny would lead the largest group, carrying the needed slammers over land to the tip of the Abaddon strait. Pyle would sail the skiff hidden at the base of the peninsula.

Nicholas and Sam would each sail separate vessels out of Pirate's cove. All would then rendezvous at the cape for a night of work.

Chris was concerned that another diver would again slash their work. They decided to deploy the slammers at a deeper level. To do so they added additional stone ballast bringing the number of stones per device to five. With several more pounds of ballast added to each slammer sack, the weapons would now float at a much deeper location. They hoped that no diver could successfully descend to that depth efficiently.

The work went on without incident through the balance of the night. From the cape, they would load one of the three skiffs in rotation. Two skiffs then would be deploying the slammers as the other took on a fresh supply. The work was long, the winds strong and searing, and the boys frozen to the gullet by the exposure. They were near completion when the eastern sky began softening with the first signs of sunlight.

Nicholas and Chris were in the strait for their last trip when trouble began. They were both tired as they deployed their payload at the southern edge. Chris saw something flash out of the corner of his eye. Turning to the east, he thought at first that the flash was the rising sun. Soon he realized another cause. "Nick!" he yelled as he realized his mistake.

A tremendous blaze began to explode through the dry needles of evergreen undergrowth and the long branches of the mighty trees on the peninsula. The bulldogs that patrolled the land devoutly began to howl. The dogs quickly became hysterical barking, jumping, and growling as they ran like darts to the edge of the trees.

With the shout of his friend, Nicholas turned startled. From their position in the strait a blazing fire could be seen racing through the trees with the band of boys trapped on the tip of the rocky peninsula, their escape quickly eaten up by the spreading fire.

"My worst fear!" Nicholas shouted to no one but himself. "I should have known as such." He turned immediately, hoisted his sail and jumped to the stern of the small vessel. Chris rolled quickly windward as the skiff took off making a dart for shore. Nicholas sailed through the strait hoping to evacuate his friends by sea on the protected northern coast. Catching the blistering wind, the skiff roared away in defense of the stranded boys.

The source of the blaze was obvious for as the boys rounded the point an ominous silhouette appeared against the rising sun. The warship had silently moored in the shallow waters of the northern Abaddon peninsula, hidden from detection by the dense tree cover. It had taken some tossed fuel and a small fire to begin a blaze which now roared out of control cutting a swath across the width of the peninsula. They were trapped; the fire cut off a retreat by land and any possible sea escape for the warship. Their only option was to stand and fight, hopelessly outnumbered.

Beaching the craft quickly, Nicholas was up and running with Chris close behind. Sitting just offshore, the ship was silent no more. As the boys arrived a blast of cannon fire accompanied them, landing on the beach with violence tossing sand and debris. The sound of the fire was overwhelming as it roared through the forest consuming the dry underbrush and trees. With hysteria, yelling screams of fear and howling dogs filled the morning air.

While the band worked in the strait, sailors from the enemy ship silently rolled barrels of oil, spilling their contents out over the dried underbrush. A torch quickly brought the fire, which then spread spontaneously. Nicholas looked at the overturned barrels in anger.

Nails ran past them up the beach, howling and looking for blood. Nicholas signaled to Chris who grabbed the dog's collar, dragging the brave animal back as he barked.

"Nicholas, we are trapped!" Pyle said, looking to his leader for hope.

Little Andy pulled back his patch and it lay carelessly within his hair. "The forest will soon be shut off completely. We can't escape along the beach. They will destroy us. They will blow us out of the water if we leave by sea! I say fight them now!"

Nicholas kicked one of the barrels as he thought. As he did, he saw that the cask was nearly full. Nick grabbed a burning branch and quickly rolled the barrel down the width of the beach to water. Touching the oily trail with flame, he soon had a firebreak between the ship and his boys.

As he turned to run, a cannon ball hit, throwing him awkwardly to the ground. The three bulldogs followed the boy against orders. Barking, the dogs grabbed Nick by the collar, dragging him to safety.

Chris saw Nicholas's plan, an idea coming to fruition. He turned and ran full speed down the beach to the skiff. One round from the ship struck close, and Chris hit the ground and covered his head as the sand cast upwards now rained down on him. Cannon blast after canon blast continued, peppering the beachfront, rocking the group of bewildered boys.

Drooling licks revived Nicholas as only a bulldog can. He was up now and ran back to the peninsula tip when Chris arrived, winded from his run to the boat and back. Chris had gathered up the few remaining slammers. "Here, we fill these with oil and they're like a bomb." He said, swinging the empty slammer on its ballast line around his head.

Nicholas liked the idea and the boys began filling the slammers with oil from the discarded casks. Plugging the inflation port with a strip of torn shirt, a Molatov cocktail was born. Chris then began twirling the slammer around and around in the air by its securing line, and like a cowboy lasso let the burning slammer go far off down the beach and towards the ship. As it hit, a loud explosion occurred, and burning oil and sand flew into the air. A much-needed cheer went up from the boys as they too began to throw the devices up the beach. They quickly littered the beach with burning oil explosions, one after the other, between themselves and the enemy. However, they had only bought some time for the cannon fire continued and the ship still lay off the coast.

"What now dude?" Chris said to his friend.

Nicholas thought for a moment. He dropped to his knees trying to attract as little attention from the enemy as possible. Biting the corner of his lip he then responded, "I am going to try and throw these last two slammers upon their deck. Let their fireman fret for a time."

Nicholas ran down the beach towards the firebreak. Moving to the water, he placed himself as close as possible to the enemy ship. Lighting the first slammer he spun and spun the globe and let loose. Before it dropped, he loaded and tossed the second slammer. Both crashed with a fiery explosion along the mizzen deck. The cannon fire stopped, and yells from the stern galley signaled a direct hit.

As Nicholas returned, a cheer rose up from his friends. The boys took this success as a boost of confidence to their cause.

Christopher congratulated the leader. "Great throw, Nick. Their ship will burn now. The cannons, they stopped dude!"

Nicholas looked seriously into the boy's eyes. Turning away from the others, he placed an arm around him. "Their fireman will make quick of that. Their ship will not burn for long. Remember faith? We could use a measure of that now my friend!"

Christopher looked seriously into the eyes of his friend. "Yes," he said very meekly.

"It is best to pray," Nick said now, scanning up the beach. "We will have to fight them, and come they will, Christopher of Temecula."

Chris pondered the question as Nicholas returned to the rocky clearing and his band of boys. They all surrounded him, each boy aware of the situation. There was a sense of calm in their leader. Each of the boys believed as always that Nicholas would lead them out of this tight situation.

As the ship began hurling cannon fire again, the situation looked hopeless. A huge enemy ship stood to their left, canon shot after canon shot landing at their feet. The forest, which had offered them cover in the past, was engulfed in an uncontrollable fire. After softening up and scattering the boys, the enemy would come, landing scores of sword-laden soldiers. How could they last? How could they repeal such a force?

Nicholas showed no such reservation to his small band of boys. Here he was smiling and calm as he wiped the perspiration from his brow. He directed each boy to dig in at locations in the path of the intended assault.

It could have been another canon blast except for its intensity. Just when all looked hopeless, their answer came. Along the beach directly in front of the evil ship, one of the giant trees had fallen. It originated from the edge of the forest, bordering on the beach. Its length was such that its fall was a direct hit, spanning the now smoldering beach, and crashing down with an explosive blast, tearing across the midsection of the warship.

The first hit could be random, but as a second, third, and then fourth tree crashed in sequence, chance began to look less plausible. With each crash a fiery explosion from a barrel of oil lashed to the tree's tip. These oil-laden casks exploded on contact, ripping and tearing deck and rigging without mercy.

With each crashing tree, a gasp followed by a cheer rose from the pirate band. Now with elation, the boys began jumping up and down understanding this change in fortune. Their nemesis ship was now in tortuous shape. Yelling men filled the air as the crew abandoned ship and the vessel tore apart in a blazing fireball.

The band rose to their feet yelling and shouting for joy as they embraced each other. The bulldogs sensed victory as well, jumping, barking, and racing back and forth.

Nicholas stood aside staring intently at the destroyed sinking ship. Down the beach, the remains of the vessel twisted in the wind as a blazing fire engulfed it. The coincidence seemed to bother the boy.

His silence brought Chris to his side. "What is it Nicholas. We won, didn't we?" Seeing the silent confused look, Chris began to think of the coincidence.

"I smell some treachery," Nicholas said, laughing from his belly. "Only my brother could steal such a stage as this!"

Alexander was walking down the beach surrounded by his band of boys. The Pitlings had drawn swords and bows expecting a fight, but the battle was over as the warship gasped its last breath. Alexander quietly looked on the wreckage of the burning vessel. A satisfied smile came upon his countenance. Nodding his head he turned and walked up the beach to his brother.

"Alexander!" Trevor yelled with joy. The pirate boys brandished their swords in victory, jumping and yelling with joy. As the Pitlings walked up the beach, the pirate boys met them with excitement. Smiles not seen for many a time in this bewildered land were present once more.

Chris ran to his former friend's side. Hugging him he said quietly, "I never thought you were dead dude!" Letting loose of Alexander, Chris turned and yelled in joy at the next boy. "Manzell!" He said as he recognized his cross-bow toting friend. "What took you so long?"

Nicholas moved to his brother. As the fire roared and the ship's bow slipped below the sea, Alexander put out his hand in friendship. Nicholas grabbed his hand and pulled the taller boy to himself in embrace. A tear trickled down the cheek of the royal boys.

"I find my brother in a fine mess," Alexander said with a laugh.

"Yes, and with it you appear," Nicholas said, rustling his brother's hair.

"Nicholas, there is too much evil in this Kingdom."

Nicholas turned to the band of boys with an arm around his brother. Cheers went up from the two groups of boys. Nicholas quieted the crowd and said, raising his sword to the sky, "As Christopher of Temecula would say, let's kick some butt...dude!"

CHAPTER 17
A Twisted Quirk of Fate

> WHEN A COUNTRY IS REBELLIOUS,
> IT HAS MANY RULERS,
> BUT A MAN OF UNDERSTANDING
> AND KNOWLEDGE MAINTAINS ORDER.
> PROVERBS 28:2

Chris was not alone in his beliefs; his false judgments formed from anecdotes of treacherous twists and mistruth. The intention here was simply to muddy the water and quench all hope. The breakup of the first family and the treasonous murder was the narrative, an impression of a concerted plot constructed by evil minds to discredit the royal family and discourage the populace.

The consensus was that Alexander's camp was overrun, captured, or scrutinized by an evil eye. For this reason, the newly reunited militia gave up on Alexander's camp as unsafe. They returned that morning to the pirate cove exhausted and seeking out sleep. The next night they found a roaring fire in the pit, a festive atmosphere, with food, stories and laughs filling the night air.

Chris was quiet throughout most of the night. Silently, he pondered events he had witnessed, and those he was led to believe. The boy observed the beginnings of an overwhelming trap before being carted away by the Autumn. Had Alexander bested the culprits? Surprise and massive numbers on the part of the enemy led him to believe not. Subsequently, he was prisoner in the castle. At the time while he was bound and gagged he witnessed a meeting where they openly discussed Alexander's demise. After his escape, he had seen a posted notice accusing Nicholas of Alexander's death and offering a hefty reward for his head. No matter the evidence, Alexander stood in living proof that he and his Pitlings had survived.

They roasted a wild boar in celebration, a new and delicious meal for the boy. Christopher was quietly looking into the fire, satisfied and comfortable, deep in thought when Alexander and Nicholas came and sat next to the boy.

"Christopher of Temecula, our last visit was on the LionBall field. You were gone, and now what luck, we find you with my brave brother," Alexander said. With that he placed his arm briefly around Nicholas.

"He was making trouble in town. Sorely in need of a home, he was. I venture he has more than paid his board since, with his bravery that is," Nicholas added, smiling and rubbing the boys head.

The mention of the game brought up the topic that Chris was pondering. He was embarrassed, thinking all this time that Alexander was dead and not being able to help the boy that day. Explaining himself he spoke, "That girl with the cold hands, she grabbed me, drug me away." Chris said apologetically, turning to Alexander, "I wanted to fight with you, believe me Alex!"

"Autumn," Alexander said remorsefully. He hung his head for the moment and closed his eyes. Silence spread around the group. "Autumn? Autumn Bienville. With her brave father's demise, I believed she was no more," Nicholas said sadly, breaking the mood of the group.

"Yes, her father rests in peace, but she is an apparition walking the back woods in torment. She has befriended our modern day friend," Alexander responded.

"Alexander, I really wasn't a coward, I would have fought! She is a strong chick. She surprised me and I couldn't get away until I was so far lost, and it--you know the ambush was over. I heard the screams and explosions. Then I fell asleep; this dude took me to the castle. I was in the dungeon, rats, bones, smells." Christopher in his blunt way then blurted out the question that was bothering him, "Why are you alive anyway?"

Alexander left his question unanswered. Turning for information he asked, "In the castle, Christopher of Temecula? We must know everything that you witnessed."

Chris now realized that he might be able to supply some important information. Beginning his story, Manzell, Little Andy, and the others sat with them around the fire to listen.

"I was just returning with the ball. I was at the edge of the field when I saw the Pitlings surrounded. Then Autumn appears from nowhere, right at my side." Chris stood as he described the scene to the others. "Then that chick, you know…she's kind of crazy. She drags me back away from the field, pulls me through the bushes and trees until I was way away. We could hear explosions and stuff, but she kept pulling me away."

Chris moved, now standing directly in front of Alexander. He knew that he could not have helped, but his disappearance at this critical time had weighed on him ever since that day. "I tried Alex, but I couldn't get away from her. Then she leaves me, and dude then I was totally lost."

"Just why would she leave you?" Nicholas asked.

Chris turned to the pirate-boy. He laughed and shook his head with some embarrassment. "I was mad, she took me away, you know—I—I--guess I called her a name." The boy dropped his head as he added, "I guess I called her something bad, I didn't' know. Dude, she didn't like that at all. She slapped me and poof she was out of there! Then I'm really in trouble. All alone, out somewhere, I had no idea where I was, dude."

"All right Christopher, what did you call her?" Nicholas inquired, smiling.

With some reluctance Chris said, "A ghost. I called her a ghost. She was so mad that she hit me with a right jab. I fell to the ground and poof, she was gone."

The entire group began laughing. Chris turned with a smile beginning on his face. Soon he was shaking his head and laughing as well. "Dude, that chick is tough. I kid you not; she dragged me on my back for maybe a mile. I got rocks and dirt and stickers all over me. Then she socks me one and she's gone."

Alexander eventually quieted the group. "Quite a fine story that is. Yes, Autumn is tough; and a fine soccer player as well. Is she not Nicholas?"

Nicholas smiled and let out a small chuckle. "Aye, she plays a good defender, Christopher of Temecula."

Alexander returned the group to the subject. "Christopher, how did you get to the castle?"

"Well after she disappeared, I looked around, and I was in a forest. I was totally lost. So I started walking. I ended up slipping onto one of those moving hay carts, you know like a hay ride, except this dude didn't like it when he found me and had me put into the dungeon. That's when I got into the castle."

"So you were a stowaway on a hay cart. Is that right?" Alexander asked.

"Ya, that's it, I was a stowaway."

"What did you see in the castle?" Nicholas asked carefully.

"Well I was tied up and brought to some sort of meeting. It was a meeting with a bunch of people. The Mayor was there and everything."

"That would be the town meeting. Oh what a farce! This meeting, it was run by the Boar I venture," Nicholas added.

Chris quickly responded. "Yes, that's the dude. And you know what! That guy, the Boar, he's Hurley, my bus driver in my home, you know Temecula."

"Bus driver!" Nicholas began laughing uncontrollably. "That's Michaelis. He's no more than a pig, but he has an evil grip upon the kingdom."

Alexander questioned the boy again. "At the town meeting, tell us, what activities did you see?"

"Well, first this old pirate dude, he said that he had wasted Nicholas," Chris said with some trepidation.

"Balaam! He lied. His ship sunk and gave up nice treasure," Little Andy said proudly to the group.

Nicholas smiled at the boy and added, "That was before Christopher of Temecula was a pirate."

"Ya, well I thought he was lying because the Boar kicked his butt and made him look like a fool. Then that guy--Alexander, you know the black horse guy!"

"Fordem," Alexander added.

"Ya, that's him, and you know what?" Chris said excitedly, turning now to Manzell. "Manzell, he said he wasted Alexander and brought the imploders to the castle. I knew it was a lie because I was there!"

Until this point Manzell sat quietly on the ground listening. The boy looked up at Chris with a knowing smile. He held out his hand. Chris slapped it, then turned with a knowing glance to Alexander.

"Did not the Boar punish him like Balaam?" Alexander asked.

"No, he believed the dude. Then they said Alexander was a goner. I believed them cause of what I saw." Christopher remembered his original question and turned to the boy. "Alexander,w,hy are you alive anyway?" Chris said again with emphasis, staring at the boy.

Alexander was thinking, staring into the fire and did not answer. "The Boar thinks I am captured, imprisoned somewhere. He does not know my fate!"

Nicholas added, "Fordem was lying. The Boar did not catch his untruth, or he would have bloody punished Fordem as well. We deal with a cruel creature."

"Ya...but why are you alive anyway?" Chris asked Alexander again loudly.

"I will tell you the story. The LionBall field is a perfect site for ambush. Nicholas, remember the field, surrounded by trees and gently sunken."

"Aye," Nicholas responded.

THE SUN WAS SHINING, AND a beautiful day was before the Pitling band. Manzell let fly with a fastball, and Alexander connected with a towering foul ball off to the right into the brush. With the crack of the bat Christopher was off. He was next at bat and feared the loss of their only ball.

The Pitlings took the opportunity to rest, now sitting on the field enjoying the rare reprieve from serious times. They were laughing and childhood was present once more, lighthearted times building memories.

FORDEM CLENCHED HIS JAW AS the lookout reported the magnificent news. The fool he thought, playing in the sun without a care in the world. Children disgusted the man acutely. His unblemished reputation had been slurred by this monster one time too many. He would take the boy alive for he was worth more as a prisoner. However, he would lose no sleep if an accident occurred, and secretly the man preferred the alternative. His capture would thrill him, the vaunted precocious little horror, knighted by his imbecile father. What an insult, the result of an inbred spoiled brat. Where was his impotent father now? The man's plight brought a joyful tear to his eye. Today, Alexander would be all over.

THE WHINEY OF A HORSE was the first sign that not all was secure that day.

"Whhhhhhhhh. Scott let ring a shrill whistle as the sentry realized their fate. For the first time, horsemen were seen, and they soon encircled the field. Quickly the periphery was flooded with mounted soldiers and archers, weapons drawn for battle.

Manzell yelled to the others, and ran to southern edge of the field. Dropping to his knees, he threw back a camouflaged drape and dropped to the floor of a small cache of weapons. Tossing arms to each of the Pitlings, the boys were now equipped and prepared to fight.

HOW PITIFUL IT IS TO see the band of monsters, surrounding their leader and drawing their swords. Children are undisciplined, not like the military men that Fordem represented, he thought with hate. Play, now that is the sordid extent of their talents. Alexander was repugnant, spoiled beyond illusion by his so-called royal but truly repulsive family.

Fordem had never played, for he worked throughout his childhood. Driven to support his family he rose only by brut determination with no one but himself to thank. The royalty looked down on him; they hated his common fiber deep down. They were the inferior breed, however. He had come to respect the Queen for her character, but she as well was mediocre and soft. It would eventually spell her destruction; it was only a matter of time. He laughed when he remembered her inquiries concerning her lost boys. "Boo Hoo, tell me of my sons, Richard!" How sad, he hoped to tell her of today's victory and watch her agonizing loss.

ALEXANDER CALLED IT A FUSE-MIX. He had developed a semi-liquid fuse that would burn quickly where poured. It consisted of oil mixed with finely ground tree bark. When decanted onto the ground, the mixture would conduct a flame for miles if needed. Alexander had dug a shallow trench completely encircling the field. The trench was then filled with fuse-mix, and covered with the leafy residue of the forest. Imploders were buried periodically, their fuses of twisted twine laid out in the mixture.

James reached the ignition site out of breath. He had strolled off watch just minutes before his call, and now he hoped his return was not too late. Pulling away the concealing tree branches, a large pool of the fuse-mix filled a bowl-shaped recess in the ground. Trying to create a light using the flint had never been James's forte, but today his life depended upon it. Striking the flint with a slicing action eventually fired a spark, and the fodder caught. Blowing softly a blaze was soon present. As he detonated the bowl of fuse-mix, Pitling fortunes changed quickly.

Pirates, Scoundrels, and Kings

Fordem turned in horror as the first explosion rocked his supply wagon. To his rear and racing around the southern edge of the field was a blaze that soon encircled the entire field and his army of men. As the conflagration raced, periodic explosions occurred sending dirt and debris into the air and covering his forces. The horses became hysterical with the deafening blasts, and the fiery silhouette raced out of control. Horses bucked and threw his mounted soldiers to the ground as the fire encircled the field. Billowing smoke filled the area and the dry forest floor went up in flames. The fire quickly roared on catching ground cover and overlying branches as the ambusher became the ambushed.

Fordem regained his control and insisted that his men press on. Through the smoky clearing, his foe was no longer visible. He pushed his jaundiced-eye mount on and rode quickly to the center of the field. Dismounting he turned around and around dizzying himself in anger, his sword drawn hoping for a fight. The Pitlings were gone however, and Fordem threw his sword down in disgust. He ran to the east, the last place he had seen the monster boy.

When he arrived at the last seen location, he screamed in the air. He then stood silent calculating his newest embarrassing loss. Looking at the ground, he spied a canvas tarpaulin covered over with brush. Kicking back its corner revealed a small underground cave. The man tossed the cover sharply, and jumped to the bottom. What had been an arms cache was also the opening of a dark tunnel, which led from the battlefield. Fordem searched but never found his nemesis.

The event was such an embarrassment for the man. He would never report or speak of this again. From that moment in his mind, more than anything that he believed, this disaster became his finest moment in his mind. This overwhelming humiliation began at that instant to be a brilliant defeat of his enemy. Subterfuge, lying, dodges, deception; Fordem chose to begin what came naturally to the man, a kingdom full of lies. Alexander did not escape, but of course, how simple, Alexander was no more. He would add the fact that his brother was the culprit. Sir Alexander dead at the hands of Nicholas the Blue.

Chapter 18
The Cloaked Rider

> IN YOUR MAJESTY RIDE FORTH VICTORIOUSLY,
> IN BEHALF OF TRUTH, HUMILITY AND RIGHTEOUSNESS;
> LET YOUR RIGHT HAND DISPLAY AWESOME DEEDS.
> **PSALM 45:4**

The fortress Alucemet towered above the northern edge of the kingdom, abutting the brutal western sea. To its east, the plain of Rochelle spread for leagues gently rolling and punctuated by scattered outcroppings of trees. This wide grassy prairie had been theatre to many historical battles, the kingdom's grip seemingly dependent upon its control. To the eastern and southern edge of the plain a dense forest stood through which lay the eastern sea and beyond the kingdom of Ateirrum. A narrow gorge wove its way through the forest to the continent's eastern port, a strategic point known as the Devil's Pass.

Their target that morning was the plain of Rochelle. Alexander and Nicholas led the cohort, riding rapidly along the dusty trail accompanied by Manzell and Little Andy. Though still unsure of his horsemanship, Chris had lobbied at the last moment to be included, and he bounced along uncomfortably at the rear. Safety dictated stealth; they assumed spies everywhere for the trees had ears and soaring birds reported to the growing evil of the kingdom. A dense dawning fog covered their path as they hurried northward through the southern forest heading for Rochelle. The wind was scathing and cold coming off the plain, and as the riders exited the forest they bore their hoods for protection. The group was fearsome cloaked as they were, shirking enemy eyes, and riding silently in the wind.

Pirates, Scoundrels, and Kings

Through scattered trees, the path emptied out onto the southern border of the plain, and the group halted for the moment resting their mounts. The sun had appeared over the eastern horizon slipping scattered rays of welcome warmth against the cold bracing wind.

Nicholas saw the lone horseman first, off in the distance racing like the wind. The group pulled back into the cover of the trees as the rider approached. The equestrian mounted a dark horse, hunched forward with a black cloak trailing like a cape, and rode against the elements in secret transit. As the rider approached, the horse gradually slowed and stopped to rest the mount just yards from the hidden group.

"A steed from the kingdom, see the Lion's brand upon his haunches," Manzell whispered. Alexander nodded silently having noticed the same. "I can take him now, before discovery," Manzell said, drawing his crossbow.

Alexander quickly placed his hand on his bow and stopped him. "No, Manzell. We must speak to him. We can have our way later. That is one of the Queen's mounts!"

The dark equestrian's mind seemed to have drifted elsewhere. Gazing across the plain, the lone horseman eyed the distant forest and its route to the sea.

Nicholas took Little Andy and Chris to the right, moving silently within the edge of the forest, while the rest surrounded the rider to the left. Without communication the boys fanned out planning to surround and capture their prey.

"Crack." The sound split through the forest like a shot as a branch broke under the hoof of Chris's horse. The cloaked rider was startled, sensed the trap, and was off with the wind before the boys could spring their trap.

"No, I'm sorry, the stick, I didn't see it," Chris yelled with anger.

Alexander was off like bullet, spurring his horse forward and chasing the rider. The others soon followed as they blew out of their hiding place pursuing with abandon.

For the modern day boy it was a frustrating event. "Wait up," Chris yelled, turning his mount and trying to keep up with the group.

There was no turning back now. The rider was from the castle and had probably guessed the boy's identity. If this horseman eventually escaped one could assume that information concerning their location and numbers would come upon evil ears. They must ride on, intercept, and silence this rider.

They rode in harried pursuit along the northern edge of the plain with the scattered trees of the forest whipping by to their right. The cloaked rider had a jump on them but with time the lead shortened. A look over the rider's shoulder showed concern, and then with a spur encouraged the horse onward. Abruptly the horseman veered to his right, jumped a small stream, and was soon into the protection of the forest. The pursuit continued, the path now tortuous with the path taking them around and between the trees. Deep within the forest their pursuit would likely fail, the dense forest at this point giving many places for the rider to hide.

Nicholas took off to his right riding like the wind. "Meet up ahead," Nicholas yelled, signaling to his brother as he shot away trying to flank their prey. The others pursued on, following the horseman's path.

They had made some progress when the rider pulled a sword and hacked branches down into their path, hysterically trying to escape. Slowed now by the obstacles, the boys jumped the brushwood and continued their pursuit.

Nicholas looked to overtake and pass the horseman. He darted away and made for a well-trodden path. Once upon the trail, he made quick progress and forged ahead of his prey. At this point he circled ahead, came to a halt, and shoed away his horse to cover. Jumping to an overhanging branch, he quickly disappeared into the overhead foliage.

Alexander knew the area and his brother's intentions well. From behind, he drove the horseman along, secretly herding the rider towards the point of interception.

As the rider approached, Nicholas launched himself, grabbing the rider around the neck and dragging them both to the ground in a kicking cloud of dust. The horseman was up with sword drawn before the boy could stop rolling. Alexander and the others slid to a stop, dismounted with weapons drawn surrounding the outnumbered horseman. The rider would fight, however, first knocking away Manzell's crossbow with the sword's hilt and then turning to take on anyone who would approach.

Nicholas was yelling as his momentum carried him sprawling into the brush. Falling through the briars, his cloak tore free and he lost his sword. Pulling himself up quickly, he jumped to confront the rider with his bare hands. The rider now loomed over the boy threatening with drawn steel. With a gasp, the rider stepped back from the boy as he recognized his identity. The rider now dropped the blade, stepped forward, and touched the boy's hair with tenderness.

"My son, Nicholas, oh Nicholas," she said as she pulled back her hood.

"The Queen," Little Andy gasped, dropping to his knee in honor.

"Mother!" Alexander cried now running to her side. The three embraced for the longest time with tears coming to each pair of eyes.

"Oh Alexander," the Queen cried. "I was trying to free you. Nicholas, why did you leave me? And you Alexander, I have missed you sourly. The kingdom is in ruins. I am so glad to be with you both."

"The Mom Queen!" Chris said, shaking his head, speaking loudly but to himself. "I know her," he said proudly. He looked very relieved as the Queen pulled back her hood and brushed a braid of hair away from her brow.

The Queen looked up from her children for the first time. Eyeing the band of boys with suspicion, her beautiful smile returned after seeing the modern day boy. "I see you survived your fall. I wished to say the same of my scalp, Christopher of Temecula," the Queen laughed.

"Sorry dude—err--sir, I mean I mean Queen. How goes your dew? You ride like Zorro, and your sword, wow you are a bad, I mean--you're a good Mom." Chris babbled looking more and more uncomfortable now that he was the center of her attention.

"Alexander, these must be Pitlings," she said, approaching Manzell who knelt before her. "A rougher group I shan't recall, but as horsemen they have learned well."

Alexander introduced the group. "He is Manzell, a better crossbow in the entire Kingdom there is not. Little Andy kneels. He is the person with the patched eye before you. And Christopher of Temecula, I sense you have been introduced before."

"Wssssss." Nick let out a long whistle. Within seconds, his three bulldogs appeared and sat at attention.

"Where did they come from?" Chris wondered as they had traveled miles with no apparent dog in sight.

"Where Nicholas goes, they soon will be found," said Little Andy quietly.

With the Queen present, the three bulldogs behaved impeccably. While bulldogs cannot help but drool, especially after such a long run, they kept that to a minimum as they sat on their haunches eyeing the Queen, hoping for her approval.

"These mongrels must be yours Nicholas," she said with a humorous but approving smile. She walked over and laid a soft hand on each dog's head. "And I would risk my skin with the likes of them."

The Queen made her way back to the group. Turning to the boys, she continued. "You both have chosen your friends well. Nicholas, as always, you have chosen your dogs well. And Little Andy, the left eye should be patched. Oh, and as well a pirate I hear!" The Queen inquired , turning again to her youngest son.

"I return fortunes of the sea to their proper owner. We are trustee for the Laughing Lion, that is all Mother." Nicholas grinned mischievously.

"Yes, I am certain of that," she said, chuckling to herself. "Quite the spoils of war, that is, if half of what I hear in court is true, my adventurous son. Enough however, your presence here changes quite drastically that to which I come in secrecy today. For your interception has made my journey none to meaningful for now. For that I am glad."

"And to where was your journey, Mother?" Alexander questioned quietly.

"I was on a journey to the sea and beyond. For you see, I was led to conclude that my oldest son was prisoner in Ateirrum. Rumors of your death Alexander were myriad. However, my sources said no. As if I could believe in the murderous behavior of my youngest son, never!" she said, grabbing Nicholas and hugging him. "Many led to believing your capture and imprisonment with Lithotomy, the king of Ateirrum."

"So your journey was to free me Mother?" Alexander asked.

"Yes. Sewn for safety within my cloak are the crown jewels. I hoped such a ransom would free you Alexander. However if not, I would offer myself come that be Lithotomy's demand."

"And what of Father?" Nicholas inquired.

The Queen dropped her head with sadness and did not speak for the longest time. Raising her face and looking intently into her boy's eyes, she continued, "His fate is unknown to me. I have searched, inquired, and prayed in earnest. He seems to be no longer," she whispered.

"I cannot believe that Mother! Fret not, we will take back our castle and free our king!" Nicholas said steadfastly, his brave soul determined to right this wrong. He moved to the Queen, and gently kissed her brow.

"Yes, I know you will Nicholas," the Queen now raised her head and said with resignation.

"It seems then, Mother," said Alexander, "someone has led you to believe that imprisonment across the sea was my fate. Who led you to believe this?"

"The story was that you had been slain by the Pirate Nicholas. Refusing this as rubbish, I was led to believe of your imprisonment."

"Does the Boar believe that I am in fact dead, or in prison?" Alexander questioned.

"In prison, of that I am certain. Death is the convenient story to discourage our populace," the Queen responded.

"How are you certain that the Boar knows not of Alexander's freedom, Mother?" Nicholas asked.

"Fordem defends his victory over Alexander vehemently. He is very certain and maintains this daily. However, when forced he admitted your survival to me alone. I am certain the porcine menace believes Alexander captured and imprisoned beyond trouble across the sea. I dare say, however, Fordem is quite sensitive when pushed upon this matter. I see why now--he is lying as has always been his nature!"

"The entire picture fits," Alexander concluded, nodding his head affirmatively. "Mother, as the hours pass your safety away from the castle becomes questionable. When your absence comes to their attention, they may know your plan. You must return without delay. I will escort my Queen!" said Alexander.

"And I as well!" Nicholas added, bravely kissing his mother's hand.

"NO. I shall not hear of it and will return alone as I left. If pressed, a long lonely ride will be my account. The danger for all of you on the open plain of Rochelle is such that I cannot countenance this. Nicholas, take my cloak!" she said, handing her garment to Nicholas. "Within the hem you will find more than all your fortunes of the sea! You must keep these, for soon the evil will have all."

With reticence the boys agreed to allow the Queen to return to the castle. Discussion and plans were spoken about quickly. As the sun rose over the horizon, embraces and goodbyes were exchanged.

With that the Queen bridled her horse and mounted the saddle. "It is with you Alexander and Nicholas that our fate lays. Return as I know you will and our Kingdom may be saved," she said as she turned and rode away.

The group followed the women to the edge of the forest, and then after embracing and tears, the Queen departed making her long journey back to the castle.

"Wow, what a mom!" Chris said, staring earnestly as the rider disappeared.

Chapter 19
The Cautious Messenger

> LIKE THE COOLNESS OF SNOW AT HARVEST TIME
> IS A TRUSTWORTHY MESSENGER TO THOSE WHO SEND HIM;
> HE REFRESHES THE SPIRIT OF HIS MASTERS.
> PROVERBS 25:13

It was dawn when Christopher dressed as a crier for the kingdom of Ateirrum, mounted his horse carefully and rode out of camp. He was to carry two messages this morning, the first for the Mayor of Alucemet, the second aimed at misleading leadership deep within the castle. These assignments brought some concern and outright fright to the boy. Chris was determined, however, to do his duty and return unharmed to the camp where his newly found friends awaited his timely reappearance.

His path that morning led him through the mountainous caves surrounding the pirate-boy's hideout, down the rocky slopes, and out onto the grassy region where his escape from the spilith had occurred. As he rode towards the city, he remembered his flight, running for his life within the foul smelling slime and ooze.

As Christopher entered the capital city of Alucemet, he noted that it was looking none the better since his last visit. Muddy streets lined by poorly maintained deserted cottages sat sadly, as the boy galloped slowly along. On the street corner he saw an ironic site, a freshly tiled mud hole beautifully installed and awaiting the porcine population of the city.

Chris rode through the city center and then out to the eastern end of town on a wide worn road lined by decrepit cottage dwellings. Years before, a quaint city had boomed with activity, but with the evil of late, attention had waned. Shutters stood boarded, and as the sun began to appear that morning, no one was in sight. His destination was one of the larger dwellings with blue-stained gingerbread trim upon graying white walls and a thatched roof. Here, he had been told, was the Mayor's home, and he hoped that the man was both present and responsive to his cause.

Robyn of Hobinsiefken had given up journeying to his office in town, concluding months before that it was a useless exercise. The city was a shambles; evil events occurred non-stop, and his ability to lead anyone, least of all himself, was seriously shaken. He was depressed, ate little, and carried the stubble of unshaven cheeks. A habitual early riser in good times, he was turning in just after nightfall, consuming a stale piece of bread or spoon of cold broth, and staying in bed until late afternoon. He could see no good reason to rise.

It was over, his lovely fairy tale world gone with the recent events. Rumors swirled that the King was dead. The Queen was functionally imprisoned and impotent in her protests. When he heard of Alexander's death, he wept with inconsolable tears. That the royal brother was responsible plagued the man's every dream.

Since then, it was a precipitous fall into the pits of black despair and self-reproach. Citizens day by day disappeared. Men in trancelike states and clipped ears policed the streets. The only thriving group, pigs.

This troubled soul was the man that Chris sought. Robyn heard the gentle knock on his door. He was in bed but awake. He had not been sleeping well but dwelling in bed as his only site of security. The knock continued and continued until the Mayor forced himself to rise.

He opened his front door just the smallest crack. The light hurt his eyes, and his only response was, "leave, I have nothing for you." Seeing the odd boy, Robyn quickly closed the door.

"Please sir, I have something of great importance for you!" Chris said as the mayor rudely shut the door in mid sentence. Chris knocked repeatedly, banging on the heavy door until it cracked open once more.

"Are you deaf? I told you to leave!" the mayor screamed. As he shouted, he pulled the door open widely. In his night clothes he bridled a sword to chase away his pursuant. "Leave me now, or I'll run in your measly body and leave you for the pigs that run this town. What is that you wear?" Robyn for the moment softened as he noticed the young boy's uniform.

The boy stood upon the man's portico. He was dressed in a well-cut leather coat, with a belt of thick dark leather and a shiny silver buckle. Embroidered on his chest was the crest of the Eagle. A hood covered his head against the cold, hiding blond hair and shadowing his face. He wore forest-colored tights and his boots were oxen blood leather cut to mid-calf. To the mayor he looked his part, a courtly messenger from the kingdom across the sea.

"Mr. Mayor, I have important information for your eyes only!" Chris said as he looked first right and then left, obviously worried about standing in the open.

"Well, what is it young boy?" Robyn said with some anger.

"Well, umm you see--" he said, pulling on his ear lobe. "I ah--" He whispered with a hand cupped to his mouth. "I have a message from-- two royal boys."

The Mayor stared at the boy in amazement. Thoughts of traps and practical jokes filled his suspicious mind. Sensing the messenger's sincerity, however, he reached out and grabbed the boy, pulling him through the entry with haste. Turning to the door, he quickly secured it with three heavy deadbolts in succession. Throwing a hinged hasp across the door, he locked it with a large padlock using a key pulled from inside his tunic.

The man and the boy now stood alone inside of a darkened parlor. Carelessly tossed papers and rotting food covered the floor. Dust and cobwebs engulfed everything in sight. Robyn turned to an oil lamp sitting on a wooden stool. He lit the wick, picked the lantern up, and returned illuminating the boy. A deep grimace overcame the man's countenance, emphasized by the shadows of the lamp. He eyed the boy with a deep suspicion as he thought about his remarks. Mr. Hobinsiefken was a tall man and he towered over the boy looking quite ominous. "Well how do I know you come from whom you refer?" the man asked.

Chris dug into his sleeve and produced a parchment for the Mayor. The man looked closely at the rolled document. Bringing his lamp closer, he examined the wax seal securing it.

It was a time where authenticity of documents was difficult to prove. In the modern day, a sworn seal from a notary authenticated important manuscripts. In these times, a wax seal impressed by the person's signet ring served the same purpose. Alexander's ring was lost when he left the castle in haste. This document bore the seal of the Laughing Lion superimposed on Nicholas's initial.

"Nicholas!" Robyn of Hobinsiefken gasped. He turned to the boy with some anger on his face. "What does this mean? Make good of yourself, or I will run you in!" he said grabbing his sword again.

Calming the man, Chris quickly tried to explain. "Sir, Alexander is alive. Nicholas never was a traitor. He didn't do it dude...it's a farce!"

Robyn now turned in thought, leaving the boy in shadows. Speaking to himself, he said, "I never believed that Nicholas could do such as that." Ignoring the boy he walked deeper into the parlor, lost in thought.

As he pulled away from the boy, Chris for the first time could really look at the man. Upon his back, his tunic hung open, the straps dangling down his naked backside in disarray. His hair receding in the front was tossed and disheveled from a lack of brushing. He walked with his right foot in an openheeled slipper, the left bare on the wooden floor.

With that, the man turned back to the boy. "If I were to believe such a story, and mind you, you're quite a suspicious looking character... but if I take this story as true, what is it to me?" the mayor wondered.

"Well, Alexander is here. Well not here in this very place, but he's alive! And--and he lives at Nicholas's camp. Oh-- but don't tell anyone!" Chris added with second thoughts. "The paper dude, open the paper! There's something inside that's important!"

Robyn slit the wax and unrolled the manuscript. Holding the document over to the lamp he saw, written in quill pen and ink, a brief message that read:

All is not lost!
Be ready, the battle will soon begin.

Signed Alexander of Alucemet Signed Nicholas the Blue

(This message will self-destruct. Strike it once.)

The mayor considered the short message reflecting upon each word. The wax imprint and signatures convinced him of its authenticity. Perhaps--all is not lost, he thought to himself. Their leadership would excite the countryside. Their source of control in this world had always surprised the man. How could they have succumbed to such a foul and ignorant bunch in the first place? Perhaps God was giving them another chance. While he knew not the plan, he did trust the royal boys. If they still had their senses and determination, Robyn would once more lead his citizens.

The mayor dropped the document to the floor and turned from the boy to think for what seemed the longest time. Finally, a much more responsive man turned from his deliberation to Chris. "Relay this message to the royal boys. Robyn of Hobinsiefken and the citizenry of our brave city Alucemet are ready whenever and wherever our call to duty leads us."

Chris walked to the mayor, bent and picked up the document. Turning to the wooden stool, he spread the rolled manuscript flat. Taking a small dagger from his sleeve, he struck the parchment with its hilt. The spark ignited gunpowder imbedded in the paper. A quick controlled fire quickly destroyed the document to leave no evidence but ash and melted wax. Subsequently, he brushed up the ashes and returned them to his sleeve. His last word before leaving the mayor on his journey was, "We will let you know when. Be ready."

With this, Chris turned. The mayor unbolted the door and the boy quickly disappeared into the fog. The mayor latched his door using just one lock. He turned from the door with a smile not seen upon his countenance in months. With his hand, he smoothed his disheveled hair. He said to himself with an air of excitement, "I must shave today! Yes." Nodding his head to just himself a small smile crossed his disheveled face. With more energy than he had felt in many months he said to himself, "We have work to be done. Yes, Alexander and Nicholas have returned."

"Alright dude--" Chris said to himself as he rode away. "Mission Impossible, this message will self destruct, sic, it worked just like Alexander said!" Chris had played his first role perfectly. He was proud of himself and quite relieved for the moment. As he rode, he shook his sleeve, scattering the ashes to the wind.

Chris was concerned to some extent by the mayor's disheveled appearance. The man was depressed and had given up, reflected by his countenance and the unkempt appearance of his home. However, Chris drew some encouragement; the message seemed to revitalize the man. Perhaps that message was all it would take. One thing was sure; the boy-led militia would need the help of loyal citizens sometime in the near future. The Mayor was the key to organizing them.

As he rode, he remembered that the greater of his two tasks still lay ahead. The castle awaited him, and he could not help but remember his last visit. Save for the Queen's brave help, Chris would still be in that dark dungeon. With only bread and water for sustenance, his skinny body would dwindle to nothing among the bones of other unfortunate souls.

Alexander and Nicholas felt that only Chris had a chance for a private audience with Fordem. The boy knew facts that Fordem did not wish revealed; he would see the boy. While he might wish the boy silenced, the message that he carried required a response. Fordem then would release him. The two boys assured Chris of his safety. "Give a message to Fordem alone!" they had said. He could expect rough treatment, but they promised he would return. Chris was not real sure how they knew this, but he trusted their judgment. Now the rough treatment was easy for them to dismiss, Chris thought. By reflex, Chris felt for his two intact earlobes. He shuddered, speaking to himself. "What if that means an ear job?"

The sun was just above the horizon and the fog dense as he began the second leg of his journey. It was cold and wet with an icy wind blowing from the east as the boy tried his best to ride out of the town and along the road to the Castle. Once out of the town, he could see his destination, a menacing fortress covered with rusting clouds high upon a rocky precipice. He rode as fast as he could along the dirt lane, kicking up dust and mud as his horse galloped. Chris took heart in meeting no traffic that day, for the once heavily traveled path drew little interchange in this age of evil.

The castle Alucemet stood upon a rocky crag, towering above the grassy plains to the east. Reaching its base, Chris began his ascent along a twisting road doubling back and forth through a rocky pass. As he neared the castle, he could not help but anticipate something malevolent awaiting him.

The fortress sat on a carved plateau, its dirty rose-colored stonewalls pushing to the sky and dominating the horizon. The western border of the castle opened like a clam clasping the eastern edge of the harbor. Surrounding the rest of the castle was a deep dark moat, over which a huge wooden drawbridge lay, meeting the twisting road.

Chris rested his horse after reaching the castle plateau, reining the mount aside and observing quietly. It was here that he began to see the first sign of human life since leaving the city. Villagers returning to the castle's central mall were scattered along the lane, crossing the drawbridge on small horse-drawn carts or on foot with merchandise loaded upon their backs. There was a curious silence here. Everyone seemed alone, looking directly at no one, each seemingly resigned to a meager existence and hopeful just to survive. Posted along the drawbridge, dressed in black with the typical marked ears, castle guards roughly audited the entering crowd. Chris wondered how they would treat a crier from the distant kingdom. Drawing up every inch of the boy's height and a courageous countenance, he silently rode back to the lane. Turning carefully, he directed his horse to lope over the drawbridge, his iron-shod hoofs clopping past the guards.

As expected, one of these marked sentinels stepped forward, grabbing the bridle of the horse, roughly stopping the boy.

"Not so fast lad," the castle guard said to Chris. "You're an odd one you are. What have ya to say fer yourself?"

He had memorized his response. "I am from the mighty kingdom of Ateirrum. Loosen me now! I carry a message from my King addressed for the eyes of master Fordem alone. You best not interfere!" Chris said with his bravest and most pompous air.

"Ha—Ha—Ha--" The man laughed till Chris thought he would fall down. With his reaction several other guards approached wanting to join in. "Fordem, Ha, as if the likes of you could see the master. You best be on your way lad, or your ears shan't welcome their treatment!"

FORDEM HAD ARISEN WITH AN unsettling feeling in his gut, a dyspeptic affliction that was increasingly common of late. A brief wave of nausea overcame the man as he recalled that recent mishandled machinations were not a product of rum-induced dreams but real. He refused to accept the blame for these unfortunate events, for he was a military genius, a victim of tawdry fate. Fordem saw his failings as the result of providence, and explained away recent catastrophic campaigns on the failure of others. First, there was the loss of precious munitions within the pass to the oldest princely brat. Here his team of horses bore fault for the loss of these weapons. Secondly, the dratted Queen interfered in his dealings with the odd boy, allowing him to escape just through his fingertips. Alexander's recent escape from the man's brilliant ambush capped off a trilogy that had to end. Here it was a failure of underlings. His subordinates allowed the spoiled boy to disappear as a coward might, surrounded by blazing fire and smoke. Fordem viewed himself the victim of treacherous larceny, the tragic antihero surrounded by incompetence.

He took his recent losses as dangerous, however, for if failure continued his charge would soon fail as well. To this point he had successfully conducted himself in court, leading the bumbling Michaelis to faulty conclusions. How wrong was it to mislead the foolish pig into actually celebrating Fordem's false success? Right and wrong, such a silly distinction, Fordem thought. For the time he would continue supporting the conclusion that Alexander was across the sea in chains, a mistruth for now, but easily corrected when his due providence arrived. With a spot of warm milk laced with rum, the man felt some relief in the pit of his gut. "Executions, yes maybe a few executions today." Perhaps the day would turn in his favor after all.

Fordem was dressed and on his way along the western breezeway, followed dutifully by his servant, when he caught site of the morning visitor. A scuffle had broken out in the courtyard, and he stopped with curiosity watching the scene from the window. He wondered why the courier was present, dressed in leather coat baring the Ateirrum eagle crest. His castle guards were handling him roughly as they should, laughing and pulling the boy from his horse. Then the visitor's hood shook loose, revealing an identity that startled the man. Here again his bane, the blond-haired mongrel that had escaped his clutches more than he cared to admit. His presence reminded him that the truth behind his stories was precarious indeed. The boy knew too much, one word of which could undermine his tenuous survival. He would dispose of the worm before he could expose Fordem's duplicity.

"Bring me that devil!" the man yelled, calling for his minion and pointing a long finger through the window to below. "Bring me that termite, that worm, that dog. Why waste such time, do so immediately!" Fordem screamed at the top of his lungs to the intimidated servant.

"To which worm do you speak, sire?" the man asked, head bowed. Fordem grabbed the unfortunate servant, dragging him to the window pointing again at the boy. "That spilith rat! Bring him, make quick of it." Stopping the man as he moved to leave, he added staring straight into his eyes for emphasis, "And to no other eyes but mine if you know what is good for you. Now be off!" With a shove down the breezeway, the man was off for the castle courtyard.

In the meantime, Chris fared poorly with the castle guards. He began to fear the worst, his private audience and subsequent release a distant promise. His claim of a message for Fordem did nothing but increase the laughter and derisive treatment that he received. To believe that the thug Fordem would be his savior seemed at this time a ridiculous belief. Reviewing his assignment from his present perspective, Chris thought it now more untenable moment by moment.

"Off that mount ya slug!" the guard said as he grabbed the boy pulling him off the horse to fall face down in the mud. Several of the sentries now encircled the boy, laughing as they kicked dirt on Chris. The first guard grabbed the boy and began to roughly drag him away.

"Stop at once!" the minion shouted, pushing back Chris's assailants one by one. Reaching the boy, he grabbed his collar and pulled him to his feet. "Your purpose escapes me, but Fordem demands your presence." As he led the boy away, he spat at the lowly guard. "You filthy leech, why must you never know the Master's desires? Is it not obvious even to your dust filled brain?"

When Chris finally realized that Fordem was to see him, his bravery began to fail. He recalled images of a dark man with flowing cape, towering over him upon horseback. Chris now strongly wished to be somewhere else. The servant pushed the boy along, entering the castle and climbing rock-hewn stairs. Opening a door, they both entered a foyer, the man shoving Chris to the floor. Turning, he left the room, closing the oaken door. Turning a key in a heavy lock with a thud, Chris was alone and a prisoner again.

"Oh freaking great!" Chris whispered to himself. "Private audience, roughly treated, then released right? Wrong." He got to his feet slowly as he accessed his position. "The sad end to a measly life. Why me?" he cried, panicking and pacing the floor. Dropping again to the floor, Chris sat to wait for his ultimate fate.

Fordem entered by a side entrance. The tall man strode in and looked down on the pitiful boy. "Rise you cow!" he said.

Chris did not stand quickly enough to please the man. Fordem grabbed the front of his tunic and lifted him to eye level, examining his crest closely. Once sure of his observations he dropped Chris to the floor again and began to laugh with an ominous tone. "Your stupidity is astounding. Here is the last place for you. You're a fraudulent fool! Ha, Ha--! Providence shines brightly this day." An evil smile came upon the man, and he turned on his heel speaking with his back to the boy. "Could you possibly believe I would not see through this miserable disguise? You are a problem for me; your story needs burying. And now you fall into my hands." Fordem turned and once again looked upon the boy. "You have not your princely guard. More than their foolery will be needed to save you this time."

Chris looked away from the man as he continued questioning his mission. He trusted the prince boys, but had they sent the wrong person? *He knows me. He sure knows I'm not from Ateirrum, or Kansas.* "Give a message to Fordem alone," they had said. He could expect rough treatment, but they promised, "Chris would return." Well the first two promises had held, but how could this man possibly release him. Then he remembered the message.

"Sire—sir--I mean your highness, whatever. From across the sea I come, with a message for your superior eyes only!" Chris quickly said in his most humbling and cowering voice. As he spoke, he pulled from his sleeve the second parchment, sealed once again with wax. This seal was different, however, a crudely drawn eagle, an obviously forged copy of the royal seal of Ateirrum.

Taking the parchment from the boy, Fordem turned and examined it. He moved first to the window, then for more privacy moved away and lifted an oil lamp. Chris could see the man concentrating upon this seal, touching the wax and viewing it carefully beneath the illumination from the lamp.

Fordem turned back to the boy. "Fool" was his only word as he sliced open the seal spreading the parchment out upon a wooden table. In the dim light, the man read from the document.

> **The Queen and the crown jewels in exchange for Alexander of Alucemet. Make good upon our agreement within a fortnight, or the boy dies.**
>
> Signed: King Lithotomy of Ateirrum

Fordem left the document to curl upon itself. The man turned walking around the room in deep thought for quite some time. As he did, Chris tried to regain his composure. The boy was shaking and knew he would vomit soon.

Fordem now stood in front of the boy, his face steeped in anger. Composing himself, he forced an insincere smile "It is agreed. In one fortnight. 14 days to you maggot! Now return and plague me no longer."

Chris forced himself to calm down. He still had the last and most dangerous step to perform. He quickly produced his dagger, and jumped past the stunned man to the document. As at the mayor's home, he struck the document once with the hilt of the knife, and it went up in flames. Chris stepped back, afraid of Fordem's response.

Fordem looked puzzled staring at the burning parchment. "An odd one you are!" Taking the boy by the hair he threw him out of his chamber door. The man yelled at the boy as he quickly slammed the heavy door in his face. "Now get out of my sight!"

Gathering himself from the floor, Chris was off and running down the breezeway and stairs to the central courtyard. "Mission accomplished!" Chris said as he bridled his horse, turned and rode quickly over the drawbridge to safety.

Had the boy seen her it would have given him some peace. The Queen had heard of his arrival and the disturbance. From her lofty chamber, she now stood in the shadows, looking down upon the central foyer expectantly. She smiled to herself as she saw the boy mount up and quickly disappear over the drawbridge.

Chapter 20
Digital Severance

> Even youths grow tired and weary,
> and young men stumble and fall;
> but those who hope in the Lord
> will renew their strength.
> They will soar on wings like eagles;
> they will run and not grow weary,
> they will walk and not be faint.
> Isaiah 40:30-31

It was another luxuriant lunchtime, and the Boar's location could be predicted, his palate so obvious and opulent. Cooks were sweating, caterers running, and the Boar, with disgusting sounds and flatus, could eat and keep up with whatever arrived at his table. The desperately tiny napkin, sitting ajar within his collar, seemed hopelessly out of place. The two fisted feast had just begun and would continue for hours.

Fordem took this opportunity to enter the chamber causing the Boar a start. As a result, a poorly aimed spoon of boiling broth came to land squarely on his abundant waist. "Ow...you fool, you interrupt me," Michaelis yelled to his visitor as he rose, stomping up and down in pain. As he stomped, his foot slid off its sole onto the polished boot shank. With great experience he righted himself with skill, covering deftly that his foot did not fill the entire boot.

This bore of a Boar had never intimidated Fordem. His distress was humorous, the man thought, bringing some welcome relief to his burning gut. He stood in front of the Boar, tightly parsing his lips and hiding his smile. "I have had a visitor today, Michaelis." Fordem said as soon as the Boar stopped his stomping.

"We need not know of your concubines and their gypsy appearances, Fordem, now let me eat in peace!" Michaelis responded as he sat back down to his feast.

"The visitor is a messenger--that is a crier from across the sea." Leaving the statement in the air, Fordem waited to see if he recalled their story, testing the inferior intelligence of this disgusting superior.

The Boar looked up from his plate. His chin was awash with stained bits and pieces of the meal as greasy fingers began rubbing his unkempt and shabby clothes. He was curious and thinking about the remark when he dismissed it. "A cry-er." the man said with a knowing smile. "Your concubine is a crying wench from across the sea? I care not for your pleasures, just keep the wench quiet." With this the man returned to spooning anything in sight into his maloccluded jaw.

Fordem seemed to enjoy this misunderstanding for as the Boar concentrated upon his meal, the man smiled and laughed quietly to himself. "Michaelis, I received a messenger from Ateirrum this day. Ateirrum! Recall, if you will, who we have interned on that inferior rock of a kingdom."

With this Michaelis stopped, and looked up reluctantly from his meal. Given the significance of his meal, his attention suggested that something of the importance was at issue here. He thought to himself, rubbing his oily fingers upon his chin, silent and not acknowledging the military man for the moment. He rose now, pushing away from his table. The man began to pace, occasionally slipping off of the high heeled exquisitely polished boots, righting himself with nary a thought.

"Alexander, the smart-Alec prince?" The Boar said, turning to Fordem.

"Yes. The crier brings a written message complete with royal seal reminding us of the agreement."

"Give it to me with haste," the Boar demanded of Fordem, walking in his odd manner to the man who towered over the pock-faced being.

"Burnt to ashes, forgive me for saying," Fordem responded.

"Burnt! Why would one even as foolish as you do such as that?"

"The messenger destroyed it. The parchment ignited somehow with just a blow from the hilt of a dagger. It is sorcery of which I know not, but destroyed it is!"

"Fool, rot in the spilith, my brilliance is dashed by the likes of you. Did one happen to read such a document?" criticized Michaelis.

"To memory I committed it. In one fortnight it is demanded that we make good our arrangement," Fordem responded.

Standing now on both shanks of his boots the boar questioned, "Arrangement, and what might this arrangement be?"

"As our leader will recall," Fordem responded slowly, "Alexander was entombed for future exchange of the Queen and the crown jewels."

"The boy can rot! The Queen and the crown jewels, what folly. Fordem of course I recall our arrangement with that stone of a so-called man, Lithotomy, but living up to and actually obeying an agreement, why that is just not right! You should have slain that tumorous prince when you had him."

"Not with the Queen still surviving as we have discussed. Imprison the brat, and then later dispose of them both as you so brilliantly concluded," Fordem said, reminding the Boar of their prior plan.

"Yes, yes that was the plan but Lithotomy was not privy to his eventual loss." The Boar retrieved a fowl leg covered with sauce. He took a huge bite finishing his thought with food in his mouth. "And what of the jewels," he said, pointing with the near eaten stub of the leg. "We have searched; torture the Queen until she produces them. That is an order master Fordem."

"The Queen will suddenly recall the jewel's location when she can rescue her son with them, to that I am sure. Within a fortnight we move with a mobile army; the Queen and the jewels, through the Devil's pass to the port. Once all three, Queen, jewels, and Alexander, are within sight we take them all. The Queen and Alexander will sadly be lost in the battle. King Lithotomy will easily fall. Everything will then be ours and consolidation complete," Fordem concluded proudly.

"Yes, yes--a brilliant plan that I had considered long ago. Be certain that the smart-Alec prince, wench, and jewels are properly cared for. Remember, the jewels are mine and nary a one may you keep from my, I mean the royal treasury." Sitting down again and pulling his heaped plate before him he queried Fordem. "You consider not one point. What of the pirate-brat boy?"

"A matter of simplicity, we will sink him upon his beloved sea. You must see, my fearless one, there are absolutely no deficiencies in your brilliant plan. Your cunning victory is only a fortnight away," Fordem said. The Boar was now fully engaged in his meal. Bowing and walking backwards, Fordem exited his chamber deferentially.

The following morning found Fordem thrilled by his position. The military man was renewed, the burning feeling in his gut gone for the time being. He was excited and knew that with the information in his possession, he would easily ambush, steal, and kill, and do so reasonably. Here was an act that was truly worthy of him. Of course, Alexander was not interned across the sea but free. The fact was unfortunate, but Fordem now saw the opportunity to turn this in his favor. He saw easily through the thin disguise of the odd boy messenger, an individual he hated but would soon destroy. The document was such an obvious forgery it was laughable. Their wizard-like destruction of the document was actually favorable, for had Michaelis seen the parchment, even that ignorant being would have guessed the ploy. How lucky it was that Fordem had intercepted the message. He figured that Alexander was now sure that the kingdom's force would march through the sole route to Ateirrum, the Devil's Pass. The boy would believe their purpose was to exchange Queen and jewels for the smart-Alec prince. Fordem knew that this thinly disguised plot was an attempt to ambush him, the Devil's Pass the location, and the date, one fortnight. His gut was healing quite nicely with this joyous turn of events. And so

Pirates, Scoundrels, and Kings

with fresh villainous renewal, thoughts of joyous infamous victory, and blessed deadly results for his enemies, Fordem began the day with a joyful bliss, only partially tempered by the arrival of his two stooges, the Ogre of 'O' and the pirate Balaam.

"As you know." Fordem announced to the two men. "The smart-Alec prince, Alexander, awaits his demise within the dungeons of the weakling stone of a king, Lithotomy. This ridiculous monarch wishes to exchange the boy for our Queen and the royal jewels."

"The boy can rot," the Ogre laughed. As was his practice his laugh led to more laughs and he forgot what he was laughing about, entertained now by a personal humor apparent only to him. "Jewels, the brat, and the Queen, ha—ha—ha—"

As for the pirate captain, he was skeptically silent save his typical stridorous rhonchi, carrying his ever-present spittoon that was unusually empty this morning.

"Silence!" Fordem could not take anymore! He took his sword from its hilt and struck the Ogre on his head, silencing the incessant laughing. This fool, why must I deal with such drivel, he thought to himself? Speaking now to the two men he said, "We will have all three at one time you drips! You must understand that once through Devil's pass, Alexander will fall, the Queen and the smart-Alec boy meeting their untimely demise. We will overpower Lithotomy; the weakling king will fall as well. Our return will be less those two nemeses, and richer the crown jewels."

"She will, he will, and they will as well," the Ogre agreed, as agreeing to such a plan seemed to be what was expected of the Royal Guard Grand Am.

With a deep cough, the captain produced some sputum whose quality seemed to disappoint the man. With little ceremony, nary any force, he drooled said hawk into his brass spittoon. "But what of the crown jewels?" Balaam said. "Our search has yielded nothing of such, we've exhausted every possibility mate."

"That is where your cunning persuasion fits in, captain Balaam," Fordem reported with an unusual kindness for the despised seafarer. "With your clear diction you will educate the Queen. With your help, she will find that producing the crown jewels and saving her spoiled prince's life are inextricably dependent," Fordem said.

The captain seemed suspect as he eyed the man, pushing a stubby finger into his mouth and loosing a particularly tenaciously adherent wad of spittle. He seemed to wonder about his claim and influence upon a Queen who seemed to be detest the man, but something more sinister as well was percolating within the mind of Balaam.

Turning now to the Royal Guard Grand Am, Fordem instructed the man. "Ogre of 'O', prepare three legions of tested men for a battlefield march. This is to occur a fortnight less one from this exact moment. Prepare as well two hundred artillery pieces and required supplies. See to this without fail!" He finished his instructions with a flurry, a wave of his right hand dismissing the man.

Laughing wildly the grotesque man left the chamber with excitement. "We're going to go to war, we're going to war!" he mumbled with insane merriment.

Balaam offered little to this point. With the Ogre's departure, the pirate was now alone with Fordem. He was meditating pensively upon the discussion, staring at the floor, and chewing on his next projectile. "Three legions, that leaves the castle unprotected, does it not mate?" A hawk rang musically into his spittoon. "Truth be, the Ogre is a grand fool, but not captain Balaam," the pirate said confronting the man. With a sly smile, he looked directly into the eyes of Fordem.

"You dare challenge me!" Fordem yelled. With second thoughts, the man calmed his violent outburst. It was a practice in this evil empire, no one trusting the other, the other trusting no one, and each trusting themselves least of all. Double speak and spin could help, for saying your thoughts could land one within the dungeon or worse. "Out with it man, to what do you refer?"

"We both know the foul truth. The smart-Alec prince is free, mate. Oh and such an army for the likes of the stone of a king, Lithotomy? He is a coward and weak!"

"Watch what you say, Captain. I have little patience for a foul expectorant such as you. Your ultimate demise by consumption would be easy to arrange! Take heed of my threats. I seldom fail to make good of them," Fordem whispered to the pirate, controlling his anger.

"You have not considered the pirate-brat boy. Will he be silent? And to what naval mind do you turn but captain Balaam. And what of the Boar? What say he of your failure with those pitiful Pitlings? Threaten me not Richard of Fordem!" Balaam made his points, ticking them off on his fingers. The man did not intimidate him. He casually dug deep and produced a foul greenish wad rattling in his upper airway. Without looking, the man deftly delivered it into the spittoon, punctuating his argument.

The two stared at one another, neither breaking eye contact. Fordem was the first to do so, turning and walking slowly in thought. He was troubled by someone who could out blackmail a blackmailer, for he took such pride in the skill. He turned now to the pirate with all the sincerity and reluctant admiration that he could muster, a tight smile plastered upon his double-crossed and disgusted countenance. "Of these issues we, such as ourselves, need not be troubled. Captain Balaam speaks correct; we must deal with the pirate-brat boy for he will support his bastard brother. You will have your day with the blue-belted brat. We both can agree then; share our story only with those of us that can understand such issues?"

"Agreed...but the treasure the sea dog stole from captain Balaam," the pirate demanded, "they be—well--for retirement so to speak. And the Queen as well, to me you leave her to my discretion?"

"You may have those diffident jewels for yourself. Do what you will with the Queen. Leave me out of that. Ready your fleet for support seaside of the Devil's Pass, a fortnight less one. You may do as you choose with the Queen, but the Crown jewels, obtain them before she is of no worth to us."

With this temporary and precarious truce based upon mutual distrust, Balaam was dismissed. He turned and walked from the chamber.

CRYSTAL HAD LOVED THE QUEEN her entire life. She was the only daughter of her dedicated mother, who until her death the year before had been the Queen's lady in waiting. To this proud position Crystal ascended, and she did so with total commitment, her life given for the Queen.

Sewing and appareling her beloved lady violated her natural tendency, however, for Crystal was at heart a tomboy. She had sun-bleached, tightly curled, brown hair, cut in a short bob. With sparkling blue eyes and a slightly mischievous smile, she found herself out of place with the other girls in court. Soccer was her passion, and what a waste to score unopposed when the girls met for this purpose. The lack of challenge troubled her, and so she played and scored quite often with the boys, a fact that galled her less confident male teammates.

Gidget considered herself the *royal dog in waiting*, a princess of the loftiest breed of Shar Pei. She was proud of her wrinkles, blessed with enough skin for two dogs and a shiny, full, reddish-brown coat. She attended the Queen with diligence, missing very dearly her beloved King and waiting for his return. That morning the royal dog was her most dutiful, lying at the Queen's foot, her wrinkly face on her front paws as she eyed the proceedings with interest.

A messenger preceded the pirate's audience with the Queen. Knocking politely on the Queen's chamber door, the clipped-ear man with message in hand waited patiently for the Queen's lady to answer. Crystal opened the chamber door and smiled at the unfortunate boy. "Boy, why do you disturb the Queen?" she proudly demanded.

As was the marked men's pattern, silence was the answer. With a distant stare the man handed a written message to the girl, turned, and disappeared down the candle-lit hall.

Pirates, Scoundrels, and Kings

Crystal returned to the Queen's waiting. "Queen Patrice, a messenger brings this unto you."

Taking the document from the girl and thanking her for her efforts, the Queen unrolled the message and read it silently to herself. The message announced captain Balaam's desired audience. A scowl came over her brow as she read, and a brief shake of her head testified to her disapproval. She considered her response. The message related the crown jewels to her son Alexander. Reluctantly, she instructed Crystal to usher in the captain.

Before she could finish the message, the lumbering bronchiectatic foul of a man appeared, not waiting for his announcement.

"My Queen," he said. "An important matter we have before us. Scoot my lassie," the pirate scowled at Crystal.

"Never will I leave my Queen with the likes of you, you foul and virulent beast!" Pulling herself as tall as possible, she interposed between the man and her beloved Queen. Gidget was up with alarm, standing and sniffing the leg of the captain.

"It is fine, Crystal. Wait for me in my sitting room. The captain has just a brief message for me," directed the beautiful Queen.

Twisting up a disapproving scowl, and shaking her head in a defiant manner to the pirate, Crystal pleaded. "My lady, this villainous slug smells of old excessive rum and crotch rot. His presence in the Queen's chamber will never be in order. I shan't leave you to this degenerate worm"

Standing now, the Queen placed a caring hand upon the girl. She wished to protect the girl from the twisted affairs of the kingdom. "Crystal await me in the sitting room. You may listen at the door if it is your desire."

Defeated but not retreating, Crystal turned from the man in disgust. Looking at the Queen's quiet determination and sensing her certain judgment concerning this issue, she lifted her billowing floor length skirt and with deliberation moved to the adjoining room begrudgingly. "Watch thy manners or you'll have me to answer to!" she added as she passed the man in a huff. Gidget lay distrustfully at the foot of her Queen.

The Queen now sat upon her velveteen lounge. Turning to the captain with patience, she asked, "And to what subject brings you directly within my personal chamber? Speak up, for this is quite unusual. Only the mention of my son Alexander by your messenger has gotten you this far, captain Balaam."

Balaam spoke in the king's finest English, barring at the door his broken sea dialect. "Please, call me Cap--your majesty, and may I say such a beautiful dress upon your fairness this morning. Excuse my intrusion, but I have been charged with relaying a matter of high national security to your royal highness."

"Go on captain," the Queen politely responded.

"That fragrance, my Queen. A rose never blessed this old seafarer as the bouquet pervading your chamber." The pirate now moved to her side, rubbing his greasy fingers upon his tunic. Absent his trusted spittoon and not wanting to disgust the Queen, he rumbled a fine sputum and swallowed it delicately.

"Thank you captain, thou art too kind," the Queen said with some impatience. "Of this matter of national security, please continue."

"Alexander of Alucemct has been located my most fair sovereign." The captain was now towering over the Queen. Moving within inches of the sitting woman, he looked down upon the royal cleavage.

This statement worried the Queen, knowing what she knew of her children's location, and not wanting to betray this knowledge, she begrudgingly left the captain's disrespectful presence stand for the moment. "My sons, of what news have you," she asked with a strained smile on her face.

"The unfortunate boy is imprisoned beyond the sea. A ransom of the crown jewels has been demanded by the King Lithotomy. With those jewels, if I might be so bold your majesty, I captain Balaam; supreme commander of the royal fleet will lure that inferior King, and rescue the boy. Oh, and certainly the jewels will return to my Queen by her most trusted, and hungry, I—I--mean humble, yes humble servant." With one bold finger, the pirate began to outline the crested bodice, which held her royal bosom.

His finger was detached before the pirate knew what displeasure his actions had caused the Queen. She was not to be beguiled, and certainly his charm was such that this was an insult. A jewel-laden dagger lay within the sleeve of her gown. Like the strike of a cobra, the violating digit was severed without delay.

Crystal was in the room as the finger hit the floor. "What have you done you dribbling fool?" she yelled at the top of her lungs as she ran to the Queen's side. Standing a full foot shorter and at least one hundred stone lighter, the fearless girl now pushed and hit the dumbfounded man. She began kicking him with her best soccer kicks. "You--I suspected foul play—beast--be gone or below your waist more than a finger you will lose."

Gidget, the royal Shar Pei, was at her Queen's side, growling, barking, and drooling in defense of the Queen.

The pirate roared in pain. With a frightened grimace the man pulled back his bloody hand absent one digit. Closing his one good hand on the finger's remnant, the pirate tried to stop the pumping blood. He looked back at the Queen, blood now bedecking the entire front of his pirate attire. The man spit out his response. "You will live to regret this rebuke. Produce those jewels within a fortnight less two, or Alexander is fodder." With that, he was off, running out of the chamber to the royal surgeon with his bleeding hand.

"You must do something for me, Crystal," the Queen said, grabbing the girl with intensity. "Go to Nicholas. It is he who has said jewels. I must have them at once." After embracing and relating the Queen's appreciation, the girl left the chamber for the royal stable.

CRYSTAL WASTED LITTLE TIME, MOVING to her modest quarters and ridding herself of her bothersome dress. Leather breeches and tunic quickly replaced this, and then upon horseback while no one was aware, she was gone.

She had little trouble finding Nicholas's pirate camp for she was one of a rare number of individuals who had seen the place before. Nick had taken the girl to the water slides just before he had disappeared for good that sad day sometime in the past. The mountainous rocky slopes were perfect for hiding from the growing evil that seemed to be spreading like mercury into every corner of the once proud and free country. She knew exactly where to enter the northern side of the mountainous caves, but once inside a few twists and turns and she was lost. Getting off her mount, she turned first right and then left in the dark, totally lost and beginning to doubt her resolve. It was in this darkened spot and with one of her turns to the right that the boy ran smack into the girl, face into face, before either could see the other.

"Ouch!" Crystal yelled, raising a hand to her face. She soon felt blood run down her hand from her mouth. Feeling with her tongue, she realized the problem. "My tooth!" she screamed as she realized that the impact had dislodged her left incisor, dropping the tooth to the ground, forever changing her mischievous smile.

Chris was startled as much by this as Crystal, and he held his forehead in pain. Bright lights and stars appeared before his eyes as he hopped around trying to make the pain go away quickly. "Why don't you look where you are going?" Then for the first time realizing that his assailant was a girl, added, "And who are you!"

Crystal just kept shouting. "My tooth, my tooth...why don't you look out odd boy!" When she finally calmed down, she looked at the boy. The small amount of bleeding had stopped. Crystal never really cared much about looks anyway, and the loss of a tooth, well perhaps people will take her more seriously she thought. She apologized to the boy who she noticed was a tanned boy with blond hair and blue eyes, and cute. "I am the Queen's lady in waiting. My name is Crystal," she said. Showing her broad smile less one incisor, she now looked even younger than her age.

There it was again: "odd boy." Chris was almost getting use to the description. "What's a lady in waiting?" Chris questioned. Chris had recovered by now, stars fading, and the pain tolerable.

He thought about this girl. Her reference to the Queen was good, and he had to laugh as she smiled with a toothless grin. "I am Christopher of Temecula. Quite a rude way to meet I would say, Crystal, your Queen-ness in waiting."

These were serious times, and quickly their banter became solemn. Crystal briefly explained her presence. "It is imperative that Nicholas return to the Queen the royal jewels. I am not privy to the reason, but I come from her directly, and she was quite certain about the immediate need!"

Chris knew that the Queen had given these to Nicholas for his keeping, and had in fact accompanied the boy when he deposited them in his oubliette. "Let me take you to him Crystal. You are probably quite lost."

"I am of course most certainly not lost! How rude an assumption you make, odd boy. And besides, I must return. My absence speaks poorly for the Queen's safety." Addressing the boy with her mischievous smile she asked, "Please, with haste return to Nicholas this very moment, and have him deliver these said jewels in person tonight. I will wait in the bowery hold. He will know where. I will then deliver the jewels to my Queen."

"Okay sure, I'll go now," the boy responded. He turned around and was off before the girl could stop him.

"Christopher of Temecula," she yelled as she ran after him. The boy stopped, turning a questioning eye to the girl. "But which way do I go; you know to get out of here?"

"I thought you weren't lost," Chris responded, smiling at the cute girl.

"Of course not odd boy, but...tell me anyway."

Chris laughed to himself. He took a brief moment to lead her on her proper way down the cavern to the outside world. He turned and walked back inside the cave. After a few turns he saw it. Returning to the cave exit he yelled out at the girl. "Crystal—ah--Queen in waiting!"

The girl turned curious as to his return.

"Your tooth!" the boy said, smiling with pride having found such a prize. He held up the incisor for the girl to see, not realizing the degree of dental expertise practiced in a land such as this.

"Christopher of Temecula, you may keep that given that it was your hard head that traumatized me so." With a broad toothless smile and a wink she turned, mounting her horse and picked her way down the mountain to her home.

Chapter 21
The Spilith Shoot

> I WILL DRIVE THE NORTHERN ARMY FAR FROM YOU,
> PUSHING IT INTO A PARCHED AND BARREN LAND...
> AND IT STENCH WILL GO UP;
> ITS SMELL WILL RISE.
> JOEL 2:20

Christopher smiled privately when he thought about Nicholas growing gum in the form of a tree. He thought that gum came from a tree, but was the chewable part the seed? Chris thought not. However, Nicholas was so sincere and dedicated that the boy began to question this assumption. He was not surprised then when one day as he watched Nicholas watering and caring for his project, the tip of burgeoning plant growth appeared.

Nicholas was always silent as he watered. He smiled at the boy as he finished his care, leaving the site, bound for things that pirates do.

Chris walked to the spot and dropped to his knees. "A weed," Chris said to assure himself as he examined in detail that day's first growth. As the days passed however, more than a weed sprouted. Soon the first sign of a trunk appeared, followed by branches and then leaves. Soon the tree's product was obvious.

"Gum!" Chris said to himself one day as he reached to the tip of the lowest branch. Squeezing the globular white product with its gum-like sticky and spongy texture, the boy was impressed.

The tree produced gum prodigiously, enough for a small country to chew night and day. The product was quite tasty, and chew they did. Nicholas, however, had much more than culinary use in mind for the product that he personally harvested daily. He saw the product as an adhesive to be used in many future ways. Sealing the inflation port on his slammers was just the beginning for this newly discovered treasure that Nicholas referred to as just *chew*.

It was dark and the moon full as Chris and the patched boy silently entered the back streets of Alucemet. Riding to accomplish a task outlined by Alexander, they rode on horseback keeping to the shadows. The horse's hooves echoed upon the dusty cobblestone streets that night with nary a sound as the two rode in stealth.

Nicholas had sent Nails in support, the trusted dog flanking the boys and keeping just out of sight, for trouble that night was expected. Returning now to the area where Fordem ruthlessly chased Chris and Little Andy brought back a frightening remembrance to the modern day boy. Neither Little Andy nor Nails seemed so affected, the dog afraid of no place in this world, Chris realized.

"We go down this lane, then starboard down the alley," little Andy said, lapsing into maritime language as all the pirate boys did from time to time. "The cobbler will have a package ready for us, Christopher of Temecula," little Andy whispered in preparation for their arrival at the night's destination.

For what they sought with the cobbler, Alexander had not said, but peach cobbler had always been one of the modern day boy's favorite desserts. He hoped, but for some reason internally doubted that the cobbler here would produce the same.

Tonight Nicholas was on the move as well, a high-risk mission to accomplish under cover of dark. The task required extreme caution, so the boy was on foot and alone, save his two remaining bulldogs, Spike and Smasher. A horse was out of the question for where his dogs and he headed evil eyes were certain. The full moon lighted the night, so for secrecy the boy stuck to the shadows. Upon foot, flanked by two bulldogs, the boy now moved in silence.

Nicholas was dressed as usual in black, and on his feet pointy elf-like shoes for silence replaced his usual barefooted state. He had darkened his face with ashes, and on his shoulders, a burgundy tunic dirtied as well from the hearth. The bulldogs were camouflaged with darkened mud from the bottom of the Pirate's Cove rubbed snout to tail, blackening them like nuggets of coal. They moved as a trio, silently making their way, dipping in and out of shadows and making good time.

The sewer system of the kingdom, or spilith, was far beyond its time, a product of the inventive Sir Alexander. Not only was the city built over a subterranean system of huge drains, but that system connected even a more complex drainage scheme within the royal residence. Royal refuse was treated royally on its way to the sea, the use of the chamber pot left to the less civilized.

Beginning part way up the northern precipice of the fortress was a chiseled stone tunnel. Opening near sea level at high tide, it was wedged between towering pointed crags and rocks. The bird population of the sea had a field day here, swooping, cawing, and nesting, making cliff dwellings and sewage all the more compatible. Built with roman style arches and tightly fitted stone, the tunnel was bored deeply within the rocky mount of the castle, climbing at a steep incline from the sea, then deep to the castle moat and under the western end of the castle.

A moat is an island of water that surrounds a fortress, its purpose in battle to place a last obstacle between the attacker and the castle occupants. Many moats were stagnant, depending upon nature and precipitation for its water supply. The moat surrounding the castle Alucemet was circulating, fresh water supplied by a diverted portion of the country's main river entering the southeastern edge over rocky falls. Once within the moat, the fresh river water circulated, eventually disappearing under the northern wall of the castle. Once under the castle the rapidly moving water spilled and cleansed the castle spilith system, the water washing all residues out the incline to the sea.

In medieval England, the royal rump fell upon an oval stool that stool open to the world beyond. Gravity had its inevitable way with the regal product of the royal high-nee. However, the high-nee received the whipping wind, chill, and the occasional projectiles from surrounding children. The Alucemet upgrade was not so antiquated.

Within the residence of the castle at discrete locations, an early variation on the water closet sat. Small rooms complete with a door for privacy included oval gateways over stone chutes that fell, carrying waste to the spilith system below.

Nicholas had used the system to his advantage in better days of the past, his plan tonight simple in origin. Sticking to the shadows, the boy and his companions made good time as they moved across the plain, staying off the more traveled roads. Nearing their destination, they jogged to their right through dense willows arriving at the river.

It was a freezing night when the boy and his two dedicated bulldogs dove into the river. Staying near the shore overhang, they drifted quietly towards the southeastern edge of the fortress. As they neared the castle, the palace sentries would begin to be seen, their job to patrol the path to the castle. The river was relatively safe, however, for at this point, overhanging weeping willows nearly covered the waterway.

When they neared the fall, Nicholas steadied himself upon the rocks and signaled his dogs to exit the river. Moving on the riverbank, the three quietly made their way to the crashing sound ahead. Here the tree cover thinned out, leaving the band exposed. Nicholas was fully aware of this, and so with caution he inched ahead. The bulldogs with their blackened coats were silent save their necessary drooling as they inched along behind their trusted leader. At just the right moment, Nicholas signaled to Spike who signaled to Smasher and all three dove with a quiet splash over the falls and into the moat below.

Moonlight came from the eastern edge of the world tonight, illuminating the southeastern moat. At this point, they swam deep to the surface, making their detection difficult. As they rounded the northern moat, they were now hidden in deepening shadows of moonlight, cast by the castle's silhouette. Making the northwest portion of the moat, they arrived at their destination without detection.

Nicholas climbed out of the water, sticking close to the castle wall and the shadows. Vegetation had grown to cover the moat where it entered under the castle, affording more cover for the marauding band. It was here that the dogs were counseled to stop.

"Spike, Smasher," the boy whispered. "Stayeth here, and be out of site. I will return shortly. Make short work of anyone who enters. But stay down." The boy signaled, holding his hand close to the ground. The dogs watched the boy closely, understanding his directions. "The guard will take your presence none too lightly my trusted boys." Spike and Smasher eyed the boy with approval, tongues and tails wagging. They moved to the brush-covered opening and began to scout the area intent upon guarding their master's life. Nicholas pulled a dagger from beneath his tunic and placed it in his mouth. Turning from his dogs, he dove with a silent splash into the moat and disappeared under the castle wall.

It was dark and vile within that waterway. The overlying castle left little headroom for the boy as he made his way deep under the stone fortress. The water route would lead him to his destination where the subterranean moat crashed over a rocky fall to the spilith below. An opening into the castle used in its original construction persisted here. It would be simple work then to enter and move to the bowery hold where Crystal would be waiting.

The foul air became stifling as the boy floated along his journey. He was at a point where he had to turn his head to keep from dragging it along the overhead stone roof of the canal. Nicholas swept along without control as he neared the crashing falls ahead. Once upon them, the rapids threw him up and over, where he crashed in a heap to the spilith system below.

The stench was horrible, much more so than he remembered from his last secret journey from the fortress. The boy picked himself up, moved to the edge of the channel, and began ascending to the spilith origin trying to put the smell out of mind. Ahead a heavy oaken cover barred the hold, but once moved allowed an easy climb into the bowery of the castle. Nicholas pulled the heavy cover aside; things at that point had changed. Across the spilith origin, cutting off access to the castle, was a heavy iron grate running from side to side and floor to ceiling secured with a heavy iron padlock. The boy lifted the lock hoping that it was unlocked. Finding it secured, he flung it back in place. Nicholas stomped his foot dejected. His planned entry was now impossible.

"Drat!" Nicholas spoke quietly to himself. He grabbed the grate and shook, hoping against hope that he could budge the substantial door without success. He sat for the moment on the edge of the spilith with his back supported by the enemy gate. "Now what, he said to himself?"

THE TWO BOYS MADE THE starboard turn off the lane and rode into the narrow alley. Deep shadows filled the way, cast from the adjacent buildings that nearly touched. Filled with trash, the passage was a haven for carelessly cast broken crates of liter and reeked of decaying filth. Chris could imagine hordes of rats running across at their feet unseen. The boys dismounted and led their horses along, winding among the scattered debris. Nails kept to the darkest shadows as the two boys made their way down the alley. "A moment more, Christopher," little Andy whispered, pointing out a small back alley door down the way as their destination.

They hurried, longing to finish their chore when at their back horse's hooves rang out on the masonry road. At a gallop, the rider jerked the bridle, bringing the horse to a grinding stop at the head of the alley. The two boys pulled their mounts into the shadows and pressed themselves against the wall between scattered crates and trash. A quiet growl from the shadows located Nails who was ready to defend his sworn friends if need be.

The rider sat upon his mount and turned for the moment looking down the alley. He seemed to sense something staring long and hard into the shadows near the boys. Chris felt an uncomfortable stare cross his silhouette that gladly left him as quickly as it appeared. Satisfied, the horseman turned to leave but his horse hesitated for the moment, pawing with his left hoof. The man looked again into the alley. His suspicion quelled, the man jerked the bridle across and spurred the horse to exit down the cobblestone road. As he rode away, the horse threw one last look down the alley and into the deep shadows that protected the boys. The snap of a whip rang out as the man disappeared; apparently more pressing matters awaiting him down the way.

Chris wiped his brow with the back of his hand. The two boys looked at each other and sighed in relief. The low growl disappeared, replaced by a vigorous pant as Nails left his hiding place and began to lead the boys again down the alleyway.

Ahead a partially open door stood, leading into one of the shop rears that bordered on the alley. As they arrived, the two boys secured their horses. Little Andy opened the door, and the two boys quickly disappeared inside. Nails continued for a short distance, jumping to an elevated position on discarded crates in the shadows. The dog now lay down, head on his paws, his eyes carefully scanning for any trouble.

"Here, take all and be gone. Evil runs everywhere tonight," the cobbler spoke out of the shadows before the boy's eyes had adjusted. Shoving two burlap bags at the visitors, the cobbler said, "I know not of why, but give these to Sir Alexander. Each is finished to his exact instruction. Let him realize our hopes are upon him and his trusted brother, now go in silence, and God be with you." The man was in obvious fear as he turned over the two satchels of items and guided Chris and Little Andy back out the door to the alley. Once within the alley, the man was gone, quickly shutting the service door with a final thud. With a whistle for Nails, the two mounted, each carrying a sack, and like the wind they were off now using speed to distance themselves from the decaying and evil occupied city.

"CHUTES," NICHOLAS SAID TO HIMSELF with reluctance, replacing his dagger and staring down at his wet shoes. "Spilith chutes! Up and out the bloody jake," he said shaking his head with disgust. He was sitting on the edge of the spilith thinking when the idea came to him quickly; enthusiasm, however, was far behind. The water closet, or jake in the vernacular, stood high above the boy in the royal residences. They consisted of a small wooden closet with an oval seat. Beneath the oval chair was a rock-hewn shoot allowing refuses to drop by gravity to the spilith system below. If one was bold or more likely crazy, one could use the shoot for access to the residential section of the castle above.

Nicholas stood and walked slowly down the spilith with his eye to the ceiling above. Here he could see the series of chutes entering the chamber roof periodically along its length. There was one in particular he hoped to find, but they all seemed the same: dark and gloomy, foul and rank with slick chiseled sides that climbed to the residences above. The boy paced off some distance along the spilith and chose an especially dark square opening as his target.

Nicholas pulled the dagger from his sash and eyed with determination the chute overhead. With a strong jump, the boy drove the knife into the stone mortar just inside and pulled himself up into the stone opening. He wedged himself into the small chute, his back against one wall and feet holding his position on the opposite side.

While the spilith was rank, the closed confines of the chute made conditions markedly worse. With no air circulation, the overpowering smell made the boy lightheaded for a moment. Looking upwards in the dark shaft with disgust, the boy could just make out the hint of oval shaped illumination confirming this jake's present empty state. Nicholas stabbed his dagger into the mortar above and pulled himself in this fashion slowly up the chute.

Could he squeeze through the oval opening once upon his goal? What if that oval portal to freedom, now empty, became occupied and used in the mean time? The thought was so vile and repugnant to the hero boy that it made him shutter as he continued his reluctant ascent.

He was now nearly to the top of the spilith chute. Above, the oval seat appeared as a halo begging him on. Nicholas took solace from the fact that the closet remained empty for the present time. He took a moment to rest, drawing deep breaths through his mouth, bypassing his sensitive nose. His legs were shaking with fatigue and his back cramped and burned, rubbed raw by the sharp rock. Thinking to himself, he decided that he would not describe this portion of his quest when finally back to his friends.

In a tale of twists, turns, excitement, evil, and heroism, that his path would come cross an obstacle so vile, so wretched and vulgar that one shudders to think of the consequences of the poor boy's much maligned timing. The oval light suddenly extinguished, and he was within a dark and reeking chamber. To his horror, the opening was now occupied by a slightly spread and hairy crack. "Oh...no!" Nicholas whispered to himself, as he looked above at the revolting and repulsive sight.

The man had brought a newspaper and sitting with a sigh, opened it anticipating an enjoyable evening. He was not about to hurry his relaxing nighttime pursuit, and while reading, the expectant bombs did not fall. However, as the man read, he also began to worry. A strain here and a grunt there: tonight would be a struggle, the visitor deduced as he tossed his paper to the floor to concentrate upon the job that was at hand.

Nicholas continued to eye the crack with repulsion, grimacing, gagging, and trying to make himself as small as possible. Turning and judging gravity and trajectory of the crack, the boy anticipated a bombardment of evil and vile proportions.

"Ahhhhhhh--" The sound came from above as the man began to show a frustrated side. Repositioning, he began fretting as the visitor realized that tonight would be a tougher job than he had estimated.

Nicholas could do nothing but listen to the straining character whose better part separated the boy from his freedom. Flatulence escaped from above with a sigh of ultimate relief. This encouraged the boy; perhaps just gas he thought as the dropping of the largest log this side of the black forest broke that thought unceremoniously. Nicholas saw it coming and lifted his right leg. Jamming his dagger into the mortar and repositioning, he was just able to miss the plummeting missile that fell striking the chute side, dropping with a silent splash below.

"No pee please!" Nicholas prayed, hoping for a quick end to this dilemma. "That log was close, no more Lord, I can take no more!" he continued in silence.

As he hoped for deliverance it started, a trickling hesitant stream that shot and splashed off the wall of the spilith chute as it gained momentum. Had Nicholas not been so quick, his left leg would have been soaked, but with a quick turn to his left, he straddled the stream, pinning his back against the wall and striking his head with a thud. Nicholas closed his eyes with disgust as the man splashed off the chute wall.

The voiding continued, and then with a shiver, the man finished. Rising from his throne, the light now descended through the chute. With a blast of fresh air, Nicholas gained some relief. Shadows hung above the oval portal for the time, as the man reached for his fallen breeches and freshened himself. The door to the closet opened and slammed closed with a thud.

"Gone, thank you!" Nicholas said, closing his eyes with relief. He would have to get out of here quickly before another visitor entered. He reached up with his dagger, drawing himself along, inching with back and feet to the top of the chute. Once at the oval seat, an unsteady hand emerged, taking hold of the first solid object he had access to since trapped within the chute. The other hand soon followed, and after tossing his dagger to the floor of the Jake, an exhausted boy pulled himself through the oval window to the freedom of the enclosed room.

"Ohhh—" Nicholas moaned and stamped his feet with disgust, shaking his hands and rubbing them on the wall with vile distaste. Vomiting was out of question here in the name of time and the tight enclosure, but the feeling welled up within him. Taking a deep breath, the nausea passed the boy. However, a pirate must sacrifice and his goal this night was important. Soon he was the composed and determined boy once again. Leaning his ear against the door, Nicholas listened, hoping for no more surprises.

Now the water closet stood ready for only those people of importance. To secure such a pompous site as a jake, the closet door closed locked after each use, a key necessary to gain admittance. The prior occupant, more pompous than most, had made sure that the door locked upon his exit. Confirming his suspicion, Nicholas quietly tried the door's handle to no avail. The boy had expected this, for with some deft work of his dagger he was certain to make quick work of the door's lock. Stooping to pick up the weapon, however, he heard boots approaching within the hall.

Nicholas moved quickly to the side of door anticipating another occupant. He raised his dagger in defense. The boots stopped outside of the door and with a gentle twist back and forth of the knob confirmed its locked condition. Evidently satisfied, the boots marched off probably to check the security of other prestigious doors.

"Whoo!" Nicholas shook his head with relief as beads of sweat appeared upon his brow. Had his hands not been so vile he would have wiped them away. "Now what!" Nicholas said as he moved to conceal himself again behind the door and listen carefully. The noise occurred once more, a scratching sound at the bottom of the closet's wooden door. A quiet whine, a lick of the wood on the opposite side, and then more scratching followed. A smile came to the boy. Gidget the *royal dog in waiting;* it must be Gidget, Nicholas thought, now missing his mother's devoted pet.

"Gidget?" Nicholas whispered through the door.

With that, the scratching increased in intensity, and the dog whined with anticipation, somehow guessing the room's occupant. Nicholas grabbed his dagger, and made quick work of the lock. He slowly opened the door a crack, and the wrinkled face and black tongue of the royal Shar Pei appeared. Silently Nicholas grabbed the dog by her pink collar, and pulled her through the door and into the jake.

The dog was ecstatic, whining, and licking every inch of the boy.

"Gidgey-- how are you? I missed you. Spike and Smasher are outside!" With the mention of her male heroes, Gidget was even happier, lapping and jumping at the boy. "Where is the Queen, Gidget?" Nicholas asked the hound as he scratched her wrinkled head.

Gidget turned and began to scratch the door and then turned back to the boy with anticipation. She knew exactly what the boy had asked, and as a dog thinks, wanted to take Nicholas to her lady. She kept turning from the boy to the door, from the door to the boy. She knew that quiet was in order, but could not help herself. Gidget whined with excitement as she thought of rejoining two of her favorite people this evening.

Nicholas took off the darkened tunic. Rolling it into a small bundle, he thrust it into the willing mouth of the drooling dog. "Take this to Mother Gidget. It's important. Can you do that?"

The dog seemed to shake her head affirmatively. Nicholas was well versed in dog lingo and knew that the royal dog understood exactly his intention. The boy quietly turned the door handle, and cracked the door. Staring with caution into the hallway, the boy confirmed its empty state.

"The hallway is empty Gidget, now go!" he said, opening the door just slightly. Grabbing the dog by the collar, he led her out through the door into the hallway. It was here that she stopped, turning and looking up at the boy. Sitting upon her haunches, her curly tail wagging, the wrinkled-face dog with the rolled up tunic within her capacious mouth just looked at the boy with sadness.

"Go girl--you must--the jewels--bring this tunic to the Queen."

The dog looked to her left down the hall, and turned back to the boy, her tail still wagging but now with reluctance. "But why?" Her sad eyes seemed to say as she realized that while she had found one of her close friends he for some reason would not be staying.

"Gidget, now go to the Queen. I will be fine, girl. I'll be back I promise you!"

With that, now resigned to her disappointment the dog turned. She jogged off turning sadly to look at Nicholas just once. With her tail twisting back and forth and her silent paws padding their way down the hall, she left the scene bringing the treasured package with loyal duty to her lady with pride.

Nicholas turned and with a deep and disgusting breath entered the chute, dropping quickly to the spilith below. Running and diving into the moat, he swam away with his bulldogs at his side.

IT WAS EARLY MORNING BEFORE Chris and Little Andy returned to camp. Their last escape from Alucemet had forewarned the boy, but this time only minor disturbances had blocked their retreat. The trip was not without disturbing sites, however, for the Boar personified in youth was on the prowl. As they exited the city, three boys no older than themselves had tried to stop their retreat. The boys were unsettling, for while they did not have the clipped earmark of the Boar, something about their affect reminded Chris of his contacts within the castle. When he looked at them he saw glassy, empty-eyed gazes, and evil: unusual for those so young. They were dressed in high, shiny, black boots with black breeches ruffling at the knee. Upon their chests they wore black tunics fastened at the waist with a leather thong and dagger. The front of their tunic bore a complimentary likeness of the Boar's hoof, signaling a ruthless, evil, and foreboding philosophy. The boys appeared to be the city guards, or at least they considered themselves as such. It took Little Andy's sword, Nails' toughness, and swift horses to elude these would-be police. The boys escaped without further incident, but the youths left a feeling of sadness and ultimate demise of the once proud and youthful kingdom which was being overcome by an evil force whose source of power to persuade continued to baffle the modern day boy.

Chris was glad to be out of the evil and back to camp. As the two dismounted and tied their horses, they realized that the contents of their jaunt were unknown. Neither of the two boys had bothered to inspect the contents of the two burlap sacks, being so cautious and concerned with their cover. Alexander now met them, and asked of their journey. He was very interested in the two sacks, and taking them from the boys, he turned to the rest of the Pitlings and pirate group.

"Skateboard shoes!" Chris said to himself as Alexander began to pass around the chosen footwear. Chris remembered now how interested Alexander had been in the boy's shoes. He remembered as well seeing their prototype briefly in the shop window, quickly removed from view when the keeper sensed his interest. In these times and before, a shoe such as these were unique. They did have their advantage, thick spongy soles with cloth uppers, all dyed the same dark blue with their thickly padded insoles and a wide tongue. These shoes would be much more tolerant on long marches than their historical equivalent; were there long marches in their future? Chris stood off to one side and watched the boys. All were delighted as they discarded their elf-like shoes or barefooted condition and laced up the new items. Orphan boys with leather coats and hose, the skateboard shoes made the ensemble. By the way, and where was his skateboard? he wondered. He had used the board very little recently, but it was still a possession that was dear to his heart.

Alexander broke Chris's concentration. He stood in the middle of a clearing and signaled for the boys to surround him. Speaking now to the excited boys, he began: "In a fortnight less seven we will begin our destined march. Much needs to be accomplished. Bravery is required of all. We will band together to rid our world of the evil that has been growing. We have a simple plan. God belies the cause. Victory is certain."

With this, a cheer went up from all. The boys crowded around Alexander with smiles and shouts of determination. With new footgear, the group would follow their leader to the ends of the earth. "Speaking of leaders, where was Nicholas?" Chris wondered.

Chris had trouble with a television-less world. He found himself often wondering of the medieval boy's education, how could they know anything without videos and movie theatres? He had taken to describing for the group his favorite films, down to the last detail. While having no visual footage to accompany him, his mastery of all the classics had come in handy. The group was now quite responsive, and *Mission Impossible*, *The Rock*, *Bill and Ted's Excellent Adventure*, and more, soon became his friend's favorites as well.

Alexander in his quiet way was telling the group of a dangerous task ahead, one with opportunity for confrontation. While the leader was confident, could it really be that certain? Chris for one was not sure, he being cautious by nature, and admittedly, he had come across a spree of bad luck lately. So given his movie talents, and the moment that now seemed to beg for some entertainment, Chris moved to the front after Alex's speech and gave his best and most motivating tirade possible.

Rocky Balboa, the group took to the hero straight away. From the worn Philadelphia slums, the man was a boxer short one big break. He received the chance of a lifetime, to fight the world's heavy weight champion none other than Apollo Creed. The champion gave the challenger very little respect. Rocky's training was moving, socking it out with huge slabs of meat and the self-victorious ascent of the city chamber stairs while jogging. The boys fixed on every word, certain that this underdog could overcome all odds. Chris then described in detail the blistering fight. Rocky had a rough start, but the champion had underestimated not the skill, but the will of the hero. As the rounds advanced, Rocky was bludgeoned but never gave up. In the exiting finish, the last round would decide this match. Here the two warriors slugged it out until both dropped to the canvas knocking each other out simultaneously to the screams and cheers of an adoring crowd.

Sensing the boy's excitement, Chris figured that now they were ready for their own underdog victory. Nicholas would cement that theory.

NICHOLAS KNEW WHERE TO FIND Chris's skateboard. He had returned and from a foul place indeed. Swimming in the river had helped, but some more water fun was in order, thought the boy. He stood now at the top of his cave-enclosed water slides, skateboard in hand, and staring at the whipping water with anticipation. He didn't really know what Chris did with the wheeled board, but from the moment he had seen it visions of speeding along his twisting water slides had seemed like such a good idea to the athletic boy. With nary a care, the boy was off.

The water slides began deep within the caves, twisting and turning, and the boy deftly sped along gaining experience as he raced. Exiting the enclosure of the caves now, the boy was roaring at top speed with a trailing spray of icy water. It was just what this boy loved: daring and speed, and he would jump the small rocks landing each time back upright upon the speeding board.

As Chris completed his story, Michael Shaun was the first to see the speeding boy. "Nicholas!" he yelled, running to the promontory and pointing with excitement. The others followed him, laughing and yelling their appreciation as Nicholas sped down the rocky path, turning and rolling his way down the mountain to the cove. He was nearing the end of his ride when he squatted down upon the board maximizing his speed. At the ride's end the slide abruptly disappeared launching the boy high in the air. Nicholas reached down in mid-air, grabbed the skateboard, and with a flip dove into the waters of the cove below.

It was a sight that did the group and their confidence well, what with Alexander's motivating speech, then Rocky Balboa, and now a speeding, skating pirate. How could they not hope but to succeed? Nicholas surfaced, holding the skateboard overhead, shaking his arm in success. The boys yelled their admiration and the young pirate swam with strong strokes to the shore.

Chapter 22
Once a Fool

> As a dog returns to its vomit,
> So a fool repeats his folly.
> **Proverbs 26:11**

The parrot fooled some, some of the time, and better men most of the time, but not even Balamn could be fooled all of the time. It seems certain that these thoughts survived through history, for a variation of the adage survives to be quoted by Lincoln some nine centuries later. The boy, however, was not one for speeches and so deferred, unknowingly, to the future president of Civil War fame.

It was one fortnight less ten (four more days for those with calendars) until the battle for freedom, and Nicholas considered this proverb. While the Captain was a fool, fooling him again in the same way with his valuable bird was definitely out, a true liability. However, he needed reconnaissance information, and Rainbow, like his bulldogs, was always willing and able. Therefore, before his flight, the pirate boy spoke of caution to his trusted friend, and then giving him leave, the huge parrot flew away.

BALAAM ADMIRED HIS POWERFUL NAVY, anchored and supplied in the royal harbor. Here was the perfect deep-water port, with a narrow northern portal, the bay nearly encircled otherwise by the rocky precipice upon which the castle lay. A stone-carved stairway spiraled from the water up the rocky cliffs, allowed a rear entry to the imposing fortress. Within the port multiple long and wide docks stood, complete with equipment for repair and supplying the maritime needs of the country. Strewn across the port were sailing ships of all sizes, as busy men bustled and strained, fitting the fleet of warships under the captain's watchful eye. This was the pirate's world. He dealt little with the fools running the court now, his intellect so superior in his mind. Had it not been for the brat boy's theft of his rightfully stolen treasure, he would have nothing to do with Fordem's plan. It was risky, their flank left so unprotected. He had his own reasons, however, and he was anxious to right unfair wrongs. His recent defeat and torment which yielded the treasure required return to the rightful owner: him. Then there was the loss of his three-masted man-of-war, the fiery destruction of his crown ship, and his recent digital amputation all ruining his victorious glory, which was his destiny. The man planned to right these painful losses and very soon.

"Ah--blasted bird!" the captain grunted, reaching to his shoulder with his good left hand in disgust. Looking like one of the Captain's favorite spittle wads, a perfectly placed bird dropping now clung to the shoulder of the commander of the royal navy. Raising his heavily bandaged right hand and blocking out the sun, he turned his attention to the sky above. "Dratted worthless species!" he continued. The sun was blazing this morning, and the prior owner of the avian projectile was not visible, having flown at quite an altitude and now perched upon the rocky crags above. The pirate Captain would not let this minor nuisance, the brat boy, or his throbbing finger ruin his morning, however. Balamn continued down the central dock, yelling his instructions between gasps to the longshoremen. The men ran too, some avoiding the captain's spittle, loading ammunitions and supplies under his distrustful eye.

The bird dropping had reminded him of that traitorous parrot, and Balamn wondered, stopping for the moment to reexamine his stained shoulder. He was wheezing and rattling today in the best tradition, and his thoughts brought up sputum much to the man's liking. It would be a good day he felt. "But that bird--I wonder?" he thought again, turning and scanning the cliffs.

Pirates, Scoundrels, and Kings

THE PARROT HAD BEEN SURVEYING the harbor, taking in details of ships, canons, and munitions. His brain functioned like an Intel chip, very superior to the average parrot and most men. He would occasionally repeat, *"Polly want a cracker,"* but he did so for humans who expected such a ridiculous statement from a feathered creature such as himself. He saw that captain once again with his lumbering breathing, staring up to the cliffs.

Nicholas had reminded the bird of the man, and with a sly smile and wink pointed out such a wise and experienced spy the bird was. Letting the outmatched man see him, and he had had to drop his load upon the man to get his intention, could do well in the future. The pirate had proven how easily a trap closed upon him. Well the bird had seen what he came for, and he took this opportunity to swoop down, bare south, and fly back for debriefing.

HIS VISION HAD BEEN BETTER in days of his rum-loving youth, but the bird had made a mistake as far as the captain was concerned. He could not make out much of his shape, but the unmistakable reds, green, yellow, and blue that gave the parrot his name was unmistakable. "That fool," the captain smiled, following the bird's path.

THE HISTORY OF ARTILLERY HAS a very proud tradition in military actions. Envision the modern equivalent, powder and projectile within one shell, loaded by the breach or rear of the canon. It was centuries until similar designs appeared, but Fordem's armory was a dangerous and huge arsenal, and combined with his large cavalry, victory seemed certain. The artillery was mobile, each of the two-hundred cannons supported upon wooden wheels, making their deployment versatile and sudden. They were new, shiny, and treacherous, and Fordem paraded up and down the columns inspecting his possessions. The artillery sat on the plains surrounding the castle for last minute preparations and deployment early the following morning. Fordem looked over the shining forest of barrels with satisfaction.

Across the way, the Ogre sat upon his horse laughing to no one but himself. The man's visage troubled Fordem and interrupted the military man's fine review. Two battalions of cavalry and artilleries left little for the castle's defense. And leading this entire military to the Devil's Pass himself left the 'O' alone to defend the citadel.

"Look at the fool!" Fordem said to himself. He had serious questions of the man's ability as he sat upon the jaundiced-eyed horse, examining his subordinate across the field. The Ogre was laughing as usual and about what and to whom was not particularly obvious to Fordem.

"And look upon his mount, the horse out thinks the man I am certain."

Pushing his doubts deep to his bloated ego, Fordem stomped a spurred boot into his similar-minded evil stallion, and returned to other duties within the walled fortress. Deep in thought, the man did not look up as a brightly colored bird flew south above his head. "Drat!" Fordem cursed, turning to his right shoulder, realizing that a well-aimed bird dropping from above had struck and stained his fearsome purple cape.

It was a fortnight less eleven as Alexander led his men in the direction of the castle. Nicholas had made known the findings of the parrot's reconnaissance to his brother, the information helping to assess timing and the strength of their enemy. Moving through the night with Manzell and Michael Shaun, their horses were loaded down with the harvested product of Nicholas's gum tree. Skateboard shoes upon the trio, dressed in black, with ash-darkened faces, they would move in stealth, an important assignment for the night.

In silence they exited the rocky caves, rode along the trail, bypassing the city Alucemet to its east. Looking now across the plains, the castle stood high upon its rocky perch. Alexander stopped the group for the moment, in silent thought and a touch of melancholy resulting from the site of his beloved home. "We will not risk horseback from here on." Turning now to the group he led them on foot silently just within the edge of the forest.

The river was deep and cold as the boys entered the body of water that night. They had tied their horses at that point, hoping to return sometime for them. The satchels were buoyant, and Alexander, Manzell, and Michael Shaun floated with them ahead, kicking their way down the river. As the river moved northward, its speed picked up markedly and they made good time. Their destination was well short of the river's diversion into the castle moat, and they quickly arrived at a predetermined point. Alexander signaled in silence to his dedicated partners, and after kicking to the side of the river, all were up and out now hiding within the dense willows of the riverbank.

The site across the plain was staggering. Over two hundred long-barreled canons on mobile wheels sat in the shadows, signaling destruction. The amassed artillery would easily outnumber the boy's canons four or five to one. Something must shift the odds. Alexander thought he had the answer, if only their mission went safely as planned.

It was a cloudy, overcast, and brutally cold night. The wet boys kept to the shadows, crawling most of the way across the clearing to their target. In a few hours, these munitions would be on their way to the Devil's Pass, the enemy expecting to ambush the ambushers.

Arriving at the first canon, Alexander opened his pack. He removed a handful of the sticky material and pushed it deep within the bronze barrel up to his elbow. After inspecting the project he instructed his men, "Spread out now. Keep to the shadows. A guard is certain. Do each barrel thusly. We will meet at the river's edge. No one leaves until the others arrive."

With that, they were off, silently dragging their precious gum-laden sacks, stopping at each cannon for sabotage. There were guards assigned as Alexander had cautioned, and the boys made use of their size and the deep darkness to avoid them. As the night passed, Alexander and the others attended each canon. It was an untested theory, but Alexander prayed that the sticky material would turn the tide in favor of the over matched boy's direction.

Alexander had his arm within the barrel, pushing and shoving the very sticky gum as far as possible down the muzzle of the canon. He had lost track of caution, and when he saw the guard, it was almost too late. Alexander's eyes were big as he pulled his stuck hand out of the canon barrel and crashed in a heap alongside the armor. The guard was just a boy as well. His crudely clipped ears and affect a sign of his devotion to the Boar. Sitting right above the hiding boy on the canon barrel, the guard stared across the plains. Had he heard something? Alexander wondered, hiding in the shadow of the canon. Rolling and placing in his mouth a smoke, the guard lit the tobacco and inhaled deeply. Sniffing the air suddenly, he said quietly, "Mint? Where in the devil is that minty smell coming from?"

The smell must have been overpowering for the guard crushed out his smoke, and turned to the canon, sniffing all the time. He was down on his knees now, opposite Alexander, as he sniffed vigorously smelling the muzzle of the canon. "Sniff—sniff-- the smell seemed to be in the barrel. "A lubricant, I never noticed that before," the guard said, now down on his hands and knees. He was about to reach down the barrel when something touched his right hand interrupting him.

Alexander had seen the problem from the moment the smoke went out. "Mint, why does chew smell as such?" he quietly thought in a panic. The boy looked frantically around him for a silent weapon, anything to save his quest. Then the answer appeared, lit in the moonlight just for him. Before the boy was a crop of the best looking mint sprigs he had ever seen. Picking them quickly, he slowly advanced his hand and dropped them over the hand of the curious guard.

"The guard was startled, and looking up to the sky as if the minty present had descended from heaven, he scowled in question. Lifting the sprigs to his nose, he was satisfied, now certain that the smell was natural. Taking the mint and rising to his feet, the guard was off enjoying his minty package throughout the remainder of the boring night.

Alexander was as done as he wished to be. Brushing the sweat from his brow, he picked up his satchel, ran in the shadows, and signaled to the others to follow him to the riverside. The three reached the water through the willowy bank. They dropped huffing, puffing to their backs as they stared up at the night sky. "That was close!" Alexander said between deep breaths. "Nicholas must get rid of his gum's smell if we are to use it to set traps." He laughed deeply at his narrow escape, and thanked God for the minty growth, which had appeared out of nowhere.

"I think we got nearly every barrel, Alexander," Manzell said, turning to the boy leader. "It was close," he said between deep breaths recanting his own close call as the boys lay upon the riverbank catching their breaths. "He was there before I knew it, he was. But luck got me hidden. He was one of those odd boys, with them strange ears, and he sat right down on the canon he did."

The trio's breathing and hearts slowed down. It was peaceful lying on the muddy riverbank and looking up at the overcast nighttime sky. "Lucky his choice was not to sleep, Manzell!" Alexander replied. "My nemesis had quite a nose for mint." It was late and the dark would not last. "We best return," Alexander said, and standing up he dove silently into the river.

It was just Nicholas and Chris that night, crouching in the dark, hidden by brush and looking out towards the harbor. A fleet of thirteen sailing ships they counted, all riding low in the water from the day's loading of munitions. Chris had no idea what the pirate boy had in mind, but he carried the gunpowder while Nicholas carried the gum. "We'll start with the three-masted ship, the crown ship. That one," he said, pointing to the largest and the most distant ship. "Keep the powder dry. We'll hit them all," the pirate boy said to Chris. Nicholas had his usual big smile, anticipating and looking forward to the danger.

Christopher proved his swimming ability to Nicholas within the strait, and the boy remembered this when tonight's job had arisen. Nicholas had discussed the plan with Alexander but no one else. Chris had just an inkling of the danger they were heading toward. It was too dangerous for the duo to use a skiff, so directly into the harbor water they moved. Chris kept his pouch of powder dry, holding it high above his head. Nicholas then pushed a satchel of buoyant gum to the boy and Chris placed the gunpowder on the bundle above the waterline. The two silently kicked, moving to the ship with their special products.

The plan was to place a burlap sack of gun powder just above the waterline, attached to the ship's hull with the adhesive properties of homegrown chew that Nicholas had come to depend upon. To the largest ship, they moved first, Chris removing a pouch of powder, and Nicholas chewing up some gum. It worked perfectly. The sack was the same color as the hull and secured with a large wad of chewed gum.

"We are setting charges, dude!" Chris said as he realized the intended result. The two finished and turned quickly, swimming and pushing along their valuable goods to the next ship.

They had gotten to the ships in the entire harbor without incident. Both boys were tired for it was quite a swim, and their load was heavy. With the last of the ships, Nicholas said, "That does it, mate." Chris had the duty of smoothing out the gum and putting the final touches on their night's work. "Sink what's left, and let's get out of here, but give me a pinch." Nicholas dug deep within the gum bag, grabbing a huge chunk, and dropping it into his mouth with a satisfied smile. He left Chris to finish the last ship, diving deeply and swimming away.

Chris turned to his work but was startled a few seconds later by Nicholas's yell. "Christopher of Temecula!" With that, skimming just by the boy's left ear, a dagger thrown by Nicholas spun, sticking into the wooden hull and vibrating back and forth. Chris turned in frightened surprise to the boy. Nicholas was several yards off.

Smiling mischievously he said, "For you my friend. Make good use of it, you promise?"

Not waiting for an answer the gum chewing pirate-boy turned, dove deep within the water and was off. Chris was still shaking as Nicholas surfaced, swimming away with strong strokes. The boy reached to the dagger. Working it back and forth, he was able to dislodge the deeply drilled blade from the wooden hull. Christopher looked over the dagger. Its jewel bedecked handle and long double-edged blade shone in the moonlight. "Sic blade!" Chris finally concluded in admiration. He sheathed the dagger within his tunic and turned to finish his job.

It was getting cold, and Chris was beginning to really feel the work of that night. The powder encased with burlap and attached to the hull would be used later he decided. He hoped to not be close to such a ship, for a real fire would occur if these charges ever caught. He turned now, finished, and filled the nearly empty sack with water and sunk the remainder of his package.

It is all in the eye of the beholder. The bird reminded the pirate of the boy, and the parrot told the boy of the pirate. And who had the advantage, Chris would never know, but he had come to the practice of never doubting either of the royal boys. As he turned from his job and pushed off, swimming for shore, Nicholas was a good deal ahead of him.

The captain looked quite rickety in the little dinghy, as he stood scanning the dark water ahead. He was sure that the boy would return, and if not this night then tomorrow, for the date was now a fortnight less two and little time remained. Therefore, when he rowed out to the center of the harbor and saw the boy swimming, he knew that luck was upon him and the boy was his.

Balamn rowed up alongside the boy and struck him on the back with his paddle. Nicholas was startled, and he looked up at the captain who began thrashing him with abandon. The captain's balance was suspect as he stood in the tiny dingy with his paddle splashing and crashing down on the boy. Nicholas swam away. The captain seated himself, and with both paddles rowed again to the boy. While paddling the captain could catch the boy, but once he stopped to thrash him, Nicholas could easily swim away.

"Dratted boy, there you are," he said, standing and striking the boy a good blow with the paddle. Nicholas, however, was quick, and while hit, his deep dive dissipated it. Diving now, he went under the skiff and was up on the other side. Before the pirate was aware, Nicholas pulled from his mouth a huge wad of chewed gum, placed it upon the wooden slat seat of the dingy, and dove again.

The captain turned and slashed with his paddle, his lumbering breathing now loud and distressful. "I'll have you, brat boy!" The captain sat down, directly on the gum, and rowed with fury after his prey. He was quicker this time and decided against the paddle. With his one good hand, he moved next to the boy and grabbed him by the scruff of the neck as he tried to swim away from his foe. "Got you!" The pirate screamed with satisfaction as he pulled the boy kicking and fighting over the side. Nicholas resisted, now with his back to the pirate, his shirt in the man's hand. The boy was kicking at the side of the dingy, hoping to free himself. Behind him, he reached out swinging his arms trying to strike his enemy anywhere, but it was futile. The man was eventually able to drag the water-soaked boy inside the craft, but it was a fight the man would remember for some time.

Once in the skiff, the boy was at the pirate's mercy. He pulled the boy to his lap, locked one arm around his head, and used his blade to threaten his neck. It was at this time that the boy saw the dressing on the man's hand, wrapping his mother's handiwork up in a blood-soaked bundle of gauze. Nicholas was quick, and with his jaw strong from gum exercise, he bit the man's hand with all that he could muster.

"Ohhhh!" the man screamed. Releasing the boy for just a moment, he quickly regained control now choking him and scraping his blade along the boy's neck.

Like the blowhole of a whale, with a single blow the blade blasted its way through the wooden floor at the pirate's feet. Water gushed in, soaking the two struggling enemies. Before the captain knew what had happened, his little dinghy was half full of water and dangerously listing to its starboard.

"Blasted!" the captain said, releasing the boy slightly. He dropped his blade and turned his attention to the rapidly sinking boat. The rising water worried the seaman for his ability to survive on shore was suspect and his pulmonary disease deadly under the water. As his defeat became clear, he released the boy, screaming in defeated agony and stamping his feet with disgust upon the wooden floor. The boy had bitten through his dressing and his stub was bleeding again

As the craft sunk, Nicholas jumped over the side and swam several feet away. Turning to the defeated pirate, he watched the man's fate. As the skiff rapidly sunk, the pirate tried to loosen himself from his seat. The gum was adherent to the man though, and as he realized that his escape was not likely he turned to the boy, shook his hand-less-one-digit with disgust and yelled in indignation.

CHRIS HAD SEEN THE STRUGGLE across the harbor, and he swam with determination to the site. "What to do?" he thought. Remembering the slammers, an idea came to the boy. "Here goes," he said as he dove deep, holding his breath. He kicked under the water surfacing right alongside of the craft. The man was screaming bloody murder as Nicholas was biting down on his bloody hand. The two wrestled and jostled, but the man had a sword. Chris dove down, coming under the dingy. Pulling his dagger out, he drove the sharp blade through the bottom of the wooden hull up to its hilt, twisting the blade to widen the hole. He pulled the dagger out leaving a wide hole rapidly filling with rushing water. He then turned and kicked to the surface.

"Christopher of Temecula!" Nicholas yelled. Chris had just surfaced, heard his name, and turned to see Nicholas now free of his predicament. He replaced his dagger and stroked over to his friend.

"The dude's going down," Christopher said to the boy as he swam up to him. They both now steadied themselves, kicking and floating as they watched the small craft sink. The captain was yelling but unable to free himself from the gum trap. "Dude, why doesn't he get out of that boat?" Chris wondered, turning to his friend. Nicholas just looked back the boy and smiled. Spontaneously they both broke out in hysteria as Chris guessed the answer.

"This dagger came in handy," Christopher said. He pulled out his dagger and waved it in the air above his head.

"For what other purpose would I present it to you, Christopher of Temecula," Nicholas said with assurance. With this, the pirate-boy dove and kicked off, swimming for the shore.

Chapter 23
Ambush in Devil's Pass

> THE HORSE IS MADE READY FOR THE DAY OF BATTLE,
> BUT VICTORY RESTS WITH THE LORD.
> **PROVERBS 21:31**

With the sun still well below the eastern horizon, the army began its day. Richard of Fordem led the assembled troops, complete with destructive mobile artillery and two battalions of archers, all loaded and marching east across the plain of Rochelle. It was one fortnight since the interception of the brat's message, the date for Fordem's total victory, the date to settle his score. The man had some unfinished business and was about to spring the greatest trap, in a trap-filled saga.

Fordem sat with pride upon the jaundice-eyed stallion, leading an unprecedented legion. The foolish Boar! He had little to do with such important maneuvers, but then he did not know the truth. The fall of the boy and the Queen was to the Boar's liking, but he left intricate details to his trusted agent. Fordem would not fail to sack the older brat, sink the pirate-boy, and do in the Queen all in one day.

The Queen hid her anxiety well that morning, Fordem decided. He actually felt some old affection for the woman, recalling the days when he was her First Aid. Fordem had changed, however, and affection had no place in life anymore. He watched the woman out of the corner of his eye as she rode to what would be her ultimate death. Dressed in her royal riding garments- rose-colored textile, tipped with gold piping, and sitting sidesaddle upon her white stallion-she looked proud and would put a fine image on the demise of the Royal family. The end of this saga would be his masterpiece, something the entire world would truly appreciate.

The monarch thought that her jewels would be exchanged for the life of her precious oldest son. "Look at her misplaced trust," Fordem thought to himself with disdain. He watched the Queen galloping with pride, crown jewels within an oaken chest, and her lady in waiting riding at her side. Running alongside the Queen was her trusted Shar Pei, leashed, and leading with such force that it seemed as if Gidget's collar would choke the excited dog. As with most things associated with the Royal family, the dog disgusted Fordem. He would feed her to his carnivorous horse after all this was over and the kingdom under proper control.

The wrinkly dog was very sure of her position, some would say affected, that is for a dog. She was dressed this morning in rose-colored cover, her Queen's color, embossed with the crown's insignia in gold. Running along proudly with her Queen's mount, the dog smelled the morning air and every inch along the path.

Fordem made some pleasantries to her majesty as he passed her for his place at the lead of the column. It was the least he could do for this doomed monarch, for this was to be her last official function. Properly dealing with the royal family came to the man with great satisfaction. He alone could lead such a force of formidable power and destiny, he thought, smiling to himself.

The disappearance the prior night of Balamn, his navy leader, troubled the commander. Where was the man and what had happened to him? The answer to these questions was not clear. He had little respect for the man, but his mighty navy was essential in Fordem's plan. Led by the crown ship, the navy was to flank his cavalry, sailing eastward along the northern sea, rounding Fool's Point, and waiting for Fordem's signal on the eastern edge of Devil's Pass. The navy would then close the rearward escape out of the pass, cutting off the foolish Prince's retreat to the sea with mighty canon fire and surprise. He had inquired all day of the captain's location, all to no avail. No one had seen him, the fool. What a time to be drunk, lying with lues-infested wenches throughout the night. However, the plan had to proceed with or without him, and Pruneshench was a capable enough sort. They would be sailing about now, Fordem imagined, and he pushed a nagging feeling of anxiety behind him. Turning to one of his commanders, the man cleared his thoughts by leveling some instructions in a rude manner about the transport of this fearsome military force.

THE NIGHT BEFORE THE BATTLE, one fortnight less 13 in the calendar of the day, Captain Balaam had nearly drowned. His swimming was suspect and his lungs much more so. The struggling boy was in his clutches when his revenge disappeared in a moment. The blade burst from nowhere, stabbing through the bottom of his dingy and the water swamped the vessel quickly. As he released the struggling brat-boy, defeat faced the man again. On the seat of the skiff was an incredibly sticky, dratted, white substance that the pirate was not familiar with. The man wrestled with his bum securely fixed to the rapidly sinking craft; as the water rose he realized his situation was critical. Being pulled down, the man spat and struggled, his wrestling and kicking just enlarging the hole in the skiff's floor. If it had not been for the dreadful condition of his britches, the pirate would have been doomed. He struggled and finally succeeded in tearing out the entire rear end of his squalid pirate pants. As they tore free, he was already fully under the water and in near respiratory failure. A hysterical fear was upon him as the sputtering captain struggled to the surface and dog paddled to the shore of the harbor. Reaching dry ground, the gasping man clawed up onto the shore and deposited himself behind some vegetation. It took a full day for the debilitated man to even partially recover. Here he lay behind bushes not realizing where, when, or who he was till late the next night.

IT WAS ONE FORTNIGHT AFTER the delivery of the boys' message. Nicholas and Manzell stood in the shadows surrounding the darkened harbor, the day of the battle. Manzell would normally be at Alexander's side, but Nicholas needed his deadly crossbow today. With their service needed elsewhere, neither bulldog was present. Rainbow was high above, watching Fordem's force march away and returning to the side of his master with reconnaissance information worth its weight in gold doubloons to the pirate-boy. As they predicted, Fordem led a huge force away from the castle that morning.

The boys were dressed in dark clothing. They had blackened their faces with fresh ash. They now lay hidden waiting for the foe to disappear eastward across the plains leaving this small force to its own exploits.

Nicholas took his spyglass, looked across the darkened harbor, and quickly noted the expected activity. The docks were alive with people moving to and fro as the fleet flying the Boar's Hoof standard prepared to sail in the early hours of dawn. Nicholas smiled with anticipation as officers and sailors lent attention to the last minute loading of the thirteen-shipped armada. The remainder of his group, led by Little Andy, were away, scheduled to rendezvous on the southern side of the Alucemet Castle after Nicholas finished his duty.

"Make way now, Manzell," Nicholas said as they ran in silence along the harbor shore ducking within the shadows. Manzell had his trusted crossbow, Nicholas shouldering a longbow. Both boys carried an unlit torch. The two boys made their way in silence along the water's edge keeping the growing naval force in their sites and laying low so as not to tip their presence before the proper time.

Pruneshench was in joyous ecstasy, his peg leg unusually respondent this important morning. He was in command now, for the spittle spitting Captain Balaam had disappeared curiously during the prior night. He cared not for the man; Balaam could rot, the man felt. Where he went, what happened to him, or any other details; the man's demise was Pruneshench's triumph. Balaam's death was in fact a rumor started by the man, suggesting that it was none other than the mighty Pruneshench who had bested the laboring captain. Better to lie than let an excellent piece of propaganda go to waste, he thought.

Pruneshench received a briefing on the simple plan just hours ago. He was now quite sure of his position. With Balaam's disappearance, Fordem needed the man as much as Pruneshench needed Fordem. His victory as the commander of the royal navy would elevate him to his due place in history. Commanding the royal crown ship, with its three masts and battery of canons, he was to lead the other twelve ships through the narrow portal of the harbor, then along the northern coast making for the eastern edge of the Devil's Pass. Why that fool of a king, Lithotomy, would exchange the Queen for the boy was not apparent to the sailor, but he was certain that his superior skills would crush the foreign King's tiny navy. The man calculated in his mind every inch of the journey. As he calculated his mind drifted off with thoughts of conquest where he maneuvered his navy ships, surrounded the outgunned ignorant king, and closed the Devil's Pass to any retreat. Pruneshench was in command as his subordinate rowed to the crown ship, the man sitting in a small skiff as he gloated victoriously to himself.

Sam was a humble boy, born of poverty, but descended of good honest stock. He was proud to serve his countries' royal family in any manner possible. He had become an accomplished sailor since his induction into Nicholas's navy. He was now entrusted with the command of the boy's fleet. Sam was excited but had a realistic sense of danger as well.

Sam sailed off in the night as instructed, exiting pirate's cove and making for open sea. Nicholas had captured and refitted Balaam's three-masted ship. When run aground, the vessel had flown the flag of the Boar's Hoof. It was a beautiful sailing craft and a formidable man-of-war. Sam was at its helm, followed by a small but quick fleet of three ships. The small armada sailed along the western edge of the country. Today's fleet had just hoisted the Laughing Lion, and the crown ship, christened *Her Royal Majesties Ship, Patrice*, was tacking full of sail to and through the strait of Abaddon. With his life, Sam would accomplish Nicholas' assignment, so with determination he set a course to blockade the portal of the royal harbor. If successful, the fleet would remove the Boar's navy from the conflict, building momentum eastward in the Devil's Pass.

When the *HRMS Patrice* made the bend, it bore down upon the portal of the royal harbor. As the ship rounded the point, Pruneshench saw the outgunned fleet immediately. Using his ship's horn, he began his fleet's sail from the harbor to the open sea. The man was full of glee as he looked upon his pitiful opponent, for the pirate-boy had made a big mistake, hoping to block the fleet's exit from the harbor. Pruneshench's quick mind and powerful navy would never let that occur.

THE THREE BULLDOGS SAT POLITELY on their rear haunches, waiting eagerly on the gingerbread-trimmed cottage's front stoop. Spike somehow struck the doorknocker as the trio now sat, trying their best not to drool, expecting the occupant to answer.

Robyn of Hobinsiefken felt rejuvenated with some purpose in his life since the message from the two princes. Over the fortnight he met with the city and in secrecy organized the populace, readying them for anything that could be in the offing. Originally reluctant, the man used all of his political shrewdness, and soon the citizens were determined to play a role in the defense of the kingdom.

Robyn heard the knock on his heavy oaken door that morning. He was beginning to have more visitors now that the city was rallying once more. However, upon opening the door the sight certainly surprised him.

Sitting on the stoop were three of the largest dogs the man had ever seen. They were silent as they sat staring at the man, with an occasional tongue to catch the inevitable salivary secretions. It was curious, the mayor thought, as he racked his brain wondering what was up with this canine reception. It dawned on him then and lit a smile upon his countenance. "The younger boy, he loves four-footed friends!" the man concluded.

Spike lifted a paw in the air and stood at attention on his other three legs.

"Oh, nice to meet you as well," the mayor responded, reluctantly shaking the dog's extended limb.

Spike extended his paw again. Smasher stood and nudged the man with his nose. Nails sat with tail wagging and added a single muffled bark to the project.

The mayor now examined the leg of the bulldog. Tied on his paw was a note, which Robyn quickly removed, unwrapped, and read aloud. "The time is now!" the note simply read. At its bottom were the signatures of Alexander and Nicholas. The seal was again that of the younger boy, guaranteeing its authenticity.

Nails reached up with his sticky mouth, grabbed the note from the startled man, and dropped it to the ground. The dog struck the document with his heavy paw, dragging his nails diagonally across the parchment. Immediately, the message began burning until only ashes alone remained. The three bulldogs turned in unison and suddenly they were gone, leaving the pajama-clothed mayor alone on his front step. A smile came over the man as he turned back to his cottage and shut the heavy door. He did not close the bolt for the first time in many months.

THE ARMY TRAVELED THROUGH THE night, arriving at their destination with the sun now just visible below the eastern horizon. The Devil's Pass loomed across the way, and Fordem felt their timing was critical. The pass was the sole mass exit to the eastern coast. A natural ravine cut by nature in the dense rocky mountains, it was a narrow and treacherous site to lead an army, prone historically to ambush. To his right the southern edge of the pass was the edge of a mountainous chain with scattered trees emptying onto the dense southern forest. To his left the mountainous edge of the pass led to the dense northern mountain chain and the northern woodland. A single man could ride through those trees to the coast. To confirm his navy's presence, Fordem would send a courier soon.

The pass was at the present time visibly empty as Fordem had hoped. They were early and this assured him of success. Perhaps if Fordem had word of the events within the royal harbor he would not have been so confident. Communications were not as in today's world, however, CNN and fax machines being a foreign concept

The plains of Rochelle through which the troops had traveled led naturally to this point, ending in rolling hills covered with thick crops of grass. Fordem halted his troops, and using his eyeglass examined the pass and surrounding area. Turning to his subordinates, he commanded the deployment of his mobile artillery to the rolling hills just adjacent to the pass, keeping their muzzles well within range of the intended site of battle.

"Fools!" he said as he focused on an obvious collection of boulders and rubble, recently stacked high above the pass on its southern edge. "So simple and obvious! The child believes he can crash boulders down, closing us within the pass. How futile their miserable efforts!"

There was no sign of his enemy this early morning. The southern forest, however, could hide the small band of men that he expected to oppose him. Fordem sensed their presence; his adversaries were here, just well hidden for the moment. The man was joyous; here was his chance to undo all of the wrongs inflicted on his noble cause by these two ignorant boys. Their birthright claimed the throne, a fact that he detested.

It was a little known fact that the King had bypassed Richard of Fordem as the Royal Guard Grand Am, appointing in his stead the late Louis Bienville. Fordem took this to heart, keeping it within his vengeful mind forever. This single decision squandered his loyalty to the king. Fordem smiled his dreaded arrogant smile as he reviewed the event whereby the man was slain. Bienville was blissfully trampled to death just one year before. "Who still survives?" he whispered to himself gleefully.

Louis Bienville was easy prey, Fordem having led the man to this very pass. In a fair fight, the outcome may have been different, but Fordem always sliced the odds in his favor. Trapping the man unknowingly, he was easy prey, especially with the use of his vile daughter. Using Autumn as bait, he led the valiant man to the pass. The rumor of his stomping by boar hooves was just that: a rumor.

The man's death was Fordem's doing, and he was forever proud of it. He felt very little sympathy for his daughter as she ran to the side of her dying father. It was unfortunate the event remained secret, and so with quick work the man ended her short pitiful life as well.

The recurrent nightmare was a small price Fordem was to pay for this refreshing demise. Here her apparition would sit within his chamber at his bedside night after night, crying and calling out for her father. Shuddering, he distracted himself, turning now to the highly anticipated slaughter of those two spoiled-brat princes.

In preparation, the soldiers rubbed down the artillery's brass barrels with ashes, for the rising sun could reflect their position. Fordem had considered everything, and with pride, he reviewed the awesome collection of canon power. The artillery was aligned and concealed, ready to close the western opening to the Devil's Pass. As far as the rest of his vaunted military, to the southern edge of the pass his archers were deployed, to the north his cavalry and mobile artillery. It was still dark in the early dawn and soon his ambush would be ready.

Fordem finished his review of the troops and rode his black stallion to his commander. "Send a scout on horseback through the forest to the sea." the man said, pointing to the path through the northern forest. "Captain Pruneshench will soon approach and seal the eastern edge of the pass. Have that scout return quickly after confirming the Captain's position. Without fail I must be signaled when his forces are in place!" With that Fordem spurred his horse away, turning his attention to the southern flank.

The Northern forest began at the northern edge of Devil's Pass. Here dense woods ran for some distance, ending at a rocky coastline and the crashing waves of the sea. A messenger that picked his way through these trees would soon observe any fleet closing down on the eastern opening of Devil's Pass. The commander instructed a mounted soldier on Fordem's assignment, and having impressed on the man the importance he was off, making for the forest.

Fordem arrived at the southern flank, his Boar's Hoof forces already victorious in his mind. The collection of boulders and debris was a sure sign of the enemy's plan. Alexander and Nicholas led a treasonous force, which must be dealt with decisively. The rebellious group was not visible to the man, but the obvious ploy indicated that they were hidden in the southern forest. The enemy's apparent plan was to allow Fordem's forces to enter the Devil's Pass. The rubble would then be rolled down behind them, closing off any retreat. Evidently, Alexander's forces wished the battle to occur within the pass. The rebellious youths apparently believed that at this site the odds were in their favor. This seditious group would then make their last stand, mistakenly confident of their victory.

Fordem felt that Alexander was not aware of the depth of his villainy. He would flood the pass with only a fraction of his contingent. "Let the boy close off their retreat and face his diversionary force," he thought. The brats were not aware of his mighty canons, archers, and cavalry left in waiting. Once the brat boy showed himself, Fordem planned to sacrifice the entire expeditionary force. With murderous volleys from his archers and deafening canon blasts, he would turn the pass into a burning hell. The eastern escape would soon be cut off by Pruneshench's fleet. With burning fury unleashed upon them, his men would not escape, but victory would be his as the entire brat-boy contingent would meet their demise as well. Fordem was certain of the outcome. The day was the beginning of a well-deserved and glorious victory.

THE WIND WAS WHIPPING OFF the icy sea. The sun would bring welcome warmth after dawn, but that would be some time from now. High above the western side of Devil's Pass Alexander knelt with his eyeglass looking down upon the entry. Surrounding the leader were a number of cold boys who warmed themselves as best as they could by marching and rubbing their hands. Piled ahead of them was a collection of boulders, logs, and stones, perched on the edge of the sheer rocky slope of the pass. Waiting to roll down into the pass's western opening, the pile stood against stout wooden posts wedged into the ground.

Pirates, Scoundrels, and Kings

THE LAUGHING LION'S SMALL ARMADA sailed to the portal of the castle's harbor. Sam let loose a volley of canon shots which struck the water exploding and tossing sea water everywhere. He continued to the harbor entry, but the sight of the huge navy had him very worried; could he truly cut off their access to the open sea? Flag signals flew between ships. Sam instructed the small fleet to circle and enclose the entry. As they did so a huge salvo of canon fire from the lead three enemy ships let fly too close for comfort. It was going to be quite a fight.

PRUNESHENCH WAS IN THE MIDDLE of glory. The man pegged his way along the deck to his ship's bow, signaling for more canon fire. He would quickly blow their tiny fleet from the water and send that infant crew to the bottom. He had roused his mighty navy, and with a strong trailing wind made the portal of the harbor before the pirate boy's fleet. He turned broadside, both banks of canons now open and loaded. The captain gave an enthusiastic order, and all the canons let loose with thunder, lifting the edge of his ship from the recoil. His fire drenched the boy's fleet. Soon enough they would shred their sheets, flatten their decks, and pierce their hulls, sinking all that he could catch to the ocean floor cemetery. Flag signals ran between ships, and the royal navy's second ship let loose with an entire bank of explosives. It was still dark, and the roar and fire from the broadside canon battery filled the air with stifling smoke and thunderous noise.

    The bow of the Boar's Hoof crown ship exploded with pieces of wood and brass careening high into the air. The concussive impact resounded through the ship, and its sailors were tossed around the sinking ship like twigs. Pruneshench had just come forward when the impact hit, tossing him to the deck and drenching the man with seawater and debris. The entire forward one-third of the ship was on fire, the forward mast was listing, its sail swallowed up by the icy sea. The vessel sank quickly as water rushed into the shredded hull of the huge man-of-war.

NICHOLAS AND MANZELL MADE THEIR way around the harbor, and now stood behind a rocky outcropping, hidden by the shadows of early dawn. With his eyeglass, the pirate-boy spied across the harbor, through its portal, and out to sea. He could just make out the ship *HRMS Patrice* right on schedule and speeding full of sail from the open ocean towards the harbor entry. The royal navy moved as expected, quickly returning volley and sailing towards the boy's fleet. Once right within the portal the time was perfect.

An agile flint strike struck the oily torch and blazed it aflame quickly. Manzell loaded an oil-tipped arrow on his trusty crossbow. Nicholas took the torch and lit its tip. With no hesitation Manzell let fly with his fiery arrow, winging in silence across the harbor and striking the royal crown ship's hull-bound packet of powder. The gunpowder exploded and tore through the bow of the doomed ship.

"Dead center, Manzell!" Nicholas yelled with glee. He shoved the unlit end of the torch in the ground before him. Reaching behind, he removed an arrow from his quiver. "Hit every last ship, Manzell," the boy yelled to his partner over the explosions. Nicholas loaded his arrow, turned to the torch, and lit its tip. Taking sight on the second ship he let the flaming arrow fly.

FORDEM'S OUTLOOK RODE QUICKLY; HE knew that the man demanded perfection in all of his soldiers. Dressed in the loosely-fitting tunic of the troops, the scout rode with haste through the northern forest, carrying a staff with the Boar's Hoof waving in the wind. As he arrived on the coast, the soldier realized that something was very wrong. Before him lay the mighty ocean, but where was the royal navy? Sweat began to form on the man's brow as he scanned northward and then to the horizon. "Perhaps the navy was late," he thought. "How late would they b,e however, and when would they arrive?" His heart rate was racing as he concluded, "Oh dear, Fordem will not be pleased." The soldier jumped off his mount and led the beast up and down the beach. It was a futile search and he was afraid of wasting much more time. The sun was just rising on the horizon and the darkness fading; the battle would soon be upon them. In disgust he turned and swinging himself up on his horse quickly returned to the forest, making a quick disturbed path back to his vengeful leader.

He was galloping like the wind down a narrow lane lined by the dense forest of the area. The assailants came from nowhere, crashing down on the messenger and dragging him from his horse. They held a burlap sack between them as they jumped down on the man, pulling the sack over his head and upper chest locking his arms. With the sack in place he was wrestling against two strong boys in darkness.

"Christopher of Temecula, lets drag him--bind him over there," Scott yelled as the two lugged the sack-enclosed man to the nearest tree. Now with his back against its trunk, they wrapped the stunned man with a stout rope, around and around his chest securing him to the tree.

"That will hold the dude!" Christopher whispered to Scott as they finished, tying the free end around the man's wrists tightly.

"That's it, friend," the boy jeered as they stood back and admired their work.

Christopher was dressed as the scout with a loosely fitting tunic, complete with a crudely drawn hoof upon his chest. He ran down the man's horse, returning now with a broad smile to the site of their captured prey. Chris straightened the saddle, and then the boy bounded up on the mount.

"Be off now, Christopher," Scott said. The boy picked up the man's flag and handed it to his accomplice.

Christopher held up his hand. "Wait a minute, dude!" he said. From his sleeve he removed a leaf-wrapped package and broke off pieces of the white material. Chris leaned over from the horse and pressed the burlap-covered face of the man, locating his mouth with his fingers. Lodging a huge wad of gum within the opening, he made sure that the man could not call out. Chris broke off two other wads, and affixed them to each side of the man's head. "Ears, what do ya think Scott? Kind of cute I think!"

With that, Scott started laughing uncontrollably. "A better Boar I have nary seen. A serious day, Christopher of Temecula, but we can't miss our fun!" The two took a moment to consider the man, each admiring their catch and smiling. "Now be off my modern day friend," Scott said to the mounted boy as he was off on foot, moving south to his next assignment.

The man was beginning to struggle against his bindings, and muffled grumbling came deep to the gum and burlap. His heart was not in this resistance, however. He was the first of Fordem's forces defeated that day, but his halfhearted resistance demonstrated that the enemy's use of fear and hatred produced an army that would quickly scatter and give up in many confrontations.

"Again on a horse, in disguise, and heading for Fordem" Chris said to himself aloud as he bounced over the trail with the flag held high in his right hand. He recalled his last similar experience, and the memory of the rude reception by the castle guard did not warm his heart. Fordem had let him go, but not before tossing the boy out of his chamber on his chin. As with all of his new friends, however, Chris had grown to trust the two boy leaders whose plan had put Scott and himself in just the right position to intercept Fordem's scout.

He was almost out of the forest now, and as he rode, he could see the grassy plains ahead. Coming to the edge of the forest the sight shocked the boy, and he bridled his horse, sliding to a stop. Before him, concealed from the pass, sat a large multitude of cavalry, the horse-mounted soldiers surrounding hundreds of huge canons. Each weapon sat on wooden wheels, manned by several artillerymen, and ready to rapidly respond.

"Dude--" Chris said to himself, staring with wide eyes at the horrible site. The numbers frightened the boy; Alexander must certainly not be expecting such a potent force! As he sat on the horse, he debated. Alexander was south, high above the Devil's Pass. He could ride quickly to tell the boy leader of his findings. However, Alexander was a journey away, and he had expressly sent Chris to intercept the scout. Fordem's messenger was to inform the man of their navy's position. Alexander did not want Fordem to realize the absence of naval support, hence the messenger's interception. What if Chris turned and rode south to warn the boy. Fordem would eventually realize that his navy was not present. The man would know of his situation; at least he would suspect! Chris concluded that the man would use the information to his advantage. He quickly weighed the advantages and disadvantages. Trusting his assignment, the boy spurred his horse forward. He rode out of the protective forest, onto the grassy plain, and signaled to the enemy's troops by raising the Boar's Hoof standard.

FORDEM WAS IMPATIENT AS HE waited for the return of his scout. He had assembled a meager force, which he would sacrifice to his right flank, ready with his word to march into the pass.

"What keeps the fool?" Fordem thought silently to himself as he sat upon the jaundiced-eyed stallion, who seemed unusually disturbed for some reason. "Ah, there he is!" he said, spying the man exiting the northern forest. The man was now waving the standard, albeit reluctantly, just as he was instructed. The navy should have easily made the eastern border of the pass hours ahead of his infantry. Now encouraged by the flag waving scout, Fordem signaled to his commander. As instructed, the diversionary battalion began marching quickly. Within minutes his men would be inside of the pass, and the battle would begin.

ALEXANDER AND HIS PITLING FORCE arrived several hours earlier. In silence they waited, watching and ready, positioning them above the southern edge of Devil's Pass. The enemy's troop movements were visible in the last few minutes, the surrounding plains still darkened by the night. To their left approximately one hundred enemy soldiers could be seen riding in formation and entering the narrow western opening of the pass. Turning now to his boys, Alexander signaled them to flank the group. When in position, they would descend the slopes cutting off the army. Alexander turned to Martin. He shook his head and smiled quietly. "It is now time to rumble."

Martin limped to the wooden grate, and with his good leg kicked out the first wooden post that wedged the boulders. This created a chain reaction as the mass of rock and lumber crushed the remaining posts. With a huge explosion like noise, the collection rolled out of control down the sheer side of the pass's southern wall. Bouncing and crashing like a freight train, this destructive force picked up momentum as it made its way down to seal the entry to Devil's Pass.

It was no surprise when Fordem heard the crash of rock and debris tumbling down on his troops. His decoy army had just entered the pass and triggered the meager response from Alexander's band, a most obvious juvenile ploy. He smiled a twisted smile, mimicked exactly by his evil horse whose satisfaction returned. With a quick bridle, the man rode to command the archers who were deployed in the foothills. Reaching them, he was ecstatic as he looked into the pass seeing his seemingly trapped army now engaged with the treasonous-boy army in battle. He shook his fist in victory, and circled to the archery command, instructing them to commence launching their deadly arsenal down upon the engagement. He would sacrifice his own men in the melee, but Alexander's force would be devastated. The foolish boy had deployed his force to his decoy. Turning with glee, he rode westward to his artillery.

The archers shot their arrows, one after the other, in banks of ten men. After launching their shot, another group would take their place. In this manner, wave after wave of deadly projectiles twitched into the air, bound for the fighting men.

Scott arrived as the boys descended on the enemy cavalry. As they did, enemy arrows began cascading down, surrounding the battling men and boys. As planned he took command of the boys. He turned the group around quickly and retreated back up the southern side of the pass away from the arrows and the trapped men. Had they stayed much longer, these hundreds of archers who now were getting their range would have decimated the small band, but to retreat now was to survive. As Fordem had planned, however, these arrows bound for Alexander's men would and did strike his own meager force now trapped in the pass behind the rocky avalanche.

Alexander did not wait for the planned faint assault and subsequent retreat, for he knew that the true battle was elsewhere. So as the boulders made their way down into the pass, he turned, mounted his steed, and descended into the southern forest. The boy was breathing hard when he reached his objective: his ready canon arsenal. Perhaps meek and pitiful in comparison with his foe's artillery, the canons and his men were trusted and dedicated. Alexander liked his odds this morning, his plan being one step ahead of the enemy. Touching off a volley, the canons roared as they sent their projectiles out over the plains, crashing within the major portion of the enemy army. Cannonballs striking the field, blasting up dirt and debris with concussive force, announced their presence.

THE BLASTS COMING FROM THE southern flank startled Fordem. The fire was from the enemy, hidden from view in the southern forest. They seemed intent upon blowing away the bulk of his force, deployed and waiting here in the foothills, preceding the entry to the Devil's Pass. His arrogance returned quickly, however; the man knew that his foe would have a desperate trick here and there. With his diversionary force holding Alexander's men within the pass, he could make quick work of this pitiful artillery package. He signaled to his artillery commander who now deployed his mobile force to deal with the southern flank. Fordem rode upon his evil stallion, making straight for the center of the action.

The Boar's artillery was greatly superior to the boy's in number, size, and mobility. Mounted on four huge wooden wheels pulled by a set of horses, each canon barrel could be deployed quickly.

Receiving Fordem's orders, the group moved to the south. Once deployed, they would begin to shred this inferior artillery formation with ease. The commander quickly mobilized the artillery and gave the order to fire on the enemy at will.

When the first of the Boar's Hoof canons went off, Fordem appreciated the huge explosion. These were great weapons, their blast was deafening, and Fordem's excitement moved the man to tears. He raised his fist in victory and looked to the forest edge expecting fire and destruction of the brat's outnumbered defenses. As he watched through his eyeglass, however, he was horrified. Fordem expected blasts to the southern forest and the boy's outnumbered artillery; instead it was his weaponry that was on fire. Another explosion occurred to his right, then another to his left. Turning to yells of anguish, Fordem realized that it was his canons that were exploding. His men were screaming and running from their artillery; for as each was lit, the canon exploded in a ball of flame, casting shrapnel and blistering heat not on the enemy but on the enemy's enemy, Fordem's force.

Artillery propels the projectile by using a controlled explosion in the barrel. The rapid expansion of exploding powder forces the lead projectile out of the muzzle, the only planned escape route for this force. However, with a barrel filled with gum, the explosion expands the barrel to the breaking point, each canon exploding in a ball of flying metal and fire. One after the other, the men would light the wick of their artillery, and soon find themselves running for their lives as their canon exploded; ear drums blasted, many caught in their own fire.

"BLAST, BLAST-- FOOLS!" FORDEM YELLED in anger as he turned to his vaunted artillery in horror. "Stopppppp--" he yelled, hoping to save some of his canons. All the artillery continued firing, however, as none of his soldiers had the nerve to disobey the proceeding order. The Boar's Hoof military was instructed and drilled to perfection on the art of war and following military protocol to the letter. Fordem had taught them well, using fear to crush any independent thought on the part of his troops. So while the more intelligent of the cannonneers noticed the odd misfire of their neighbors, not one of them would cease firing, for fear was a tradition of the Boar's military supplanting constructive thought.

"You incompetent fools!" Fordem yelled as he rode frantically back and forth among his exploding artillery. The man pulled his sword and began striking any man he could lay his hands on. The jaundice-eyed horse was equally shocked and showed a look of horse horror as well. Snorting and blinking his yellow eyes, the horse mirrored his master's disgust.

Alexander's canons were now shredding their defenses with one well-placed blast after another. Fordem's canons were exploding like timed devices right in the mist of the army. The force was riddled by enemy artillery blasts and unable to return the fire. The Boar's Hoof forces were scattered, each man running for his life. Fordem was furious as he saw the destruction of his vaunted military. He sheathed his sword, bridled the stallion sharply, and turned exiting the fiery debacle, making for his archers.

CHRISTOPHER SAT UPON HIS HORSE at the edge of the battle. The sun was rising, and a deafening roar was beginning across the way. He had seen the enemy artillery move south, and now he saw the horrible explosions and scattering of the enemy cannonneers, screams rising as they tried to avoid their own shrapnel. "All right!" the boy yelled, raising his fist, aware of Alexander's trap. The man was upon him before he could escape.

FORDEM HAD A SINKING FEELING as he rode across the plain, and the sight of the blond-haired boy infuriated the man. Veering from his men he pulled up to the boy, drew his sword said, "Blond haired rapscallion; you vile miserable creature, you! I will finally finish you off, you brat! Always in the thick of things, are you not. You will loath your end, boy. Prepare for death!"

Wide eyed, Chris's mouth dropped open when he saw his foe. He dug into the sides of his horse, turning now to just avoid the man. Chris still had the flag, and as he turned he struck out with its tip jamming the man in the chest. It was not enough to stop the enraged man, however. The man righted himself and turned to chase the hated boy.

THE SOLDIERS SENT TO THE pass found themselves alone and in trouble. The small band of boys they pursued was in fact a ploy, a fact the leader realized when he saw them escape up the southern slope of the pass. Trapped from escape to the west by the fallen rocks; his own troop's incoming arrows were soon decimating the group. The leader pulled an arrow from the ground. The Boar's Hoof insignia was obvious. Waving the arrow to his men he signaled their retreat and led all the angry and now actively traitorous men out the eastern opening to the sea.

ALEXANDER HAD SEEN, HEARD, AND felt the implosion of canons on the battlefield before him. With each explosion, a tremendous force was unleashed, tossing the canon in the air like a small toy, scattering dirt, rock, and debris. Before him the battlefield had changed; where once an imposing weapon stood, an excavated cavern was the result. With the enemy artillery in total disarray, Alexander now moved his forces across the frontline. He turned his canons on the enemy soldiers and made quick work of the helpless men. Scattering, the bulk of Fordem's army disintegrated in chaos and ceased being an organized opposition.

THE QUEEN WAS FORGOTTEN DURING the confused melee. Her assigned guard had left her long ago, realizing the unfolding disaster about them. Crystal and the Shar Pei were at her side, but the noise and smoke were overpowering and freighening. The lady sat upon her horse looking unsettled as she viewed the carnage surrounding the area.

"We must leave this open area Crystal!" the Queen said to her lady in waiting Around them were explosions, scurrying men, screaming, and fire everywhere.

"Over thusly, you're Majesty," Crystal suggested, pointing across the plain toward the northern forest. With her Queen's leave, they shot off for their target. Within moments, however, a huge explosion to the rear rocked the girl. With tremendous force, the projectile went off casting dirt and debris on her; surrounding the girl with smoke, heat, and disorientation as she was thrown from her mount. The royal dog had followed closely behind the girl. She too met this explosion, and now Crystal saw the dog tossed through the air landing at her feet. Gidget was up in a moment, barking and growling at the explosion and frantically looking for her Queen. As the smoke was clearing, Crystal realized that the battle raged around her. "The worst has happened and where is the Queen," she frantically considered. Crystal was distraught as she yelled for her sovereign. The Queen had disappeared in the melee; now alive or gone Crystal was not sure. Whistling for the dog, Crystal remounted and raced towards the forest.

As the smoke cleared it became clear that two were engaged in combat ahead. Gidget started growling as they made their way. Before Crystal could stop her, she was off and running toward the two. The dog was barking, growling, and jumping over obstacles. Crystal yelled for the dog. Not knowing where her Queen was, she turned her horse and chased after the determined dog.

CHRISTOPHER HAD STUNNED THE MAN with his staff, buying enough time to turn and ride for his life as Fordem raced after the boy. The boy was no match for the evil obsession of the man and steed, however, and he soon was overtaken. Fordem was yelling for the boy's head. Reaching out with a strong hand the man pulled the boy off his mount and up onto his own horse. Here the man began choking the boy hysterically. "You, you, everywhere it's you!" Fordem screamed over and over at the suffocating boy. Chris wrestled and struggled in vain to free himself.

Crystal was alongside the two, sliding with her horse to a stop, before Fordem could defend himself. The girl launched herself off the horse, landing now without fear behind the evil man. Fordem clung to Christopher's throat and screamed at the girl behind him. Crystal struggled to free the boy, kicking the man with her spurred shoes. Fordem began to realize his quandary. He continued to choke the boy and tried to shake the girl away as she kicked him mercilessly. The girl yelled and bit the man and grabbing for his head, pulled out a wad of graying hair. Fordem screamed in agony. He loosened his grip temporarily on the boy but would never let go. He shook and struggled while holding the boy, using his elbows to flail the willful girl.

Gidget was upon the horse in the next moment. The dog flew through the air, locking her jaw onto the right rear haunch of Fordem's evil horse and not letting go. With her teeth buried in horseflesh, the dog tore a huge chunk of the horse free. Biting again she ripped and tore the horse's thigh, blood now all over the dog.

The horse convulsed in agony, the jaundice-eyes staring back in disbelief. He rose up violently on his rear hooves, tossing the three passengers to the ground and whinnying in agony.

Gidget had tremendous disdain for horsemeat, and she spit the shreds that she had torn away from the horse unceremoniously on the ground. Kicking the pieces away with her rear paws, the dog ran with a gleeful dog smile to help the fallen girl. "Action," she thought as she growled in excitement.

Fordem had lost his grip upon the boy now as the three rolled free from the stomping stead. Chris was the first to his feet, grabbing the girl and dragging her away from the man. The girl was yelling, "Leave me to him! Leave me to him! I will tear him apart, Christopher of Temecula!"

The boy succeeded in pulling the girl away. He drew the dagger presented to him by Nicholas, and moved determined to face down this wretched man.

A gleeful smile now rose upon the countenance of the man. He stood slowly and walked to face Christopher of Temecula.

Measuring the slight boy, Fordem sneered; he spat upon the ground and drew his long sword with glee. "First I'll slash your skinny body and then I'll do the wench," the man yelled with satisfaction, slashing the shining blade back and forth, showing his skill to the outmatched boy and frightened girl. "You've crossed me one time too many; you vile, wretched, child!" He lunged forward slashing at Christopher. Christopher was quick, and he sidestepped him easily. The man was at him again, slashing with his sword as the boy back peddled.

"Stop Richard of Fordem, Alexander ordered with authority!"

The hero boy arrived after riding across the plain. He had seen his mother, and now the two arrived on this cowardly scene. Alexander dismounted from his horse, her majesty sitting sidesaddled on her royal steed. Crystal ran to her side, hugging her with relief.

Gidget jumped up, running to the long lost boy. Meeting him, she jumped up and down at his side, licking and biting the boy, whining and crying. "Alexander is back," she thought

Fordem turned with the sound of the boy. Seeing Alexander, he now left Chris to himself and moved to finish off one of his prime nemeses.

"It was always about power, was it not Richard of Fordem!" Alexander said in defiance of the man. "You have no guilt, you are beyond that. Our family, all of us trusted in you, and look at the destruction that you bring."

The fencing skills of the royal prince were legend in the kingdom. From birth, he received daily instruction, and along with his brother Nicholas, the two were felt to be without match. However, Fordem was one of those tutors. The man saw himself as superior in skill to the prince boy. He would take this boy with glee, then finish Christopher and salvage his evil scheme.

A sour but assured smile came upon the man, as Alexander drew his sword and walked slowly to meet him. The duel began furiously, with clashing metal clanging and echoing across the plains. Alexander was much quicker, eluding all of his attempted rushes at the boy with ease. Fordem had backed the boy up against the forest trees. Alexander avoided one swing at his legs with a quick jump. He avoided a swing at his neck by ducking. Fordem made one last desperate thrust. Alexander turned to his right, and with a swing of his sword amputated the man's outstretched arm just below the elbow. Fordem roared in pain. He dropped to his knees and in horror looked upon his slashed arm.

Alexander dropped to his knees looking on the shattered man. The boy placed a comforting arm on his victim's back. Reaching for Fordem's sword, which remained in the detached hand, he discarded it, throwing the blade deep into the forest. "Fordem, I am sorry--"

Fordem interrupted the apology with a shout. The man bolted to his feet and turned in a threatening manner to the boy. Holding the stump tightly in his one good hand he spit, "You vile and spoiled rat, you shan't have seen the last of me!" Turning now from the group, the defeated man turned and ran to the forest, yelling vulgarities as he disappeared.

THE HARBOR WAS EXPLODING, GREAT warring ships torn to shreds and sinking. It advanced the cause tremendously for with one deft stroke a huge sailing force was now removed from the conflict brewing in the Devil's Pass.

Little Andy knelt in the shadows. He was without his patch today, the culmination of all of his training. With an eye towards the imposing southern wall of the Fortress Alucemet, the boy considered his assignment. Little Andy and a small band of boys were to scale the sheer face of the castle with grappling hooks. Once accomplished, they were to drop the drawbridge, allowing an all out assault for the kingdom. With the fire growing in the harbor, the signal was clear; Little Andy and his boys were on.

The castle was secured, drawbridge high as they approached the towering wall. They quickly crossed the enclosure to the moat, and waded across to the sheer wall of the castle. Each boy grabbed his rope and tossed it high above. Catching the grappling hook on a solid purchase of the wall, the boys began climbing.

Pirates, Scoundrels, and Kings

Their ascent was not to be without conflict, a long blast of the castle horn announcing their presence. Following this, castle guards dropped debris, cascading down upon them with bruising force. As they climbed, the wind began whipping making each foot of ascent more troublesome.

SHE SEEMED TO APPEAR FROM nowhere, and perhaps in fact she had. The young girl dressed in the lavender dress arrived standing alone at the foot of the great drawbridge.

The girl was determined but had a hint of sadness on her face. From where she came, and to where she would go was not obvious, but she now found herself in the middle of a battle. The girl did not seem bothered at all by being so out of place.

It was still dark that morning, the dawn sun rising in the east behind the mountain and cloud cover, but the small girl was not. As a visage, she was lit up like a shining star in the night, almost translucent in the chilly morning air. The girl walked forthright to the castle front, crossed the moat quickly, and stepped intact through the thick wooden drawbridge gate.

"Did you see that, Tyler?" Little Andy said to his friend as they both struggled up the wall of the castle.

"See what?" the boy responded between straining and huffing as the boys continued to climb. Tyler turned for the moment. Seeing nothing he returned to his overwhelming task. The boy put up a hand to deflect a well-placed brass pan cascading down upon him. Soon the group was again making slow painful progress.

Autumn was aware of the preparations and had hoped for some role in the fun. Alexander and Nicholas were her friends, but they seemed to not notice her much lately. In the early morning light, she saw the scaling of the castle, and immediately knew what she might in fact do. How she had learned to move through items that used to be solid, she did not know. She had acquired the knack, however, and she used this to walk through the heavy wooden drawbridge. Once past this it was easy to squeeze between the iron grate, openings that used to be too small for her.

It had been sometime since she had entered the castle, but the works that lifted the heavy bridge and gate were always fascinating to her. She crossed to her left, and entered the guard tower. An odd man with flattened ears was within, but he seemed to not care much about the girl. "You, sir, raise the bridge for the boys!" the girl said. Moving to the man now, she tugged on his tunic and finally the man looked down upon her. She was cold, and the touch of the girl must have sucked some heat from the man because suddenly he was horrified by her presence. Screaming in fright the man turned around and ran out of the room.

This happened all too often to the girl. Something about her was frightening to everyone and she was becoming quite tired of this. No one to talk to she thought, and turning to the lift, she began to struggle with the mechanism to the bridge. It was all that she could do to get the handle moving, but she did; soon the mechanism was dropping the drawbridge, and raising the grated gate.

"Little Andy look!" Tyler yelled as he looked down on the opening gate. "The bridge is opening up," he yelled with excitement.

"Careful Tyler, a trap it is!" Little Andy responded with suspicion.

Autumn was quite pleased with herself. She had dropped the bridge and raised the gate. The girl glanced down at her hands with a grimace. She was very happy to help, but the greasy residue now on her hands would require washing after she alerted the boys. She moved now from the mechanism housing, under the castle wall, and walked out along the wooden bridge.

Raising her hands to her mouth she turned to the scaling group and yelled, "Boys..., Boys... you're silly for climbing, come this way." Dropping her hands, she waved to the group directing them in her direction.

"Who is that?" Little Andy yelled to his friends as he looked down on the young girl. In a moonless sky, this girl shone as if illuminated by the moon. The boy had heard of an apparition but never believed in them. Shaking his head he debated; he was no longer sure of a trap. Even if behind the girl lay soldiers, these soldiers would soon appear and make easy prey of the hanging boys. Little Andy left his rope and dropped to the ground below. He looked up at his partners and signaled them to follow. They made their way to the drawbridge with no interference. As they climbed over its side, the little girl began to lead the group over the bridge under the castle wall and into the foray of the fortress without opposition.

As sudden as she appeared, she was gone, leaving the group alone. The girl had pierced the rocky fortress of castle Alucemet without blood. Now just as any girl would, she left to find somewhere to wash her greasy hands.

NICHOLAS AND MANZELL WERE VERY successful. With a few choice arrows they utterly destroyed the enemies' fleet. The huge vessels blew up in a fiery ball, its bow bursting off like a balsa wood model. As the water flooded the ship, it sank like a stone to the bottom of the harbor. This was the crown ship, and it had just made the portal to the sea. As the second and then third ship followed, the boys had fiery target practice. Exploding the powder packets one after the other, they created a cemetery blocking any exit from the royal harbor. The sky lit up with fire as they continued. Arrow after arrow struck the enemy ships; sinking them to a watery end and scattering the frightened crew.

The two were quite pleased with themselves as the surveyed their work from the harbor's shore. Here lay in ruins a most powerful navy, the thirteen vessels burning and sinking to the floor of the sea. The Boar's fleet would not be available to reinforce forces at the Devil's Pass.

Manzell was laughing and jumping for joy. The fire in the harbor lit the faces of the two tanned boys who had just destroyed their enemy's powerful force. "Dude--" He laughed, realizing he spoke as would his friend Christopher. "It is done!" Manzell yelled in joy, slapping the prince upon his back.

"Well done, trusted friend!" Nicholas said. "Return now to the fortress gate and lead the others on the frontal assault. I will take the castle rear. I have plans for the Boar, and he will not be fond of them. We will meet within the castle courtyard, Manzell."

Manzell turned, raising his hands to the air. He holstered his crossbow and the remainder of his arrows, and ran to the plains surrounding the castle.

Nicholas turned to his next objective. He had destroyed the Boar's entire fleet and now the boy wanted the man. Running in the shadows of the harbor, his smiling countenance became one of quiet determination. Reaching the castle precipice, he struggled up and over the rocky wall, dropping to the main dock below. Ahead of him was the secluded inner port of the castle, surrounded on three edges by fingers of the castle wall. Ahead was a rocky stairway, leading to the rear entry of his former residence. Nicholas drew his sword; he knew that he would have to fight his way into the castle.

THE FIRST EXPLOSION SHOOK THE ground as the ship went up in a fiery ball. In shock, Captain Balaam rolled over and pulled himself along the ground. Looking out across the harbor, the pirate was horrified. Before him was his powerful navy in destruction. When he saw the brat-boy laughing and running along the shore, he knew he was defeated again. Anger burst out of the man and he was exhausted no more. With disgust his temper returned, and he thought that he must do in this insolent fool of a boy. The pirate righted himself, turned, and ran after the boy, climbing the rocks along the castle wall. He saw Nicholas drop over the side to the dock, and moving quickly, he descended and made his way to intercept the vile boy.

Nicholas was running along the dock under the huge boom used to load ships as a huge obese man, dressed in tattered and soaked clothes, dropped with a hideous yell to the dock in front of the boy. Stopping suddenly, Nicholas took stock of the man who was struggling to his feet. It was Balamn, back from the dead, with his hairy bum hanging out of the torn rear of his britches.

"Oh!" Nicholas yelled in disgust. He could have easily lived his entire life without the sight of the man's bum, the boy thought. Drawing his sword from his blue scabbard, Nicholas yelled to the man. "Captain Balamn, from what crack have you crawled this dawn?"

The pirate turned and laughed in derision. "Funny boy, always so funny," he said, shaking his head angrily. He glanced above and jumped quickly to the overhanging boom, swinging and springing himself, boots held high towards the smaller boy. He was unusually nimble for a stridorous mass of a man, and he succeeded in knocking Nicholas to the ground, dropping his sword. The boy was scattered back along the dock, spinning and skidding up to several barrels. The pirate was up, grabbed the boy's sword, and covered the distance to the boy with amazing quickness.

"Vile, wicked, brat!" the captain spat, reaching deep in his diseased lungs and launching the perfect projectile upon the boy. "Last rights, and how pitiful the royal son, alone on the dock laying sprawled upon your back." The pirate lunged at the boy, jabbing with the sword.

Nicholas spread his legs quickly, and the Captain buried the blade's tip into the wooden dock. Struggling to free the blade the Captain sputtered and looked anxiously down on the boy. As the man struggled with the sword he yelled, "Depraved and wicked urchin!"

Nicholas quickly reached up and grabbed the pirate by his collar. Using his legs, he buried his feet into the man's belly. Lifting him, he launched the man over his head. Crashing head first, Balaam found himself buried in a barrel of gunpowder right up to his middle. His exposed buttocks smiled over the edge of the barrel as his spindly legs kicked furiously in the air.

The boy looked for a moment at the site, laughing and shaking his head. Here an obese man struggled, buried head first in a barrel with buttocks exposed, as he hysterically wrestled to free himself. Nicholas grabbed his sword, turned, and ran down the dock to where he had dropped his bow. Reaching them now, he grabbed an oil tipped arrow, lit it, and let it fly. Striking the barrel, a huge explosion sent the pirate back to the sea for good.

Robyn of Hobinsiefken had immediately understood the dog-delivered message. He dressed quickly and ran down the lane to the center of the city. Rousing his civil leaders, the entire town was quickly awake, ready and willing to defend the kingdom. With picks, shovels, and sickles, the citizens marched with the Mayor towards the castle. It was about time, many of them were thinking.

The Mayor seemed alive again for the first time in quite some time. He had felt paralyzed as the demise around him had risen. He wondered if he could have done something to stop the evil, and when unable to change, guilt overpowered the man. This was all gone now, and he was again leading his dedicated citizens, feeling more and more certain of the outcome.

Once inside the castle Little Andy and the band found intense resistance. The explosions in the harbor had alerted the Royal Guard, and the defense of the castle had begun. The castle guard was mounted and while they had not anticipated the lowering of the drawbridge, they were ready for the meager force. Along the castle escapement, scaffolding stood. Those who were dropping debris upon the boys before were now launching arrows towards them. The Ogre of "O" had appeared, and he was yelling instructions to his men.

Little Andy and Tyler had managed to turn over one of the scaffolds, and down it tumbled men and all. This created quite a disturbance in the castle courtyard as yelling and screaming continued to pierce the dawn air.

Alexander led the group from the battlefield. With the Queen, Crystal, and Chris in the lead, they raced westward across the plains of Rochelle towards the expected conflict for the castle. Gidget raced ahead, her royal crest of arms flying in the breeze. She tasted the battle, and was eager for more.

Alexander and his group arrived as the mayor-led citizens appeared. Alexander looked to the mayor, smiled, and raised his hand in acknowledgement. He rode with the army over the wooden drawbridge into the castle foray. There was hand-to-hand fighting going within the castle courtyard. With the entry of Alexander's army and the citizenry, simply by numbers the tide began to turn. These citizens were angry. They were striking the guards with their shovels and turning over scaffolding. The Ogre was concerned as he looked about him.

NICHOLAS HAD A REASON FOR entering the castle from the rear. After making work of the pirate, the boy picked up his bow, sheathed his sword, and ran along the dock making his way towards the stone stairway. There was no resistance to his entry, and entering the stairway, the boy made good time circling to his left and climbing high over the harbor. The gate at the top of the stairway stood closed; the boy, however, was up over that gate and running along a corridor quickly. As he ran he jumped and grabbed a torch out of its fitting upon the wall. Exiting the corridor now he was high atop the castle circling the wall, his goal now in site. Ahead of him waved the Boar's Hoof, the flag flying high above the castle courtyard.

THE BATTLE IN THE COURTYARD raged, continuing with hand-to-hand combat. The arrival of Alexander with his troops and the Mayor's citizens began to turn the tide. The castle guards, so long held to task by fear, were aware and their resistance was waning. Many began dropping their weapons, turning and running away over the drawbridge. The encouragement of the people was growing with each moment.

The Ogre of "O" did not like the turn of events and he searched for anything to gain some advantage. The Queen had just appeared over the drawbridge, and a cursory thought dawned on the meager mind of the man.

He was off, and before Crystal could intercept the man, the O had reached the Queen. The laughing fool gathered up the Queen and pulled her away to his horse. The battle stopped as the vulgar man yelled in satisfaction, all eyes now upon the two. Laughing like the fool he was, he rode with Queen in hand to the center of the courtyard. The battle gradually halted as the boys and the guard realized what the Ogre was doing.

Nicholas reached the base of the flagpole, barring the torch in hand. At the top of the castle, the wind was fierce, and the Boar's Hoof waved in the breeze. Nicholas studied the flag, and with a sneer turned and mounted his last arrow. With his free hand raising the torch to the arrow, he lit the tip. The boy sighted down the arrow aiming for the flag flying high above his head. Nicholas let the flaming arrow fly, sailing off with a swish. Striking the flag dead center, the enemy flag went up in flames with pieces of burning cloth cascading down upon the castle escarpment.

Nicholas jumped in the air in victory, and celebrated the symbolic end to a despotic rule. The boy now moved to the edge of the wall, and looking down upon the courtyard began yelling and waving. He then saw the problem. The Ogre of "O" had the Queen and was gleefully displaying her to the crowd. Crystal had ridden to her side and was now cussing and hitting the man. Gidget was at the man's feet, barking loudly and drooling. Alexander rode to his mother's side and drew his sword.

"The coward! He uses the Queen as a shield." Nicholas was livid as he viewed these events. The victory that just moments before had been his, came crashing down. He was high above the scene, and no one knew of his presence. The enemy flag was in flames, but their quest was not through.

Nicholas quickly assessed the situation as he ran back to the flagpole. Drawing his sword with one swipe, he severed the rope which had elevated the flag. Pulling this down, he now had a long segment of stout cord. Tying a quickly made lasso he took some practice. Swinging the rope around his head, he was ready. He would have only one chance.

The Ogre was laughing hysterically, shrugging off Crystal's blows, and really enjoying tussling with the Queen. Nicholas jumped up to the edge of the wall and walked along the narrow precipice now standing above the man. He did so quietly, and looking the several stories down hoped that his rope was long enough for the job. The boy began by circling the lasso in the air, and then with a deft strike he let loose, sending the noose below. The shot was perfect, encircling the Ogre around the shoulders. Suddenly, the man realized that he was not in control.

Nicholas quickly dropped from the wall and began winding in the slack from the rope. Once tight, the noose was secured around the surprised man. The boy then reeled in the slack and tied the loose end to the closest battle escarpment.

Alexander was upon the man as soon as the noose was secured. He reached the Queen and freed her, pulling her down off the Ogre's horse and onto his. He sat there on his horse with sword draw as the rest of the play unfolded.

Nicholas had made similar moves many times before, always on his ships however, never over solid ground. Without time to think he grabbed his leather sheath and slid down the rope. As he made his way towards the Ogre he lifted his feet, and after having picked up some momentum hit the enemy squarely in the face knocking the man backwards and down on the ground in a ball of dust. The man was hog-tied and hopelessly stuck.

The crowd swelled towards the man. The Royal Guard Grand Am lay on the ground staring in horror at the gathering swelling about him. Nicholas brushed himself off and, smiling, began to roll the man in, pulling up the rope. The entire courtyard was in an uproar as the boy drug the obese man forward. The few castle guards that remained were the ones now laughing at the man the most loudly.

Chris could not keep away. After seeing Nicholas rope the man he rode up and jumped from his horse. Turning to Nicholas, Christopher said, "Dude, let's roll him over the drawbridge. I was in that moat once. This dude will not like it one bit!"

It struck Nicholas as a good idea. Running along the rope he reached the last place that he could grasp before it ascended to its anchor above. With his dagger, he cut the rope, and tossed the free end to Christopher. Nicholas grabbed the "O" and righted him to his feet. Chris now began winding the rope around the captured man ensnaring him tighter and tighter. The two tipped the man over and began rolling him along the central courtyard to the drawbridge. The crowd surrounded them, clapping and laughing and encouraging the boys. The bulldogs were barking their agreement, and Gidget chased them. The Ogre was yelling and struggling as he was rolled to the bridge. With a final kick Nicholas dumped the man upside down into the foul moat below.

It was over for the time. The boys won the day. Fordem was an armless man. Balaam had ceased to exist. The resisting castle guard ran for their lives. Only the Boar was left to attend to.

Chapter 24
The Beast

> Under three things the earth trembles,
> under four it cannot bear up:
> a servant who becomes king,
> a fool who is full of food,
> an unloved woman who is married,
> and a maidservant who displaces her mistress.
> Proverbs: 30:21-23

As times before, the Boar's own snoring woke himself up just before dawn. He felt regal sleeping in a four-point poster bed with three down mattresses. Michaelis preferred the term gathered rather than stolen from the King, but then the monarch had no further need of such items, did he? The thought made him roar and snort as he climbed out of bed, his own jokes always so funny.

The Boar's legs were unusually short, and each morning he would dangle them from the bedside before having the nerve to drop to the ground. This morning was different; he bounded out of bed like a youngster afraid of missing Saturday morning cartoons. He was in a hurry for today destiny would shine on him. Of that he was certain.

Michaelis pulled off his night cap, discarding it carelessly as always. Picking up was the maid's problem, he concluded as he struggled out of his nightshirt into his black tunic and riding britches. "BELCH!" Like clockwork his first of the morning, and to this one he added a second with a flurry. He reasoned that today he was destined for greatness, and he hurried to his favorite application, breakfast.

For effect, he sat upon the high-backed golden chair with a daunting flourish and slipped into his prized, black, shiny jackboots. The Boar was nearly blind, as those of his species tend to be, but he would inspect these boots closely each day, looking at his reflection in the spit and polish. Heaven help his clothier if he discovered any defect, but today everything looked in order, and what a day it was to be.

While Michaelis passed and presented himself as a man of the military, complete with a metal bedazzled chest, he truly was a man who knew only the vagaries of refuse management. He had shown little interest when Fordem had explained his plan, but inside, the consolidation of his rightful kingdom looked to finally be his. He had risen like a meteor taking the country for his own, but many details remained aloof. He did not like having that vile brat Alexander within the idiot King Lithotomy's control. He hated the fact that the Queen was free, she being too popular to deal rightly with her for the time being. He detested the pirate-boy's freedom as well. This latter item was neutralized somewhat, for the Boar had succeeded in convincing everyone of the prince's traitorous execution of his equally disgusting brother. For while the obnoxious boy was in fact free. This traitorous rumor was a canard that cheered him deeply. For to the Boar, a lie was noble, and a noble lie such as this much more noble than the truth could ever be.

"Ha—Ha—Ha---" he roared, entertaining himself. Michaelis loved his wickedness more than wickedness itself, and today finally the kingdom would be all his.

Fordem had assembled the largest army ever seen. For the simple capture of Alexander from that fool of a King it was somewhat overkill Michaelis thought, but better to be safe than sorry he concluded. The Queen would be safely away from civilization's protective eye when she met her fate. He had left it to Fordem to set such a trap, and he felt very confident with the events, every item twisted now to his advantage. He was very encouraged then as he moved to his chamber window that dawn and saw the huge ground force led by Fordem marching eastward: cavalry, archers,

Pirates, Scoundrels, and Kings

and artillery for certain victory. This victorious sight produced his most valued feeling: hunger. Michaelis now listened with joy as his stomach growled. He turned and yelled with indignation for his breakfast. Yes, how dare his servant to be just a moment late! The man would suffer the consequences.

The explosion in the harbor rocked the man, sending him tumbling backward, his face full of pastry. "What was that," he yelled as he lay on the floor straddling his chair.

The Boar was up and moving to the western end of the castle in the early daylight. Here he could see the entire harbor, the obvious source of this noise. Squinting, Michaelis struggled to make out the action that was occurring below. "Some fires, some explosions, ships sinking." Yes everything seemed just right to the nearly blind man.

His navy was obviously destroying the pirate-boy's fleet, and he jumped for joy. Just one last look to be sure, he thought, and he squinted down to the water below. Yes, the sinking ships were the pirate boy's. his eyes were straining now, but he was certain. Turning he strutted back to his royal chamber. Grabbing a fresh towel he wiped the pastry from his face, righted his chair, and sat down to finish his huge meal.

The rest of the events that day fell right in step with his expectations. The lowering of the drawbridge and the return of his victorious army into the courtyard were all in order and gave little concern to Michaelis. He took little stock in anything that day, thinking continually of his greatness. The Boar was full of bliss as he envisioned the destruction of the Queen and the deserved punishment of her royal brats. The mirrorlass's power had eluded him for now. Soon, however, his brilliant mind would sort out its mystery, and the device's unlimited power would then be his.

Had he been able to see clearly he might have been concerned as one flaming arrow burnt down his precious Boar's Hoof flag. He would have been concerned as well when the boy used a rope to lasso and tie his royal Guard Grand Am. The increasing noise within the courtyard should have been of some concern to him as well. The Boar, however, knew his victory was certain, and he would let nothing dissuade his growing vision of grandeur.

When he realized the truth of the situation, it was very much too late. The truth manifested itself in the way of an innocent quiet knock upon his chamber door. Opening the door he expected a message of victory; instead, he was shocked. Sitting before him were three growling and drooling bulldogs. Quickly the Boar closed the door, turned, and leaned against it. He was sweating now and trying to think. A look out to the courtyard confirmed his worst fears. His flag was burning, and the Ogre was hog-tied and being rolled out of the castle. Yes, there was some trouble brewing, and only he could do something about it. Wondering, he turned to action; he ran and hid.

Spike's first job upon taking the castle was to locate the Boar. With Nails and Smasher, a quick trip up the rear donjon, led by their canine sense of smell, led them without much difficulty to the Boar's chamber. They had mastered a human-like knock, and they were not surprised when the door opened, and before them stood their prey. As the door shut, the dogs began to bark and howl. They were striking the door now with dog-like determination, clawing at the wood, trying to get at the man. Spike backed up, and then running and jumping struck the door with a heavy thud. Soon the other two were doing the same. Smasher had an idea. Standing with his flank against the door the other two dogs would take turns running, jumping on his back and launching themselves with intense power against the top of the door. Within minutes, the heavy door came crashing down. Once inside they searched and sniffed. The man was gone, and they were after his ample scent down the back stairs, tracking their prey.

The dogs raised attention with all their barking and thrashing of the chamber door. Nicholas and Chris had just rolled the Ogre down the drawbridge. Alexander had just triumphantly returned from the Devil's Pass. Banding together the three began running across the courtyard. Once inside the castle the noise led them down a flight of stairs, up the rear donjon, along a torch lit hallway, and to the Boar's chamber.

"Dude--" Chris said, staring in disbelief at the mess before them.

The door was destroyed, torn apart from its hinges and lying on the floor. Alexander and Nicholas crashed over the door into the chamber and soon all three were back down the rear stair exit running hard towards the barking and growling of the three bulldogs. They took the stairs in a few jumps, circled around, and took off running down the hallway.

The dogs had cornered their prey, and they were barking and growling voraciously. In the upper bowery, the three dogs sat upon their rear haunches with tails wagging. As the boys entered the room, the dogs looked over their shoulders, tongues dripping with pride. Against the wall, a table was turned over with pots and pans dislodged and piled up around it.

The three boys walked to the site. Nicholas reached his dogs, stroking their fur and telling them, "Good boys."

The Boar had tried to get away from the three monster dogs. Throwing everything he could find and running, he was now caught. Tossing over a table and dragging it to a corner, the Boar had jumped behind it hiding, crying, and whining.

From the position of the boys, the man was well-hidden, except for one curly tail that stuck up in the air above the edge of the table. Nicholas was laughing loudly, and he turned to Alexander and pointed to the tail. The boy walked to a bowl of overturned nuts. Grabbing a nutcracker he returned to the side of the others. Placing the nutcracker around the tail, and handing one of the two handle grips to his brother, they simultaneously crushed the tail in the vise of the device.

"Ahhhh--" The Boar screamed in agony. He lifted up, striking his head on the table, and tossing it aside. Standing now, confronting his victorious opponents, Michaelis was holding his tail, stamping and cussing. "Wretched brats, I curse you!"

With that, he was off running to the window, hurling himself out of the frame. The man had miscalculated his girth, however, and was now lodged midway through the window. Michaelis was shouting, screaming, and kicking trying to escape. His right boot hung, toe pointing up while his left boot was twisted and hanging from his ankle. Chris shook his head. He was perplexed, and he walked to the foot of the frantic beast. Removing one boot, his confusion was cleared.

"Hooves!" he said as he examined the toeless foot of the man. "Hurley," the boy said to himself, turning to his friends.

Michaelis managed to struggle free, pulled himself through the window, and launched himself down to the moat below. As he fell his voice trailed off, "I will never give up..."

The man was gone. Fordem and his forces were scattered and defeated. The Queen was safe, triumphantly returning to the fortress in victory. It had been a good day.

Chapter 25
Dogs are People Too

> A RIGHTEOUS MAN CARES FOR THE NEEDS OF HIS ANIMAL,
> BUT THE KINDEST ACTS OF THE WICKED ARE CRUEL.
> **PROVERBS 12:10**

The Queen's return in victory that day created hysteria among the good citizens of Alucemet, who packed the castle courtyard for brief sightings of the Royal Family. There was cheering and waving, complete with the bountiful flow of alcoholic spirits. They carried Alexander and Nicholas high above the crowd as returning defenders of the crown. The evil that had dominated the Kingdom had taken its toll, but perhaps the good times of the past had returned.

It was evening as the Queen took court. She wanted a private time for she had not been able to properly reunite with her precious sons. Assembling in the royal sitting room, Alexander, Nicholas, as well as Crystal and Christopher were all present. It was a treat for the three bulldogs to be in the royal chambers, but they had given to the effort, and Nicholas bade them to enter and sit quietly. Present as well was Gidget, the royal dog in waiting. The Shar Pei had a secret crush on the leader bulldog Spike and would smile her way upon him on occasion, emboldening the larger dog. .

"Alexander my son and prince, I have missed you so. And Nicholas, you royal boy, please give me a hugs!" the Queen said.

"Mother, you embarrass me!" Nicholas smiled as the Queen grabbed the two boys in her arms. She was crying with joy, so proud and happy. If only the King had returned as well, she thought to herself. "The beast! Tell me again, is Michaelis truly gone?"

"Unless he can swim he still is in the moat. Methinks he can paddle, however, and was happy to leave us. Is it not true Alexander?" Nicholas said.

"It is true Mother, and a happier Boar there might never have been to make an escape. But had he carried just one stone more of gut his fate would still be stuck in the bowery window I venture."

The Queen embraced the two boys again. It was as if she was not sure that the scene was true. Would the joy truly last? It would be some time before she felt comfortable with this return to good fortune. She turned now to Chris. The boy was sitting proudly to Crystal's left, quietly smiling, happy and contented. "Christopher of Temecula," she said, embracing the boy and bringing a bright blush to his face. "You are so handsome and in much better condition than with your last visit to our castle I venture to guess."

Alexander could not wait any longer, and disobeying tradition interrupted the Queen with a question. "Mother, our Father, what has become of him?" Alexander asked.

The question put a damper on the scene. The Queen hung her head with this question. "Alexander, King William is gone," she said quietly. Patrice began to sob, covering her eyes with her hand. The happy reunion now became a somber one. An icy silence pervaded the room. Nicholas, who always wore a smile, did not do so now.

Christopher wished he could say something, anything, but he certainly did not encourage the group with his next line. "Nicholas grew a gum tree," he said, looking hopeful. No one responded. "Oh, I forgot," the boy said, dropping his head. "Your Queen, I mean Majesty, you don't know what gum is."

Had anyone been looking at the Shar Pei, had someone been able to read the mind or the facial wrinkles of the dog, they would have noted a change come over the canine with the mention of her master, King William. Gidget knew, however, that humans did not show the proper respect to people like her. In situations like these, the dog was fond of saying, of course to herself, "Dogs are people too."

Pirates, Scoundrels, and Kings

Gidget reminded the gathering of her presence with a loud bark, and having done so ran to the door. No one really paid the dog much notice, so she ran back to the middle of the room and barked again. The dog garnered no response and so repeated this act over and over again.

Nicholas was the first to notice the dog's actions. "What is it girl?" the boy said, walking behind the dog to the chamber door.

"Finally," the dog seemed to be thinking. With finality she turned and ran out of the royal chamber with Alexander, Nicholas, and Christopher of Temecula following her down the hallway.

A castle, while serving as a home to the royal family and others, is much more than a residence. A city perhaps would be a better analogy. A castle is a huge complex of areas sitting upon a deep foundation dug well into bedrock.

Many different contractors, each with their own agendas, construct the castles, none allowing the other access to his own section. The true anatomy of a medieval castle is often discovered in the distant future by a modern anthropologist. While the boys had visited nearly every area of the castle, the area to which the dog led them that day was new to all. Down they went, first in the traveled areas of the castle, but soon to cracks and corners within the bowels of the stone fortress.

When the boys caught up to her, Gidget was standing with her little curled tail wagging, and staring into the blackness of a large crack in the rock floor. "What do you see girl?" Alexander wondered. The boy got down on his knees and looked directly into the wrinkled face of the black-tongued canine.

Gidget kept looking into this deep and black crack and panting. The boys and dog were now deep within the castle, and though not knowing it at the time, they were staring directly into the actual wall that made up the outer foundation of the western side of the castle.

Castles are heavy, and the requirement of the lowermost foundation requires it to be built in sections, each the size of a small room. It was dark and damp, and a foul stagnation to the air seemed to bother them all.

Gidget sat on the edge of the crack, staring downward and panting. "What is it girl?" Alexander asked again.

The dog looked to him one last time, and then standing jumped deep through the crack and disappeared. The boys fell to their knees and stared after the dog, their eyes now straining to see in the dim light. "Help me down," Alexander said, lifting an arm to Nicholas and readying himself to slide down after the dog. Gidget was barking, sounds of her digging coming from below.

"Alex, here I will help you first, but then Chris and I will follow," Nicholas said.

"Down there?" Chris said with a foul look. It was dark and cold, snakes and bats coming to the mind of the modern day boy.

Alex was off, first hanging then dropping into the blackness below. The dog was interested in a small hole in a crudely constructed wall just above the dirt, and she was digging and barking when the boys reached her. The opening was large enough to admit the medium-sized dog, but nothing larger. At the time, they were within the wall at the base of the castle foundation. This was deep below ground level, the wall really consisting of stones arranged in large cubicles to sustain the massive weight of the castle above. The crack had given them access to the very bottom of one of these chambers. The room consisted of stone and mortar, and across its center, a crudely plastered wall lay closed except for the small hole to which the dog was drawing the boy's attention.

"What's inside Gidget?" Alexander inquired. The dog looked up at the boys. She knew they could not fit through the opening, but something was very important to her, and so she disappeared through the hole. In a moment she was back, her head looking back out with black tongue panting.

"We must get some light and tools. We need to break more of this plastered footing," Alexander said, looking up and kicking the wall. Turning to the others he said, "We'll leave and return. Something or someone is within here, I am convinced of that much."

Pirates, Scoundrels, and Kings

"I'll help you up Alexander," Nicholas said. Chris and the boy made a saddle, lifting the foot of the boy above so that he could climb out of the crack. Once he was above, he held his hand down and helped the others.

The boys were back quickly, carrying torches and pick axes. Gidget was now out of the opening, sitting upon her haunches patiently, her tail wagging as the boys returned. With the light, they found her sitting and staring at the small opening. Nicholas took one of the torches, got down on his hands and knees, and looked within. "I can't see anything," he said in frustration. "Hand me that ax," Nicholas said as Chris handed him a large handled pick ax.

The three boys began cracking the plastered wall and widening the hole. It raised dust and dirt filled the air. Piece by piece they cracked away, opening up access slowly. All three were filthy by now, sweat and dirt sticking like Nick's favorite gum to everyone and every place in this wretched hole. Nicholas was the smallest of the three, and soon he felt that he could crawl through the opening. "I am going through. Hold the light," he said. The boy was down on his belly and inched his way through the tight opening. Once inside he yelled back, indicating a space on the other side. Alexander handed the boy a torch through the hole and Nicholas was gone for the moment.

Nicholas returned. "Give me that ax," he said with determination.

"What is it Nick?" Alexander said, now on his knee looking through the opening at the dirt-stained face of his brother?

"Father!" Nicholas said. "He is still alive, but just by so much!" Nicholas now disappeared and began to frantically crack at the foundation from within with his pick ax. Alexander and Chris looked at each other in surprise. The two boys grabbed their axes and began work on the other side, all three boys now swinging and breaking the plastered wall in the small space. Gidget was excited, and she barked and went back and forth through the opening, deftly missing the swinging axes.

"Gidget, we'll hit you." Chris said as he tried to keep the excited dog away from their work.

KING WILLIAM AND HIS QUEEN, Patrice, had ruled the Kingdom of Alucemet for fifteen years. They were good monarchs as well as good parents. Their marriage was exemplary, both loving each other. Their kingdom flourished as they ruled with wisdom and kindness. However, something had happened to the good King over the last few years. It started slowly, with even the Queen not noticing, but as the time went on it became obvious to all. Decisions were made, errors in judgment began to occur that would never have happened in the past. And why was this happening, you might wonder? The answer was simple, yet so hard to predict. Sleep deprivation!

In beauty there was not a match for Queen Patrice. Her long beautiful brown hair and green eyes had won William the moment they had met years before. As she aged and became a mother, her beauty grew along with her wisdom. But Patrice snored, quiet at first, but for someone who slept so poorly the years took their toll on King William. It began by waking him at night, with his fitful attempts at going back to sleep. Soon the Queen would fall asleep before the King, and he would not be able to drop off. William had tried to awaken the Queen. "Stop snoring Patrice," he would say gently.

Unlike her regal daytime countenance, if the Queen would wake, she would yell back at the man in a combative fashion. "You woke me! I snore not." Immediately the Queen would drop back to sleep while the King lay frustrated and of course still awake. Then it would begin again so that soon the King would not try to stop the noise. He tried to get to sleep first, but this seldom worked anymore, and as the years passed, falling asleep became a major problem for the King.

"Dratted Woman," William would whisper as he lay in the royal bed next to his bride. I love you so, but snore-- oh for one night of silence," he would say in anger, turning first on one side then on the other. If he lay with his back to the Queen it was quieter, but soon he would open his eyes and have to move. He tried remembering his youth and remembering meeting the Queen and it would help, but soon the noise would break through and sleep would elude him again. The King would get up and pace, run in place trying to tire himself. On occasion, a servant would draw a hot bath for him, and after returning he would be relaxed, but sometimes nothing would help.

When Gidget became the royal dog, she too began to suffer; at least it seemed as such to the King. "Can't sleep either I see, Gidget." William would say as the concerned pet would follow her master night after night as he paced. It gave the King some solace to have his dog at his side as he would get out of bed, pace, or read by candlelight night after night. However, the dog learned a trick that the King could never quite master. It was late one night. The night had not gone well for sleep. Sitting off the royal chamber he read the Holy Word. Soon he became aware that the sound at his feet had changed. William noticed one late night that the dog had dropped off to sleep, now in majestic dreams upon her stuffed cushion. More to his amazement, the dog snored timing her inhalation and exhalations perfectly with the Queen. William hung his head in dejection, his last nightly friend now asleep, and the King wide awake.

King William would usually drop off just as the sun was rising on the next day for a few minutes. As the years went along his youth did as well, and with the chronic lack of sleep, he began to make mistakes. William knew he was not thinking well when he appointed that Michaelis, the minister of refuse, and replaced the suddenly slain Bienville with the Ogre de Oppenhoffer, but it seemed a good idea at the time. Fordem seemed to consent to the decision with ease, and while the mayor voiced some opposition, William was King. He was sleeping more and more during the day now, and before he knew it he was gone, plastered deep within the foundation of the castle, left there to die of starvation. And he would have except for one brave dog, which dug and dug under the corner of the wall and gained access to the King. She would bring him water and scraps of food each day, and on these meager portions, the King survived, but just by so much.

"It is large enough now," Alexander said, dropping his ax to the ground. He grabbed a torch, and dropping to his knees was through the opening. "Nicholas, stop your pounding before you behead me," he said as his head appeared upon the other side.

Christopher, Nicholas, and Gidget followed through the opening and they stood now within the space which was just high enough for Alexander to stand with his neck bent. They all stood holding torches and examining what was before them. Across the way was a man, his long dirty hair hanging over his face. He was dressed in what used to be a white open-necked shirt, which hung down over a rotting pair of greasy dirty britches. He was without shoes, and he hung his head low down upon his neck. His face and hands were covered with months of grim, and long nails betrayed the time he had suffered alone. The man sat lifelessly, his right hand shackled to the wall behind him. Gidget ran to his side and began licking his leg. It seemed to revive the man, for he lifted his head and whispered in a horse voice, "Good girl, have you some water my dog?"

Nicholas was the first to the man's side and with his ax broke the shackle on the man's right hand. Collapsing, the two other boys arrived and supported the man. Within seconds he was free, unable to support himself without the help of the three boys. Gidget started barking, licking, and biting the legs of the man as Shar Pei's show their affection and it seemed to revive the man again. He looked up, first at Alexander, and then turning his head slowly with great difficulty, he saw Nicholas.

"Father," Nicholas said as the three now helped the man up. "What has happened to you?"

"The Boar? Did he plaster you within this hole?" Alexander said, his voice rising with anger.

"Alexander," the man said, for the first time appearing to comprehend his situation. "Nicholas, I am very tired," he said.

Pirates, Scoundrels, and Kings

Chris lowered himself to the dirt where the man had sat. The boy picked up a small glass container of water, and with his torch he observed a few scraps of old bread. The glass was stained with dirt on its outside, and the neck was invested with marks suggesting the dog had dragged this to the man. Turning now with the container, he dropped to his knees before the man and held the jar to his parched lips.

The man drank with great thirst. "Yes, the Boar. Had not my dog found me, well, it would have been disastrous. Gidget, she saved me. And now you have found me." Tears came to the corner of his eye as he spoke. "She came each day dragging that dirty jar of water and whatever scraps of food she could find." Gidget now jumped up and began to lick the man in the face. He was very unsteady but lifted a filthy hand to pet his royal dog.

"What is this, Father?" Alexander said, seeing a stained cloth within the man's hand? The boy reached out and the King handed him the item. Alexander examined it closely under the light of the torch. It was a torn piece of cloth, filthy and rotting now, but he was certain that it was at one time a very distinct color: blue. "Nicholas!" he said now turning to his brother and comparing the cloth to the blue sash that the pirate-boy always had around his waist. "My tunic!" Nicholas responded, taking the dirty piece of cloth that had been left on the drawbridge spike as Nicholas had escaped that day so long ago. "Father," he said now grabbing the grizzled man. "You held this for so long?" A tear came to the boy's eye; he had thought things about his father that now brought shame to the proud boy.

"Yes, Nicholas," The man said. "Never did I wish your departure," he said with a dry whisper.

He now raised his closed left hand and picking up Alexander's right hand slowly opened his grimy fingers, dropping a small item into the boys open hand. "My ring!" the boy said with surprise, remembering his sudden pressured departure. He had left the diamond ring after cutting the Mirrorlass even longer ago than

427

Nicholas's departure. "Father, my ring," he said, looking now at the disheveled broken man.

"I think you forgot that," the King said. For the first time a small smile came to the corner of the man's mouth.

Chapter 26
We'll Play in Heaven

> But whoever drinks the water
> I give him will never thirst.
> Indeed, the water I give him
> will become in him a spring of water,
> welling up to eternal life.
> John 4:14

The next day was beautiful, stunning sunlight ringing off the brilliant colors of the native shrubbery. Mixed with a lighthearted ocean breeze, the world was calm in a manner not seen for years. The castle was polished to a brilliant hue, revealing the inherent rose color of its natural stone. Flowers adorned each of the many windows. The Laughing Lion flew proudly above, reinforcing a long lost pride.

They let the drawbridge down early in the morning. The courtyard buzzed with festive activities for today was a day long in coming. How long had the evil covered this once wonderful Kingdom? The answer was a difficult one for no one really remembered its beginning.

The sky was a beautiful clear blue this wonderful morning, the rust-colored hue absent, hopefully for good. Today was a day for celebration and fun; today was a day for recognition of service and Knighthood.

Alexander was up early as well this fine morning, returning to the castle after a brisk ride. The boy crossed a meadow full of bright smells, the dew clinging to the fresh grass as his proud horse pranced in celebration. Autumn was sitting on a small boulder along the side of the roadway. Alexander was surprised when he saw the girl. Turning his horse, he rode to her side. "Autumn, a beautiful morning is it not?"

Autumn looked at the boy with a sad smile. "I can't tell anymore Alexander. Is it such?" the girl said. She dropped her head and brushed an unseen object from the surface of her lavender dress.

Alexander dismounted and stood in front of the girl. He was concerned for her, knowing her plight. Today was a happy day and should be so for the young girl as well. Alexander sat on the boulder next to her. As he did he could feel an intense cold associated with the girl. "Autumn, you should not be here," the boy said quietly as he too found an object to brush from his pants.

"Where should I be Alexander?" the girl asked sadly.

"Heaven of course!" the boy said.

"But I'm just a young girl, Alexander. I want to find my father and I want to have fun again!"

"Yes, I know," Alexander said. The boy waited for a moment, then looked up and turned to her. "You know where your father is. You cannot have fun on the earth anymore. Autumn, don't you know, our true Father has prepared a mansion for you. In this mansion are many, many rooms. There are tables filled with lots of food, and many places to play."

The girl turned to the boy and asked, "Alexander is that true? But I am so scared." Autumn dropped her head and began sobbing.

Alexander placed his arm around the girl. "It is so, the Word states as much. Our earthly life is nothing, Autumn! Today is a happy day in our Kingdom, but in yours it is always so," the boy said.

"Will I see my father?" she asked.

"You will see our Heavenly Father and your earthly one. And Autumn your mother will be there as well. All of them are there already, of that I am certain."

The two sat in the sunlight for a few minutes in silence. Suddenly, Autumn stood up. She brushed the wrinkles from her dress and shook out her long brown hair. "Yes, I am ready Alexander," she said, looking down at the boy. A happy smile crossed her face as she added, "but I am still scared."

Alexander stood slowly with a smile on his face. He embraced the young girl and kissed her on her forehead. "Good bye, Autumn, I will see you in heaven soon, I look forward to that day!"

"Yes Alexander, can we play then?"

Alexander thought for a moment. A big smile crossed his face. "I may be very old then, Autumn! But yes, I think everyone plays in heaven." The boy touched the girl on her shoulder. "You kept the battle for the castle from becoming a bloody one. As it was, it was taken without violence. We have you to thank you for that, sweet Autumn."

Autumn turned now with a smile. She said good-bye and began to skip away down the trail. Turning one last time she waved at the boy. "There is an odd boy, a Christopher of Temecula. Say hello to him for me will you? Oh, and Alexander, did we win?"

"Yes we won, Autumn. I will give your regards to him. You know, he really is not odd at all, just from the future."

"Yes, I know." With that the girl turned and began skipping away down the tree lined path and was soon gone.

The King and Queen sat proudly upon their thrones. Each smiled and held the other's hand tightly. The throne room was decorated for the celebration of the year. Alexander stood in his finest silk stockings and britches. A beautiful brown and gold trim coat made him quite the noble figure. At his side was his golden sword, holstered for the celebration.

Gidget sat upon a rose-colored cushion at the foot of the first lady. The dog was freshly scrubbed and dressed in her rose colored coat. She was excited and showed as much, by panting briskly with her black tongue.

Fine ladies dressed in billowing dresses, accompanied by their gentlemen, lined the walls of the chamber. At the back three freshly cleaned bulldogs sat on their haunches, minimally drooling on their best behaviors, proud and trying to be quiet. Little Andy without an eye patch, Manzell, and the other boys stood as well. Each was clean and dressed as best a common boy could.

The crier announced the beginning of the ceremony with a long blast upon his horn. "Here yea, here yea! All please remain silent in the presence of King William and Queen Patrice of Alucemet. Today we celebrate the dubbing of three new Knights of the realm!" And with that the audience applauded politely but with great anticipation. "Nicholas of Alucemet, please enter!"

Nicholas entered with some show of discomfort through the curtained door. For a boy so used to commanding his fleet he was blushing, smiling but proud. He was dressed finely as well. Shiny black shoes with polished silver buckles adorned his feet. White silk stockings covered his lower legs. Brilliant blue velvet pants, cut to just below the knee with blue and silver trim and embroidery finished his stunning costume. The boy made his way through the audience and stood in front of the King and Queen.

The King had made a miraculous recovery. Now little resemblance of the disheveled prisoner remained, and he was smiling with tears of joy coming to his eyes as he looked at his youngest son. "Nicholas of Alucemet, known commonly as Nicholas the Blue. A friend of the kingdom, a defender of the crown. Our Kingdom is indebted to your bravery and patriotic defense of our borders." With this, the King nodded to the boy who took the cue to descend to one knee. The King stood in front of the boy, a magnificent jeweled sword in his right hand. "With this I dub you, Sir Nicholas the Blue of Alucemet." Taking the sword the King touched briefly the right then the left shoulder of the boy. The Queen had tears of joy in her eyes. She was overcome with pride.

"Thank you, father," was Nicholas's only answer. The boy stood with a big smile upon his face. He backed away slowly and stood next to his brother. Quickly he was back with his friends, pulling at his collar and loosening his shirt. Little Andy patted the boy on the back. The three bulldogs, while still silent, sat proudly, unable to control their drooling with quite the same authority.

Pirates, Scoundrels, and Kings

The crier now silenced the crowd. Taking again the scroll he read. "Here yea, here yea! All in attendance please remain silent in the presence of the King and Queen of Alucemet. Robyn of Hobinsiefken, please enter."

The mayor entered through the same curtained door. He was a proud man, his life's goal of knighthood finally here. It had taken only one day for the King to take control of the kingdom. One of his first acts was the revoking of the provision, which forbade knighthood for anyone not of porcine blood. The mayor was delighted, not knowing until today though that he too would be bestowed with Knighthood. Moving now to the King, Robyn stood in front of the two monarchs.

With a nod from the King, the mayor knelt. "Robyn of Hobinsiefken. For your bravery and devotion to the Kingdom I hereby dub you, Sir Robyn of Hobinsiefken." Repeating as he did with Nicholas the King used his decorative sword to Knight the excited man.

The crowd could not help itself, and with less fanfare than for Nicholas, applauded strongly as the blushing man made his way through the audience. The crier had confirmed that three were to be knighted that day. Most in the crowd were not aware of who that third person would be. A hush fell over the audience. All looked to the curtain with great anticipation.

They had worked all morning with the boy. He had seen Nicholas and Alexander, and while what they were wearing was okay, it was certainly not his style. He knew, however, that he could not insult the King and Queen. Therefore, a compromise was arrived at. No stockings, that was for sure. He exchanged his knee length shorts for britches, and with some distaste wore the silk shirt and embroidered coat. But the shoes never were right, and at the last minute Nicholas tossed his beloved skateboard style well worn shoes to the boy along with a new wad of his best gum. It satisfied the modern day boy, and he accepted a good tousling of his spiked hair by the former pirate-boy and friend.

"Here yea, here yea. All please be silent in the presence of the King and Queen of Alucemet. Christopher of Temecula," the crier struggled, "please enter."

The boy entered through the curtain as the others. When he saw the large group he stopped suddenly. "Whoa--" he thought to himself. His mind returned to his real home, visualizing himself in front of the multipurpose room. Chris's face blushed, and he dropped his head trying to give himself a moment. Taking a few chews of his gum, he felt more confident. The boy slowly walked forward very slowly to address the royal family. When he saw the Queen he smiled. "She's not half bad--for a mom," he thought silently to himself. "A little old--well like his real mom," the boy said to himself with a smile. He thought the King was old as well. He noticed that the man looked much better than when they had rescued him from that closet. "Dude--." He thought again silently. "The dude doesn't look like the same person. Maybe a facelift," the boy thought trying not to laugh.

It took a little encouragement, but eventually Chris knelt as the others in front of the King. The King rose once more. "Christopher of Temecula, for your bravery in defense of the Kingdom and Crown I hereby dub you Sir Christopher of Temecula."

Christopher had seen this before, in movies of course. "The sword is way bad," he thought again to himself. Like the others before him, the King used his sword and the ceremony was soon over. Christopher turned, thanking the King and Queen. A cheer went up through the crowd as the boy raised his clutched fist. "All right--" the boy said as he walked towards his friends at the back of the hall.

Chapter 27
Good Bye

> THE HOUSE OF THE WICKED WILL BE DESTROYED,
> BUT THE TENT OF THE UPRIGHT WILL FLOURISH.
> **PROVERBS 14:11**

The pageant had been wonderful, full of fun, food, and crowds. Roast pig was once more cooked in the kingdom, and Christopher had stuffed himself. There was something wrong, however; the boy was not home. It came back to him slowly. Throughout the festivities the boy was excited. He was a Knight and could not believe it. There was recognition and excitement within the crowds now milling around in the courtyard. Flags were flying, fun and games were for everyone, and Christopher was quite a celebrity with the townspeople. He realized though that it was not real, and for the first time in a while he missed his real family. He walked slowly by himself across the courtyard deep in thought.

"Christopher of Temecula," Nicholas said as he rode up on horseback to the boy. Nicholas was dressed for jousting. He was holding his staff and he invited the boy for a friendly game. Nicholas could tell something was wrong with his friend as he approached, however, and he dismounted driving his staff into the ground and placing his helmet on the horse's saddle. He moved to the boy and placed his arm around him. "What is it, Christopher of Temecula?" the pirate-boy inquired with concern.

"Home, I'm not home, Nicholas. Remember I don't live here like you," Christopher said sadly.

Nothing fazed Nicholas. He was always smiling, and fun was his middle name. He was not real concerned this time as well as he escorted his friend across the courtyard. "Let me show you something my friend," he boy said to Christopher.

The entrance to the castle, constructed in the Roman arch fashion, was just ahead. The drawbridge was down, and there was a small amount of traffic traversing the opening. The two boys walked together along the bridge, and Nicholas directed the boy to a table that stood directly in front of the stone archway. On the table, the Mirrorlass was displayed. The object was a perfect sphere of a mirror-like glass that gleamed in the brilliant sunlight.

In the days that followed the battle, Alexander had repaired the device. Taking the piece that had long been around his neck, he fitted it back into the device, cementing it with perfection using what else: gum.

Nicholas took the boy around the table. The two stood now between the Mirrorlass and the stone archway. "See Christopher, it was always there!" Nicholas said pointing to the Mirrorlass.

"What do you mean, dude?" Christopher said, staring now into the reflective surface and searching for Nicholas's point. It took a moment to see. He had to look deep within the sphere and concentrate, but eventually Chris realized it definitely was there! "T e m e c u l a--" Christopher read from the Mirrorlass with a curious twist to his face. "Temecula--dude?" The boy now turned to Nicholas and examined the boy with curiosity.

Nicholas smiled and he turned his head to the stone archway at their back. Pointing he said, "Look."

It took Christopher a moment but eventually he too turned, facing the archway. He had not noticed it before, but inscribed in that archway with chiseled letters was the name of this kingdom, ALUCEMET, making a perfect half circle around the archway. "Hmm," the boy said, staring at the inscription for a moment. He turned now again and stared into the Mirrorlass. The word TEMECULA was definitely there. And then it dawned upon the boy; the shape of the mirrored sphere turned the letters of the stone archway around. Alucemet was Temecula spelled backwards. The word was obvious now. He turned to Nicholas with a questioning frown. "Dude, what does it mean?"

"You can always go back," Nicholas laughed. "You always could!"

"But how?" Christopher asked the boy.

"The Mirrorlass! Remember, I believe the song went. Alexander will show us how. Do you wish to return, Christopher?" Nicholas added.

Christopher was now not so certain. He dropped his head deep in thought. "Home," he thought silently. There were cars, candy, CD's, but then again there was school! The last thought brought some doubt to the boy. Christopher was homesick, however. Even school did not seem so bad he thought. Thinking now of his family he knew he must return.

Lifting his head he looked at his new pirate friend. "Ya--dude, I got to get home." Laughing now he said, "You know my mom will kill me."

"We don't want that!" Nicholas said, laughing in return.

THEY LEFT EARLY THE NEXT morning upon horses. Alexander led the way with Christopher and Nicholas following closely behind. The modern day boy was excited about his return, but the change brought fear as well. Manzell and Little Andy rode silently, having mixed emotions for their new friend.

When Crystal heard that Christopher might leave she had insisted on coming as well. Riding now sidesaddle, the young girl pranced her white stallion along with the boys. The bulldogs cleared their path, sniffing and running as were their natures. Rainbow sat in a spot of prominence on the shoulder of his master Nicholas.

It was important, according to Alexander, to find that exact location where so long ago the boy had entered this world. "I have no idea," Christopher had said. But Manzell knew, and the others seemed to know exactly as well. It was to this site that the group now rode, arriving upon a dusty road with dense vegetation.

As they rounded a bend in the road, Nicholas pointed. "Ahead it should be thusly," he said.

Manzell agreed. "It is just over the ridge," he said.

They came to a widening in the road, and the group slowed. Alexander got off his horse, tying the beast's reign to a piece of brush. "Here," he said, turning to Manzell.

"Exactly where you stand, Alexander," the boy responded to his leader.

Alexander looked down at his feet. Something seemed to be missing. The boy looked around the site coming eventually to an area just to the edge of the dirt road. Pulling now the brush aside, he found what he was looking for. "Remember thust Christopher of Temecula?" He said pointing to a small sapling growing within the dense brush.

"What dude?" The boy said. Then it came to him. The oak tree, the small sapling was the tree but one thousand years earlier. "Whoa—yes—dude--the tree!"

"An oak sapling, it must be quite large in your world, is that not right, Christopher of Temecula?" Alexander questioned, turning to the boy.

"Very big, gnarly, old, but that's it. I can see it now." Christopher said from his saddle.

"You must stand exactly where you were, then with the Mirrorlass you will return. Are you quite sure my friend?"

"I stand there, and you zap me back?"

"Something like that," Alexander said, smiling at the boy. "I ask again though, are you sure?"

Christopher took a deep breath. He looked around at the group. Nicholas returned his stare as did the others. He then turned to Crystal who was smiling her usual big smile, less one small tooth.

"Yes I'm sure. I'm really late dude. I've slept over at my friend's house before, you know Michael down the street, but this is ridiculous. My Mom-- she will be so mad."

"Then you stand thusly," Alexander said, pointing to the area right in front of the sapling.

Pirates, Scoundrels, and Kings

Chris got off his horse slowly. He turned to Alexander and smiled. He looked up at Nicholas and slapped him on his thigh. Manzell and Little Andy each gave him a hand, and Chris slapped their palms. Spike had come to his side and was lifting his paw. "Shake?" Christopher questioned. As he did so he grabbed the dogs paw and shook it briskly.

Once he was at the site it was quick. He awoke with just the slightest of headaches. He was on his belly, his face turned, and his tongue again in the dirt. To his right, the shade of the old oak tree could be seen. The sun was setting and it was quite late in the day. Chris lifted up, shaking his head. Spitting he cleared his dirt-filled mouth. It was all the same. He could not believe it. The tree was unchanged. Sitting next to it was the same rotting branch. Chris looked warily to the sky; luckily there was no cloud. Rising now he looked down the slope towards his house. Reaching down he found his beloved basketball, skateboard, and backpack all neatly resting as if placed there by his friends. Without hesitation, he picked them up and ran racing towards his house.

His brothers were in the driveway as he approached. Alexander was standing next to his skateboard. Nicholas was sitting on his board, pushing off with his hands and riding like the wind down the driveway. "Alex—Nick." Chris yelled as he ran down the dusty hillside towards his brothers. Both waved to the boy without a thought. Maybe his brothers were okay, he thought to himself. Nomatter, neither seemed to have missed him at all!